Praise for #1 *New York Times* bestselling author Debbie Macomber

"No one writes better women's contemporary fiction."
—*RT Book Reviews*

"It's impossible not to cheer for Macomber's characters…. When it comes to creating a special place and memorable, honorable characters, nobody does it better than Macomber."
—*BookPage*

"As always, Macomber draws rich, engaging characters."
—*Publishers Weekly*

Praise for *New York Times* bestselling author Lee Tobin McClain

"Lee Tobin McClain's books make my heart sing."
—Debbie Macomber,
#1 *New York Times* bestselling author

"Lee Tobin McClain dazzles with unforgettable characters, fabulous small-town settings and a big dose of heart. Her complex and satisfying stories never disappoint."
—Susan Mallery, #1 *New York Times* bestselling author

Debbie Macomber is a #1 *New York Times* bestselling author and a leading voice in women's fiction worldwide. Her work has appeared on every major bestseller list, with more than 170 million copies in print, and she is a multiple award winner. The Hallmark Channel based a television series on Debbie's popular Cedar Cove books. For more information, visit her website, www.debbiemacomber.com.

New York Times and *USA TODAY* bestselling author **Lee Tobin McClain** read *Gone with the Wind* in the third grade and has been an incurable romantic ever since. When she's not writing angst-filled love stories with happy endings, she's probably Snapchatting with her college-student daughter, mediating battles between her goofy goldendoodle and her rescue cat, or teaching aspiring writers in Seton Hill University's MFA program. She is probably not cleaning her house. For more about Lee, visit her website at www.leetobinmcclain.com.

DEBBIE MACOMBER

FALLEN ANGEL

**HARLEQUIN
BESTSELLING
AUTHOR
COLLECTION**

**HARLEQUIN®
BESTSELLING
AUTHOR
COLLECTION**

Recycling programs
for this product may
not exist in your area.

ISBN-13: 978-1-335-00754-4

Fallen Angel
First published in 1990. This edition published in 2023.
Copyright © 1990 by Debbie Macomber

The Soldier's Secret Child
First published in 2017. This edition published in 2023.
Copyright © 2017 by Lee Tobin McClain

For questions and comments about the quality of this book, please contact us at CustomerService@Harlequin.com.

Harlequin Enterprises ULC
22 Adelaide St. West, 41st Floor
Toronto, Ontario M5H 4E3, Canada
www.Harlequin.com

Printed in U.S.A.

CONTENTS

Visit her Author Profile page at Harlequin.com,
or debbiemacomber.com, for more titles!

FALLEN ANGEL

Debbie Macomber

Chapter 1

The least it could do was rain! What was the use of living in Seattle if it wasn't going to so much as drizzle? And Amy was in the mood for a cloudburst.

She bought herself an order of crispy fried fish and chips simply because she felt guilty occupying a picnic table in the tourist-crowded pier along the Seattle waterfront. The mild June weather had refused to respond to her mood and the sun was playing peekaboo behind a band of thin clouds. No doubt it would ruin everything and shine full force any minute.

"Excuse me—is this seat taken?"

Amy glanced up to discover a man who looked as though he'd just stepped out of a Western novel and was searching for Fort Apache standing opposite her. The impression came from a leather band that was wrapped around his wide forehead and the cropped-waisted doeskin jacket.

"Feel free," she said, motioning toward the empty space opposite her. "I'll be finished here within a couple of minutes."

"It doesn't look like you've even touched your meal."

"I couldn't possibly eat at a time like this," she said, frowning at him.

His thick brows shot upward as he lifted his leg over the wooden table and sat opposite her. "I see."

Amy picked up a fat French fry and poised it in front of her mouth. "I've been home exactly two weeks and it hasn't so much as rained once. This is Seattle, mind you, and there hasn't even been a heavy dew."

"The weather *has* been great."

"I'd feel better if it rained," she returned absently. "It's much too difficult to be depressed when the sun is shining and the birds are chirping and everyone around me is in this jovial, carefree mood."

The stranger took a sip of his coffee, and Amy suspected he did so to cover a smile. It would be just her luck to have a handsome stranger sit down and try to brighten her mood.

He set the cup on the picnic table and leveled his gaze at her. "You look to me like a woman who's been done wrong by her man."

"That's another thing," Amy cried. "Everything would be so much simpler if I'd been born a male."

Her companion's brown eyes rounded. "Is that a fact?"

"Well, of course, then I wouldn't be in this mess… well, I would, but I'd probably be happy about it."

"I see."

Feeling slightly better about the situation, Amy tore off a piece of fish and studied it before popping it into her mouth. It tasted good, much better than she'd anticipated. "It wouldn't be nearly this difficult if I didn't have the most wonderful father in the world."

His dark eyes softened. "Then you shouldn't need to worry."

"But it just kills me to disappoint him." Amy took another bite of the battered fish. "After all, I am twenty-three—it's not as though I don't know what I want."

"And what *do* you want?"

"How would I know?" she muttered. "No one even asked me before."

Her newfound friend laughed outright.

Amy smiled, too, for the first time in what seemed like years. "If I'm going to be spilling my guts to you, I might as well introduce myself. I'm Amy Johnson."

"Josh Powell." He held out his hand and they exchanged quick handshakes.

"Hello, Josh."

"Hello yourself," he returned, grinning broadly. "Are you going to be all right, Amy Johnson?"

She expelled a harsh sigh, then shrugged. "I suppose." Another French fry made its way into her mouth. When she reached for the fish, she noted that Josh had stopped eating and was studying her.

"Is there a reason you're wearing that rain coat?" he asked.

She nodded. "I was hoping for a downpour—something to coordinate with my mood."

"I thought you might have heard a more recent forecast. An unexpected tropical storm or something."

"No," she admitted wryly.

"Frankly, I'm surprised by the weather myself," Josh

stated conversationally. "I've been in Seattle several days now, and the sun has greeted me every morning."

"So you're a tourist?"

"Not exactly. I work for one of the major oil companies, and I'm waiting for government clearance before I head for the Middle East. I should fly out of here within the week."

Her father owned a couple of oil wells, but from what Amy could remember they were in Texas and had been losing money for the past few years. If her father was experiencing minor financial problems with his vast undertakings, then it was nothing compared to what was bound to happen when *she* stepped into the picture. He had such high hopes for her, such lofty expectations. And she was destined to fail. It would be impossible not to. She had about as much business sense as Homer Simpson. Her college advisers had repeatedly suggested she change her major. Personally, Amy was all for that. She worked hard and even then she was considered borderline as to whether she would be accepted into the five-year joint BA and MBA program. She'd been number three on a waiting list. Then her father had donated funds toward a new library, and lo and behold, Amy and everyone else on the list had been welcomed into the prestigious school of business with open arms.

"I'm impressed with what I've seen of Seattle," Josh went on.

"It's a nice city, isn't it?" Amy answered with a soft smile. She leaned forward and plopped her elbows on top of the picnic table. "Do you think it would work if I feigned a fatal illness?"

"I beg your pardon?"

"No," she said, answering her own question. "It

wouldn't." Knowing her father, he would call in medical experts from around the world, and she'd be forced into making a miraculous recovery.

Josh's amused gaze met hers.

"I'm not making the least bit of sense, am I?"

"No," he admitted dryly. "Do you want to talk about it?"

Supporting her cheek with the palm of one hand, she stared into the distance, wondering if discussing the matter with a stranger would help. At least he would be unbiased.

"My father is probably one of the most dynamic men you'll ever meet. Being around him is like receiving a charge of energy. He's exciting, vibrant, electric."

"I know the type you mean."

"I'm his only child," Amy muttered. "You may have noticed that Dad and I don't share a whole lot of the same characteristics."

Josh hedged. "That's difficult to say—we only met a few minutes ago, but from what I've seen, you don't seem to lack any energy."

"Take my word on this, Dad and I aren't anything alike."

"Okay," he said, then gestured toward her. "Go on."

"I recently acquired my MBA—"

"Congratulations."

"No, please. If it had been up to me I would have hung around the campus for as many more years as I could, applied for a doctorate—anything. But unfortunately that option wasn't left open to me. According to my father, the big moment has finally arrived."

"And?"

"He wants to take me into the family business."

"That isn't what you want?"

"Heavens, no! I know Dad would listen to me if I had some burning desire to be a teacher or a dental assistant or anything else. Then I could talk to him and explain everything. But I don't know what I want to do, and even if I did, I'm not so certain it would matter anyway."

"But you just said—"

"I know, but I also know my father, bless his dear heart. He'd look at me with those big blue eyes of his, and I'd start drowning in this sea of guilt." She paused long enough to draw in a giant breath. "I'm the apple of his eye. According to him, the sun rises and sets on my whims. I can't disappoint him—Dad's got his heart set on me taking over for him."

"You've never told him this isn't what you want?"

She dropped her gaze, ashamed to admit she'd been such a coward. "Not in so many words—I just couldn't."

"Perhaps you could talk to your mother, let her pre- pare the way. Then it won't come as any big shock when you approach your father."

Once more Amy shook her head. "I'm afraid that won't work. My mother died when I was barely ten."

"I see—well, that does complicate matters, doesn't it?"

"I did this to myself," Amy moaned. "I knew the day was coming when I'd be forced to tell him the truth. It wasn't like I didn't figure out what he intended early enough. About the time I entered high school, I got the drift that he had big plans for me. I tried to turn the tide then, but it didn't do any good."

"Turn the tide?" Josh repeated. "I don't understand."

"I tried to marry him off. The way I figured it, he could fall in love again, and his new wife would promptly give birth to three or four male heirs, and then I'd be off the hook. Unfortunately, he was too busy with the business to get involved with a woman."

"What if *you* married?"

"That wouldn't…" Amy paused and straightened as the suggestion ricocheted around the corners of her brain. "Josh…oh, Josh, that's a brilliant idea. Why didn't I think of that?" She nibbled on her lower lip as she considered his scheme, which sounded like exactly the escape clause she'd been wanting. "If my father would be willing to accept any excuse, it'd be something like that. He's a bighearted romantic, and if there's one thing he wants more than to see me in the business—it's grandchildren." Her blue eyes flashed with excitement as she smiled at Josh. Then it struck her, and she moaned. "There's one flaw to this brilliant plan, though." She raised her fingers to her mouth and stroked her lips while she gave the one weakness some thought.

"What do you mean there's a flaw?" Josh repeated, sounding impatient.

"I'm not in love."

"That's not such a difficult hang-up. Think. Surely there's one man you've met in your life that you like well enough to marry?"

She considered the list of men she'd dated and her shoulders sagged with defeat. "Actually, there isn't," she admitted reluctantly. "I dated in college, but only a little, and there was never anyone I'd seriously consider spending the rest of my life with."

"What about the boys who attended high school with you? Five years have passed, and things have changed— perhaps it's time you renewed those old friendships."

Once more Amy frowned, then regretfully shook her

head. "That won't work, either. I attended a Catholic girls' school." She closed her eyes, prepared to mentally scan through a list of potential men she might consider marrying. Unfortunately, she couldn't think of a single one.

"Amy," Josh whispered, "are you all right?"

She nodded. "I'm just thinking. No," she said emphatically, as the defeat settled on her shoulders like a blanket of steel, "there's no one. I'm doomed."

"You could always have a heart-to-heart talk with your father. If he's as wonderful as you claim, then he'll be grateful for the honesty."

"Sure, and what exactly do I say?"

"The truth. You might suggest he train someone else to take his place."

Despite the fact that Josh was serious, Amy laughed a little. "You make it sound so easy...you couldn't possibly realize how difficult telling him is going to be."

"But necessary, Amy."

The second to the last thing Amy needed was the cool voice of reason. The first had been a handsome stranger introducing himself to her. When a person is depressed and miserable, she decided, everything seems to fall apart!

"Talk to him," Josh advised again.

As much as Amy wanted to argue with him, he was right. Her eyes held on to his as if she could soak up his determination.

"The sooner you get it over with the better," he added softly.

"I know you're right," she murmured. "I should do it soon...before I find myself behind a desk, wondering how I ended up there."

"What's wrong with *now?*"

"Now?" Her startled gaze flew to Josh.

"Yes, now."

Her mouth opened to argue with him, but she realized there really wasn't any better time than the present. The corporate headquarters was within walking distance, and it would be best to face her father when she was charged with righteous enthusiasm. If she delayed the confrontation until dinnertime, she might chicken out.

"You're absolutely right. If I'm going to talk to my father, I've got to do it immediately." In a burst of zeal, she charged to her feet and offered Josh her hand. "Thank you for your advice."

"You're most welcome." He smiled and finished his coffee. "Good luck."

"Thanks, I'm going to need it." Securing the strap of her purse over her shoulder, she deposited what remained of her lunch in the trash and marched toward the sidewalk in smooth strides of military precision. When she reached the street, she turned to find Josh watching her. She raised her hand in a gesture of farewell, and he did the same.

An hour later, Amy sat in the back row of the Omnitheater at the Seattle Aquarium, slouched down as far as she could in her seat without slipping all the way out of it and into the aisle. Her hand covered her eyes. A documentary about the Mount St. Helen's disaster was about to start.

Disasters seemed to be the theme of Amy's day. Following her trip to the Rainier Building on Fifth Avenue, she'd walked to the waterfront area where her car was parked. The thought of returning home, however, only added to her misery, so she'd opted for the documentary.

Her bravado had been strong when she reached the fifty-story structure that housed Johnson Industries. She'd paused on the sidewalk outside and glanced up at the vertical ribs of polished glass and concrete. About half of all the people inside were a part of the conglomerate that made up her father's enterprise.

Her mistake had been when she'd started working with the figures. Calculating two hundred people per floor, that came to twenty thousand workers inside the Rainier Building—when full—of which a possible ten thousand were Johnson employees.

Of all those thousands, very few would stand equal to or above Amy in the capacity her father had chosen for her.

She wasn't exactly stepping into an entry-level position. Oh, no, she'd been groomed for a much loftier point on the corporate scale. Her father's idea had been to place her as a director, working her way through each of the major sections of the company until the most important aspects of each department had been drilled into her. Naturally, Harold Johnson planned to stay on as president and chief executive officer until Amy had learned the ropes, but "the ropes" felt too much like a hangman's noose to suit her.

The lights lowered in the Omni-theater, and Amy heard someone enter the row and sit next to her.

"I take it the confrontation with your father didn't go well."

Amy's hand flew away from her face. It was Josh. "No," she whispered.

"What happened?"

She flopped her hands over a couple of times, searching for a way to start to explain. "It's a long story."

The man in front of them twisted around and glared, clearly more interested in hearing the details of the natural disaster than Amy's troubles.

"I've already seen the movie once," Josh said. "Do you want to go outside and talk?"

She nodded.

As she suspected, the sun was shining and the sky was an intense shade of blue. Even the seagulls were in a jovial mood.

"Do you want some ice cream?" Josh asked when they reached the busy sidewalk. He didn't wait for her reply, but bought them each an enormous double scoop waffle cone, then joined her in front of the large, cheerful water fountain.

Amy sat on the edge of the structure, feeling even more pathetic than she had earlier that afternoon.

"I take it you talked to your father?"

"No," she muttered. "I didn't get past Ms. Wetherell, his executive assistant." She lapped at the side of the cone, despite everything enjoying the rich, smooth taste of the vanilla ice cream. "I don't think I've ever really looked at that woman before. She reminds me of a prune."

"A prune?" Josh repeated.

"She might have been a pleasant plum at one time, but she's been ripened and dried by the years. I think it might be the fluorescent lighting." Amy knew she would look just like Ms. Wetherell within six months. She was going to hate being trapped indoors with no possibility of escape.

"The prune wouldn't allow you to talk to your own father?"

"He was in an important meeting." She turned to Josh and shrugged. "I was slain at the gate."

"Amy..."

"I know exactly what you're going to say, and you're absolutely right. I'll talk to my dad tonight. I promise you I will."

"Good."

He looked proud of her, and that helped. "How'd you happen to be in the Omni-theater?" she asked. It had to be more than coincidence.

"I saw you go inside and was curious to find out what happened."

He'd removed the leather jacket and draped it over his shoulder, securing it with one finger. His eyes were deeply set, his nose prominent without distracting from his strong male features. His ash-blond hair was longer than fashionable, but well kept. It seemed to Amy that calendar and poster manufacturers were constantly searching for men with such blatant male appeal. Men like Josh.

"Is something wrong?" he asked her unexpectedly.

"No," she said, recovering quickly. She hadn't realized she'd been staring quite so conspicuously.

"Your ice cream is melting," he told her.

Hurriedly, she took several bites to correct the problem. The green-and-white ferry sounded its horn as it approached the pier. It captured Josh's attention.

"Did you know that Washington has the largest ferry system in the United States and the third largest in the world?" Amy asked, in what she hoped was a conversational tone.

"No, I didn't."

"When you consider someplace like the Philippines

with all those islands, that fact is impressive." Amy realized she was jabbering, but she wanted to pull attention away from herself and her problems. "Our aquarium is the one of only a few in the world built on a pier," she said, adding another tour-guide fact. "Have you been up to the Pike Place Market yet?"

"Several times, and I've enjoyed it more each visit."

"It's the largest continuously operated farmers' market in the nation."

"You seem to be full of little tidbits of information."

She smiled and nodded. Then she closed her eyes and expelled her breath in a leisurely exercise. "I really do love this city."

"It's home," Josh said quietly, and Amy sensed such a longing in his voice that she opened her eyes to study him.

"Would you like to walk with me?" he asked her unexpectedly. Standing, he offered her his elbow.

"Sure." She tucked her arm around his, enjoying the feeling of being connected with him. Josh had been a friend when she'd needed one. They barely knew each other—they'd exchanged little more than their names—and yet she'd told him more about her problems than she had anyone. Ever. Even her closest college friends didn't know how much she dreaded going to work for her father. But Josh Powell did. A stranger. An unexpected friend.

It took them forty minutes to walk from the waterfront area to the Seattle Center on Queen Ann Hill. They stood at the base of the Space Needle, which had been built for the 1962 World's Fair and remained a prominent city landmark. Feeling it was her duty to relay the more important details, Amy told him everything she could remember about the Space Needle, which wasn't much. She finished off by asking, "Where's home?"

"I beg your pardon?"

"Where are you from?"

He paused and looked at her for a tense moment. "What makes you ask that?"

"I… I don't know. When I told you how much I love Seattle, you claimed that was because it was home. Now I'm curious where home is for you."

His eyes took on a distant look. "The world—I've taken jobs just about everywhere now. The Middle East, South America, Australia, Europe."

"But where do you kick off your boots and put up your feet?"

"Wherever I happen to be," he explained.

"But—"

"I left what most others would consider home several years ago. I didn't ever intend to go back."

"Oh, Josh, that's so sad." Her voice sounded as if she'd whispered into a microphone, low and vibrating.

"Amy…" He paused, then chuckled softly. "It wasn't any big tragedy." Burying his hands in his pockets, he strolled away, effectively ending the conversation. He paused and waited on the pathway for her to join him.

Glancing at the time, Amy sighed. "I've got to get back to the house," she said with reluctance.

"Tell me what you're going to do tonight."

"Nothing much," she hedged. "Watch a little television probably, read some—"

"I don't mean that, and you know it."

"All right, all right, I'm going to talk to my father."

"And then tomorrow you're going to meet me at noon at the seafood stand and tell me what happened."

"I am?"

"That's exactly what you're going to do."

Her heart started to pound like an overworked piston in her chest, but that could have been because she would soon be confronting her father, and her success rate with making dragons purr was rather low at the moment. But the reaction could well have been due to the fact that she would be meeting Josh again.

"Any questions?" he asked.

"One." She paused and looked up at him, her eyes wide and appealing. "Will you marry me?"

"No."

"I was afraid of that."

Chapter 2

Manuela had served the last of the evening meal before Amy had the courage to broach the subject with her father. She looked at him, watching him closely, wanting to gauge his mood before she unloaded her mind. His disposition seemed congenial enough, but it was difficult to tell exactly how he would respond to her news.

"Did you have a pleasant afternoon?" Harold asked his daughter, glancing at her.

His unexpected question thumped her out of her musings. "Yes... I took a stroll along the waterfront."

"Good," he said forcefully, and nodded once. Harold Johnson took a bite of his shrimp-stuffed sole. He was nearly sixty-five and in his prime. His hair had gone completely white in the past few years, but his features were ageless, as sharp and penetrating as Amy could ever remember. He watched what he ate, was physically and mentally fit and lived life to the fullest. Nothing had ever been done by half measure. Harold Johnson was an all-or-nothing man. There were few compromises in attitude, health or personality.

He was the type of man who, when he saw something he wanted, went after it with everything he had. He would never accept defeat, only setbacks. He claimed his greatest achievements had been the result of patience. If ever he would need to call upon that virtue, it was now, Amy mused. She loved him just the way he was and prayed he could accept her for who she was, as well.

"Ms. Wetherell said you stopped in to see me," he added, when he'd finished his bite of fish.

"You were in a meeting," she answered lamely.

Her father's responding nod was eager. "An excellent one as it turned out, too. I told a group of executives in five minutes how they can outsell, outmanage and outmotivate the competition."

"You said all that in five minutes?"

"Less," he claimed, warming to his subject. "Mark my words, Amy, because you're going to be needing them soon enough yourself."

"Dad—"

"The first thing you've got to do is set your goals— you won't get any place in this world if you don't know where you're headed. Then visualize yourself in that role."

"Dad—"

He held up his hand to stop her. "And lastly, and this is probably the most important aspect of success, you must learn to deny the power of the adverse. Now you notice, I didn't say you should deny the negative, because there's plenty of that in our world. But we can't allow ourselves the luxury of thinking adversity can get control over us. Because the plain and simple truth is this—misfortune has power only when we allow it to. Do you understand what I'm saying?"

Amy nodded, wondering if she would ever get a word in edgewise and, if she did, how she could possibly say what she needed to tell him.

"You come to the office tomorrow," her father went on to say, smiling smugly. "I've got something of a surprise for you. I was saving it for later, but I want you to see it now."

"What's that?"

"Your own office. I've hired one of those fancy interior decorators and I'm having the space redesigned. Nothing but the best for my little girl. New carpet, the finest furniture, the latest technology, the whole nine yards. Once that's completed, I want you working with me and the others. Together, you and I are going to make a difference in this country—a big one." He paused and set aside his fork. When he looked up, his gaze was warm and proud. "I've been waiting for this day for nearly twenty years. I don't mind telling you how proud I am of you, Amy Adele. You're as pretty as your mother, and you've got her brains, too. Having you at my side will almost be like having Mary back again."

"Oh, Dad…" He was making this so much more difficult.

"These years that you've been away at school have been hard ones. You're the sunshine of my life, Amy, just the way your mother always was."

"I'd like to be more like her," she whispered, knowing her father would never understand what she meant. Her mother had always been behind the scenes, acting as a sounding board and offering moral support. That was where Amy longed to be, as well.

Her father reached for his wineglass. "You're more and more like Mary every day."

"Mom didn't work at the office though, did she?"

"No, of course not, but don't you discount her worth to me. It was your mother's support, love and encouragement that gave me the courage to accomplish everything I have done over the years. Never in all that time did Mary and I dream we'd come so far or achieve so much."

"I meant what I said about being more like her," Amy tried once again. "Mom…was more of a background figure in your life and I…think that's the role I should play, too."

"Nonsense! You belong at my side."

"Dad, oh, please…" Her voice trembled like loose change in an oversize pocket. "You just finished telling me how important it was to visualize yourself in a certain role, and I'm sorry, but I can't see myself cooped up in an office day in and day out. It just isn't me. I—"

"You can't what?"

"See myself as an important part of Johnson Industries," she blurted out in one giant breath.

Her announcement was followed by a short silence.

"I can understand that," Harold said.

"You can?"

"Of course. It's little wonder when all you've done, so far is book learning," her father continued confidently. "Business isn't sitting in some stuffy classroom listening to a know-it-all professor spouting off his views. It's digging in with both hands and pulling out something viable and profitable that's going to affect people's lives for the better."

"But I'm not sure that's what I want."

"Of course you do!" he countered sharply. "You wouldn't be a Johnson if you didn't."

"What about Mom, and the support she gave you? Couldn't I start off like that… I mean…be a sounding board for you and a helpmate in other ways?"

"Years ago that was all you could have done, but times have changed," her father argued. "Women have fought for their rightful place in the corporate world. For the first time in history women are getting the recognition they deserve. You're my daughter, my only child—everything I've managed to accumulate will some day belong to you."

"But—"

"Now, I think I understand what you're saying. I should have thought of this myself. You're tired. Exhausted from your studies. You've worked hard, and you deserve a break. I wasn't thinking when I suggested you start working with me so soon after graduation."

"Dad, I'm not *that* tired."

"Yes, you are, only you don't realize it. Now I want you to take a vacation. Fly to Europe and soak up the sun on those fancy beaches. Then in September we'll talk again."

"Vacationing in Europe isn't going to change how I feel," she murmured sadly, her gaze lowered. The lump in her throat felt as large as a grapefruit. She loved her father, and it was killing her to disappoint him like this.

"We aren't going to talk about your working until September. I apologize, Amy, I should have realized you needed a holiday. It's just that I'm a bit anxious to have you with me—it's been my dream all these years and I've been selfish not to consider the fact you're in need of a little time to yourself."

"Dad, please listen."

"No need to listen," he said, effectively cutting her off. "I just said we'd talk about it in the fall."

It took everything within Amy just to respond to him with a simple nod.

"You don't understand," Amy told Josh the following afternoon. "Before I could say a word, Dad started telling me how I was the sunshine of his life and how he'd waited twenty years for this day. What was I supposed to do?"

"I take it you didn't tell him?"

"I did—in a way."

"Only he didn't listen?"

Her nod was slow and reluctant. "It's obvious you've met my father, or at least someone like him. I don't blame Dad—this isn't exactly what he wanted to hear. The best I could do was to admit I couldn't see myself working with him in the office. Naturally, he didn't want to accept that, so he suggested I take the rest of the summer off to unwind after my studies."

"That's not such a bad idea. You probably shouldn't have expected anything more. Frankly, I think you did very well."

"You do?" she asked excitedly, but her mood quickly deflated. "Then why do I feel so rotten?"

"It's not going to get any easier. Last night was difficult, but at least you've gotten yourself a two-month reprieve. Perhaps, in the coming weeks, you'll come up with some way of making him understand."

Amy lowered her gaze and nodded. "Maybe." She raised the cup to her mouth and took a sip of coffee. "What about you, Josh? Did you hear about the government clearance?"

"No—nothing." His voice was filled with resignation.

"I know it's selfish of me," she admitted with a soft smile, "but I'm glad."

"It's easy enough for you to feel that way, you're not the one sitting on your butt waiting."

They exchanged smiles, and Josh brushed a stray strand of hair from her cheek. His fingers lingered as his eyes held hers.

"I'm grateful you came up and asked to share that table with me," Amy admitted. "I was feeling so low and miserable and talking to you has helped."

A reluctant silence followed, before he said, "Actually, I'd been watching you for some time."

"You had?"

Josh nodded. "I waited around for ten minutes to see if someone was going to join you before I approached the table. I was pleased you were alone."

"I wish there was more time for us to get to know each other," she whispered, surprised by how low and sultry her voice sounded.

"No," he countered bluntly, "in some ways it's for the best."

They stood at the end of the pier behind a long row of tourist shops, and Amy walked away, confused and uncertain. She didn't understand Josh. There wasn't anyone else nearby, and when she turned around and looked up, prepared to argue with him, she was taken aback to realize how close they were to one another—only a scant inch or two separated them.

Josh took the coffee from her hand and set it aside. Then he settled his hands on top of her shoulders, and his spellbinding gaze was stronger than the force of her will. His eyes searched hers for a long moment. She knew then that he intended to kiss her, and her immediate response was pleasure and anticipation. All morning, she'd been thinking about meeting Josh again and her heart had leaped with an eagerness she couldn't explain.

With unhurried ease, he lowered his head to settle his mouth over hers. He was surprisingly gentle. The kiss was slow and thorough, as if rushing something this sweet would spoil it. Amy sighed, and her lips parted softly, inviting him to kiss her again. Josh complied, and when he'd finished, a low moan escaped from deep within his throat.

"I was afraid of that," he said, on the ragged end of a sigh.

"Of what?"

"You taste like cotton candy…much too sweet."

Amy felt a little breathless, a little shaken and a whole lot confused. In one breath Josh had stated that it was better if they didn't get to know each other any better, and in the next he'd kissed her. Apparently, his mind was just as muddled as hers was.

"Amy, listen—"

"You don't like the taste of cotton candy?" she interrupted, her eyes still closed.

"I like it too much."

"Then maybe we should try kissing one more time… you know…as an experiment."

"That might be a bad idea," Josh countered.

"Why?"

"Trust me, it just could."

"Okay," she murmured, disappointed. He placed his fingertips to the vein that pounded in her throat and his thumb stroked it several times as if he couldn't help touching her.

"On second thought," he whispered, a little breathlessly, "maybe that wouldn't be such a big mistake after all." Once more his mouth settled over hers. His kiss was a leisurely exercise as his lips worked from one side of her lips to the other. The heat he generated within her was enough to melt concrete.

He was so tender, so patient, as if he understood and accepted her lack of experience and had made allowances for it. Timidly, Amy slid her hands up his chest and clasped them behind his neck, and when she leaned into him, her breasts brushed against him. He must have felt them through her thin shirt because he moaned and reluctantly put some space between them.

Amy struggled to breathe normally as she dropped her hands.

"You taste good, too," she admitted. That had to be the understatement of the year. Her knees felt weak, and her heart—well, her heart was another story entirely. It seemed as though it was about to burst out of her chest, it was pounding so hard and fast.

Josh draped his wrists over her shoulders and supported his forehead against hers. For a long time he didn't say a word.

"I've got to get back to the hotel. I have a meeting in half an hour."

Amy nodded; she was disappointed, but she understood.

"Can I see you tomorrow?"

"Yes. What time?" How breathless she sounded. How eager.

"Dinner?"

"Okay."

He suggested a time and place and then left her. Amy stood at the end of the pier, her gaze following Josh for as long as he was within sight, then she turned to face the water, letting the breeze off the churning green waters cool her senses.

With his hands buried deep in his pants pockets, Josh stood at the window of his hotel room and gazed out at the animated city below. His thoughts were heavy, confused.

He didn't know why he was so strongly attracted to Amy Johnson, and then again he did.

All right, he admitted gruffly to himself, she was different. Her openness had caught him off guard. From the first moment he'd seen her, something had stopped him. She had looked so miserable, so troubled. He wasn't in the business of counseling fair maidens, especially blond-haired, blue-eyed ones. Even now he was shocked at the way he'd stood and waited for someone to join her and then did so himself when he was certain she was alone. Somehow, the thought of her being friendless and troubled bothered him more than he could explain, even to himself.

It wasn't his style to play the part of a rescuer. Life was complicated enough without him taking on someone else's problems. He'd convinced himself the best course of action was to turn and walk away.

Then she had looked straight at him, and her slate-blue eyes had been wide with appeal. He had realized almost immediately that although she had been staring in his direction, she wasn't seeing him. Perhaps it was then that he recognized the look she wore. Resignation and defeat flickered from her gaze. It was like looking in a mirror and viewing his reflection from years past.

In Amy he saw a part of himself that he had struggled to put behind him, to bury forever. And there it was, a look in a lovely woman's eyes, and he couldn't refuse her. He waited for a moment, not knowing what to do, if anything, then he had ordered the fish and chips and approached her table.

Now the travel clearance he had been waiting for had arrived. For the past fourteen days, he had been looking for government approval before he headed for the oil-rich fields of Saudi Arabia. By all rights, he should be taking the first available flight out of Seattle. He should forget he had even met Amy Johnson, with the blue angel eyes and the soft, sweet mouth. She wasn't the first woman to attract him, but she was the first to touch a deep part of himself that he'd assumed was beyond reach.

In many ways Josh saw Amy as a complete opposite to himself. She was young and vulnerable. The world hadn't hardened her yet, life hadn't knocked her off her feet and walked over her. Her freshness had been retained, and her honesty was evident in every word she spoke.

Yet, in as many ways as they were different there was an equal number that made them similar. Several years back, Josh had faced an almost identical problem to Amy's. He'd loved his father, too, longed to please him, had been willing to do anything to gain Chance Powell's approval.

It was his father's betrayal that had crippled him.

For Amy's sake, Josh prayed matters would resolve themselves differently for her and her father than they had for him and his own. He couldn't bear the thought of Amy forced to face the world alone.

Moving away from the view of downtown Seattle, Josh sat at the end of his mattress, where his suitcase rested. The problem was, he didn't want to leave Amy. His mistake had been kissing her. It was one thing to wonder what she would feel like in his arms, and something else entirely to have actually experienced her softness.

When he had suggested she tell him what had happened once she talked to her father, he had promised himself it would be the last time. Then he had kissed her, and even before he realized what he had been saying, he had suggested dinner. She had smiled at the invitation, and when she spoke, she had sounded eager to see him again.

Only he wouldn't be there. Josh had decided not to show up for their dinner date. It wouldn't take Amy long to figure out that his visa had been approved and he'd had to leave. He was being cruel in an effort to be kind. Funny, the thought of disappointing her troubled him more than anything he had done in a good long while.

"Amy," her father called, as she rushed down the curved stairway. "Why are you running like a wild animal through this house?"

"Sorry, Dad, I'm late," she said with a laugh, because he tended to exaggerate. She hadn't been running, only hurrying. She didn't want to keep Josh waiting.

"Late for what?"

"My date."

"You didn't mention anything about a dinner date earlier."

"I did, at breakfast."

Her father snorted softly. "I don't remember you saying a word. Who is this man you're seeing? Is he anyone I know?"

"No." She quickly surveyed herself in the hall mirror and, pleased with the result, reached for her jacket.

"Who is this young man?" her father repeated.

"Josh Powell."

"Powell… Powell," Harold echoed. "I can't recall knowing any Powells."

"I met him, Dad, you didn't."

"Tell me about him."

"Dad, I'm already five minutes behind schedule." She grabbed her purse and dutifully kissed him on the cheek.

"You don't want me to know about him? This doesn't sound the least bit like you, Amy. You've dated several young men before, but you've always told me something about them. Now you don't have the time to talk about him to your own father?"

"Dad." She groaned, then realized what he said was partially true. She was afraid he wouldn't approve of her seeing someone like Josh and hoped to avoid the confrontation—a recurring problem with her of late.

Dragging in a deep breath, she turned to face Harold

Johnson. "I met Josh on the waterfront the other day. He's visiting Seattle."

"A tourist?"

She nodded, hoping that would satisfy him.

"How long will he be here?"

"I...don't know."

Her father reached for a Havana cigar and stared at the end of it as if that would supply the answers for him. "What aren't you telling me?"

It was all she could do not to groan. She was as readable as a first-grade primer when it came to her father in certain areas, while in others he had a blind eye. "Josh works for one of the oil companies—he didn't mention which one so don't think I'm hiding that. He's waiting for his visa to be approved before he leaves."

"And when will that be?"

"Anytime."

Her father nodded, still gazing at his fat cigar.

"Well?" She threw the question at him. "Aren't you going to tell me not to see him, that he's little more than a drifter and that I'm probably making a big mistake? Josh certainly doesn't sound like the kind of man you'd want me to become involved with."

"No. I'm not going to say a word."

Amy paused to study him. "You're not?"

"I raised you right. If you can't judge a man's character by now, you'll never be able to."

Amy was too shocked to say anything.

"So you like this oil worker?"

"Very much," she whispered.

A smile came over Harold as he reached for a gold lighter. The flames licked at the end of the cigar and he took two deep puffs before he added, "Frankly, I'm not surprised to discover you met someone. Your eyes are as bright as sparklers on the Fourth of July, and you can't get out of this house fast enough."

"I'd leave now if one nosy old man wasn't holding me up by asking me a bunch of silly questions."

"Go on now, and have a good time," he said with a chuckle. "I won't wait up for you."

"Good."

Her father was still chuckling when Amy hurried down the front steps to her car. She felt wonderful. Just when she was convinced her life was at its lowest ebb, she'd met Josh. He was a cool voice of reason that had guided her through the thick fog of her doubts and worries. She had opened up to him in ways she hadn't with others, and in doing so, she had unexpectedly discovered a rare kind of friend. His kiss had stirred up sensations long dormant, and she held those emotions to her chest, savoring them until she was able to see him again.

Fifteen minutes after she left home, Amy walked into the French restaurant near the Pike Place Market. A quick survey of the dim interior confirmed that Josh hadn't arrived yet.

Her heart raced with excitement. She longed for him to kiss her once more, just so she'd know the first time had been real and that she hadn't built it up in her mind.

"May I help you?" the maître d' asked when she stepped into the room.

"I'm meeting someone," Amy explained, taking a seat in the tiny foyer. "I'm sure he'll be along any minute."

The man nodded politely and returned to his station. He paused, glanced in her direction and picked up a white sheet of paper. "Would your name happen to be Amy Johnson?"

"Yes," she said and straightened.

"Mr. Powell phoned earlier with his regrets. It seems he's been called out of town."

Chapter 3

"Do you mean he's left?" Amy's voice rose half an octave with the question. A numb feeling worked its way from her heart to the ends of her fingertips.

The maître d' casually shrugged his thin shoulders. "All I know is what the message says."

He handed it to her, and Amy gripped the white slip and glared at the few words that seemed so inadequate. "I see," she murmured. They hadn't exchanged phone numbers so there'd been no way for him to contact her one last time and let her know his clearance had arrived.

"Would you like a table for one?" the maître d' pressed.

Amy glanced at the angular man and slowly shook her head. "No. Thanks." Her appetite vanished the moment she realized Josh wouldn't be joining her.

The man offered her a weak smile as she headed for the door. "Better luck next time."

"Thank you." The evening had turned exceptionally dark, and when Amy glanced toward the sky, she noted that thick gray thunderclouds had moved in. "Just in time," she mumbled toward the heavens. "I didn't think it was ever going to rain again, and if I was ever in the mood for it, it's now."

With her hands buried in the pockets of her long jacket, she started toward her car, which was parked in the lot across the street.

So Josh was gone. He had zoomed in and out of her life with a speed that had left her spinning in its aftermath, and in the process he had touched her in ways that even now she didn't completely understand.

She recalled the first time she had seen him standing above her, holding an order of fish and chips, wanting to know if he could share the picnic table with her. The look in his expressive dark eyes continued to warm her two days later.

Alone now, she stood at the curb, waiting for the light to change, when she heard her name carried in the wind. Whirling around, she noticed someone running toward her with his hand raised. Her heart galloped to her throat when she realized it was Josh. Briefly, she closed her eyes and murmured a silent prayer of thanksgiving. Turning abruptly, she started walking toward him, too happy to care that it had started to rain.

Josh was breathless by the time they met. He stopped jogging three steps away from her, and when he reached her, he wrapped his powerful arms all the way around her waist, half-lifting her from the sidewalk.

His hold was so tight that for a second Amy couldn't breathe, but it didn't matter. Happiness erupted from her, and it was all she could do not to cover his face with kisses.

"What happened?" she cried when her feet were back on the ground.

The rain was coming down in sheets by this time, and securing his arm around her shoulders, Josh led her into the foyer of the restaurant.

"Ah," the maître d' said, looking pleased. "So your friend managed to meet you after all." He lifted two oblong menus from the holder on the side of the desk and motioned toward the dining room. "This way." His voice took on a formal tone and relayed a heavy French accent that had been noticeably absent earlier.

Once they were seated and presented with the opened menus as if there was insider information from Wall Street to be mindfully studied, Amy looked over to Josh. "What happened?" she asked again. "I thought you'd left town."

His smiling eyes met hers above the menu. "I'm still here."

"Obviously!" She was far more interested in talking to him than scanning the menu. Their waiter arrived and introduced himself as Darrel. Holding his hands prayerfully, he recited the specials of the day, poured their water and generally made a nuisance of himself. By the time he left their table, Amy was growing restless. "Your clearance came through?"

"Yesterday afternoon."

"Then you *are* leaving. When?"

He glanced at his watch as the waiter approached their table once more. "In a few hours."

"Hours," she cried, and was embarrassed when the conversations around them abruptly halted and several heads turned in her direction. Feeling the heat creep into her cheeks, she felt obligated to explain. "I… I wasn't talking about our dinner."

A couple of heads nodded and the talk resumed.

"Would you care to place your order?" Darrel inquired, his eyes darting from Amy to Josh and back again.

"No," she said forcefully. "Could you give us ten more minutes?"

"Of course." He dipped his head slightly and excused himself, looking mildly irritated.

Amy smoothed the white linen napkin onto her lap as the realization hit her that if Josh was scheduled to depart in several hours, then he must have decided earlier not to meet her. But for some unknown reason, he'd changed his mind. "What made you decide to see me?" she asked starkly.

Josh's eyes clashed with hers, and a breathless moment passed before he answered her. "I couldn't stay away."

His answer was honest enough, but it did little to explain his feelings. "But why? I mean why did you want to leave Seattle without saying goodbye?"

"Oh, Amy." He said her name on the end of a troubled sigh, as if he didn't know the answer himself. "It would have been best, I still believe that, but heaven help us both, here I am."

The look in his eyes caused her to grow hot inside, and she reached for her glass, tasting the cool lemon-flavored water.

"I knew the minute I kissed you I was in trouble." He was frowning as he said it, as though he couldn't help regretting that moment.

"Despite what you think, our kissing wasn't a mistake," she said softly, smiling, "It was fate."

"In any case, I'm flying out of Sea-Tac in a little less than seven hours."

Amy's eyes sparked with eagerness as she leaned toward him. "You mean, we have seven whole hours?"

"Yes." Josh didn't seem to share her excitement.

She set her menu aside. "Are you really hungry?"

Josh's gaze narrowed. "I'm…not sure. Why are you looking at me like that?"

"Because if we've got seven hours, I don't think we should waste them sitting in some elegant French restaurant with a waiter named Darrel breathing down our necks."

"What do you suggest?"

"Walking, talking…kissing."

Josh's Adam's apple moved up his throat as his eyes bored straight into hers. "I don't think so… Besides, it's raining." He dismissed her idea with an abrupt look of impatience.

Darrel returned with a linen cloth draped over his forearm, looking more like an English butler than ever.

"I'll have the lamp chops," Josh announced gruffly, handing him the menu. "Rare."

"Escalope de veau florentine," Amy said when their waiter looked expectantly in her direction. She would rather have spent these last remaining hours alone with Josh, but he was apparently going out of his way to avoid that.

Twice now, he'd claimed that kissing her had been problematic, and yet she knew he'd enjoyed the exchange as much as she. In fact he looked downright irritated with himself for having changed his mind about coming this evening. But he'd professed that he couldn't stay away. He was strongly attracted to her, and he didn't like it one bit.

"Amy, would you kindly stop looking at me like that?"

"Like what?" she asked, genuinely confused.

"You're staring at me with my grandmother would call 'bedroom eyes.'"

He was frowning so hard that she laughed out loud. "I am?"

He nodded, looking serious. "Do you realize I'm little more than a drifter? I could be a mass murderer for all you know."

"But you're not." Their salads arrived and she dipped her fork into the crisp greens.

"The fact that I wander from job to job *should* concern you."

"Why?" She didn't understand his reasoning.

"Because just like that—" he snapped his fingers to emphasize his point "—I'm going to be in and out of your life—I won't see you again after tonight. I don't intend on returning to Seattle. It's a nice place to visit, but I've seen everything I care to, and there isn't any reason for me to stop this way again."

"All right, then let's enjoy the time we have."

He stabbed his salad with a vengeance. "I don't know about you, but I'm having a fantastic time right here and now."

"Josh," she whispered. "Why are you so furious?"

"Because." He stopped and inhaled sharply. "The problem is, I'm experiencing a lot of emotions for you that I have no right feeling. I should never have come here tonight, just the way I should never have kissed you. You're young and sweet, and most likely a virgin."

Despite herself, Amy blushed.

"I knew it," he muttered, setting his salad fork aside and sadly shaking his head. "I just knew it."

"That's bad?"

"Yes," he grumbled, looking more put out than ever. "Don't you understand?"

"Apparently not. I think we should appreciate what we feel for each other and not worry about anything else."

"You make it sound so simple."

"And you're complicating everything. You were there for me when I needed a friend. I think you're marvelous, and I'm happy to have met you. If we've only got seven hours—" she paused and, after glancing at her watch, amending the time "—six and a half hours left together, then so be it. I can accept that. When you're gone, I'll think fondly of you and our brief interlude. I don't expect anything more from you, Josh, so quit worrying."

He didn't look any less disturbed, but he returned to his salad, centering his concentration there as if this was his last meal and he was determined to enjoy it.

They barely spoke after their entrées arrived. Amy's veal was excellent, and she assumed that Josh's lamb was equally good.

When Darrel carried their plates away, Josh ordered coffee for them both. When the bill arrived, he paid it, but they didn't linger over their coffee.

"The dinner was very good," Amy said, striving to guide them naturally into conversation. "I'm glad you came back, Josh. Thank you."

He looked as if he was tempted to smile. "I've been rotten company. I apologize."

"Saying goodbye is never easy."

"It has been until now," he said, his eyes locking with hers. "You're a special lady, Amy Johnson, don't sell yourself short. Understand?"

Amy wasn't sure that she did. "I won't," she answered.

"You're far more capable than you give yourself credit for. I don't think your father is as blind as you believe. Once you're in the family business and get your feet wet, you may be surprised by how well you do."

"Et tu, Brute?"

Josh chuckled. "Do you want any more coffee?"

She shook her head.

Josh helped her out of her chair and they left the restaurant.

The rain had stopped for the moment, and a few brave stars poked out from behind a thick cluster of threatening clouds.

With her hands in her pockets, Amy stood in front of the restaurant. "Do you want to say goodbye now?" He didn't answer her right away and, disheartened, Amy read that as answer enough. Slowly, she raised her hand to his face and held it against his clean-shaven cheek. "God speed, Joshua Powell." She was about to turn away when he took hold of her wrist and closed his eyes.

"No," he admitted tightly. "I don't want to say goodbye just yet."

"What would you like to do?"

He chuckled. "The answer would make you blush. Let's walk."

He looped her hand in the crook of his elbow and pressed his fingers over her own. Then he led the way

down the sidewalk, their destination unknown, at least
to her. His natural stride was lengthy, but Amy managed
to keep pace with him without difficulty. He didn't seem
inclined to talk, which was fine, since there wasn't anything special she wanted to say. It was such a joy just
to spend this time with him, to be close to him, knowing that within a matter of hours, he would be gone forever from her life.

After the first couple of blocks, he paused and turned
to her. His eyes were wide and restless as they roamed
her features, as though setting them to memory.

"Do you want to talk?" she asked, looking around
for a place for them to sit down and chat. The area was
shadowy, and most of the small businesses had closed
for the day. The only illumination available was a dim
streetlight situated at the end of the block.

He shook his head. "No," he said evenly, his gaze effectively holding hers. "I want to kiss you."

Amy grinned. "I was hoping you'd say that."

"We shouldn't."

"Oh, I agree one hundred percent. If it was cotton
candy the first time, there's no telling what we'll discover the second. Caramel apples? Hot buttered pop-
corn? Or worst of all—"

He chuckled and silenced her by expertly fitting his
mouth over hers. His kiss was so unbelievably tender
that it caused her to shiver. His grip tightened, bringing her more fully into the circle of his arms. Amy
linked her hands to the base of his neck, leaning into
him and letting him absorb the bulk of her weight. She
strained upward, standing on the tips of her toes, naturally blossoming open to him the way a flower does to
the summer sun.

When they broke apart, they were both trembling.

It had started to rain again, but neither of them seemed to notice. Josh threaded his fingers through her hair as he kissed her once more, rocking his lips slowly back and forth, creating a whole new range of delicious sensations with each small movement.

He shuddered when he finished. "You're much too sweet," he whispered, taking a long series of biting kisses, teasing her with his lips and his tongue.

"So you've said...just don't stop."

"I won't," he promised, and proceeded to show her exactly how much he enjoyed kissing her.

A low moan escaped, and Amy was surprised when she realized the sound had come from her.

"You shouldn't be so warm and giving," Josh continued. He held her close as if loosening his grip would endanger her life.

Amy felt her knees about ready to give. She was a rag doll in his arms. "Josh," she pleaded, caressing the sides of his face and the sharp contours of his jawline.

He continued to mold her softness to him and braced his forehead against hers while he drew in several deep breaths. Amy couldn't stop touching him; it helped root her in reality. Her hands cherished his face. She ran her fingertips up and down his jaw, trying to put the feel of him into her memory, hoping these few short moments would last her for all the time that would follow.

"It's raining," Josh told her.

"I know."

"Cats and dogs."

She smiled.

"You're drenched."

"The only thing I feel is your heart." She flattened

her hand over his chest and dropped her lashes at the sturdy accelerated pulse she felt beneath her fingertips.

"If you don't get dry, you could catch cold," he warned as if he were searching for an excuse to send her away.

"I'll chance it."

"Amy, I can't let you do that." He slipped his arm around her shoulders and guided her east, toward the business-packed section of the downtown area. "I'm taking you to my hotel room. You're going to dry yourself off, and then I'm going to give you a sweater of mine."

"Josh…"

"From there, I'll walk you to your car. We'll be in and out of that hotel room in three minutes flat. Understand?"

Her eyes felt huge. He didn't trust himself to be alone with her in his room, and the thought warmed her from the inside out. Amy didn't need his sweater or a towel or anything else, but she wasn't about to tell him that.

By the time they reached the lobby of his hotel, her hair was so wet that it was dripping on the carpet. She was certain she resembled a drowned muskrat.

Josh's room was on the eighteenth floor. He opened the door for her and switched on the light. The suite was furnished with a king-size bed, chair, television and long dresser. His airline ticket rested on the dresser top, and her gaze was automatically drawn to that. The ticket forcefully reminded her that Josh would soon be out of her life. The drapes were open, and the view of the Seattle skyline was sweeping and panoramic.

"This is nice," she said, smiling at him.

"Here." He handed her a thick towel, which she used to wipe the moisture from her face and hair.

"What about you?" she asked, when she'd finished.

He stood as far away from her as he possibly could and still remain in the same room. His eyes seemed to be everywhere but on her.

"I'm fine." He scooted past her, keeping well out of her way. His efforts to avoid brushing against her were just short of comical. He seemed to breathe again once he was safely out of harm's way. From the way he was acting, one would suspect she carried bubonic plague. He opened the closet and took out a long-sleeved sweater. "There's a mirror in the bathroom if you need it."

She actually did want to run a comb through her hair and moved into the other room.

"Do you remember the other day when you asked me if I didn't go in to my father's business what I wanted to do instead?"

"I remember." His voice sounded a long way off, as though he was on the other side of the room.

"I've given the question some thought in the last few days."

"What have you come up with?"

She stuck her head around the door. She was right; Josh stood with his back to her in front of the windows, although she doubted that he was appreciating the view. "If I tell you, do you promise not to laugh?"

"I'll try."

She eased his sweater over her head and smoothed it around her hips, then gingerly stepped into the room, hands dangling awkwardly at her sides. "In light of all the advancements in the feminist movement, this is going to sound ridiculous."

"Try me." He folded his arms over his broad chest and waited.

"More than anything, I'd like to be a wife and a stay-at-home mother." She watched him carefully, half expecting him to find something humorous in her confession. Instead, his gaze gentled and he smiled.

"I treasure the memories of my mother," she continued. "She was so wonderful to me and Dad, so loving and supportive of everything we did. I've already explained my father's personality, so you know what he's like. Mom was the glue that held our family together. Her love was the foundation that guided him in those early years. I don't know if she ever visited his office, in fact, I rather doubt that she did, and yet he discussed every decision with her. She was his support system, his rock. She was never in the limelight, but she was a vital part of Dad's life, and his business."

"You want to be like her?"

Amy nodded. "Only I'm more greedy. I want a house full of children, too."

Josh's gaze moved deliberately to his watch. "I think we'd better go," he said, sounding oddly breathless.

"Josh?"

He stiffened. "I promised you we'd be in and out of here in a matter of minutes. Remember?"

"I'd like to stay."

"No," he said forcefully, shaking his head. "Amy, please, try to understand. Being alone with you is temptation enough—don't make it any more difficult."

"What about the sweater?" She ran her fingers down the length of the sleeves. "Won't you want it back?"

"Keep it. Where I'm headed it's going to be a hundred degrees in the shade. Trust me, I'm not going to miss it."

"But—"

"Amy!" Her name was a husky rumble low in his chest. "Unless you'd like to start that family you're talking about right now, I suggest we get out of here."

"Soon," she told him firmly, refusing to give in to the shock value of his statement.

Twin brows arched. "Soon?" he repeated incredulously.

"Come here." Her back was pressed against the door, and her heart was pounding so hard that it had long since drowned out what reason remained to her. She had never been so bold with a man in her life, but she knew if she was ever going to act, the time was now. Otherwise, Josh was going to politely walk her to her car, kiss her on the cheek and wish her a good life and then casually stroll away from her and out of her world.

"Amy." His mouth thinned with impatience.

"Say goodbye to me here," she said, smiling, then she motioned with her index finger for him to come to her.

He shoved his hands into his jeans pockets as if he didn't trust them to keep still at his sides. He paused and cleared his throat. "It really is time we left."

"Fine. All I'm asking is for you to say our farewells here. It will be much better than in a parking lot outside the restaurant, don't you think?"

"No." The lone word was harsh and low.

She shrugged and hoped she looked regretful. "All right," she murmured and sighed. "If you won't come to me, then I guess I'll have to go to you."

Josh looked shocked by this and held out his hand as if he were stopping traffic.

The action did more to amuse her than keep her at bay. "I'm going to say goodbye to you, Joshua Powell. And I'm warning you right now, it's going to be a kiss you'll remember for a good long while."

Everything about Josh told her how much he wanted her. From the moment they had stepped into his room the tension between them had been electric. She didn't understand why he was putting up such a fight. For her part, she was astonished by her own actions. Until she had met Josh, she had always been the timid, reserved one in a relationship. Two minutes alone with him and she had turned into a hellcat. She wasn't sure what had caused the transformation.

"Amy, please, you aren't making this easy," Josh muttered. "We're playing with a lighted fuse here, don't you understand that? If I kiss you, sweetheart, I promise you it won't stop there. Before either of us will know how it happened, you're going to be out of that dress and my hands are going to be places where no one else has ever touched you. Understand?"

She felt the blood drain out of her face as quickly as if someone had pulled a drain from a sink. Blindly, she nodded. Still, it didn't stop her from easing her way toward him.

Josh groaned. "I knew it was a mistake to bring you up here." His face was tight, his eyes dark and brilliant. "We're going to end up making love, and you're going to give me something I don't want. Save it for your husband, sweetheart, he'll appreciate it more than I will."

Her heart went crazy. It felt like a herd of charging elephants was stampeding inside her chest. She moistened her lips, and whatever audacity had propelled her into this uncharacteristic role abruptly left her at the threat in his words. Pausing, she drew in a deep, calming breath and forced a smile.

"Goodbye, Josh," she whispered. With that, she turned and bolted for the door.

He caught her shoulder and catapulted her around and into his chest before she made it another step. He cursed under his breath and locked her in his arms, rubbing his chin back and forth over the crown of her head in a caressing action, silently apologizing for shocking her.

"Oh, Amy," he groaned, "perhaps you're right. Maybe it *is* fate." She felt his warm breath against the hollow beneath her right ear.

Her head fell back in a silent plea, and he began spreading warm kisses over the delicate curve of her neck. With his hands holding each side of her face, he ran his lips along the line of her jaw, his open mouth moist and passionate. When she was sure he meant to torment her for hours before giving her what she craved, he lowered his mouth to hers, softly, tenderly in a kiss that was as gentle as the flutter of a hummingbird's wings. A welcoming rasping sound tumbled from her lips.

He made a low, protesting noise of his own as his lips caressed hers, tasted her, savored her, his mouth so hot and compelling that she felt singed all the way to the soles of her feet. When they broke apart, they were both breathless.

"Amy... I tried to tell you."

"Shh." She kissed him to silence his objections. She had no regrets and longed to erase his. "I want you to touch me...it feels so good when you do."

"Oh, angel, you shouldn't say things like that to a man."

"Not any man," she whispered, "only you."

Josh inhaled a sharp breath. "That doesn't make it any better."

"Why don't you just shut up and kiss me again?"

"Because," he growled, "I want so much more." He ground his mouth over hers as if to punish her for making him desire her so much.

Amy bit into her lower lip at the powerful surge of sensations that assaulted her like a tidal wave. Before she knew what was happening, he had removed the sweater he had given her to wear. His fingers were poised at the zipper at the back of her dress when he paused, his breathing labored. Then, with a supreme effort, he brought his strong loving hands to either side of her face, stroking her satiny cheeks with the pads of his thumbs.

"It's time to stop, Amy. I meant what I said about saving yourself for your husband. I won't be coming back to Seattle."

She dipped her head and nodded, accepting his words. "Yes, I know." Gently she raised her lips to his and kissed him goodbye. But she kept her promise. She made sure it was a kiss Joshua Powell would well remember.

Josh secured the strap of his flight bag to his shoulder and glanced a second time at his watch. He still had thirty minutes before he could board the plane that would carry him to his destination in Kadiri. He had been filled with excitement, eager for the challenge that awaited him in this Middle Eastern country, and now he would have gladly forfeited his life savings for an excuse to remain in Seattle.

His mind was filled with doubts. He had said goodbye to Amy several hours earlier and already he was being eaten alive, caught between the longing to see her again and the equally strong desire to forget they had ever met.

His biggest mistake had been trusting himself alone with her in his hotel room. The temptation had been too much for him, and she certainly hadn't helped matters any. The woman was a natural-born temptress, and she didn't even know it. She couldn't so much as walk across the room without making him want her. All his life, he would remember her leaning against his door and motioning for him to come to her with her index finger. She was so obviously new to the game that her efforts should have been more humorous than exciting. Unfortunately, everything about her excited him.

To complicate matters, she was innocent. When she started talking about building a secure home life for her husband and wanting children, he knew that she was completely out of his league. They were as different as fresh milk and aged Scotch. She was hot dogs and baseball and freshly diapered babies. And he was rented rooms, a dog-eared passport and axle grease.

He had to bite his tongue to keep from asking for her number. He didn't often think of himself as noble, but he did now. The sooner he left Amy, the sooner he could return to his disorderly vagabond lifestyle.

However, Josh was confident of one thing—it would be a long time before he forgot her.

As Josh stood in the security line at Sea-Tac Airport he checked the flight time and gate number on his ticket.

"Josh."

He jerked around to discover Amy hurrying down the concourse toward him. For one wild second, Josh didn't know if he should be pleased or not.

It didn't take him long to decide.

Chapter 4

"**A**my." Josh rushed out of the line at security and gripped her shoulders as his eyes scanned hers. "What are you doing here?" She was still breathless and it took her several moments to speak. "I know I shouldn't… have come, but I couldn't stay home and…and let it all end so abruptly."

"Amy, listen to me—"

"I know." She pressed the tips of her fingers over his lips, not wanting him to speak. He couldn't say anything that she hadn't already told herself a dozen times or more. "I'm doing everything wrong, but I couldn't bear to just let you walk out of my life without—"

"We already said goodbye."

"I know that, too," she protested.

"How'd you know where to find me?"

"I saw your airline ticket on the dresser, and once I knew which airline, it wasn't difficult to figure out which secrurity checkpoint you'd be going through. Oh, Josh, I'm sorry if this embarrasses you." She was so confused, hot and cold at the same time. Hot from his kisses and cold with apprehension. She was making a complete idiot of herself, but after weighing her options, she'd done the only thing she could.

"Here," she said, thrusting an envelope toward him.

"What's this?"

"In case you change your mind."

"About what?" His brow condensed with the question.

"About ever wanting to see me again. It's my contact information, and for good measure I threw in a flattering photo of myself, but it was taken several years ago when my hair was shorter and…well, it's not much, but it's the best I have."

He chuckled and hauled her into his arms, squeezing her close.

"You don't have to email me," she told him, her voice steady with conviction.

"I probably won't."

"That's fine…well, it isn't, but I can accept that."

"Good."

He didn't seem inclined to release her, but buried his face in her neck and drew in a short breath. "Your scent is going to haunt me," he grumbled. "I'm going halfway around the world and all I'll think about is you."

"Good." Her smile was weak at best. She'd done everything she could by pitching the ball to him. If and when he decided to swing at it, she would be ready.

The security guard tapped him on the shoulder. "Are you going or not, cause you're blocking the line." Moving over slightly, Josh wrapped her in a warm embrace, he brushed his hand across her cheek, his touch was tender, as though he was caressing a newborn baby. "I have to go," he said, his voice low and gravelly.

"Yes, I know." Gently she smoothed his sweater at his shoulders and offered him a feeble smile. "Enjoy the Middle East," she said, "but stay away from those belly dancers."

Amy dropped her arms and stuffed her hands inside her pockets for fear she would do something more to embarrass them both. Something silly like reaching out and asking him not to leave, or pleading with him to at least contact her.

She did her utmost to beam him a polished smile. If he was going to hold on to the memory of her, she wanted to stand tall and dignified and give him a smile that would make Miss America proud. "Have a safe trip."

He nodded, turned and took two steps away from her.

Panic filled Amy—there was one last thing she had to say. "Josh." At the sound of her voice, he abruptly turned back. "Thank you...for everything."

He offered her a weak smile.

She nodded, because saying anything more would have been impossible. She kept her head tilted at a proud angle, determined to send him off with a smile.

"Amy." Her name was a low growl as Josh dropped his flight bag and stepped toward her.

"Go on," she cried. "You'll miss your plane."

He was at her side so fast she didn't have time to think or act. He hauled her into his arms and kissed her with a hunger and need that were enough to convince her she would never find another man who made her feel the things this one did. His wild kiss was ardent, but all too brief to suit either of them.

Josh pulled himself away from her with some effort, picked up his bag and headed into the security checkpoint. Amy stood frozen to the spot he'd left her, following him with her eyes, until he was out of sight, her head demanding that she forget Joshua Powell and her heart claiming it was impossible.

Harold Johnson was sitting in the library smoking a cigar when Amy quietly let herself into the house. The lights from the crack beneath the door alerted her to the fact her father was up and waiting for her return.

"Hi," she said, letting herself into the room. She sat in the wingback leather chair beside him and peeled off her coat. Slipping off her shoes, she tucked her feet beneath her and rested her eyes.

"You're back."

She nodded. "I saw Josh off at the airport. I gave him all my contact information and for good measure a photo of myself."

"Smart idea."

"According to Josh it was a mistake. I can't understand why he thinks that way, but he does. He made it clear he has no intention of keeping in touch."

"Can you accept that?"

To Amy's way of thinking, she didn't have a choice. "I'll have to."

Her father's low chuckle was something of a surprise. "I don't mind telling you that your interest in this young man is poetic justice."

"Why's that?"

"All these years, there've been boys buzzing around

this house like bees in early summer, but you didn't pay a one of them a moment's heed. For all the interest you showed, they could have been made of marble."

"None of them was anything like Josh."

"What makes this one so different?" her father asked, chewing on the end of his cigar.

Amy swore he ate more of it than he smoked. "I don't know what to tell you. Josh is forthright and honest— to a fault sometimes. He's the type of man I'd want by my side if anything was ever to go wrong. He wouldn't back away from a fight, but he'd do everything within his power to see that matters didn't get that far."

"I'd like him, then."

"I know you would, Dad, you wouldn't be able to stop yourself. He's direct and sincere."

"Pleasant to look at, I suspect."

She smiled and nodded. "He wears his hair a little longer than what you'd like, though."

"Hair doesn't make the man." Harold Johnson puffed at the cigar and reached for his glass of milk.

"What are you doing up this late?" she asked after a moment of comfortable silence.

"After we talked when you came home from dinner, I heard you roaming around your bedroom for an hour or two, pacing back and forth loud enough to wake the birds. About the time I decided to find out what was troubling you, I heard you leave. Since I was awake, I decided to read a bit, and by the time I noticed the hour, it wasn't worth going back to bed."

"I'm sorry I kept you awake."

"No problem." He paused and yawned loudly, covering his mouth with the back of his hand. "Maybe I *will* try to get in an hour or two of rest before heading for the office."

"Good idea." Amy hadn't realized how exhausted she was until her father mentioned it.

They walked up the stairs together and she kissed his cheek when she reached her bedroom door. "Sally and I are playing tennis tomorrow morning, and then I'm doing some volunteer work at the homeless center later in the afternoon. You didn't need me for anything, did you?"

"No. But I thought you were going to take the summer off?"

"I am," she said, and yawned. "Trust me, Dad, tennis is hard work."

Josh had never been fond of camels. They smelled worse than rotting sewage, were ill-tempered and more stubborn than mules. The beasts were the first thing Josh saw as he stepped off his small plane that had delivered him to the oil fields. He had the distinct impression this country was filled with them. And soldiers. Each and every one of them seemed to be carting a machine gun. A cantankerous camel strolled across the runway followed by two shouting men waving sticks and cursing in Arabic.

Joel Perkins, Josh's direct superior and best friend, was supposed to meet him in the crowded Kadiri airport. Kadiri was a small town rich in oil. The company that employed Josh had recently signed a contract for oil exploration and drilling with the Saudi government.

It was like stepping back in time when Josh stepped off the plane. The terminal, if the building could be termed that, was filled with animals and produce and so crowded that Josh could barely move.

Ten minutes in this part of the country and already his clothes were plastered to his skin; the temperature must have been over a hundred degrees inside, and no telling what it was in the direct sunlight.

At six foot four, Joel Perkins was head and shoulders above most everyone, so it was easy enough for Josh to spot his friend. Making his way over to him, however, was another matter entirely.

"Excuse me," Josh said twenty times as he scooted around caged chickens, crying children and several robed men.

"Good to see you," Joel greeted him, and slapped his hand across Josh's back. "How was the flight?"

"From Seattle to Paris was a piece of cake. From Paris to Kadiri…you don't want to hear about it, trust me."

Joel laughed. "But you're here now and safe."

"No thanks to that World War II wreck of a plane that just landed."

"As you can see, the taxis are out of service," Joel explained. "We're going to have to ride into the city on these."

Josh took one look at the ugliest-looking camel he had ever encountered and let out an expletive that would have curled Amy's hair. He stopped abruptly. Every thought that drifted through his mind was in some way connected to her. He hadn't stopped thinking of her for a single minute. Every time he closed his eyes, it was her lips that smiled at him, her blue eyes that flashed with eagerness, her arms that reached toward him.

What he had said to her about her scent haunting

him had been prophetic. In fact, he had strolled along the streets of Paris until he had found a small fragrance shop. It took him an hour to discover the perfume that reminded him of her. Feeling like a fool for having wasted the proprietor's time, he ended up buying a bottle. He didn't know what he was going to do with it. Mail it to his seventy-year-old aunt Hazel?

"What's the matter?" Joel asked. "Has the heat gotten to you already?"

"No," Josh said. "A woman has."

Joel's eyes revealed his surprise. "A woman? Where?"

"Seattle."

Joel laughed.

"What's so funny?" Josh demanded.

"You. It does me good to see you aren't as immune as you'd like others to believe."

Josh muttered under his breath, regretting saying anything about Amy to his friend.

Joel slapped him across the back as his eyes grew dark and serious. "Are you going to do anything about it?"

Josh didn't need to think before he answered. "Not a damn thing."

Joel expelled his breath in a slow exercise. "Good. You had me worried there for a minute."

A week later, Josh had changed Joel Perkins's mind.

Exhausted, Amy let herself in the back door of her home. Her face was red, and she wiped it dry with the small white towel draped around her neck. Her tennis racket was in one hand, and after securing it under her arm, she poured herself a tall glass of iced tea.

"Manuela, is the mail here?"

"Nothing for you, Miss Amy," the Spanish-American housekeeper informed her.

Amy tried to swallow the disappointment, but it was growing increasingly difficult. Josh had been gone nearly two weeks, and she'd hoped to hear from him before now. No emails, no messages. She'd hoped he at least might write. Nothing yet and she was beginning to believe she wouldn't hear from him. The thought deeply depressed her.

Her phone rang, as she went to answer it she noted that the display read private. "Hello," she said, walking out of the kitchen. Her words were followed by an eerie hum. Amy blinked and was about to disconnect when someone spoke.

"Amy, is that you?"

Her heart raced into her throat. "Josh?"

"What time is it there? I wasn't sure of the time difference and I hope it isn't the middle of the night."

"It's not. It's three in the afternoon."

He sounded so different. So far away, but that didn't detract from the exhilaration she was experiencing from hearing the sound of his voice.

"I'm so glad you called," she said softly, slumping into her father's desk chair. "I've been miserable, wondering if you ever would. I'd just about given up hope."

"It was Joel's idea."

"Joel?"

"He's a friend of mine. He claimed that if I didn't call you, he would. Said I had my mind on you when I should be thinking about business. I guess he's right."

"If he were close by, I'd kiss him."

"If you're going to kiss anyone, Amy Johnson, it's me, understand?"

"Yes, sir."

"What's the weather like?"

"Seventy-five and balmy. I just finished playing two sets of tennis. I've been doing a lot of that lately... If I'm exhausted, then I don't think of you so much. What's the weather like in Kadiri?"

"You don't want to know. A hundred and five about ten this morning."

"Oh, Josh. Are you going to be all right?"

"Probably not, but I'll live." There was some commotion and then Josh came back on the line. "Joel's here, and he said I should email you."

Her heartbeat slowed before she asked, "Is that what you want?"

An eternity passed before he responded. "I don't know what I want anymore. At one time everything was clear to me, but after two weeks, I'm willing to admit I was a fool to think I could forget you. Yes, Amy, I'll be in touch. I'll try and get a message off to you now and again, but I'm not making any promises."

"I understand."

"Listen, I put something in the mail for you the other day, but it'll take a week or more before it arrives—if it ever does. The way everything else goes around here, I doubt that it'll make it through customs intact."

"Something from Kadiri?"

"No, actually, I picked this up in Paris."

"Oh, Josh, you were thinking of me in Paris?"

"That's the problem, I never stopped thinking about you." Once more there was a quick exchange of muffled words before Josh came back on the line. "Joel seemed to think it's important for you to know that I haven't been the best company the last couple of weeks."

Amy closed her eyes, savoring these moments. "Thank Joel for letting me know."

"Be sure and tell me if that package arrives. If it does, there's something else I'd like to send you, something from Kadiri." His words were followed by heavy static.

"Josh. Josh," she cried, certain she'd lost him.

"I'm here, but I can't say for how much longer."

"This is probably costing you a fortune."

"Don't worry about it. Joel's springing for the call."

A faint laugh could be heard in the distance, and Amy smiled, knowing already that she was going to like Josh's friend.

"As soon as you contact me I'll email you back, I promise." It was on the tip of her tongue to tell him how much she had thought about him and missed him since he'd left. Twice now, she had gone down to the waterfront and stood at the end of the pier where he had first kissed her, hoping to recapture those precious moments.

"I swear living in Kadiri is like stepping into the eighteenth century. This phone is the only one within a hundred miles, so there isn't any way to reach me."

"I understand."

"Amy, listen." Josh's voice was filled with regret. "I've got to go. Joel's apparently bribed a government official to use this phone, and we're about to get kicked out of here."

"Oh, Josh, do be careful."

"Honey," he said, and laughed. "I was born careful."

At that precise moment, the line was severed.

Amy sat down at the dinner table across from her father and smoothed the napkin across her lap, feeling warm and happy.

"So you got another email from Josh today?"

"Yes," she said, glancing up. "How'd you know?"

"You mean other than that silly grin you've been wearing all afternoon? Besides, you haven't played tennis all week, and before his phone call, you spent more time on the tennis courts than you did at home."

Amy reached for the lean pork roast and speared herself an end cut. "I don't know what tennis has to do with Joshua Powell."

Her father snickered softly. He knew her too well for her to disguise her feelings.

"Little things say a lot, remember that when you start working at the end of the summer. That small piece of advice will serve you well."

"I will," she murmured, handing him the meat platter, avoiding his gaze.

"Now," her father said forcefully, "when am I going to meet this young man of yours?"

"I… I don't know, Dad. Josh hasn't written a word about when he's leaving Kadiri. He could be there for several months—perhaps longer. I have no way of knowing."

Her father set the meat platter aside, then paused and rested his elbows on the table, clasping his hands together. "How do you feel about that?"

"I don't understand."

"I notice you're not dating anyone. Fact is, you've been living like a nun. Don't you think it's time to start socializing a little?"

"No." Her mind was too full of Josh to consider going out with another man, although she was routinely asked. Not once in all the weeks since Josh had left Seattle had the thought of dating anyone else entered her mind.

Harold Johnson brooded during the remainder of their meal. Amy knew that look well. It preceded a father-to-daughter chat in which he would tell her something "for her own good." This time she was certain the heart-to-heart talk would have to do with Josh.

Amy didn't have a single argument prepared. Harold was absolutely right, she barely knew Joshua Powell. She'd seen him a grand total of three times—four if she counted the fact they'd met twice that first day and five if she included her harried trip to the airport. It wouldn't have mattered if she'd seen him every day for six months, though. But her father wouldn't understand that. As far as Amy was concerned, she knew everything important that she needed to know about him.

When their talk was over, Amy went to her room, took out her computer and read the email she'd received and sat on the bed.

Dear Amy,

I opened your email this morning. There are no words to tell you how pleased I was to see it. It seems weeks since we talked on the phone, and with Joel standing over me, it was difficult to tell you the things that have been going through my head. Now, as I sit down to type, I realize it isn't any easier to find the words. I never was much good with this sort of thing. I work well with numbers and with my hands, but when it comes to expressing my feelings, I'm at a loss.

I suppose I should admit how glad I was to see you at the airport. As I headed to the airport to catch my flight I told myself it was best to make a clean break. Then, all of a sudden, you were there and despite everything, I was thrilled you came. I still can't believe you came and how you knew when and where to find me. Anyways like I said before, I'm not much good at this. Email be back when you can.

Love, Josh

Needing to think about her response, Amy waited a day to reply.

Dearest Josh,

The perfume arrived in today's mail. The fragrance is perfect for me. Where did you ever find it? The minute I opened the package, I dabbed some behind my ear and closed my eyes, imagining you were here with me. I know it sounds silly, but I felt so close to you at that moment, as if it was your fingers spreading the fragrance at my pulse points, holding me close. Thank you.

Today was a traumatic one for me. Dad brought me in to work with him to show me how he'd had an office completely remodeled for me. It was so plush, so... I don't know, elaborate. Everything was done in a dark wood, mahogany I think. I swear the desk had to be six feet long. I don't suppose this means that much unless you've ever seen my dad's office. He's used the same furniture for twenty years...same office assistant, too. At any rate, everything about my dad's office shouts humble beginnings, hard work and frugality. He should be the one with the fancy furniture—not me. I swear the guilt was more than I could bear.

It made me realize that the clock is ticking and I won't be able to delay telling him my feelings much longer. I've got to tell him...only I don't know how. I wish you were here. You made me feel so confident that I'm doing the right thing. I don't feel that anymore. Now all I am is confused and alone.

Love, Amy

P.S. You haven't been seeing any belly dancers, have you?

Dearest Angel Eyes,
I swear this country is the closest thing to hell on earth. The heat is like nothing I've ever known. Last night, for the first time since I arrived, Joel and I went swimming. We were splashing around like a couple of five-year-olds. The whole time I was wishing it was you with me instead of Joel.

Later I lay on the sand and stared at the sky. The stars were so bright, they seemed to droop right out of the heavens. I had the feeling if I reached up I could snatch one right out of the sky. First chance I get I rush to my computer at the end of the day and I'm happy as a kid in a candy store when an email arrives from you. Then the next thing I know I'm gazing at the stars, wondering if you're staring at them, too. What have you done to me, Amy Johnson?

Joel keeps feeding me warnings. He tells me a woman can be too much of a distraction, and that I've got to keep my head screwed on straight. He's right. We're not exactly here on a picnic. Don't worry about me, if I'm anything it's cautious.

I put a surprise in the mail for you today. This is straight from the streets of Kadiri. Let me know when it arrives.

Love, Josh

P.S. No, I haven't seen any belly dancers. What about you? Any guys from the country club wanting you for doubles on the tennis courts?

My dearest Josh,
I love seeing the picture of you and Joel. You look so tan and so handsome. It made me miss you all the more. I sat down and studied the photo for so long the image started to blur. I miss you so much, it seems that we barely had a chance to know each other and then you were gone. Don't mind me for complaining. I'm in a blue funk today. Dad took me to lunch so I could meet the others from the office and when I jumped on the computer I saw your email.

It made me wish I could sit down and talk to you.

By the way, Joel's so tall. I'm pleased he's there with you. Thanks, too, for your vote of confidence in handling this situation with Dad. He seems oblivious to my feelings. Come September, I probably will move into my fancy new office because I can't honestly see myself confronting him. My fate is sealed.

Your Angel Eyes

It was one of those glorious summer afternoons that blesses the Pacific Northwest every August. Unable to resist the sun, Amy was venting her energy by doing laps in the pool.

"Miss Amy, Miss Amy!"

Manuela came running toward the pool, her hands flying. She stopped, breathless, and a flurry of Spanish erupted from her so fast and furiously that even after two years of studying the language, Amy couldn't make out a single word.

"Manuela," she protested, stepping out of the pool. She reached for her towel. "What are you saying?"

"You left your phone on the counter...long distance... man say hurry."

Amy's heart did a tiny flip-flop. "Is it Josh?"

The housekeeper's hands gestured to the sky as she broke into her native tongue again.

"Never mind," Amy cried, running toward the phone in her hand. "Josh... Josh, are you still there?"

"Amy? Who answered the phone? I couldn't understand a word she said."

"That's Manuela. I'm sorry it took me so long. How are you? Oh, Josh, I miss you so much."

"I miss you, too, angel. I read your email from yesterday, and I haven't been able to stop thinking about you since."

"I was in such a depressed state when I wrote that... I should never have pressed the Send button."

"I'm glad you did. Now, tell me what's happening between you and your father."

"Josh, I can't—not over the phone."

"You're going to work for him?"

"I can't see any way out of it. Are you going to think me a coward?"

"My Angel Eyes? Never."

"I figured the least I could do was give it a try. I don't hold out much hope, but who knows, I might shock everyone and actually be successful."

"You sound in better spirits."

"I am...now. Oh, before I forget, the traditional dress from Kadiri arrived, and I love it. It's so colorful and cool. What did you say the women call it again?"

"Btu-btu."

She could hear the smile in his voice, which did more to elevate Amy's mood than anything in two long months. "It's beautiful."

"Amy, listen, I've only got a few more minutes. We were able to get use of the phone again, but I don't know how long it's good for so if we're cut off again, don't worry."

She nodded before she realized he couldn't see her gesture of understanding. She closed her eyes to keep the ready emotion cornered. "I can't tell you how good it is to hear your voice."

"Yours, too, Angel Eyes."

She laughed. "I loved the picture of you and Joel. Thank you so much for sending it. You look even better than I remember."

"I'm coming back to Seattle."

Amy's head snapped up. "When? Oh, Josh, you don't know how many times I prayed you would."

"Don't get so excited, it won't be until December."

"December," she repeated. "I can wait another five months…easy. How about you?"

"I swear to you, Amy, I don't know anymore. I've never felt about a woman the way I do about you. Half the time I'm so confused by what's happening between us that I can't understand how this company can pay me the money it does. Joel keeps threatening to fire me; he claims he doesn't need anyone as lovesick as me on his crew."

Lovesick. It was the closest Josh had ever come to admitting what he felt for her.

"Hold on a minute," Josh shouted. He came back on the line almost immediately. "Honey, I've got to go. I'm thinking about you, angel—"

"Josh… Josh," she cried, "listen to me. I love you."
But the line had already gone dead.

A man could only take so much, Josh reasoned as
he walked among the huge drilling structures that had
been brought into Kadiri by SunTech Oil. Joel, acting
as general foreman, had left his instructions with Josh,
but Josh had been running into one confounding problem after another all morning. There wasn't any help
for it. Josh was going to have to find Joel and discuss
the situation.

It was as he was walking across the compound that
he heard the first explosion. The force of it was powerful enough to hurl him helplessly to the ground.

By the time he gathered his wits, men had panicked
and were running, knocking each other down, fighting
their way toward the gates.

"Joel," Josh cried when he didn't see his friend.
Josh searched the frantic, running crowd, but battling
through the workers was as difficult as swimming up
a waterfall.

"Joel," Josh shouted a second time, then grabbed a
man he recognized by the collar. "Where's Joel Perkins?"

The trembling man pointed toward the building that
was belching smoke and spitting out flames from two
sides. Something drove Josh forward. Whatever it was
had nothing to do with sanity or reason or anything
else. The only conscious thought Josh had was the bru-
tal determination to go inside and bring out his friend.

Two men tried to stop him, screaming a word that
Josh found unintelligible. Covering his mouth with a
wet cloth, Josh shoved them both aside with a super-

human strength, then, without thought, stormed into the building.

He recognized two things almost immediately. The first was that Joel Perkins was dead. The second was more devastating than the first. The building was going to explode, and there was nothing he could do to get himself out alive.

Chapter 5

"Amy."

Her father's gentle voice stirred her from a light sleep. She rolled over onto her back to discover him sitting on the edge of her bed, dressed in his plaid robe, his brow puckered in a dark frown. He'd turned on her bedside lamp to its lowest setting.

"Dad?" she asked, softly. "What is it?"

His eyes pooled with regret, and instantly she knew. "It's Josh, isn't it?"

Her father nodded. "The call came an hour ago."

He'd waited an hour. A full hour? Struggling into a sitting position, she brushed the hair from her temples, her hands trembling. She hadn't heard from him in almost two weeks and had already started to worry. Her heart had told her something was wrong.

"Tell me," she whispered. Her tongue felt thick and

uncooperative, but she had to know even if it meant she'd lost him forever. "What's happened?"

Harold Johnson placed his hands on her shoulders. "He's been seriously injured. There was an accident, an explosion. Five men were killed. Josh wasn't hurt in the initial explosion, but he went back for his friend. Apparently, he was too late; his friend was already dead."

Amy covered her mouth with her palm and took in deep, even breaths in an effort to curtail the growing alarm that churned in her like the huge blades of a windmill, stirring up dread and fear. "But he's alive."

"Yes, baby, he's alive, but just barely. I can't even tell you the extent of his injuries, only that they're life threatening."

Fear coated her throat. "How did SunTech Oil know to contact me?" Whatever the reason, she thanked God they had. Otherwise, she might never have known.

Her father gently brushed the hair from her brow, his eyes tender and concerned. "Josh listed you as his beneficiary in case of his death. Since he hadn't written down anyone as next of kin, yours was the only name they had. I can't tell you any more than that. The line was terrible, and it was difficult to understand anything of what the official was saying."

Without waiting for anything more, Amy tossed back the covers. "I'm going to him."

Her father shook his head meaningfully. "Somehow I knew you'd say that."

"Then I suppose you also knew I'd want the next flight out of here for Kadiri?" She paused and thought for a moment. "What about a visa?"

"As a matter of fact, I thought of both those things," he admitted, chuckling softly. "There's a connecting plane in Paris, but the only flight into Kadiri flies on Wednesdays."

"But that means I'll have to wait an entire week." She used her thumb and index finger to cup her chin and frowned. "Then I'll get to Paris and hire a private plane to fly me into Saudi Arabia. If I have to, I'll walk from there."

"That won't be necessary," Harold told her.

"Why not?" She whirled around, not understanding.

"You can take the company jet. I'm not sending you off to that part of the world without a means of getting you out of there."

Despite the severity of the situation she smiled, tears glistening in her eyes. "Thank you, Dad."

"And while I was at it, I talked to a friend of mine in the State Department. You've been granted a six-week visa, but you won't be able to stay any longer—our relations with the Middle East are strained at best. Get in and out of there as fast as you can. Understand?"

Her mind was buzzing. "Is there anything else I need to know?"

"Yes," Harold said firmly. "When you come home, I want Josh with you."

When Josh awoke, the first thing that met him was pain so ruthless and severe that for a moment he couldn't breathe. He groaned and dragged in a deep breath, trying to come to terms with the fact that he was alive and not knowing how much longer he wanted to live if being alive meant this excruciating pain. Blissfully, he returned to unconsciousness.

The second time, he was greeted with the same agony, only this time there was a scent of jasmine in the air. Josh struggled to hold on to consciousness. The flower brought Amy to the forefront of his mind. His last thoughts before the building exploded had been of his Angel Eyes, and regret had filled him at the thought of never seeing her again. Perhaps it had been that thought that had persuaded death to give him a second chance. Whatever it was, Josh was grateful. At least, he thought he was, until the pain thrust him into a dark world where he felt nothing.

Time lost meaning. Days, weeks, months could have silently slipped past without him ever realizing it. All he experienced were brief glimpses of consciousness, followed by blackouts for which he was always grateful, because they released him from the pain.

The scent of jasmine was in the wind whenever he awoke. He struggled to breathe it into his lungs because it helped him remember Amy. He held on to her image as long as he could, picturing her as she stood at the airport, determined to send him off with a smile. So proud. So lovely—with soulful eyes an angel would envy. It was then that he had started thinking of her as Angel Eyes.

The sound of someone entering his room disturbed his deep sleep. He heard voices—he had several times. They disturbed him when all he wanted to do was sleep. Only this time, one soft, feminine voice sounded so much like Amy. He must have died. But if this was heaven, then why the pain?

"No," he cried, but his shout of protest was little more than a whisper. It wasn't fair that he should fall in love for the first time and then die. Life wasn't fair, he'd known that from the moment he walked out of his father's office, but somehow he'd always thought death would be...

* * *

"Josh," Amy whispered, certain she'd heard him speak. It had been little more than a groan, but it had given her hope. "I'm here," she told him, clasping his hand in her own and pressing it to her cheek. "I love you. Do you understand?"

"Miss Johnson," Dr. Kilroy, Josh's English doctor, said with heavy reluctance. "I don't think he can hear you; the injuries to his body have been catastrophic. I don't think your friend is going to make it. We've only given him a fifty percent chance to live."

"Yes, I know."

"He's been unconscious for nearly three weeks."

"I know that, too."

"Please, you aren't helping him by staying at the hospital day and night. Perhaps if you returned to your hotel room and got a decent night's sleep."

"You'll have to get used to my presence, Doctor, because I'm not budging." She turned toward the bed and swallowed back the alarm, as she had every time her gaze rested on Josh. His injuries were multiple, including second-degree burns on his arms, a broken leg, cracked ribs, a bruised kidney and other internal damage, not to mention a severe concussion. Mercifully, he'd been unconscious from the moment she arrived, which had been five days earlier. Not once had she left his side for more than a few minutes. She talked to him, read to him and wiped the perspiration from his brow, touching him often, hoping her presence would relay her love.

The weak sound he'd made just a moment before was the first indication she'd had that he was awake.

"Miss Johnson, please," Dr. Kilroy continued.

"Doctor, I'm not leaving this hospital," she returned sternly.

"Very well," he acquiesced and left the room.

"Josh." She whispered his name and lightly ran her hand across his forehead. "I'm here." His eyes were bandaged, but Dr. Kilroy had assured her Josh hadn't been blinded in the accident.

Another soft cry parted his lips, one so unbelievably weak that she had to strain to hear it. Cautiously, she leaned over the hospital bed and placed her ear as close to his mouth as she could.

"Angel Eyes? Jasmine?"

"At your service," she said, choking back the tears. She didn't know who Jasmine was, but she wasn't going to let a little thing like another woman disturb her now. "You're awake?" It was a stupid question. Of course he was.

"Dead?"

It took her a moment to understand his question. "No, you're very much alive."

"Where?"

"We're here in Kadiri."

Gently, he shook his head and then grimaced. The action must have caused him severe pain. She could tell that talking was an effort for him, but there wasn't anything more she could do to help.

"Where?" he repeated. "Hell? Heaven?"

"Earth," she told him, but if he heard her, he didn't give any indication.

She ran for the nurse but by the time they arrived at the room Josh was unconscious again.

Another twenty-four hours passed before she was able to communicate with him a second time. She had been sitting at his bedside, reading. Since his eyes were wrapped it was impossible to tell if he was asleep or awake, but something alerted her to the fact that he had regained consciousness.

"It's Amy," she said softly, taking his hand and rubbing his knuckles gently. "Here, touch my face."

Very slowly he slid his thumb across the high arch of her cheek. Amy was so excited that it was impossible to sit still. She kissed the inside of his palm. "I love you, Joshua Powell, and I swear I'll never forgive you if you up and die on me now."

A hint of a smile cracked his dry lips. "Earth," he said and his head rolled to the side as he slipped into unconsciousness.

"Dad," Amy shouted into the heavy black telephone receiver. It made her appreciate the effort Josh had made to contact her by phone, not once but twice.

"Amy, is that you?"

She could almost see her father throwing back his covers and sitting on the edge of his mattress. By now, he would have reached for his glasses and turned on the bedside lamp.

"It's me," she cried. "Can you hear me all right?"

"Just barely. How's Josh doing?"

"Better, I think. The English doctor SunTech Oil flew in says he's showing some signs of improvement. He knows he's alive, at any rate. He's said 'earth' twice now."

"What?"

Amy laughed. "It's too difficult to explain."

"Are you taking care of yourself?"

"Yes…don't worry about me."

"Amy." Her father paused and continued in his most parental voice. "What's wrong?"

"Wrong?" she repeated. "What could possibly be wrong? Oh, you mean other than the fact I've flown halfway around the world to be at the deathbed of the man I love?"

"You just told me Josh is improving."

"He is. It's just that…oh, nothing, Dad, everything is fine. Just fine."

"Don't try to feed me that. There's something troubling you. Whatever it is—I can hear it in your voice even if you *are* eight thousand miles away. You can't fool me, sweetheart. Tell me what's up."

Amy bit her lower lip and brushed the tears from her eyes. "Josh keeps asking for another woman. Someone named Jasmine. He's said her name three or four times now, and he seems to think I'm her."

"You're jealous?"

"Yes. I don't even know who she is, but I swear I could rip her eyes out." No doubt she'd shocked her dear father, but she couldn't help it. After spending all this time with Josh, praying he would live, nursing his injuries, loving him, it was a grievous blow to her ego to have him confuse her with another woman.

"Do you want to come home now?"

"Josh can't travel."

"Leave him."

Amy realized the suggestion was given for shock value, but it had the desired effect. "I love him, Dad. I'm here for the long haul. Whoever this Jasmine woman is, she's got a fight on her hands if she thinks I'm giving Josh up quite so easily."

Her father chuckled, and Amy felt rejuvenated by the

sound. It had taken her the better part of three hours to place the call to Seattle, but the time and effort had been well spent.

"Take care of yourself, Amy Adele."

"Yes, Dad, I will. You, too."

When she returned to Josh's room, she found a nurse and Dr. Kilroy with him. He was apparently in a good deal of pain and was restlessly rolling his head back and forth. Amy walked over to his bedside and clasped his hand between her own.

"Josh," she said. "Can you tell me what's wrong? How can we help you?"

His fingers curled around hers and he heaved a sigh, then apparently drifted into unconsciousness.

"What happened?" Amy asked.

The doctor lifted the patient's chart and made several notations. "I can't be sure. He apparently awoke soon after you left the room and was distressed. He mumbled something, but neither the nurse nor I could understand what he was trying to say. It's apparent, however, that you have a calming effect upon him."

It wasn't until later that night that Josh awoke again. Amy was sitting at his bedside reading. She heard him stir and set her novel aside, standing at his bedside.

"I'm here, Josh."

His hand moved and she laced her fingers with his, raising his hand to touch her face to prove she was there and real and not a disembodied voice in the distance.

"Joel's dead," he said in a husky murmur.

"Yes, I know," she whispered, and her voice caught. Instinctively, she understood that his uneasiness earlier in the afternoon had been the moment he realized his friend had been killed in the explosion.

"I'm so sorry." A tear crept from the corner of her eye and ran down the side of her face. He must have felt the dampness because he lifted his free hand and blindly groped for her nape, forcing her head down to his level. Then he buried his face in the curve of her neck and held her with what she was certain was all the strength he possessed. Soon his shoulders started shaking, and sobs overtook him.

Amy wept, too. For the life that was gone, for the man she never knew, for the dear friend Josh had tried to save and had lost.

She fell asleep that night with her head resting on her arms, which she'd folded over the edge of the mattress. She awoke to feel Josh caressing her hair.

"Good morning," she whispered, straightening.

"Thank you," he returned, his voice still incredibly weak.

No explanation was needed. Josh was telling her how grateful he was that she'd been with him while he worked out his grief for his friend.

She yawned, arching her back and lifting her arms high above her head. "Are you in a lot of pain?"

"Would you kiss me and make it better if I said I was?"

"Yes," she answered, smiling.

"Amy," he said, his voice growing serious. "You shouldn't be here. I don't know how it's possible, you being here. It took me weeks to get my visa remember?"

"I remember." She bent over and kissed his brow.

"Leave while you can."

"Sorry, I can't do that." She pressed a warm kiss along the side of his mouth. "Feel better yet?"

"Amy, please." He gripped her wrist with what little

strength he had. "I'm going to be fine...you've got to get out of here. Understand?"

"Of course."

"I thought your father had better sense than this. You should never have come."

"Josh, you don't need to worry about me."

"I do... Amy, please."

She could tell the argument was draining his strength. "All right," she lied. "I'll make arrangements to leave tomorrow."

"Promise me."

"I...promise."

Amy could see the tension ease out of him. "Thank you, Angel Eyes."

He seemed to rest after that. Amy felt mildly guilty for the lie, but she couldn't see any way around it.

The following day when Josh awoke, he seemed to know instinctively that she was there. "Amy?"

"I'm here."

"No! You promised. What happened?"

"Kadiri Airlines only flies on Wednesday."

"What day is it?"

"I don't know, I lost track." Another white lie. But the minute he learned it was Tuesday, he would get upset and she didn't want to risk that.

"Find out."

"Dr. Kilroy said he was going to remove the bandages from your eyes today. You don't expect me to leave without giving you at least one opportunity to see me, do you?"

"I'm dying for a glimpse of you," he confessed reluctantly.

"Then I'd better make it worth your while. I have

an appointment to get my hair done at eleven." There wasn't a beauty salon within five hundred miles of Kadiri. Josh had to know that.

"Any chance of getting me a toothbrush and cranking up the head of this bed?"

"I'll see what I can do."

It took Amy fifteen minutes to locate a new toothbrush and some toothpaste. Josh was asleep when she returned, but he awoke an hour later. She helped him brush his teeth while he complained about the taste of Kadiri water. She didn't have the heart to tell him he was brushing with flat soda water.

By the time they'd completed the task, Dr. Kilroy entered the room. The man reminded her of a British Buddy Holly. He turned off the lights and removed the bandages while Amy stood breathlessly waiting.

The minute the white gauze was unraveled from Josh's head, he squinted and rotated his head to where Amy was standing. He held out his hand to her. "I swear, you've never looked more beautiful."

Knowing that after weeks of having his eyes covered, she couldn't be anything more than a wide blur against the wall, she walked to his side and wrapped her arms around his neck. "Joshua Powell, you don't lie worth beans."

He curved his hand around her neck and he directed her mouth down to his. "I've waited three long months to kiss you, don't argue with me."

Amy had no intention of doing anything of the sort.

Josh moved his mouth over hers with a fierce kind of tenderness, a deep, hungering kiss that developed when one had come so terribly close to losing all that was important, including life itself. He shaped and fitted her soft lips to his own, drinking in her love and her strength.

Dr. Kilroy nervously cleared his throat, mumbled something about seeing his other patients and quickly vacated the room. Amy was grateful.

"Josh," she whispered while he continued nibbling at her lips, catching her lower lip between his teeth and tugging at it sensuously before he lay back and rested his head on the pillow. Still he didn't fully release her. He closed his eyes and his smile was slanted, full and possessive.

"Angel Eyes," he whispered. "I can't tell you how good it feels to kiss you again."

"Yes," she agreed, her own voice pathetically weak.

He brought his hand back to her nape, stroking and caressing, directing her mouth back to his own. Amy held back, fearing too much contact would cause him pain.

"I'm afraid I'll hurt you," she whispered.

"I'll let you know if you do."

"But, Josh—"

"Are you going to fight with me?"

Their mouths were so close that their breaths merged. Amy could deny him nothing. "No..."

"Good."

He touched his tongue to her lips, gently coaxing them open, and then she complied to his unspoken request.

Shudders of excitement braided their way along her backbone, and her heart was hammering like a machine gun inside her chest. When she flattened her palms against Josh's chest, she noted that his heart was beating equally strongly. The movement was reassuring.

Taking in a deep breath, Josh ended the kiss and rested his forehead against hers. Their mouths were moist and ready, their breaths mingling.

"Go back to Seattle, Amy," he pleaded, running his hands through her hair.

"One kiss and you're dismissing me already?"

"I want you home and safe."

"I'm safe with you."

He chuckled lightly. "Honey, you're in more danger than you ever dreamed. Is that door open or closed?"

"Open."

He muttered a curse.

She dipped her mouth to his and kissed him long and slow, taking delight in sensuously rubbing her mouth back and forth over his, creating a slick friction that was enough to take the starch from her knees. By the time they broke apart, she was so weak, she'd slumped against the side of the bed.

"Maybe... I should close it," she said, once she'd found her voice.

"No...leave it open," he said with a sigh as he ran his palms in wide circles across her back as though he had to keep touching her to make sure she was real. "Amy, please, you've got to listen to me."

"I can't," she told him, "because all you want to do is send me away." She leaned forward and pressed her open mouth over his, showing him all that he had taught her in the ways of subtle seduction. "Here," she whispered. "Feel my heart." She pulled one of his hands from her back and pressed it to her chest.

"Amy!" He sucked in a wobbly breath.

"Josh, I love you," she said, kissing him once more, teasing him with the tip of her tongue.

"No…you shouldn't…you can't."

"But I do."

He closed his eyes to deny her words, but he couldn't keep his body from responding. He moved his hand and lovingly cupped her chin, then brushed the edges of her mouth. "I can't get over how good it feels to hold you again."

She leaned into his embrace, experiencing a grateful surge of thanksgiving that he was alive and on the mend.

"You promised me you were going to leave," he reminded her quietly.

"Yes, I know."

"Are you going back on your word?"

"No." Eventually she would fly out of Kadiri, but when she did, Josh would be with her. Only he didn't know that yet.

"Good. Now kiss me once more for good measure and then get out of here. I don't want to see you again until I'm in Seattle."

"Josh," she argued. "That could be weeks—"

"Honey, will you stop worrying?" He was exhausted. Resting his head against the pillow, he closed his eyes.

It took him all of two seconds to fall asleep. Carefully, Amy lowered the head of his bed, then tenderly kissed his forehead before silently slipping out of the room.

Amy felt better after she'd showered and eaten. From the moment her father had come to her bedside that fateful night all those weeks ago, she hadn't done anything more than nibble at a meal.

She slept better than she had in a month. Waking bright and early the following morning, she dressed in the traditional Kadiri dress Josh had mailed her and walked down to the public market. With her blond hair and blue eyes, she stuck out like a bandaged thumb. Small children gathered around her, and, laughing, she handed out pieces of candy. The eyes of the soldiers, with rifles looped over their shoulders, anxiously followed her, but she wasn't frightened. There wasn't any reason to be.

Amy bought some fresh fruit and a colorful necklace and a few other items, then lazily returned to the hospital.

"How's Josh this morning?" she asked Dr. Kilroy when they met in the hallway.

The doctor looked surprised to see her. "He's recovering, but unfortunately his disposition doesn't seem to be making the same improvement."

"Why not?"

The thin British man studied her closely. "I thought you'd left the country."

Amy smiled. "Obviously, I haven't."

"But Mr. Powell seems to be under the impression that you're back in America."

"I let him think that. When I leave Kadiri, he'll be with me."

Dr. Kilroy lifted his thick, black-framed glasses and pinched the bridge of his nose. "Personally, I don't want to be the one who tells him."

"You won't have to be."

"Oh." He paused.

"I'm going that way myself. Is there anything else you'd like me to tell him?"

Dr. Kilroy chuckled, and Amy had the impression that he was a man who rarely laughed.

"No, but I wish you the best of luck with your friend, Miss Johnson. I fear you're going to need it."

With a smile on her lips, Amy marched down the hall and tapped lightly against Josh's door. She didn't wait for a response, but pushed it open and let herself inside.

"I told you, I don't want any breakfast," Josh grumbled, his face turned toward the wall. The drapes were drawn and the room was dark.

"That's unfortunate, since I personally went out and bought you some fresh fruit."

"Amy." He jerked his head around, wincing in pain. "What are you still doing here?"

Chapter 6

"What does it look like I'm doing here?" Amy answered, gingerly stepping all the way into the room. "I brought you some fresh fruit."

Josh closed his eyes against what appeared to be mounting frustration. "Please, don't tell me you bought that in the public market."

"All right," she answered matter of factly. She brought out a small plastic knife and scored the large orange-shaped fruit. It looked like a cross between an orange and a grapefruit, but when she'd asked about it, the native woman she'd bought it from apparently hadn't understood the question.

"You *did* go the market, didn't you?" Josh pressed.

"You claimed I wasn't supposed to tell you." She peeled away the thick, grainy skin from the succulent fruit then licked the juice from the tips of her fingers.

"You went anyway."

"Honestly, Josh, I was perfectly safe. There were people all around me. Nothing happened, so kindly quit harping about it. Here." She handed him a slice, hoping that would buy peace. "I don't know what it's called. I asked several people, but no one seemed to understand." She smiled at the memory of her antics, her attempts to communicate with her hands, which were no doubt humorous to anyone watching.

Josh accepted the slice. "It's an orange."

"An *orange*? You mean I flew halfway around the world and thought I was buying some exotic fruit only to discover it's an orange? But it's so big."

"They grow that way here."

She found that amusing even if Josh didn't. She continued to peel away the skin and divided the sections between them. After savoring three or four of the sweet-tasting slices, she noted that Josh hadn't sampled a single one of his.

"You promised me you were leaving Kadiri," he said, his words sharp with impatience. His eyes were dark and filled with frustrated concern.

"I am."

"When?"

She sighed and crossed her long legs. "When you're ready to travel, which according to Dr. Kilroy won't be for another two weeks, perhaps longer. Josh, please try to understand, you've received several serious injuries. It's going to take time, so you might as well be tolerant."

"Amy—"

"Nothing you can say or do is going to change my mind, Joshua Powell. Nothing. So you might as well be gracious enough to accept that I'm not leaving Kadiri unless you're with me."

Joshua shut his eyes so tightly that barbed crow's feet marked the edges of his eyes. "How in the name of heaven did you get to be so stubborn?"

"I don't know." She wiped the juice from her chin with the back of her hand. "I'm usually not, at least I don't think I am, it's just that this is something I feel strongly about."

"So do I," he returned vehemently.

"Yes, I know. I guess there's only one solution."

"You're leaving!"

"Right," she agreed amicably enough. "But you're coming with me."

Amy could see that she was trying his patience to the limit. His tan jaw was pale with barely suppressed exasperation. If there had been anything she could do to comply with his demands, she would have done it, but Josh was as obstinate as she, only this time she was fortunate enough to have the upper hand. He couldn't very well force her out of the country.

In a burst of annoyance, Josh threw aside the sheet.

"Josh," she cried in alarm, leaping to her feet, "what are you doing?"

"Getting out of bed."

"But you can't…your leg's broken and you're hooked up to all these bottles. Josh, please, you're going to hurt yourself."

"You're not giving me any choice." The abrupt movements were obviously causing him a good deal of pain. His face went gray with it.

"Josh, please," she cried, his agony causing her own. Gently she pressed her hands against his shoulders, forcing him down. Josh's breathing was labored, and certain that he'd done something to harm himself, she hurried down the hall to find Dr. Kilroy.

The doctor returned with her to Josh's room. Almost immediately he gave Josh a shot to ease the pain and warned them both against such foolishness. Within minutes, Josh was asleep and resting relatively comfortably.

Amy felt terrible. When Dr. Kilroy invited her to have tea with him, she accepted, wiping the tearstains from her face.

"Josh seems to think my life is in imminent danger," she confessed. "He wants me out of the country." She stared into the steaming cup of tea, her gaze avoiding his. Even if the doctor agreed with Josh, she was bound and determined not to leave Kadiri unless Josh was at her side.

The good doctor, fortyish and graying, pushed his glasses up the bridge of his nose as if the action would guide his words. "Personally, I understand his concern. This is no place for an American woman on her own."

"But I just can't leave Josh here," she protested. "Are you sure it's going to be two more weeks before he can travel comfortably?"

"Three." He added a small amount of milk to his tea and stirred it in as if he were dissolving concrete. "It'll be at least that long, perhaps longer before he can sit for any length of time."

"What about laying down?"

"Oh, there wouldn't be any problem with that, but there aren't any airlines that provide hospital beds as a part of their flying options," he said dryly.

"But we could put a bed in my father's jet. I flew into Kadiri in a private plane," she rushed to explain. "It's at my disposal for the return trip as well."

Propping his elbows against the tabletop, Dr. Kilroy nodded slowly, thoughtfully. "That changes matters considerably. I think you might have stumbled upon a solution."

"But what about when we land in Seattle? Will Josh require further medical care?"

"Oh, yes. Your friend has been severely injured. Although the immediate danger has passed, it'll be several weeks—possibly months—before he'll be fully recovered. For the next two or three weeks it is critical he gets medical care only available at a hospital."

Amy knew the minute Josh was released from the Kadiri Hospital he wouldn't allow anyone to admit him to another one stateside.

"Josh isn't one to rest complacently in a hospital," she explained.

"I understand your concern. I fear Mr. Powell may try to rush his recovery, pushing himself. I only hope he realizes that he could do himself a good deal of harm that way."

"I could make arrangements for him to stay at my family home," she offered hopefully. "Would a full-time nurse be adequate to see to his needs? Naturally he'd be under a physician's care."

It didn't take the doctor long to decide. "Why, yes, I believe that could work quite well."

"Then consider it done. The plane's on standby and can be ready within twenty-four hours. Once we're airborne and we can contact Seattle, I'll have my father make all the necessary arrangements. A qualified nurse can meet us at the airport when we arrive."

"I can sedate Mr. Powell so the journey won't be too much of a strain on him…or anyone else," Dr. Kilroy added. It was agreed that a nurse would travel with them, although Amy would have preferred it if Dr. Kilroy could make the trip with them himself.

"I believe this will all work quite well." The British man looked pleased. "Now, both you and Mr. Powell can have what you want."

"Yes," Amy said, pleased by the unexpected turn of events.

When Josh awoke early in the afternoon, Amy was at his bedside. He opened his eyes, but when he saw her sitting next to him, he lowered his lids once more.

"Amy, please..."

"I'm flying out this evening, Josh, so don't be angry again."

His dark eyes shot open. "I thought you said Kadiri Airlines only flew on Wednesdays."

"They do. I'm going by private jet."

His lashes flew up to his hairline. "Private jet?"

"Before you find something else to complain about, I think you should know you're coming with me."

If he was shocked before it was nothing compared with the look of astonishment on his face now. " Amy... how...when...why?"

"One question at a time," she said, smiling softly and leaning over him to press her lips to his. "The how part is easy. Dr. Kilroy and I had a long talk. We're flying you to Seattle, hospital bed and all."

"Whose plane is this?"

"Dad's. Well, actually," she went on to explain, "it technically belongs to the company. He's just letting us use it because—"

"Hold on a minute," Josh said, raising his hand. "This jet belongs to your father's company?"

"Right."

His eyes slammed shut, and for one breathless moment he didn't say a word. When he opened them once more, his gaze held hers while several emotions flickered in and out of his eyes. Amy recognized shock, disbelief and a few other ones she wasn't sure she could identify.

"Josh, what is it?"

"Your father's name wouldn't happen to be Harold, would it?"

"Why, yes. How'd you know?" To the best of her knowledge she'd never mentioned her father's first name. But she hadn't been hiding it, either.

The harsh sound that followed could only be described as something between a laugh and a snicker. Slowly, Josh shook his head from side to side. "I don't believe it. And here I thought your father was just some poor devil who wanted to make you a part of a wholesale plumbing business."

Josh wasn't making the least bit of sense. Perhaps it was the medication, Amy reasoned. All she knew was that she didn't have time to argue with him, nor would there be ample opportunity for a lot of explanations. He looked so infuriated, and yet she was doing exactly what he wanted. She couldn't understand what was suddenly so terribly wrong.

The red flashing lights from the waiting ambulance were the first things Amy noted when they landed at Boeing field near Seattle some fifty hours later.

Amy was exhausted, emotionally and physically.

The flight had been uncomfortable from the moment they'd taken off from the Kadiri Airport. Josh, although sedated, was restless and in a good deal of pain. Amy was the only one who seemed capable of calming him, so she'd stayed with him through the whole flight.

Harold Johnson was standing alongside the ambulance, looking dapper in his three-piece-suit. He hugged Amy close and assured her everything was ready and waiting for Josh at the house.

"Now what was this about me finding a nurse with the name of Brunhilde?" he asked, slipping his arm around her thin shoulders. "You were joking, weren't you? I'll have you know, Ms. Wetherell contacted five agencies, and the best we could come up with was a Bertha."

Amy chuckled, delighted that her father had taken her message so literally. "I just wanted to make sure you didn't hire someone young and pretty."

"Once you meet Mrs. White, I think you'll approve." Her father laughed with her. The worry lines around his mouth and eyes eased, and Amy realized her journey had caused him a good deal of concern, although he'd never let on. She loved him all the more for it.

"It's good to have you back, sweetheart."

"It's good to be back."

The ambulance crew were carrying Josh out of the plane on a gurney. "Just exactly where are you taking me?" he demanded.

"Josh." Amy smiled and hurried to his side. "Stop being such a poor patient."

"I'm not going back in any stuffy hospital. Understand?"

"Perfectly."

He seemed all the more flustered by her easy acquiescence. "Then where are they taking me?" His words faded as he was lifted into the interior of the ambulance.

"Home," she called after him.

"Whose home?"

The attendant closed one door at the rear of the ambulance and was reaching toward the second before Amy could respond to Josh's question.

"My home," she called after him.

"No you're not. I want a hotel room, understand? Amy, did you hear me?"

"Yes, I heard you."

The second door slammed shut. Before he could argue with her, the vehicle sped off into the night.

"It's good to be home," Amy said with an exhausted sigh. She slipped her arm around her father's trim waist and leaned her head against his strong shoulders. "By the way, that was Josh. In case you hadn't noticed, he isn't in the best of tempers. He doesn't seem to be a very good patient, but who can blame him after everything he's been through?" She lifted her gaze to her father's and sucked in a deep breath. "I almost lost him, Dad. It was so close."

"So he's being a poor patient," her father repeated, obviously trying to lighten her mood.

"Terrible. Mrs. White's going to have her hands full."

Harold Johnson took a puff of his cigar and chuckled softly. "I always hated being ordered to bed myself. I can't blame him. Fact is, I may have a good deal in common with this young man of yours."

Amy smiled, realizing how true this was. "I'm sure you do. It isn't any wonder I love him so much."

* * *

Josh awoke when the golden fingers of dawn slithered through the bedroom window, creeping like a fast-growing vine over the thick oyster-gray carpet and onto the edges of his bed. Every bone in his body ached. He'd assumed that by now he would have become accustomed to pain. He'd lived with it all these weeks, to the point that it had almost become his friend. At least when he was suffering, he knew he was alive. And if he was alive, then he would be able to see Amy again.

Amy.

He shut his eyes to thoughts of her. He'd been in love with her for months. She was warmth and sunshine, purity and generosity, and everything that was good. She was the kind of woman a man dreams of finding—sweet and innocent on the outside, but when he held her in his arms, she flowered with fire and ready passion, promising him untold delights.

Yet somehow Josh was going to have to dredge up the courage to turn his back and walk away from her.

If he was going to fall in love, he cried silently, then why did it have to be with Harold Johnson's daughter? The man was one of the wealthiest men in the entire country. His holdings stretched from New York to Los Angeles and several major cities in between; his name was synonymous with achievement and high-powered success.

Josh couldn't offer Amy this kind of life, and even if he could, he wouldn't. He had firsthand experience of what wealth did to a man. By age twenty-five, he had witnessed how selfishness and greed could corrupt a man's soul.

The love for money had driven a stake between Josh

and his own father, one so deep and so crippling that it would never be healed. Eight years had passed, and not once in all that time had Josh regretted leaving home. Chance Powell had stared Josh in the eye and claimed he had no son. Frankly, that information suited Josh well. He had no father, either. He shared nothing with the man who had sired him—nor did he wish to.

Josh's mother had died when he was in college, and his only other living relative was her sister, an elderly aunt in Boston whom he visited on rare occasions. His aunt Hazel was getting on in years, and she seemed to make it her mission in life to try to bridge the gap between father and son, but to no avail. They were both too proud. Both too stubborn.

"I see you're awake," Bertha White, his nurse, stated as she stepped into the room. She certainly dressed for the part, donning white scrubs with the dedication of a conquering army.

Josh made some appropriate sound in reply. As far as he was concerned, Bertha White should be wearing a helmet with horns and singing in an opera. She marched across his room with all the grace of a herd of buffalo and pulled open the blinds, flooding the room with sunlight. Josh noted that she hadn't bothered to ask him how he felt about letting the sun blind him. Somehow he doubted that she cared.

She fussed around his bedside, apparently so he would know she was earning her salary. She checked his vital signs, dutifully entering the statistics in his chart. Then she proceeded to poke and prod him in places he didn't even want to think about. To his surprise, she graciously gave him the opportunity to wash himself.

Josh appreciated that, even if he didn't much care

for the woman, who was about as warm and comforting as a mud wrestler.

"You have a visitor," she informed him once he had finished.

"Who?" Josh feared it was Amy. It would be too difficult to deal with her now, when he felt weak and vulnerable. He didn't want to hurt her, but he wasn't sure he could do what he must without causing her pain.

"Mr. Johnson is here to see you," Bertha replied stiffly, and walked out of the room.

No sooner had she departed than Amy's father let himself in, looking very much the legend Josh knew him to be. The man's presence was commanding, Josh admitted willingly. He doubted that Harold Johnson ever walked anywhere without generating a good deal of attention. Everything about him spelled prosperity and accomplishment. This one man had achieved in twenty years what three normal men couldn't do in a lifetime.

"So you're Josh Powell," Amy's father stated, his eyes as blue as his daughter's and just as kind. "I would have introduced myself when you arrived last night, but you seemed to be in a bit of discomfort."

They shook hands, and Harold casually claimed the chair at Josh's bedside, as if he often spent part of his morning visiting a sickroom.

"I'll have you know I had nothing to do with this," Josh said somewhat defiantly, wishing there was some way he could climb out of his bed and meet Johnson man-to-man.

"Nothing to do with what?"

"Being here—I had no idea Amy planned to dump me off in your backyard. Listen, I don't mean to sound like I'm ungrateful for everything you've done, but I'd like to make arrangements as soon as I can to recover elsewhere."

"Son, you're my guest."

"I would feel more comfortable someplace else," Josh insisted, gritting his teeth to a growing awareness of pain and an overabundance of pride.

"Is there a reason?" Harold didn't look unsettled by Josh's demands, only curious.

The effort to sit up was draining Josh of strength and conviction, which he struggled to disguise behind a gruff exterior. "You obviously don't know anything about me."

Harold withdrew a cigar from his inside jacket pocket and examined the end with a good deal of consideration. "My daughter certainly appears to think highly of you."

"Which doesn't say much, does it?"

"On the contrary," Harold argued. "It tells me everything I need to know."

"Then you'd better…" A sharp cramp thrust through his abdomen and he lay back and closed his eyes until it passed. "Suffice it to say, it would be best if I arranged for other accommodations. Amy should never have brought me here in the first place."

"My daughter didn't mean to offend you. In fact, I don't know if you've noticed, but she seems to have fallen head over heels in love with you."

"I noticed," Josh admitted dryly. Amy. Her name went through his mind like a hot blade. He had to leave her, couldn't her father understand that much? They were as different as the sun and the moon. As far apart as the two poles, and their dissimilarities were in ways that were impossible to bridge. Harold Johnson should be intelligent enough to recognize that with one look.

Josh would have thought the man would be eager to be rid of him.

"You don't care for her?" Harold asked, chewing on the end of the cigar.

"Sir, you don't know anything about me," Josh said, taking in a calming breath. "I'm a drifter. I'm hardly suitable for your daughter. I don't want to hurt her, but I don't intend to lead her on, either."

"I see." He rubbed the side of his jaw in a thought-filled action.

It was apparent to Josh that Amy's father did nothing of the sort. "And another thing," Josh said, feeling it was important to say what was on his mind. "I can't understand how you could have let her fly to the Middle East because of me. Kadiri was no place for her."

"I agree one hundred percent. It took me an hour to come to terms with the fact she was going no matter what I said or did, so I made sure the road was paved for her."

"But how could you let her go and do a thing like that?" Josh demanded, still not understanding. Someone like Harold Johnson had connections, but even *his* protective arm could only stretch so far.

"I was afraid of being penalized for defensive holding," Harold said firmly.

Josh was certain he'd misunderstood. His confusion must have shown in his face, because the older man went on to explain.

"Amy's recently turned twenty-four years old and beyond the point where I can tell her what she can and can't do. If she wants to take off for the far corners of the world, there's little I can do to stop her. She knows it, and so do I. For that matter, if she's going to fall in love with you, it's not my place to tell her she's making a mistake. Either the girl's got sound judgment or she doesn't."

"I'm not good enough for her," Josh insisted.

The edges of the man's mouth lifted slightly at that. "Personally, I doubt that any man is. But I'll admit to being partial. Amy is, after all, my only child."

Josh closed his eyes, wanting to block out both the current pain and the one that was coming. If he stayed it would be inevitable. "I'm going to hurt her."

"Yes, son, I suspect you will."

"Then surely you realize why I need to get out of here, and the sooner the better."

"That's the only part I can't quite accept," Harold said slowly, his tone considerate. "As I understand it, you don't have any family close at hand?"

"None," Josh admitted reluctantly.

"Then perhaps you'd prefer several more weeks in a hospital?"

"No," Josh answered.

"Then you've made other arrangements that include a full-time nurse and—"

"No," Josh ground out harshly.

Harold Johnson's eyes filled with ill-concealed amusement.

"Your point is well taken," Josh admitted unwillingly. He didn't have a single argument that would hold up against the force of the other man's logic.

"Listen to me, son, you're welcome to remain here as long as you wish, and likewise, you're free to leave anytime you want. Neither Amy nor I would have it any other way."

"The expenses...?"

"We can discuss that later," Harold told him.

"No, we'll clear the air right now. I insist upon paying for all this… I want that understood."

"As you wish. Now, if you'll excuse me I'd better get into the office before my assistant comes looking for me."

"Of course." Josh wanted to dislike Amy's father. It would have made life a whole lot easier. If Harold Johnson had been anything like his own father, Josh would have moved the Panama Canal to get as far away from the Johnson family as humanly possible. Instead, he'd reluctantly discovered Amy's father was the kind of man he would have gladly counted as a friend.

"Sir, I don't want you to think I don't appreciate everything you've done." Josh felt obliged to explain. "It's just that this whole setup makes me uncomfortable."

"I can't say that I blame you. But you need to concentrate on getting well. You can worry about everything else later."

It commanded a good deal of effort for Josh to nod. Swirling pain wrapped its way around his body, tightening its grip on his ribs and his leg. Amy's father seemed to understand that Josh needed to rest.

"I'll be leaving you now."

"Sir." Josh half lifted his head in an effort to stop him. "If you could do one small favor for me, I'd greatly appreciate it."

"What's that?"

"Keep Amy away from me."

Harold Johnson's answering bellow of laughter was loud enough to rattle the windows. "It's obvious you don't know my daughter very well, young man. If I couldn't prevent her from flying to Timbuktu and risking her fool neck to be at your side, what makes you think I can keep her out of this sickroom?"

Josh felt an involuntary smile twitch at the corners of his mouth. Harold was right. There was nothing Josh could do to keep away Amy. But that wasn't the worst of it. He wanted her with him, and he wasn't fooling either of them by declaring otherwise.

He must have fallen asleep, because the next thing Josh knew Bertha White was in his room, fussing around the way she had earlier in the morning. Slowly, he opened his eyes to discover the elderly woman dragging a table across the room with a luncheon tray on it.

A polite knock sounded on the door. "Ms. White."

"Yes?"

"Would it be all right if I came in now? I brought my lunch so I could eat with Josh."

"No," Josh yelled, not waiting for the other woman to answer. His nurse shot him a look that reminded him of his sixth grade teacher, who Josh swore could cuff his ears with a dirty look. "I don't feel like company," he explained.

"Come in, Miss Johnson," Mrs. White answered, daring Josh to contradict her. "I've brought the table over next to the bed so you can sit down here and enjoy your visit."

"Thank you," Amy said softly.

Josh closed his eyes. Even her voice sounded musical. Almost like an angel's… He might as well accept that he wasn't going to be able to resist her. Not now, when he was too weak to think, much less argue.

Chapter 7

"Hi," Amy said, sitting down at the table. She carried her lunch with her—a shrimp salad and a tall glass of iced tea. Try as he might, Josh couldn't tear his eyes away from her. If her voice sounded like an angel's, it didn't even begin to compare with the way she looked. Sweet heaven, she was lovely.

"Are you feeling any better?" she asked, her eyes filled with gentle concern.

Josh thought to answer her gruffly. If he was irritable and unpleasant, then she wouldn't want to spend time with him, but one flutter of soft blue eyes and the battle was lost.

"I'm doing just fine," he muttered, reluctantly accepting defeat. He couldn't seem to look away. She might as well have nailed him to a wall, that was how powerless he felt around her. Why did she have to be so sweet, so wonderful? Before she came to visit him, he'd tried to fortify his heart, build up his defenses. Some defenses! One glance and those defenses crumbled at his feet like clay.

"You're not fine," Amy countered swiftly, with a hint of indignation. "At least, that's not what I heard. Mrs. White claimed you had a restless night and have been in a good deal of pain."

"I wouldn't believe everything Robo-nurse says if I were you."

Amy chuckled, then whispered, "She is a bit intimidating, isn't she?"

"Attila the Hun incarnate."

Josh momentarily closed his eyes to enjoy the sound of her merriment as it lapped over him like a gentle wave caressing the shoreline. How he loved it when Amy laughed.

She hesitated before spreading a napkin across the lap of her jeans. "I thought it was best if we cleared the air," she said, stabbing a fat pink shrimp with her fork. She carefully avoided his gaze. "You seemed so upset with me when Dad met us at the airport the other night. I didn't mean to take charge of your life, Josh, I honestly didn't. But I suppose that's how you felt, and I certainly can't blame you." She paused long enough to chew, but while she was eating, she waved her fork around like a conductor, as if her movements would explain what she was feeling.

"Amy, I understand."

"I don't think you do," she said, once she'd swallowed. "You wanted me out of Kadiri, and I saw the perfect chance to get us *both* out, and I grabbed it. There wasn't time to consult with you about arrangements. I'm sorry if bringing you here went against your wishes.

I... I did the best I could under the circumstances." She stopped long enough to suck in a giant breath. "But you're right, I should have consulted with you. I want you to know I would have, except Dr. Kilroy had heavily sedated you, and he thought it best to keep you that way for the journey. Then when we arrived everything happened so fast, and you—"

"Amy, I understand," he said quickly, interrupting her when he had the chance.

"You do?"

"Yes."

The stiffness came out of her shoulders, like air rushing from a balloon as she relaxed and reached for another shrimp. His gaze followed her action, and when she lifted the fork, she paused and smiled at him. Her happiness was contagious and free-flowing. It assailed him in a whirlwind of sensations he'd desperately struggled to repress from the moment he learned she'd flown to Kadiri to be with him.

"Want one?" she asked, her voice low and a little shaky. Her lips were moist and slightly parted as she leaned forward and held the fork in front of his mouth.

Their eyes met, and obediently he opened his mouth for her to feed him the succulent shrimp. It shouldn't have been a sensuous deed, but his heart started beating hard and strong, and the achy, restless feeling of needing to hold and kiss her fueled his mind like dry timber on a raging fire.

He longed to touch her translucent skin and plow his fingers through the silky length of her hair. But most of all, he realized, he wanted her warm and naked beneath him, making soft sounds of pleasure in his ear, and with her long, smooth legs wrapped around his.

His stomach knotted painfully. He leaned back and closed his eyes to the image that saturated and governed his thoughts.

She was at his side immediately, her voice filled with distress. "Should I get Mrs. White? Do you need something for the pain?"

The idea of a shot taking away the discomfort in his groin was humorous enough to curve up the edges of his mouth.

"Josh!" she blurted out. "You're smiling."

"I've got a pain, all right," he admitted, opening his eyes. He raised his hand, and trailed his fingertips across the arch of her cheek. "But it's one only you can ease."

"Tell me what to do. I want to help you. Oh, Josh, please, don't block me out. Not now, when we've been through so much together."

Gently, she planted her hands on his chest, as if that would convince him of her sincerity. Unfortunately, the action assured him of a good deal more. The ache within him intensified, and every second that she stared down on him with her bright angel eyes was adding heaps of coal to a fire that was already roaring with intensity.

"Honey, it's not that kind of pain." He set her hand on his groin.

Amy's eyes jolted with surprise and flickered several times as she came to terms with what he was saying.

Josh, unfortunately, was in for a surprise of his own. If he'd thought his action would cure what ailed him, then he was sadly mistaken. Instead, a shaft of desire stabbed through him with such magnitude that for a wild moment it was all he could do to breathe.

Amy's hand trembled, or perhaps he was the one

shivering, he couldn't tell for sure. He released her wrist, but she kept her fingers exactly where they were, tormenting him in ways she couldn't even begin to understand.

"Josh," she whispered, her voice filled with wonder and excitement. "I want you, too…there's so much for you to teach me."

Her eyes reflected the painful longing Josh was experiencing. Knowing she was feeling the same urgency only increased his desire for her. He knew he could handle his own needs, but how was he going to be able to refuse hers?

"No," he cried desperately, his control already stretched beyond endurance. The need in him felt savage. The woman couldn't be *that* innocent not to realize she was driving him insane.

"Amy," he cried harshly, gripping her wrist once more. "Stop."

"It's…so hot," she whispered, her low words filled with wonder. "It makes me feel so… I don't know…so empty inside."

Josh had reached the point where reason no longer controlled him. All the arguments he'd built up against there ever being anything sexual between them vanished like mist under a noonday sun. He grasped her around the waist, half dragging her onto the bed beside him. Josh barely gave her time to adjust herself to the mattress before he kissed her, thrusting his fingers into her hair and sweeping his mouth over hers.

The kiss was hot and wild. Amy seemed to sense that he was giving her an example of what was soon to follow, and she slid her hand over his shoulder, digging her nails into the muscles there. Her untamed response was enough to send the blood shooting through him until he thought his head would explode with it.

He found her hipbone and scooted her as close as he could, then he gloried in the way she intuitively churned the lower half of her body against him.

"Amy," he groaned. "You don't know what you're doing to me."

She smiled, and her whole face glowed with joy as her soft, kittenlike sound was nearly his undoing. "You're wrong. I do know and I'm enjoying every second." Her hands were in his hair, encouraging him with soft, trembling sounds that came deep from the back of her throat.

The bliss was so sharp, so keen that for Josh it reached the point of pain. The ache in his loins was unbearable. It was either take her now or stop completely.

Josh didn't have long to consider his options. His shoulders were heaving when he buried his face in the gentle slope of her neck. It took him several seconds to compose himself, and even then he felt as shaky as a tree limb caught in a hurricane.

"Josh?" Amy's voice was filled with question. "What's wrong?"

Slowly, he lifted his head, struggling to maintain the last fragment of his control before it snapped completely. Gently, he kissed her lips, while he gently pushed her away, breaking their intimate hold on one another.

"Did I hurt you?" she asked, her voice low and warm, throbbing with concern.

Her question tugged at his heart, affecting Josh more than any in his life. He'd come within a hair's space of making love with her, driven to the edge of insanity by need and desire. His burning passion had dominated his every move. He might have frightened her, or worse, hurt her. The hot ache in him had been too strong to have taken the proper amount of care to be sure this first time was right. And Amy was concerned that she'd hurt *him*.

"Josh?" She repeated her question with his name, grazing his face with gentle, caressing fingers.

"I'm fine. Did I hurt you?"

"No…never. It was wonderful, but why did you stop?"

"Remember Robo-nurse?"

It was obvious that Amy had completely forgotten Bertha White by the startled look that flashed into her soft blue eyes. "Did she…is she back?"

"No, but she will be soon enough." Bertha was an excuse, Josh realized, a valid one, but she wasn't the reason he'd pulled away. He'd been about to lose all control, and heaven help him, he couldn't allow that to happen.

For two frustrating days, Amy's visits to Josh were limited to short ten-minute stays. Her father had her running errands for him. The charity bazaar she had worked on earlier that summer needed her for another project, and then Manuela had taken sick.

Everything seemed to be working against her being with Josh. It seemed every time she came, wanting to be alone with Josh, his nurse found an excuse to linger there. Amy wondered if he had put the older woman up to it. That was a silly thought, she realized, because he didn't seem to be any more fond of Bertha than Amy was.

Her thoughts were abuzz with questions. Every time

her mind focused on the things Josh had done to her, the way he had held and kissed her, she grew warm and achy inside. The pleasure had been like nothing she had ever known, and once sampled, it created a need for more. She felt as though she had stood at the precipice, seeking something she couldn't name. Now that she had gazed upon such uncharted territory she was lost, filled with questions with no one to answer them.

It was late and dark and her father had retired for the evening. Amy lay in bed, restlessly trying to concentrate on a novel. The effort was useless, and she knew it. Every thought that entered her head had to do with Josh.

Throwing aside the sheets, she reached for her satin robe and searched out her slippers, which were hiding beneath her bed. Never in all her life had she done anything so bold as what she was about to do now.

She paused outside her bedroom door in the softly lit hallway and waited for reason to lead her back where she belonged. Nothing drove her backward. Instead she felt compelled to move forward.

Thankfully, at this time of night Bertha White would be sound asleep. As silently as possible Amy closed the door, then proceeded down the wide hallway to Josh's room.

The first thing she noticed was that his reading light was on. The sight relaxed her. She hadn't looked forward to waking him.

"Hello, Josh," she said as she silently stepped into the room. She closed the door, and when she turned around, she noticed that he was sitting up, gazing at her with dark, intense eyes.

"It's late," he announced starkly.

"Yes, I know. I couldn't sleep."

He eyed her wearily. "I was just about to turn out my light."

"I won't be a minute. It's just that I have a few questions for you, and I realize this is probably pretty embarrassing, but there isn't anyone else I can ask."

He closed his book, but she noticed that he didn't set it aside. In fact, he was holding it as if the hardbound novel would be enough of a barrier to keep her away.

"Questions about what?"

"The other day when we—"

"That was a mistake."

She swallowed tightly before continuing. "I don't know why you say that. Every time you so much as touch me, you claim it was a mistake. It's unbelievably frustrating."

A hint of a smile bounced against his eyes and mouth. "What do you want to know?" he asked, not unkindly. "And I'll do my level best to answer you."

"Without making a comment about the rightness or wrongness of what's happening between us?"

"All right," he agreed.

"Thank you." She pulled up a chair and sat, her gaze level with his own. Now that she had his full attention, she wasn't sure exactly where to start. Twice she opened her mouth, only to abruptly close it again, her muddled thoughts stumbling over themselves.

"I'm waiting," he said with a dash of impatience.

"Yes, well, this isn't exactly easy." She could feel a blush work its way up her face, and was confident she was about to make a complete idiot of herself. Briefly Amy had thought that if her mother had been alive, she could have asked her, but on second thought, she realized this was something one didn't discuss with one's mother.

"Amy," he questioned softly, "what is it?"

Her gaze was lowered, and the heat creeping up from her neck had blossomed into full color in her cheeks. She absently toyed with the satin ties at the neck of her robe.

"I...when we—you know—were on the bed together, you said something that has been on my mind ever since."

"What did I say?"

Josh sounded so calm, so...ordinary, as if he had this type of discussion with women every day of the week, as if he were a doctor discussing a medical procedure with his patient. Amy's heart was thundering in her ears so loudly she could barely form a coherent thought.

He prompted her again, and she wound the satin tie around her index finger so tightly she cut off the circulation. "You were trying to undo my blouse," she whispered, nearly choking on the words.

"And?"

"And you kissed me and held me in ways no other man ever has."

"I suspected as much."

"You see I attended a private girls school and there just wasn't much opportunity for this sort of...foreplay. I realize you must think me terribly naive and...gauche."

"I don't think anything of the sort. You're innocent, or at least you were until I got my hands on you." He frowned as he said it.

"Would you do it again...touch me the way you did before."

"Amy, no..."

"Please, I need to know these things and I want you to be the one to teach me."

"You don't know what you're asking."

"I do, Josh. I'm not completely innocent and I promise you I'm a quick learner."

He closed his eyes and groaned. "I'm all too aware of that fact already."

"It felt so good to have you touch me."

"It did for me, too." Josh's voice was low and hesitant.

"Will you do it again?" she asked, her voice so quiet she could barely hear herself. Boldly she raised her eyes to his, her heart beating wildly.

She stood and walked the few short steps to his bedside and laid open her robe. Josh sat there mesmerized, his face unreadable, but he didn't say or do anything to stop her. Her fingers were trembling as she slipped the robe from her shoulders. It fell silently at her feet. She made herself vulnerable to him in ways she was only beginning to comprehend. She was so pale, she realized, wishing now that she was tan and golden for him, instead of alabaster white.

"Amy."

Her name was little more than a rasp between his lips. "Like I explained earlier you don't know what you're asking." Of their own volition, it seemed, his fingers lightly brushed the smooth skin of her throat. Instantly, her tender skin there started to throb.

His touch, although featherlight, produced an immediate melting ache in her. She pulsed in places she'd never known existed until Josh had kissed and touched her.

"Please, Josh," she whispered. "I have to know."

There was more she longed to ask, more she yearned to discover, but the words withered on the end of her tongue at the look of intense longing Josh gave her.

He reached for her waist and gently urged her forward until she was close enough for him to bury his face between her breasts. Abruptly, Josh stopped and jerked his head away. For several seconds he did nothing but draw in deep, lung-rasping breaths. "Enough," he said finally. Amy clung to him, not knowing how to tell him that he hadn't answered a single inquiry. Instead he'd created even more.

"I don't want you to stop," she moaned in bewilderment. She paused, hoping to clear her thoughts, then continued raggedly. "Josh, I want to make love with you. I want you to teach me to be a woman, your woman."

"No."

Her knees would no longer support her, and she sank onto the bed, sitting on the edge of the mattress. It was then that she realized that Josh was trembling, and the knowledge that she could make him want her so desperately filled her with a heady sense of power.

Reaching out to him, Amy wasn't about to let him push her away. Not again.

"No," he cried a second time, but with much less conviction. Even as he spoke he filled his palms with her breasts and made a low, rough sound of protest. "Amy... please." His voice vibrated between them, filled with urgency and helplessness. "Not like this...not in your father's house."

She sagged, drooping her head in frustration. Josh was right. They were both panting with the effort to resist each other as it was, and in a few seconds neither one of them would be able to stop. It took everything within her to quit now.

Amy blindly reached for her robe. She would have turned and vaulted from the room if Josh hadn't reached for her wrist, stalling her. Not for anything could she look him in the eye.

"Are you going to be all right?" he asked.

She nodded wildly, knowing it was a lie. She would never be the same again.

He swore quietly, and with a muffled deep gasp of pain sat upright in the bed and reached for her, hugging her close and burying his face in the gentle slope of her neck.

"Amy, listen to me; we've got to stop this horsing around before it kills the both of us."

"Josh," she whispered, her tone hesitant. "That's the problem. I don't want to stop. It feels so wonderful when you touch me, and I get all achy inside and out." Consternation and apprehension crept into her voice. "My behavior is embarrassing you, isn't it?"

"Me?"

"I mean, the last thing you need is me making all kinds of sexual demands on you. You're lucky to be alive. Here I am, like a kid who's recently discovered a wonderful toy and doesn't quite know how to make everything work."

"Believe me, honey, it's working."

"I'm sorry, Josh, I really am—"

He silenced her with a chaste kiss. "Go back to bed. We can talk more about it in the morning, when both our heads are clear."

"Good night," she whispered, heaving a sigh.

"Good night." He kissed her once more and, with a reluctance that tore at her heart, he released her.

"Morning, Dad," Amy said as she seated herself at the table for breakfast the following morning.

Her father grumbled an inaudible reply, which wasn't anything like him. Harold Johnson had always been a morning person and boomed enthusiasm for each new day.

Amy hesitated, her thoughts in a whirl. Was it possible that her father had heard her sneak into Josh's room the night before? That thought was enough to produce a heated blush, and in an effort to disguise her discomfort, she hurriedly dished up her scrambled eggs and bacon.

Her father didn't say anything more for several minutes. Deciding it would be better to confront him with the truth than suffer this intolerable silence, Amy straightened her shoulders and clasped her hands in her lap.

"How's Josh doing?" Harold asked, reaching for the sugar bowl after pouring himself a cup of coffee.

"Better." She eyed him warily, trying to decide the best way to handle this awkward situation. Perhaps she should let him bring up the subject first.

"I talked to Mrs. White yesterday afternoon," she said with feigned cheerfulness, "and she said Josh is doing better than anyone expected."

"Good. Good."

Enthusiasm echoed in each word. Amy was absolutely positive that her father knew the reasons behind Josh's increasing strength. The crimson heat that had invaded her face earlier circled her ears like a lariat.

She swallowed a bite of her toast, and it settled in her stomach like a lead ball.

"I had a chance to talk to Mrs. White this morning myself."

"You did?" she blurted out.

"Yes," he continued, eyeing her closely.

Amy did her level best to disguise her distress. She'd always been close to her father, and other than the business about him making her a part of Johnson Industries, she'd prided herself on being able to talk to him about anything.

"Amy, are you feeling all right?"

"Sure, Dad," she said energetically, knowing she wasn't going to be able to fool him.

He arched his brows and reached for his coffee, sipping at it while he continued studying her.

There was nothing left to do but blurt out the truth and clear the air before she suffocated in the tension. "You heard me last night, didn't you?"

"I beg your pardon?"

"Well, you needn't concern yourself, because nothing happened. Well, almost nothing, but not from lack of trying on my part. Josh was the perfect gentleman."

Her father stared at her with huge blue eyes. He certainly wasn't making this any easier on her. He continued to glare at her for several uneasy seconds until Amy felt compelled to explain further.

"It was late…and I couldn't sleep. I know that probably isn't a very good excuse, but I had a question that I wanted to ask Josh."

"You couldn't have asked me?"

Her startled eyes flew to him. "No!"

"Go on."

"How much more do you want to know? I already told you nothing happened."

"I believe the phrase you used a moment ago was 'almost nothing.'"

"I'm crazy about him, Dad, and I've never been in love before, and, well, it's difficult when you…feel that way about someone…if you know what I mean?"

"I believe I do."

"Good." She relaxed somewhat. Although her appetite had vanished the instant she realized her father was waiting to confront her about what had happened in Josh's room, she did an admirable job of finishing her breakfast.

"Mrs. White said Josh would be able to join us for dinner tonight."

Amy's happy gaze flew to her father. "That's wonderful."

"I thought you'd be pleased to hear it."

"I'll have Manuela prepare a special dinner."

Her father nodded. "Good idea." He downed the last of his coffee, glanced at his watch, then stood abruptly. "I've got to go to the office. Have a good day, sweetheart."

Amy raised her coffee cup to her lips and sipped. "Thanks. You, too."

"I will." He was halfway out of the dining room when he turned around. "Amy."

"Yes, Dad."

"I'm not exactly certain I should admit this. But I didn't hear a thing last night. I slept like a log."

Chapter 8

"It's your move," Amy reminded Josh for the second time, growing restless. Just how long did it take to move a silly chess piece, anyway?

Josh nodded, frowning slightly as he studied the board that rested on the table between them.

Amy's gaze caught her father's and she rolled her eyes. Josh was the one who'd insisted they play chess following dinner. Harold Johnson shared a secret smile with her. He pretended to be reading when in fact he was closely watching their game.

Amy had never been much of a chess player; she didn't have the patience for it. As far as she was concerned, chess was a more difficult version of checkers, and she chose to play it that way. It never took her more than a few seconds to move her pieces. Josh, on the other hand, drove her crazy, analyzing each move she made, trying to figure out her strategy. Heaven knew she didn't have one, and no one was more shocked than she was when Josh announced that she'd placed him in checkmate. Good grief, she hadn't even noticed.

"You're an excellent player," he said, leaning back and rubbing the side of his jaw. He continued to study the board as though he couldn't quite figure out how she'd done it. Amy hoped he would let her in on the secret once he figured it out; she was curious to find out herself.

Her father rose from his wingback leather chair and crossed the room to get a book from the mahogany cases that lined two walls. As soon as he was out of earshot, Amy glanced over to Josh.

"You haven't kissed me all week," she whispered heatedly.

Josh's anxious gaze flew to her father, then to her. "I don't plan to."

"Ever again?"

Josh frowned. "Not here."

"Why not?"

"Because!" He hesitated and glanced toward her father. "Can we discuss this another time?"

"No," she answered with equal fervor. "You're driving me crazy."

"Mr. Johnson," Josh said anxiously and cleared his throat when her father started toward his chair. "Could I interest you in a game of chess?"

"No thanks, son. Amy's the champion of our family, you're going to have to demand a rematch with her." He stopped and placed his hand over his mouth, then did a poor job of feigning a yawn. "The fact is, I was thinking of heading up to bed. I seem to be tired this evening."

"It's barely eight," Amy protested. She immediately

regretted her outburst. With her father safely tucked away in his bedroom, she might be able to spend a few minutes alone with Josh, which was something she hadn't been able to do in days.

"Can't help it if I'm tired," Harold grumbled and, after bidding them both good night, he walked out of the room.

Amy waited a few moments until she was sure her father was completely up the stairs. "All right, Joshua Powell, kindly explain yourself."

"The subject's closed, Amy."

She bolted to her feet, her fists digging into her hipbones as she struggled to quell her irritation. "Subject? What subject?"

"You and me...kissing."

If his face hadn't been so twisted with determination and pride, she would have laughed outright. Unfortunately, Josh was dead serious.

"You don't want to kiss me anymore? At all?"

He tossed her a look that told her she should know otherwise by now. Reaching for his crutches, he struggled to his feet. The cast had been removed from his leg, but he still had trouble walking without support.

"Where are you going?" she demanded, growing more agitated by the minute.

"To bed."

"Oh, honestly," she cried. "There's no reason to wrestle your way up those stairs so early. If you're so desperate to escape me, then I'll leave."

"Amy..."

"No." She stopped him by holding up both hands. "There's no need to worry your stubborn little head about me taking a drive alone in the cold, dark city.

There are plenty of places I can go, so sit down and enjoy yourself. You must be sick of that room upstairs." With a proud thrust of her chin she marched out of the room and retrieved her purse. Glancing over her shoulder, she sighed and added, "There's no need to fret. Seattle has one of the lowest murder rates on the west coast." She had no idea if this was true or not, but it sounded good.

"Amy," he shouted, and followed her. His legs swung wide as he maneuvered his crutches around the corner of the hallway, nearly colliding with her.

She offered him a brave smile and pretended she wasn't the least bit disturbed by his attitude, when exactly the opposite was true. If he didn't want to kiss or hold her again then...then she would just have to accept it.

"Yes?" she asked, tightly clenching the car keys in her hand as though keeping them safely tucked between her fingers was the most important thing in her life.

For a long moment Josh did nothing but stare at her. A battle raged in his expression as if he was fighting himself. Whichever side won apparently didn't please him, because his shoulders sagged and he slowly shook his head. "Do you want company?"

"Are you suggesting you come along with me?"

His smile was off center. "What do you think?"

"I don't know anymore, Josh. You haven't been yourself all week. Do you think I'm so blind I haven't noticed how you've arranged it so we're never alone together anymore?"

"It's too much temptation," he argued heatedly. "We're in trouble here, Amy. We're so hot for each other it's a minor miracle that we don't burst into spontaneous combustion every time we touch."

"So you're making sure that doesn't happen again?"

"You've got that right," he returned forcefully. He was leaning heavily upon his crutches. He wiped a hand over his face as if to erase her image from his mind. "I don't like it any better than you do, Angel Eyes."

Somehow Amy doubted that. Her tight look must have said as much because Josh emitted a harsh groan.

"Do you have any idea how much I want to make love with you?" he asked her in a harsh whisper. "Every time you walk into the room, it's pure torment. Tonight at dinner, I swear I didn't take my eyes off your breasts the entire meal."

She smiled, not knowing how to answer him.

"Then you got up and walked away, and it was all I could do to keep from watching your sweet little tush swaying back and forth. I kept thinking how good it would be to place my hands there and hold you against me. Did you honestly believe I wanted seconds of dessert? The fact was, I didn't dare stand up."

"Oh, Josh." Her smile was watery with relief.

He held open his arms for her, and she walked into them the way a frightened child ducks into a family home, sensing security and safety. Using the wall to brace his shoulders, he set one crutch aside and reached for her, wrapping his arm around her waist. Slowly, he lowered his hand, lifting her toward him so he could press himself more intimately against her. "Josh…"

"Do you understand now?" he ground out, close to her ear.

"Yes," she whispered with a barely audible release of breath. She slipped her arms around his neck.

He stroked his thumb along the side of her neck and

inhaled a wobbly breath before he spoke again. "Now, what was it you were saying about going for a ride?"

"Ride?" she repeated in a daze.

"Yes, Amy, a ride, as in a motorized vehicle, preferably with all the windows down and the air conditioner on full blast so my blood will cool."

She pressed her forehead to his chin and smiled before reluctantly breaking away from him. Josh reached for his crutches and followed her through the kitchen and to the garage just beyond.

A few minutes later, with Amy driving and Josh sitting in the passenger seat, they headed down the long, curved driveway and onto the street, turning east toward Lake Washington.

"I love Seattle at night," Amy said, smiling at him. "There're so many bright lights, and the view of the water is fantastic."

"Where are you taking me?"

"Lover's Leap?" she teased.

"Try again."

"All right, it isn't exactly Lover's Leap, but it is a viewpoint that looks out onto the lake. It's been a while since I've been there, but from what I remember, it's worth the drive."

"And what exactly do you know about lookout points, Amy Johnson? I'd bet my entire life's savings that you've never been there with a man."

"Then you'd lose." She tossed him a saucy grin, then pulled her gaze to the roadway, her love for him so potent she felt giddy with it.

He eyed her skeptically. "Who?"

"Does it matter? All you need to know is that I was

there with a man. A handsome one, too, by anyone's standards."

"When?" he challenged.

"Well," she hesitated, not wanting to give her secret away quite so easily. "I don't exactly remember *when*. Let me suffice to say, it was several years back, when I was young and foolish."

"You're young and foolish now."

"Nevertheless, I was with a man. I believe you said you'd hand over your life savings to me." She laughed, her happiness bubbling over. "I'll take a check, but only with the proper identification."

"All right, if you're going to make this difficult, I'll guess. You were ten and your daddy was escorting you around town and stopped at this lookout point so you could view the city lights."

"How'd you guess that?" she asked, then clamped her mouth shut, realizing she'd given herself away. "I should make you pay for that, Joshua Powell."

He brushed his fingers against her nape, and when he spoke his voice was low and seductive. "I'm counting on it, Angel Eyes."

"You think once I park this car that I'm going to let you kiss me, don't you?"

Josh's laugh was full. "Baby, you're going to ask for it. Real nice, too."

Laughing, she eased the Mercedes to a stop at the end of the long, deserted street and turned off the headlights, then the ignition. The view was as magnificent as she remembered. More so, because she was sharing it with Josh. The city stretched out before them like a bolt of black satin, littered with shimmering lights that sparkled and gleamed like diamonds. Lake Washington was barely visible, but the electricity from the homes that bordered its shores traced the curling banks. The sky was cloudless and the moon full.

Amy expelled her breath and leaned her head back to gaze into the heavens. It was so peaceful, so quiet, the moment serene. It was a small wonder that this area hadn't been developed over the intervening years since she'd last been here. She was pleased that it remained unspoiled, because it would have ruined everything to have this lovely panorama defaced with long rows of expensive homes.

Josh was silent, apparently savoring the sight himself.

"All right," she whispered, her voice trembling a little with anticipation.

He turned to her, his mending leg stretched out in front of him in as comfortable a position the cramped quarters of the car could afford him. The crutches were balanced against the passenger door. "All right what?"

"You said I was going to have to ask for a kiss. I'm asking, Josh." She felt breathless, as if she'd just finished playing a set of tennis. "Please."

Josh went stock-still, and she could sense the tension in him as strongly as she could smell the fragrant grass that grew along the roadside.

"Heaven help me, Amy, I want to please you."

"You do, every time we touch."

He turned her in his arms, his kiss slow and sultry. So hot and sweet that her toes curled and she twisted, wanting to get as near to him as possible in the close confines. The console was a barrier between them, and the steering wheel prevented her from twisting more than just a little.

In their weeks together, Josh had taught her the fine art of kissing, his lessons exhaustive and detailed. Tonight, Amy was determined to prove to him what an avid student she had been. His shoulders heaved, and he drew in a sharp breath.

"Amy," he warned in a severe whisper, "you should never have gotten us started. Angel, don't you understand yet what this is eventually going to lead to—"

She pressed the tips of her fingers over his lips. "Why do you insist on arguing with me, Joshua Powell?" She didn't give him an opportunity to answer, but slid her hands up his shoulders and joined them at the base of his neck, lifting her mouth to his once more, unwilling to spend these precious moments alone debating a moot point.

Josh's kiss wasn't slow or sweet this time, but hot and urgent, so hungry that he drove the crown of her head against the headrest. He grasped the material of her skirt, bunching it up around her upper thighs as he slid his callused palm over her silk panties.

Her eyes snapped open with surprise at this new invasion. He wanted to shock her, prove to her that she was in over her head. What Josh didn't realize was that with all the other lessons he'd been giving her, she'd learned to swim. So well she wanted to try out for the Olympic team. Lifting her hips just a little to aid him, her knee came in sharp contact with the steering wheel, and she cried out softly.

"Damn."

"If you think that's bad, I've got a gear shift sticking in my ribs," he informed her between nibbling kisses. "I'm too old for this, Angel Eyes."

"I am, too," she whispered and teased him with her tongue.

"Maybe I'm not as old as I think," he amended at the end of a ragged sigh.

Amy smoothed the hair away from his face, spreading eager kisses wherever she could. "You know what I want?"

"Probably the same thing I do, but we aren't going to get it in this car."

"Honestly, Josh, you've got a one-track mind."

"Me!" he bellowed, then groaned and broke away from her to rub the ache from his right leg.

"Are you all right?" Amy asked, unable to bear the thought of Josh in pain.

"Let me put it this way," he said, a frown pleating his brow. "I don't want you to kiss it and make it better."

"Why not?" She tried to sound as offended as she felt.

"Because the ache in my leg is less than the one that console is giving my ribs. If this is to go any farther, then it won't be in this car."

"Agreed." Without another word, she snapped her seat belt into place, turned on the ignition and shifted the gears into Reverse. Her tires kicked up loose gravel and dirt as she backed into the street.

"*Now* where are you taking me?" Josh asked, chuckling.

"Don't ask."

"I was afraid of that," he muttered.

A half hour later, they turned off the road onto the driveway that led to her family home. She drove past the garage and the tennis courts and parked directly in front of the pool.

"What are we doing here?" he demanded, looking none too pleased.

"I tried to say something earlier," she reminded him, "but you kept interrupting me. I think we should go swimming."

He groaned and shut his eyes, obviously less than enthusiastic with her suggestion. "Swimming? In case you hadn't noticed it's October, and there's a definite nip in the air."

"The pool's heated. Eighty-two degrees, to be exact."

"I don't have a suit."

"There are several your size in the cabana."

Josh closed his fingers around the door handle. Slowly shaking his head, he opened the door and, using both hands, carefully swung out his right leg. "I have the distinct notion you have an argument for every one of my objections."

"I do." She climbed out of the car, and with her arm around his waist, she guided him toward the changing room and brought out several suits for him to choose from. She kissed him, then smiled at him. "The last one in the water is a rotten egg."

By the time Amy came out of the cabana, Josh was sitting at the edge of the deep end, his long legs dangling in the pool. He was right about there being a chill in the night air. She kept the thick towel securely wrapped around her shoulders as she walked over to join him, but she did this more for effect than to ward off the cold.

"Hello, rotten egg."

"Hi, there," she said, giving him a slow, sweet smile before letting the towel drop to her feet.

The minute she did, Josh gasped and his eyes seemed

to pop out of their sockets. "Oh, no," he muttered, expelling his breath in a slow exercise.

"Do you like it?" she asked, whirling around in a wide circle for him to admire her itsy-bitsy string bikini.

"You mean, do I like what there is of it?"

She smiled, pleased to the soles of her feet by his response. "I picked it up in France last summer. Trust me, this one is modest compared to what some of the other women were wearing."

"Or not wearing," he commented dryly. "You'd be arrested if you showed up in that...thing on any beaches around here."

Holding her head high to appear as statuesque as possible, she smiled softly, turned and dipped her big toe into the pool to test the temperature. "I most certainly would *not* be arrested. Admired, perhaps, but not imprisoned."

His Adam's apple moved up and down his throat, but he didn't take his eyes off her. "Have you...worn this particular suit often?"

"No. There was never anyone I wanted to see me in it until now." With that, she stood at the edge of the pool, raised her arms high above her head and dove headlong into the turquoise blue waters, slicing the surface with her slender frame.

She surfaced, sputtering and angry. "Oh, dear."

"What's wrong?"

"You don't want to know." Before he could question her further, she dove under the clear blue water and held her breath for as long as she could.

When she broke the surface, gasping for breath, Josh was in the pool beside her, treading water. He took one look at her and started to laugh.

"You lost your fancy bikini top," he cried, as if she hadn't noticed.

"I suppose you find this all very amusing," she said, blushing to the roots of her hair. To her horror, she discovered that women's breasts have the uncanny habit of floating. Trying to maintain as much dignity as possible, she pressed her splayed fingers over her breasts, flattening them to her torso. But she soon discovered that without her hands, she couldn't stay afloat. Her lips went below the waterline, and she drank in several mouthfuls before choking. Mortified, she abandoned the effort, deciding it was better to be immodest than to drown.

Josh was laughing, and it was all she could do not to dunk him. "The least you can do is try to help me find it."

"Not on your life. Fact is, this unfortunate incident is going to save me a good deal of time and trouble."

"Josh." She held out her hand. "I insist that you... keep your distance." She eyed him warily while clumsily working her way toward the shallow end of the pool.

"Look at that," he said, his gaze centering on her breasts, which were bobbing up and down at the surface as she tried to get away from him.

Her toes scraped the bottom of the pool, and once her feet were secure, she scrunched down, keeping just her head visible. She covered her face with both hands. "This is downright embarrassing, and all you can do is laugh."

"I'm sorry."

But he didn't sound the least bit petulant.

"I wanted you to see me in that bikini and swoon with desire. You were supposed to take one look at me and be so overcome with passion that you could hardly speak."

"I was."

"No, you weren't," she challenged. "In fact you looked angry, telling me I should be arrested."

"I didn't say that exactly."

"Close enough," she cried, her discontent gaining momentum. "I spent an extra ten minutes in the cabana spreading baby oil all over my body so I'd glisten for you, and did you notice? Oh, no, you——"

Before another word passed her lips, Josh had gripped her by the waist and carried her to the corner of the pool, securing her there and blocking any means of escape with his body. His outstretched arms gripped the edge of the pool.

Wide-eyed, she stared at him, the only light coming from the full moon and the dim blue lights below the water. "It isn't any big disaster," Josh told her.

"Oh, sure, you're not the one floating around with your private parts exposed. Trust me, it has a humbling effect."

She knew he was trying not to laugh, but it didn't help matters when the corners of his mouth started quivering. "Joshua Powell," she cried, bracing her hands against his shoulders and pushing for all she was worth. "I could just——"

"Kiss me." The teasing light had vanished and he lowered his gaze to the waterline. His eyes were dark and narrowed, and her breasts felt heavy and swollen just from the way he was looking at her.

Timidly, she slanted her mouth over his, barely brushing his lips with her own.

"Not like that," he protested, threading his fingers

through her wet, blond hair. "Kiss me the way you did earlier in the car." His voice was low and velvety. "Oh, baby," he moaned, slipping his moist mouth back and forth over her own. "The things you do to me." Seemingly impatient, he took advantage of her parted lips, and kissed her thoroughly and leisurely. He kissed her as he never had before, tasting, relishing, savoring her in a hungry exchange that left them both breathless.

"Wrap your legs around my waist," he instructed, his words raspy with desire.

Without question she did as he asked. Slipping her hands over the smooth-powered muscles.

"Josh?"

"Yes, love."

She didn't know what she wanted to ask.

She slipped her arms around his neck and pressed her torso against the water-slickened planes of his chest.

"Are you…hungry?" she asked, her voice little more than a husky murmur.

His response was guttural. "You know that I am."

Her head spun with all the things he was doing to her, kissing her until she was senseless.

"Angel," he whimpered, "be still for just a moment."

"I can't," she cried breathlessly.

Her nails curled into his chest, but if the action caused him any pain, he gave no indication. The need to taste him dominated every thought as she ran the tip of her tongue around the circumference of his mouth. Her breasts were heaving when she collapsed on him. "Oh, Josh, I never knew… I never knew." She was just regaining her breath when she heard the sound of voices and laughter advancing from the other side of the cabana.

Josh heard it as well and stiffened, tension filling

his body. "Who's there?" he shouted, his body shielding Amy from view.

"Peter Stokes."

Josh's questioning gaze met Amy's. "He's our gardener's son," she explained in a whisper. "Dad told him he could come swimming anytime...but not now."

"The pool's occupied," Josh called out. "Come back tomorrow." A low grumble followed his words, but soon the sound of the voices faded.

The moment was ruined. They both accepted it with reluctance and regret. Josh kissed her forehead, and she snuggled against him. The water lapped against them, and they hugged each other, their bodies entwined.

"Next time, angel," he said, tucking his finger under her chin and raising her eyes to his. "We don't stop."

Chapter 9

"About last night," Josh started, looking disgruntled and eager to talk.

"That's exactly what I want to talk to you about," Amy whispered fiercely as she joined him in the dining room the following morning. "It isn't there."

Manuela had just finished serving him a plate heaped high with hot pancakes. He waited until the housekeeper was out of the room before he spoke. "What isn't there?" Josh asked, pouring thick maple syrup over his breakfast.

"My bikini top," she returned, growing frustrated. "I went down to the pool early this morning…before anyone else could find it, and it *wasn't there*." She was certain her cheeks were the same color as the cranberry juice he was drinking. It had been too dark to search for it the night before, and so cold when they climbed out of the water that Josh had insisted they wait until morning.

"I'm sure it'll show up," he said nonchalantly.

"But it's not there now. What could have possibly happened to it?" Naturally, he was unconcerned. It wasn't *his* swimsuit that was missing. The fact that he was having so much trouble suppressing a smile wasn't helping matters, either.

"It's probably stuck in the pump."

"Don't be ridiculous," she countered, not appreciating his miserable attempt at humor. "The pump would never suck up anything that big."

"Trust me, honey. There wasn't enough material in that bikini to cover a baby's bottom. Personally, I don't want to be the one to explain to your father how it got there when he has to call in a plumber."

"Funny. Very funny."

She'd just pulled out a chair to sit across the table from him when the phone rang. She turned, prepared to answer, when the second ring was abruptly cut off.

"Manuela must have gotten it," she said, noting that Josh had set his fork aside as if he expected the call to be for him. Sure enough, a couple of moments later, the plump Mexican cook came rushing into the dining room. "The phone is for you, Mr. Josh," she said with a heavy accent.

Josh nodded, and he cast a glance in Amy's direction. She could have sworn his eyes held an apologetic look, which was ridiculous, since there was nothing to feel contrite about. He scooted away from the table and stood with the aid of his cane. Her gaze followed him, and she was surprised when he walked into the library and deliberately closed the door.

"Well," Amy muttered aloud, pouring herself a cup of coffee. So the man had secrets. To the best of her knowledge, Josh had never received or made a phone call the entire time he had spent with them. But then, she wasn't with him twenty-four hours a day, either.

An eternity passed before Josh returned—Amy was on her second cup of coffee—but she was determined to drink the entire pot if it took that long.

He was leaning heavily upon the cane, his progress slow as he made his way into the dining room. This time his eyes avoided hers.

"Your breakfast is cold," she said, standing behind her chair. "Would you like me to ask Manuela to make you another plate?"

"No, thanks," he said, and his frown deepened.

Amy strongly suspected his scowl had little or nothing to do with his cold breakfast.

"Is anything the matter?" She would have swallowed her tongue before she'd directly inquire about the phone call, but something was apparently troubling Josh, and she wanted to help if she could.

"No," he said.

He gave her a brief smile that was meant to hearten her, but didn't. His unwillingness to share, plus his determined scowl, heightened her curiosity. Then, in a heartbeat, Amy knew.

"That was Jasmine, wasn't it?" Until that moment she'd put the other woman completely out of her mind, refusing to acknowledge the possibility of Josh loving someone else. It shocked her now that she had been so blind.

"Jasmine?"

"In the hospital you murmured her name several times…apparently you had the two of us confused."

"Amy, I don't know anyone named Jasmine." His eyes held hers with reassuring steadiness.

"Then why would you repeat her name when you were only half-conscious?"

"Good grief, I don't know," he returned resolutely.

He looked like he was about to say something more, but Amy hurried on. "Then I don't need to worry about you leaving me for another woman?" She gave a small laugh, not understanding his mood. It was as if he had erected a concrete wall between them, and she had to shout to gain his attention.

"I'm not going to leave you for another woman." His eyes softened as they rested on her, then pooled with regret. "But I *am* leaving you."

He stated it so casually, as if he was discussing breakfast, as if it was something of little consequence in their lives. Amy felt a fist closing around her heart, the winds of his discontent whipping up unspoken fears.

"I'm sorry, Angel Eyes."

She didn't doubt his contrition was sincere. She closed her hands deliberately over the back of the dining room chair in front of her. "I... I don't think I understand."

"That was SunTech on the phone."

Amy swallowed tightly, debating whether she should say anything. The decision was made simultaneously with the thought. She had to! She couldn't silently stand by and do nothing.

"You couldn't possibly mean to suggest you're going back to work? Josh, you can't—you're not physically capable of it. Good grief, this is only the first day you haven't used your crutches."

"I'll be gone as soon as I've finished packing."

She blinked, noting that he hadn't bothered to respond to her objections. He never intended to discuss his plans with her. He told her, and she was to accept them.

"Where?" she asked, feeling sick to her stomach, her head and her heart numb.

"Texas."

She sighed with relief; Texas wasn't so far. "How long?" she asked next.

"What does it matter?"

"I... I'd like to know how long it will be before you can come back."

He tensed, his back as straight as a flagpole. "I won't be coming back."

"I see." He was closing himself off from her, blocking her out of his life as if she was nothing more than a passing fancy. The pain wrapped itself around her like ivy climbing up the base of a tree, choking out its life by degrees.

Without another word of explanation, Josh turned and started to walk away from her.

"You intend to forget you ever knew me, don't you?"

He paused in the doorway, his back to her, his shoulders stiff and proud. "No."

Amy didn't understand any of this. Only a few hours before he'd held her in his arms, loved her, laughed with her. And now...now, he was casually turning and strolling out of her life with little or no excuse. It didn't make any sense.

Several minutes passed before Amy had the strength to move. When she did, she vaulted past Josh as he slowly made his way up the stairs one at a time. Poised at the top, she forced a smile to her lips, although they trembled with barely suppressed emotion.

"You can't leave yet," she said with a saucy grin, placing a hand on her hip and doing her best to look sophisticated and provocative. "We have some unfinished business. Remember?"

"No, we don't."

"Josh, you're the one who claimed that the next time we don't stop."

"There isn't going to be a next time."

He was so cold, so callous, so determined. Removing her hand from her hip, Amy planted it on her forehead, her thoughts rumbling in her mind, deep and dark. Lost. "I think I'm missing out on something here. Last night—"

Josh stopped her with a glare, telling her with his eyes what he said every time he touched her. *Last night was a mistake.*

"All right," she continued, undaunted. "Last night probably shouldn't have happened. But it did. It has in the past, and I was hoping—well, never mind, you know what I was hoping."

"Amy…"

"I want to know what's so different now? Why this morning instead of yesterday or the day before? It's as though you can't get away from me fast enough. Why? Did I do something to offend you? If so, I think we should talk about it and clear the air…instead of this."

He reached the top of the stairs, his gaze level with her own. He tried to disguise it, but Amy saw the pain in his eyes, the regret.

"The last thing I want to do is hurt you, Amy."

"Good, then don't."

He cupped her face in his hand and gazed deeply into her eyes as if to tell her that if there had been any way to avoid this, he would have chosen it. He dropped his hand and backed up two small steps. Once more, Amy noted how sluggish his movements were, but this time she guessed it wasn't his leg that was bothering him, but his heart. She looked into his eyes and saw so many things she was certain he meant to hide from her. Confusion. Guilt. Rationalization.

Without another word, he walked past her and to his room. Not knowing what else to do, she followed him.

"You can't tell me you don't love me," she said, stepping inside after him. Immediately, her eyes fell on the open suitcase sitting atop the bed and a sick, dizzying feeling assaulted her. Josh had intended to leave even before the phone call, otherwise his suitcase wouldn't be where it was. "You *do* love me," she repeated, more forcefully this time. "I know you do."

He didn't answer, apparently unwilling to admit his feelings either way.

"It's the money, isn't it? That ridiculous pride of yours is causing all this, and it's just plain stupid. I could care less if you have a dime to your name. I love you, and I'm not going to stop loving you for the next fifty years. If you're so eager to go to Texas, then fine, I'll go with you. I don't need a fancy house and a big car to be happy... not when I have you."

"You're not following me to Texas or anyplace else," he said harshly, his words coated with steel. "I want that understood right now." While he was speaking, he furiously stuffed clothes into the open piece of luggage, his movements abrupt and hurried.

Amy walked over to the window and gripped her hands behind her back, her long nails cutting into her palms. "If you are worried about Dad's—"

"It isn't the money," he said curtly.

"Then what is it?" she cried, losing patience.

He pressed his lips together, and a muscle leaped in his lean jaw.

"Josh," she cried. "I want to know. I have the right, at least. If you want to walk out of my life, then that's your business, but tell me why. I've got a right to know."

He closed his eyes and when he opened them again, they were filled with a new determination, a new strength. "It's you. We're completely different kinds of people. I told you when we met I had no roots, and that's exactly the way I like my life. I like jobs that take me around the world and offer fresh challenges. You need a man who's going to be a father to those babies you talked about once. And it's not going to be me, sweetheart."

She flinched at the harsh way he used the term of affection. Sucking in her breath, she tried again. "When two people love each other, they can learn to compromise. I don't want to chain you to Seattle. If you want to travel, then I'll go with you wherever you want."

"You?" He snickered once. "You're used to living the lifestyles of the rich and famous. Jetting off in your daddy's plane, shopping in Paris, skiing in Switzerland. Forget it, Amy. Within a month, you'd be bored out of your mind."

"Josh, how can you say that? Okay, I can understand why you'd think I'm a spoiled rich kid, and…and you're right, our lifestyles *are* different, but we're compatible in other ways," she rushed on, growing desperate. "You only have to think about what…what nearly happened in the pool to realize that."

He paused, and his short laugh revealed no amusement. "That's another thing," he said coldly. "You with your hot little body, looking for experience. I'm telling you right now, I'm not going to be the one to give it to you."

"You seemed willing enough last night," she countered, indignation overcoming the hurt his words caused.

He granted her that much with a cocky grin. "I thank the good Lord that your gardener's son showed up when he did, otherwise there could be more than one unpleasant complication to our venture into that pool."

"I'm not looking for experience, Josh, I'm looking for love."

"A twenty-four-year-old virgin always coats her first time with thoughts of love—it makes it easier to justify later. It isn't love we share, Amy, it's a healthy dose of good old-fashioned lust." He stuffed a shirt inside his suitcase so forcefully it was a miracle the luggage remained intact. "When it comes to making love, you're suffering from a little retarded growth. The problem is, you don't fully realize what you're asking for, and when you find out, it's going to shock you."

"You haven't shocked me."

"Trust me, I could."

He said this with a harshly indrawn breath that was sharp enough to make Amy recoil.

"Sex isn't romance, Angel Eyes, it's hot mouths and grinding hips and savage kisses. At least it is with me, and I'm not looking to initiate a novice."

"It seems we've done our share of…that."

"You wouldn't leave me alone, would you? I tried to stay out of your way. I went to great pains to be sure we wouldn't be alone together—to remove ourselves from the temptation. But you would have none of that—you threw yourself at me at every opportunity."

That was true enough, and Josh knew it.

"I'm a man, what was I supposed to do, ignore you? So I slipped a couple of times. I tried to ward you off, but you were so eager to lose your virginity, you refused to listen. Now the painful part comes, I was as much of a gentleman as I could be under the circumstances. It wasn't as if I didn't try." He slammed the lid of his suitcase closed, shaking the bed in the process.

A polite knock sounded at the door, and Josh turned slowly toward it. "Yes, what is it, Manuela?"

"Mr. Josh, there is taxi here for you."

"Thank you. Tell him I'll be down in a couple of minutes."

Amy blinked as fast as she could to keep the burning tears from spilling down her cheeks. "You're really leaving me, aren't you?" She was frozen with shock.

"I couldn't make it any more clear," Josh shouted. "You knew the score when I met you. I haven't lied to you, Amy, not once. Did you think I was joking when I told you I was walking out that door and I didn't plan on coming back? Accept it. Don't make this any more difficult than it already is."

"Go then," she whispered, pride coming to her rescue. "If you can live with the thought of another man holding and kissing me and making love with me then… go." *Go,* she cried silently, *before I beg you to stay.*

For a moment, Josh stood stock-still. Then he reached for his suitcase, closing his fingers viciously around the handle, and dragged it across the bed. He held it in one hand and his cane in the other. Without looking at her, he headed toward the stairs.

Amy stood where she was, tears raining down her face in a storm of fierce emotion. By the time the shock had started to dissipate and she ran to the head of the stairs, Josh was at the front door.

"Josh," she cried, bracing her hands against the railing.

He paused, but he didn't turn and look at her.

"Go ahead and walk out that door... I'm not going to do anything to stop you."

"That's encouraging."

She closed her eyes to the stabbing pain. "I... I just wanted you to know that you can have all the adventures you want and travel to every corner of the world and even...and even make love to a thousand women."

"I intend on doing exactly that."

He was facing her now, but the tears had blinded her and all she could make out was a watery image. "Live your life and I'll... I'll live mine, and we'll probably never see each other again, but... I swear to you...one day you're going to regret this." Her shoulders shook with sobs. "One day you're going to look back and think of all that you threw away and realize..." She paused, unable to go on, and wiped the moisture from her eyes.

"Can I go now?"

"Stop being so cruel."

"It's the only thing you'll accept," he shouted, his anger vibrating all the way up the stairs. He turned from her once more.

"Josh," she cried, her hands knotting into tight fists at her sides.

"Now what?"

The air between them crackled with electricity and the longest moment of her life passed before she could speak. "Don't come back," she told him. "Don't ever come back."

* * *

Josh rubbed his eyes with his thumb and index finger and sagged in the seat of the yellow cab.

"Where to, mister?"

"Sea-Tac Airport," Josh instructed. His insides felt like a bowl of overcooked oatmeal tossed in a campfire. Surviving the explosion had been nothing compared to saying goodbye to Amy. He would gladly have run into another burning building rather than walk away from her again. He had to leave, he had known that the minute he climbed out of the pool the night before. It was either get out of her life before their lovemaking went too far or marry her.

For both their sakes, he was leaving.

But it hadn't been easy. The memory of the way her eyes had clouded with pain would haunt him until the day he died. He shut his mind to the image of her standing at the top of the stairs. Her anguish had called to him in an age-old litany that would echo in his mind far beyond the grave.

What she said about him regretting leaving her had hit him like a blow to the solar plexus. He hadn't even been away five minutes, and the remorse struck him the way fire attacks dry timber.

She was right about him loving her, too. Josh hadn't tried to lie about his feelings. He couldn't have, because she knew. Unfortunately, loving her wouldn't make things right for them. It might have worked, they may have been able to build a life together, if she wasn't who she was—Harold Johnson's daughter. Even then Josh had his doubts. There was only one absolute in all this—he wasn't ever going to stop loving her. At least not in this lifetime.

"Hey, buddy, are you all right back there?" the cab driver asked over his shoulder. He was balding and friendly.

"I'm fine."

"You don't look so fine. You look like a man who's been done wrong by his woman. What's the matter, did she kick you out?"

Josh met the driver's question with angry silence.

"Listen, friend, if I were you, I wouldn't put up with it." His laugh was as coarse as his words.

Josh closed his eyes against fresh pain. Amy's words about another man making love to her had hit their mark. Bull's-eye. If he had anything to be pleased about, it was the fact that he had left her with her innocence intact. It had come so close in the pool. He had managed to leave her pure and sweet for some other man to initiate into lovemaking.

A blinding light flashed through his head, and the pain was so intense that he blinked several times against its unexpected onslaught.

"Hey, friend, I know a good lawyer if you need one. From the looks of it, you two got plenty of cold cash. That makes it tough. I know a lot of people who've got money, and from what I see, it sure as hell didn't buy happiness."

"I don't need a lawyer."

The taxi driver shook his head. "That's a mistake too many men make, these days. They want to keep everything friendly for the kids' sakes. You got kids?"

Josh's eyes drifted closed. Children. For a time there, soon after they had returned from Kadiri, Josh had dreamed of having children with her. He dreamed a good deal about making those babies, too. He smiled wryly. If he had learned anything in the months he had spent loving Amy, it was the ability to imagine the impossible. He would wrap those fantasies around him now the way his aunt Hazel tucked an afghan around her shoulders in the heart of winter.

"I got two boys myself," the driver continued, apparently unconcerned with the lack of response from his passenger. "They're mostly grown now, and I don't mind telling you they turned out all right. Whatever you do, buddy, don't let the wife take those kids away from you. Fight for 'em if you got to, but fight."

Josh was battling, all right, but the war he was waging was going on inside his head. It didn't take much imagination to picture Amy's stomach swollen with his child and the joy that would radiate from her eyes when she looked at him. Only there wouldn't be any children. Because there wouldn't be any Amy. At least not for him.

"Buddy, you sure you don't want the name of that lawyer? He's good. Real good."

"I'm sure."

The cab eased to a stop outside the airport terminal, and the chatty driver looped his arm around the back of the seat and twisted around to Josh. "Buddy, I don't mean to sound like a know-it-all, but running away isn't going to solve anything."

Josh dug out his wallet and pulled out a couple of bills. "This enough?"

"Plenty." The cabbie reached for his wallet. "No, sir, the airport is the last place in the world you should be," he muttered as he drew out a five-dollar bill.

Josh already had his hand on the door. He needed

to escape before he realized how much sense this taxi driver was making. "Keep the change."

"Amy." Her father tapped gently against her bedroom door. "Sweetheart, are you all right?"

She sat with her back against the headboard, her knees drawn up. The room was dark. Maybe if she ignored him, her father would go away.

"Amy?"

She sniffled and reached for another tissue. "I'm fine," she called, hoping he would accept that and leave her alone. "Really, Dad, I'm okay." She wasn't in the mood for conversation or father-daughter talks or anything else. All she wanted was to curl up in a tight ball and bandage her wounds. The pain was still too raw to share with her father, although she loved him dearly.

Contrary to her wishes, he let himself into her room and automatically reached for the light switch. Amy squinted and covered her face. "Dad, please, I just want to be by myself for a while." It was then that she noticed the illuminated dial on her clock radio. "What are you doing home this time of day, anyway?"

"Josh phoned me from the airport on his way out of town."

"Why? So he could gloat?" she asked bitterly.

Harold Johnson sat on the edge of his daughter's bed and gently patted her shoulder. "No. He wanted to thank me for my hospitality and to say you probably needed someone about now. From the look of things, he was right."

"I'm doing quite nicely without him, so you don't need to worry." And she would—in a few months or a few years, she added mentally.

"I know you are, sweetheart."

She blew her nose and rubbed the back of her hand across her eyes. "He loves me…in my heart I know he does, and still he walked away."

"I don't doubt that, either."

"Then why?"

"I wish I knew."

"I… I don't think we'll ever know," she sobbed. "I hurt so much I want to hate him and then all I can think is that the…the least he could have done was marry me for my money."

Her father chuckled softly and gathered her in his arms. "Listen, baby, a wise man once stated that happiness broadens our hearts, but sorrow opens our souls."

"Then you can drive a truck through mine."

He held her close. "Try to accept the fact Josh chose to leave, for whatever reason. He's gone. He told me when he first came that was his intention."

"He didn't tell me," she moaned. "Dad, I love him so much. How am I ever going to let him go?"

"The pain will get better in time, I promise you."

"Maybe," she conceded, "but it doesn't seem possible right now." Knowing Josh didn't want to marry her was difficult enough, but refusing to make love with her made his rejection all the more difficult to bear.

"Come downstairs," her father coaxed. "Sitting in your room with the drapes closed isn't helping anything."

She shook her head. "Maybe later."

"How about a trip? Take off with a friend for a while and travel."

She shook her head and wiped a tear from her cheek.

"No, thanks. It isn't that I don't appreciate the offer, but I wouldn't enjoy myself. At least not now."

"Okay, baby, I understand." Gently he kissed her crown and stood.

"Dad," she called to him when he started to walk out of her room. "Did Josh say...anything else?"

"Yes." His eyes settled on her and grew sad. "He said goodbye."

The knot in her stomach twisted so tight that she sucked in her breath to the surge of unexpected pain. "Goodbye," she repeated, and closed her eyes.

The next morning, Amy's alarm clock rang at six, rousing her from bed. She showered and dressed in her best suit, primly tucking in her hair at her nape in a loose chignon.

Her father was at the breakfast table when she joined him. His eyes rounded with surprise when she walked into the room.

"Good morning, Dad," she said, reaching for the coffee. She didn't have Josh, but she had her father. Harold Johnson had the courage of a giant and the sensitive heart of a child. Just being with him would help her find the way out of this bitter unhappiness.

"Amy." It looked as if he wasn't quite sure what to say. "It's early for you, isn't it?"

"Not anymore. Now, before we head for the office, is there anything you want to fill me in on?"

For the first time Amy could remember, her father was completely speechless.

Chapter 10

"There was a call for you earlier," Rusty Everett told Josh when he returned from lunch.

Josh's heart thudded heavily. "Did you catch the name?"

"Yeah, I wrote it down here someplace." Rusty, fifty and as Texan as they come, rummaged around his cluttered desk for several moments. "I don't know what I did with it. Whoever it was said they'd call back later."

"It didn't happen to be a woman, did it?" One that had the voice of an angel, Josh added silently. He'd gone out of his way to be sure Amy never wanted to see or talk to him again, and yet his heart couldn't stop longing for her.

"No, this was definitely a man."

"If you find the name, let me know."

"Right."

Leaning upon his cane, Josh made his way into the

small office. Since he was still recovering from the explosion, Josh was pushing a pencil for SunTech. He didn't like being cooped up inside an office, but he didn't know if he should attribute this unyielding restlessness to the circumstances surrounding his employment or the gaping hole left in his life without Amy. He had the feeling he could be tanning on the lush white sands of a tropical paradise and still find plenty of cause for complaint.

As painful as it was to admit, there was only one place he wanted to be, and that was in Seattle with a certain angel. Instead, he was doing everything within his power to arrange a transfer to the farthest reaches of planet earth so he could escape her. The problem was, it probably wouldn't matter where he ran, his memories would always catch up with him.

He was wrong to have abruptly left her the way he did, to deliberately hurt her, but, unfortunately, he knew it was the right thing for them both, even if she didn't.

He'd been noble, but he'd behaved like a jerk.

He had to forget her, but his heart and his mind and his soul wouldn't let him.

Wiping a hand across his face, Josh leaned back in his chair and rubbed the ache from his right thigh. The pain in his leg was minute compared to the throbbing anguish that surrounded his heart.

With determination, Josh reached for the geological report he wanted to read, but his mind wasn't on oil exploration. It was on an angel who had turned his life upside down.

"Hey, Josh," Rusty called from the other room. "You've got a visitor."

Josh stood and nearly fell back into his chair in shock when Harold Johnson casually strolled into his office.

"Hello, Josh."

Amy's father greeted him as if they were sitting down to a pleasant meal together. "Mr. Johnson," Josh replied stiffly, ill at ease.

The two shook hands, eyeing each other. One confident, the other dubious, Josh noted. Without waiting for an invitation, Harold claimed the chair on the other side of the desk and crossed his legs as though he planned to sit and chat for a while. All he needed to complete the picture was a snifter of brandy and a Cuban cigar.

"What can I do for you?" Josh asked, doing his level best to keep his voice crisp and professional.

"Well, son," Harold said, and reached inside his suit jacket for the missing cigar. "I've come to talk to you about my daughter."

Vicious fingers clawed at Josh's stomach. "Don't. I made it clear to her, and to you, that whatever was between us is over."

"Just like that?"

"Just like that," Josh returned flatly, lying through clenched teeth.

A flame flickered at the end of the cigar, and Harold took several deep puffs, his full attention centered on the Havana Special. "She's doing an admirable job of suggesting the same thing."

Perhaps something was wrong. Maybe she had been hurt or was ill. Josh struggled to hide his growing concern. Amy's father wouldn't show up without a good reason.

"Is she all right?" Josh asked, unable to bear not knowing any longer.

Harold chuckled. "You'd be amazed at how well she's doing at pretending she never set eyes on you. She hasn't so much as mentioned your name since the day you left. She's cheerful, happy, enthusiastic. If I didn't know her so well, I could almost be fooled."

Relief brought down his guard. "She'll recover."

"Yes, I suspect so. She's keeping busy. The fact is, the girl surprised the dickens out of me the morning after you left. Bright and early she marched down the stairs, dressed in her best business suit, and claimed it was time she started earning her keep. Accounting never knew what hit them." The older man chuckled, sounding both delighted and proud.

If Amy's father had meant to shock him, he was doing an admirable job of it.

"The girl's got grit," Harold continued.

"Then why are you here?" Josh demanded.

"I came to see how you were doing, son."

"A phone call would have served as well."

"Tried that, but your friend there said you were out to lunch, and since I was in town, I thought I'd stop by so we could chat a bit before I flew home."

"How'd you know where to find me?"

Harold inhaled deeply on the cigar. "Were you in hiding?"

"Not exactly." But Josh hadn't let it be known where in Texas he was headed.

"I must say you're looking well."

"Thanks," Josh murmured. Most days he felt as though he wanted to hide under a rock. At least it would be dark and cold, and perhaps he could sleep without dreaming of Amy. The last thing he needed was a con-

frontation with her father, or to own up to the fact he was
dying for news of her.

"Fact is, you look about as well as my daughter does."

Josh heaved a sigh and lowered his eyes to his paperwork, hoping Harold Johnson would take the hint.

"By the way," the older man said, a smile teasing the
corners of his mouth, "you wouldn't happen to know
anything about a swimsuit I found at the bottom of my
pool the day you left, would you?"

It took a good deal to unsettle Josh, but in the course
of five minutes Harold Johnson had done it twice. "I...
Amy and I went swimming."

"Looks like one of you decided to skinny-dip," Harold added with an abrupt laugh.

His amusement bewildered Josh even more. "We...
ah... I know it looks bad."

"That skimpy white thing must have belonged to my
daughter, although I'll admit that I'd no idea she had
such a garment."

"Sir, I want you to know I... I didn't..."

"You don't have to explain yourself, son. My daughter's a grown woman, and if nothing happened, it's not
from any lack of trying on her part, I'll wager."

Josh hadn't blushed since he was a boy, but he found
himself doing so now.

"She must have been a tempting morsel for you to
walk away from like that."

Josh swallowed with difficulty and nodded. "She
was."

Harold Johnson puffed long and hard on his cigar
once more, then held it away from his face and examined the end of it as if he suspected it wasn't lit. When

he spoke again, his voice was nonchalant. "I knew a Powell once."

Josh stiffened. "It's a common enough name."

"This Powell was a successful stockbroker with his own firm situated on Wall Street. Ever hear of a fellow by the name of Chance Powell?"

A cold chill settled over Josh. "I've heard of him," he admitted cautiously.

"I thought you might have." Harold nodded, as if confirming the information he already knew. "He's one of the most successful brokers in the country. From what I understand he has offices in all fifty states now. There's been a real turnaround in his business in recent years. I understand he almost lost everything not too long ago, but he survived, and so did the business."

Josh didn't add anything to that. From the time he'd walked away from his father, he'd gone out of his way *not* to keep track of what was happening in his life, professional or otherwise.

"From what I know of him, he has only one child, a son."

If Harold was looking for someone to fill in the blanks, he was going to be disappointed. Josh sat with his back rigid, his mouth set in a thin line of impatience.

Harold chewed on the end of the cigar the way a child savors a candy sucker. "There was a write-up in the *Journal* several years back about Chance's son. I don't suppose you've heard of *him*?"

"I might have." Boldly Josh met the older man's stare, unwilling to give an inch.

"The article said the boy showed promise enough to be one of the brightest business minds this country has ever known. He graduated at the top of his class at

MIT, took the business world by storm and revealed extraordinary insight. Then, without anyone ever learning exactly why, he packed up his bags and walked away from it all."

"He must have had his reasons."

Harold Johnson nodded. "I'm sure he did. They must have been good ones for him to walk away from a brilliant future."

"Perhaps he was never interested in money," Josh suggested.

"That's apparently so, because I learned that he served for several years as a volunteer for the Peace Corps." Harold Johnson held the cigar between his fingers and lowered his gaze as if deep in thought. "It's unfortunate that such a keen business mind is being wasted. Fact is, I wouldn't mind having him become part of my own firm. Don't know if he'd consider it, though. What do you think?"

"I'm sure he wouldn't," Josh returned calmly.

"That's too bad." Harold Johnson heaved a small sigh. "His life could be a good deal different if he wished. Instead—" he paused and scowled at Josh "—he's wasted his talents."

"Wasted? Do you believe helping the less fortunate was squandering my—his life?"

"Not at all. I'm sure he contributed a good deal during the years he served with the Peace Corps. But the boy apparently has an abundance of talent in other areas. It's a shame he isn't serving where he's best suited." He stared directly at Josh for a lengthy, uncomfortable moment. "It would seem to me that this young man has made a habit of walking away from challenges and opportunities."

"I think you may be judging him unfairly."

"Perhaps," Amy's father conceded.

Josh remained silent. He knew what the older man was saying, but he wanted none of it.

Harold continued to chew on his cigar, apparently appreciating the taste of the fine Cuban tobacco more than he enjoyed smoking it. "I met Chance Powell several years back, and frankly, I liked the man," Harold continued, seeming to approach this conversation from fresh grounds.

"Frankly," Josh echoed forcefully, "I don't."

The older man's eyes took on an obstinate look. "I'm sorry to hear that."

Josh made a show of looking at his watch, hoping his guest would take the hint and leave before the conversation escalated into an argument. Harold didn't, but that wasn't any real surprise for Josh.

"Do you often meddle in another man's life, or is this a recent hobby?" Josh asked, swallowing what he could of the sarcasm.

The sound of the older man's laughter filled the small office. "I have to admit, it's a recent preoccupation of mine."

"Why now?"

Harold leaned forward and extinguished his cigar, rubbing it with unnecessary force in the glass ashtray that rested on the corner of Josh's crowded desk. "What's between Chance Powell and his son is their business."

"I couldn't agree with you more. Then why are you bringing it up?"

Any humor that lingered in the older man's gaze vanished like sweet desserts in a room filled with children. "Because both you and Amy are about to make the biggest mistakes of your lives, and I'm finding it downright difficult to sit back and watch."

"What goes on between the two of us is our business."

"I'll grant you that much." Releasing his breath, Harold stood, his look apologetic. "You're right, of course, I had no right coming here. If Amy knew, she'd probably never forgive me."

Josh's tight features relaxed. "You needn't worry that I'll tell her."

"Good."

"She's a strong woman," Josh said, standing and shaking hands with a man he admired greatly. "From everything you said, she's already started to rebound. She'll be dating again soon."

The smile on his lips lent credence to his words, but the thought of Amy with another man did things to his heart Josh didn't even want to consider. It was far better that he never know.

"Before you realize it, Amy will have found herself a decent husband who will make her a good deal happier than I ever could," Josh said, managing to sound as though he meant it.

Harold Johnson rubbed the side of his jaw in measured strokes. "That's the problem. I fear she already has."

Amy sat in the office of the accounting supervisor for Johnson Industries. Lloyd Dickins would be joining her directly, and she took a few moments to glance around his neat and orderly office. Lloyd's furniture was in keeping with the man, she noted. His room was dominated by thick, bulky pieces that were so unlike her own ultramodern furnishings. A picture of Lloyd's wife with their family was displayed on the credenza, and judging by its frame, the picture was several years old. The one photograph was all there was to fill in the blanks of Dickins's life outside the company. Perhaps his need for privacy, his effort to keep the two worlds separate, was the reason Amy had taken such a liking to Lloyd. It was apparent her father shared her opinion.

Lloyd had welcomed Amy into the accounting department, although she was convinced he had his reservations. Frankly, she couldn't blame him. She was the boss's daughter and if she was going to eventually assume her father's position, albeit years in the future, she would need to know every aspect of managing the conglomerate.

"Sorry to keep you waiting," Lloyd mumbled as he sailed into the office.

Amy swore the man never walked. But he didn't exactly run, either. His movements were abrupt, hurried, and Amy supposed it was that which gave the impression he was continually rushing from one place to the other. He was tall and thin, his face dominated by a smile that was quick and unwavering.

"I've only been waiting a minute," she answered, dismissing his apology.

"Did you have the chance to read over the Emerson report?" he asked as he claimed the seat at his desk. He reached for the file, thumbing through the pages of the summary. The margins were filled with notes and comments.

"I read it last night and then again this morning."

Lloyd Dickins nodded, looking pleased. "You've been putting in a good deal of time on this project.

Quite honestly, Amy, I wasn't sure what to expect when your father told me you'd be joining my team. But after the last three weeks, I don't mind telling you, you've earned my respect."

"Thank you." She'd worked hard for this moment, and when the praise came, it felt good.

"Now," Lloyd said, leaning back in his chair, "tell me what you think?"

Amy spent the next twenty minutes doing exactly that. When she'd finished, Lloyd added his own comments and insights and then called for a meeting of their department for that afternoon.

When Amy returned to her office, there were several telephone messages waiting for her. She left Chad's note for last. Chad Morton worked in marketing and had been wonderful. He was charming and suave and endearing, and best of all, nothing like Josh. In fact, no two men could have been more dissimilar, which suited her just fine. If she was going to forget Josh, she would have to do it with someone who was his complete opposite.

Chad was the type of man who would be content to smoke a pipe in front of a fireplace for the remainder of his life. He was filet mignon, designer glasses and BMW personality.

"Chad, it's Amy." She spoke into the receiver. "I got your message."

"Hi, Angel Face."

Amy closed her eyes to the sudden and unexpected flash of pain. She was forced to bite her tongue to keep from asking him not to call her anything that had to do with angels. That had been Josh's line, and she was doing everything within her power to push every thought of him from her life.

"Are you free for dinner tonight?" Chad continued. "Brenn and James phoned and want to know if we can meet them at the country club at six. We can go to a club afterward."

"Sure," Amy responded quickly, "why not? It sounds like fun." Keeping busy, she'd discovered, was the key. If she wasn't learning everything she could about her father's business, she was throwing herself into social events with the energy of a debutante with a closet full of prom dresses.

Rarely did she spend time at home anymore. Every room was indelibly stamped with memories of Josh and the long weeks he had spent recovering there. She would have given anything to completely wipe out the time spent at his side, but simultaneously she held the memories tightly to her chest, treasuring each minute he'd been in her life.

She was mixed up, confused, hurting and pretending otherwise.

It seemed Josh had left his mark in each and every room of her home. She couldn't walk into the library and not feel an emptiness that stabbed deep into her soul.

Only when she ventured near the pool did she feel his presence stronger than his absence, and she left almost immediately, rather than have to deal with her rumbling emotions.

When Amy arrived home that evening, she was surprised to discover her father sitting in the library in front of the fireplace, his feet up and a blanket draped over his lap. It was so unusual to find him resting that the sight stopped her abruptly in the hallway.

"Dad," she said, stepping into the room. "When did you get back?" Still perplexed, but pleased to see him, she leaned over to affectionately kiss his cheek. He'd been away several days on a business trip and wasn't expected home until the following afternoon.

"I landed an hour ago," Harold answered, smiling softly at her.

Amy removed her coat and curled up in a chair beside him. "I didn't think you'd be home until tomorrow night. Chad phoned, and we're going out to dinner. You don't mind, do you?"

He didn't answer her for several elongated moments, as if he was searching for the right words. This, too, was unlike him, and Amy wondered at his mood.

"You're seeing a good deal of Chad Morton, aren't you? The two of you are gallivanting around town every night of the week, it seems. Things seem to be getting serious."

Amy sidestepped the question. As a matter of fact, she'd been thinking those same thoughts herself. She *had* been seeing a good deal of Chad. He'd asked her out the first day she started working at Johnson Industries, and they'd been together nearly every night since.

"Do you object?" she asked pointedly. "Chad would make an excellent husband. He comes from a good family, and seems nice enough."

"True, but you don't love him."

"Who said anything about love?" Amy asked, forcing a light laugh. As far as she was concerned, falling in love had been greatly overrated.

If she was going to become involved with a man she

would much rather it was with someone like Chad. He was about as exciting as one-coat paint, but irrefutably stable. If there was anything she needed in her life, it was someone she could depend on who would love her for the next fifty years without demands, without questions.

As an extra bonus, there would never be any threat of her falling head over heels for Chad Morton and making a fool of herself the way she had for Josh Powell. No, it wasn't love, but it was comfortable.

Her father reached for his brandy, and Amy poured herself a glass of white wine, savoring these few minutes alone with him. They seldom sat and talked anymore, but the fault was mainly her own. In fact, she had avoided moments such as this. Her biggest fear was that he would say something about Josh, and she wouldn't be able to deal with it.

"I may not love Chad, but he's nice," she answered simply, hoping that would appease the question burning in her father's deep blue eyes.

"Nice," Harold repeated, his smile sad and off-center. He made the word sound trivial and weak, as if he was describing the man himself.

"Chad works for you," she said as a means of admonishment.

"True enough."

"So how was the trip?" she asked, turning the course of the conversation. She hadn't said she would accept Chad's proposal when he offered it, only that she fully expected him to tender one soon. She hadn't made up her mind one way or the other on how she would answer such a question. A good deal would depend on what her father thought. Since the two men would be working closely together in the future, it would be best if they liked and respected each other...the way Josh and her father seemed to have felt.

Josh again. She closed her eyes to the thought of him, forgetting for the moment that he was out of her life and wouldn't be back.

Once more her father hesitated before answering her question. "The trip was interesting."

"Oh?" Rarely did her father hedge, but he seemed to be doing his fair share of it this evening.

His gaze pulled hers the same way a magnet attracts steel. "From Atlanta I flew down to Texas."

Amy rotated the crystal stem between her open palms, her heart perking like a brewing pot of coffee. Josh had claimed he was heading for Texas, but it was a big state and...

She blinked a couple of times, hoping desperately that she had misread her father, but one look from him confirmed her worst suspicion. Instantly, her throat went dry and her tongue felt as if it was glued to the roof of her mouth.

"You...talked to Josh, didn't you?"

Without the least bit of hesitation, Harold Johnson nodded, but his eyes were weary, as if he anticipated a confrontation.

Her lashes fluttered closed at the intense feelings of hurt and betrayal. "How could you?" she cried, bolting to her feet. Unable to stand still, she set the wineglass aside and started pacing the room, her movements crisp enough to impress the military.

"He put on a brave front—the same way you've been doing for the last three weeks."

Amy wasn't listening. "In all my life, I've never

questioned or doubted anything you've ever done. I love you... I trusted you." Her voice was trembling so badly that it was amazing he could even understand her. "How could you?"

"Amy, sit down, please."

"No!" she shouted. The sense of betrayal was so strong, she didn't think she could remain in the same room with him any longer. Through the years, Amy had always considered her father to be her most loyal friend. He was the safe port she steered toward in times of trouble. Since she was a child he'd been the one who pointed out the rainbow at the end of a cloudburst. He was the compass who directed the paths of her life.

Until this moment, she had never doubted anything he'd done for her.

"What possible reason could you have to contact Josh?" she demanded. "Were you looking to humiliate me more? Is that it? It's a wonder he didn't laugh in your face... Perhaps he did, in which case it would serve you right."

"Amy, sweetheart, that isn't the reason I saw Josh. You should know that."

Furious, she brushed away the tears that sprang so readily to her eyes and seared a wet trail down her cheeks. "I suppose you told him I was wasting away for want of him? No doubt you boosted his arrogance by claiming I'm still crazy about him...and that I'll probably never stop loving him."

"Amy, please—"

"Wasn't his leaving humiliation enough?" she shouted. "Who...gave you the right to rub salt in my wounds? Didn't you think I was hurting enough?" Without waiting for his reply, Amy stormed out of the library, so filled with righteous anger that she didn't stop until she was in her bedroom.

No more than a minute had passed before her father pounded on her door.

"Amy, please, just listen, would you?"

"No…just go away."

"But I need to explain. You're right, I probably shouldn't have gone to see Josh without talking with you about it first, but there was something I needed to discuss with him."

Although she remained furious, she opened her bedroom door and folded her arms across her chest. "What possible reason could you have to talk to Joshua Powell… if it didn't directly involve me?"

Her father stood just outside her door, a sheen of perspiration moistening his pale forehead and upper lip. He probably shouldn't have come racing up the stairs after her. He looked ashen, and his breathing was labored, but Amy chose to ignore that, too angry to care.

"Dad?" she repeated, bracing her hands against her hips. "Why did you talk to Josh?"

Her father's responding smile was weak at best. "I have a feeling you aren't going to like this, either." He hesitated and wiped a hand across his brow. "I went to offer him a job."

"You did what?" It demanded everything within Amy not to explode on the spot. She stood frozen for a moment, then buried her face in her hands.

"It isn't as bad as it seems, sweetheart. Joshua Powell is fully qualified. I was just looking to—"

"I know what you were trying to do," Amy cried. "You were looking to *buy* him for me!" Before it had been her voice that trembled. Now her entire body shook with outrage. Her knees didn't feel as if they were going to support her any longer.

But that didn't stop her from charging across the room to her closet and throwing open the doors with every ounce of strength she possessed. She dragged out her suitcases and slammed them across the bed.

"Amy, what are you doing?"

"Leaving. This house. Johnson Industries. And you."

Her calm, rational father looked completely undone. If he was colorless before, he went deathly pale now. "Sweetheart, there's no reason for you to move out." The look in his eyes was desperate. "There's no need to overreact... Josh turned down the offer."

The added humiliation was more than Amy could handle.

"Of course he did. He didn't want me before. What made you think he would now?" Without stopping, she emptied her drawers, tossing her clothes in the open suitcase, unable to escape fast enough.

"Amy, please, don't do anything rash."

"Rash?" she repeated, hiccuping on a sob. "I should have moved out years ago, but I was under the impression that we...shared something special...like trust, mutual respect...love. Until tonight, I believed you—"

"Amy."

Something in the strangled way he uttered her name alerted her to the fact something was wrong. Something was very, very wrong. She whirled around in time to see her father grip his chest, roll back his eyes and slump unconscious to the floor.

Chapter 11

Josh lowered the week-old *Wall Street Journal* and let the newspaper rest on his lap while his mind whirled with troubled concern. Mingling with his worries was an abundance of ideas, most of them maverick—but then he had been considered one in his time.

"What part of the world are you headed for now, dear?" his aunt Hazel inquired, her soft voice curious. She sat across the living room from him, her fingers pushing the knitting needles the way a secretary worked a keyboard. Her white hair was demurely pinned at the back of her head, and tiny wisps framed her oval face. Her features, although marked with age, were soft and gentle. Her outer beauty had faded years before, but the inner loveliness shone brighter each time he stopped to visit. Without much difficulty, Josh could picture Amy resembling his aunt in fifty or so years.

"I'm hoping to go back to Kadiri," he answered her, elbowing thoughts of Amy from his mind.

"Isn't that the place that's been in the news recently?" she asked, sounding worried. "There's so much unrest in this world. I have such a difficult time understanding why people can't get along with one another." She pointedly glanced in his direction, her hands resting in her lap as her tender brown eyes challenged him.

Over the years, Josh had become accustomed to his aunt inserting barbed remarks, thinly veiled, about his relationship with his father. Josh generally ignored them, pretending he didn't understand what she meant. He preferred to avoid a confrontation. As far as he was concerned, his aunt Hazel was his only relative, and he loved her dearly.

"What's that you're reading so intently?"

Josh's gaze fell to the newspaper. *"The Wall Street Journal."* Knowing his aunt would put the wrong connotation into the subject matter, since he normally avoided anything that had to do with the financial world, he hurried to explain. "I have a…friend, Harold Johnson, who owns and operates a large conglomerate. With all the traveling I do, it's difficult to keep in contact with him, so I keep tabs on him by occasionally checking to see how his stock is doing."

"And what does that tell you?"

"Several things."

"Like what, dear?" she asked conversationally.

Josh wasn't certain his aunt would understand all the ins and outs of the corporate world, so he explained it as best he could in simple terms. "Stock prices tell me how he's doing financially."

"I see. But you've been frowning for the last fifteen minutes. Is something wrong with your friend?"

Josh picked up the newspaper and made a ceremony of folding it precisely in fourths. "His bond rating has just been lowered."

"That's not good?"

"No. There's an article here that states that Johnson Industries' stock price is currently depressed, which means the value has fallen below its assets. With several long-term bonds maturing, the cost of rolling them over may become prohibitive."

His aunt Hazel returned to her knitting. "Yes, but what does all that mean?"

Josh struggled to put it into terminology his aunt would understand. "Trouble, mostly. Basically it means that Johnson Industries is a prime candidate for a hostile takeover. He may be forced into selling the controlling interest of the business he's struggled to build over a lifetime to someone else."

"That doesn't seem fair. If a man works hard all his years to build up a business, it's not right that someone else can waltz right in and take over."

"Little in life is fair anymore," Josh said, unable to disguise his bitterness.

"Oh, Josh, honestly." His aunt rested her hands in her lap and slowly shook her head, pressing her lips together tightly. "You have become such a pessimist over the years. If I wasn't so glad to see you when you came to visit me, I'd take delight in shaking some sense into you."

Although his aunt was serious, Josh couldn't help laughing outright. "Harold's going to be just fine. He's a strong man with a lot of connections. The sharks are circling, but they'll soon start looking for weaker prey."

"Good. I hate the thought of your friend losing his business."

"So do I." Setting the newspaper aside, Josh closed his eyes, battling down the surge of long-forgotten excitement. The adrenaline had started to pound through his blood the minute he had picked up the *Wall Street Journal*. It had been years since he had allowed himself the luxury of remembering the life he'd left behind. Since the final showdown with his father, he had done everything he could to forget how much he loved plowing into problems with both hands, such as the one Johnson Industries was currently experiencing. Before he realized what he was doing, his mind was churning out ways to deal with this difficulty.

Releasing his breath, Josh closed his mind to the thought of offering any advice to Amy's father. The cord had been cut, and he couldn't turn back now.

"Your father is looking well," his aunt took obvious delight in informing him.

Josh ignored her. He didn't want to discuss Chance, and Aunt Hazel knew it, but she did her best to introduce the subject of his father as naturally as possible.

"He asked about you."

Josh scoffed before he thought better of it.

"He loves you, Josh," Hazel insisted sharply. "If the pair of you weren't so unbelievably proud, you could settle this unpleasantness in five minutes. But I swear, you're no better than he is."

The anger that shot through Josh was hot enough to boil his blood and, unable to stop his tongue, he blurted out, "I may not be a multimillionaire, but at least I'm not a crook. My father should be in prison right now, and you well know it. You both seem to think I was supposed to ignore the fact that Chance Powell is a liar and a cheat."

"Josh, please, I didn't mean to reopen painful wounds. It's just that I've seen you fly from one end of the world to the other in an effort to escape this difficulty with your father. I hardly know you anymore... I can't understand how you can turn away from everything that ever had any value to you."

The older woman looked pale, and Josh immediately regretted his outburst. "I'm sorry, Aunt Hazel, I shouldn't have raised my voice to you. Now, what was it you said you were cooking for dinner?"

"Crow," she told him, her eyes twinkling.

"I beg your pardon?"

She laughed softly and shook her head. "I seem to put my foot in my mouth every time I try to talk some sense into you. No matter what you do with the rest of your life, Joshua, I want you to know I'll always love you. You're the closest thing to a son I've ever had. Forgive an old woman for sticking her nose where it doesn't belong."

Josh set aside the paper and walked over to sit on the arm of her overstuffed chair. Then he leaned over and kissed her cheek. "If you can forgive me for my sharp tongue, we'll call it square."

That night, Josh wasn't able to sleep. He lay on the mattress with his hands supporting the back of his head and stared into empty space. Every time he closed his eyes, he saw Harold Johnson sitting across the desk from him, discussing his current financial difficulties.

Amy's father was probably in the most delicate position of his business career. The sheer force of the older man's personality was enough to ward off all but the most bloodthirsty sharks. But Josh didn't know how long Harold could keep them at bay. For Amy's sake, he hoped nothing else would go wrong.

His first inclination had been to contact her father with a few suggestions. But Harold Johnson didn't need him, and for that matter, neither did Amy. According to her father, she was seriously dating someone else. In fact, he had claimed she would probably be wearing an engagment ring before long.

Josh hadn't asked any questions, although he would have given his right hand to have learned the name of the man who had swept her off her feet so soon after he had left. More than likely, Josh wouldn't have known the other man, and it wouldn't have mattered if he had.

When he had flown out of Seattle, Josh had hoped Amy would hurry and fall in love with someone else, so there was no reason for him to be unsettled now. This was exactly what he had wanted to happen. So it made no sense that he was being eaten alive with regrets and doubts.

The answer as to why was obvious. He was never going to stop loving Amy. For the first time since his conversation with her father, he was willing to admit what a fool he had been to have honestly believed he had meant it. Just the thought of her even *kissing* another man filled him with such anger that he clenched his fists with impotent rage.

If that wasn't bad enough, envisioning Amy making love with her newfound friend was akin to having his skin ripped off his body one strip at a time. The irony of this was that Amy had told him as much. She'd stood at the top of her stairs and shouted it to him, he recalled darkly. *If you can live with the thought of another man holding and kissing me and making love to me then...go.*

Josh *had* walked away from her, but she had been right. The image of her in the arms of another man caused him more agony than his injuries from the explosion ever had.

Harold Johnson's words came back to haunt him, as well. They had been talking, and Amy's father had stared directly at him and claimed: *This young man has made a habit of walking away from challenges and opportunities.*

At the time it had been all Josh could do not to defend himself. He had let the comment slide rather than force an argument. Now the truth of the older man's words hit him hard, leaving him defenseless.

Josh couldn't deny that he had walked away from his father, turned his back on the life he had once enjoyed, and had been running ever since. Even his love for Amy hadn't been strong enough to force him to deal with that pain. Instead, he had left her and then been forced to deal with another more intense agony. His life felt like an empty shell, as if he were going through the motions, but rejecting all the benefits.

In his own cavalier way, he'd carelessly thrown away the very best thing that had ever happened to him.

Love. Amy's love.

Closing his eyes to the swell of regret, Josh lay in bed trying to decide what he was going to do about it. If anything.

He didn't know if he could casually walk into Amy's

life after the way he had so brutally abandoned her. The answer was as difficult to face as the question had been.

Perhaps it would be best to leave her to what happiness she had found for herself.

Doubts pounded at him from every corner until he realized sleep would be impossible. Throwing back the blankets, he climbed out of bed, dressed and wandered into the living room. His aunt's bedroom door had been left slightly ajar, and he could hear her snoring softly in the background. Instead of being irritated, he was comforted by the knowledge that she was his family. He didn't visit her as often as he should, and he was determined to do so from now on.

Josh sat in the dark for several minutes, reviewing his options with Amy and her father. He needed time to carefully think matters through.

In the wee hours of the morning, he turned on the television, hoping to find a movie that would help him fall asleep. Instead, he fiddled until he found a station that broadcast twenty-four-hour financial news. The article in the *Wall Street Journal* was a week old. A great many things could have happened to Johnson Industries in seven days. It wasn't likely that he would learn anything, but he was curious nonetheless.

"Josh, what are you doing up at this time of night?" his aunt demanded, sounding very much like a mother scolding her twelve-year-old son. She stood and held the back of her hand over her mouth as she yawned. She was dressed in a lavender terry-cloth robe that was tightly cinched at the waist, and her soft hair was secured with a thin black net.

"I couldn't sleep."

"How about some warm milk? It always works for me."

"Only if you add some chocolate and join me."

His aunt chuckled and headed toward the kitchen. "Do you want a bedtime story while I'm at it?"

Josh grinned. "It wouldn't hurt."

She stuck her head around the corner. "That's what I thought you'd say."

Josh stood, prepared to follow her. He walked toward the television, intent on turning it off, when he heard the news. For one wild moment, he stood frozen in shock and disbelief.

"Aunt Hazel," he called once he found his voice. "You'd better cancel the hot chocolate."

"Whatever for?" she asked, but stopped abruptly when she turned and saw him. "Josh, what's happened? My dear boy, you're as pale as a ghost."

"It's my friend. The one I was telling you about earlier—he's had a heart attack and isn't expected to live."

For most of the evening, Josh had been debating what he should do. He had struggled with indecision and uncertainty, trying to decide if it would be best to leave well enough alone and let both Amy and her father go on with their lives. At the same time, he had begun to wonder if he could face life without his Angel Eyes at his side.

Now the matter had been taken out of his hands. There was only one option left to him, and that was to return. If Johnson Industries had been a prime candidate for a hostile takeover *before* Harold's heart attack, it was even more vulnerable now. Sharks always went after the weakest prey, and Johnson Industries lay before them with its throat exposed. Josh's skills might be rusty, but they were intact, and he knew he could help.

Amy would need him now, too. Father and daughter had always been especially close, and losing Harold now would devastate her.

"Josh." His aunt interrupted his musings, her hand on his forearm. "What are you going to do?"

Josh's eyes brightened and he leaned forward to place a noisy kiss on his aunt's cheek. "What I should have done weeks ago—get married."

"Married? But to whom?" A pair of dark brown eyes rounded with surprise. Flustered, she patted her hair. "Actually, I don't care who it is as long as I get an invitation to the wedding."

Like a limp rag doll, Amy sat and stared at the wall outside her father's hospital room. He was in intensive care, and she was only allowed to see him for a few minutes every hour. She lived for those brief moments when she could hold his hand and gently reassure him of her love, hoping to lend him some strength. For three days he'd lain in a coma, unable to respond.

Not once in those long, tedious days had she left the hospital. Not to sleep, not to eat, not to change clothes. She feared the minute she left him, he would slip into death and she wouldn't be there to prevent it.

Hurried footsteps sounded on the polished floor of the hospital corridor, but she didn't turn to see who was coming. So many had sat by her side, staff requesting information, asking questions she didn't want to answer, friends and business associates. But Amy had sent them all away. Now she felt alone and terribly weary.

The footsteps slowed.

"Amy."

Her heart thudded to a stop. "Josh?" Before she was entirely certain how it happened, she was securely tucked in his embrace, her arms wrapped around his neck and her face buried in his chest, breathing in his strength the way desert-dry soil drinks in the rain.

For the first time since her father's heart attack, she gave in to the luxury of tears. They poured from her eyes like water rushing over a dam. Her shoulders jerked with sobs, and she held on to Josh with every ounce of strength she possessed.

Josh's hands were in her hair, and his lips moved over her temple, whispering words she couldn't hear over the sound of her own weeping. It didn't matter; he was there, and she needed him. God had known and had sent him to her side.

"It's my fault," she wailed with a grief that came from the bottom of her soul, trying to explain what had happened. "Everything is my fault."

"No, angel, it isn't, I'm sure it couldn't be."

No one seemed to understand that. No one, and she was too weak to explain. Stepping back, she wiped the tears from her eyes, although it did little good because more poured down her face. "I caused this… I did…we were arguing and…and I was so angry, so hurt that I wanted to…move out and…that was when it happened."

Josh gripped her shoulders, and applying a light pressure, he lowered her into the chair. He squatted in front of her and took both her hands between his, rubbing them. It was then that Amy realized how cold she felt. Shivering and sniffling, she leaned forward enough to rest her forehead against the solid strength of his shoulder.

His arms were around her immediately.

"He's going to be all right," Josh assured her softly.

"No…he's going to die. I know he is, and I'll never be able to tell him how sorry I am."

"Amy," Josh said, gripping the sides of her head and raising her face. "Your father loves you so much, don't you think he already knows you're sorry?"

"I… I'm not sure anymore."

She swayed slightly and would have fallen if Josh hadn't caught her.

He murmured something she couldn't understand and firmly gripped her waist. "When was the last time you had anything to eat?"

She blinked, not remembering.

"Angel," he said gently, "you've got to take care of yourself, now more than ever. Your father needs to wake up and discover you standing over him with a bright smile on your face and your eyes full of love."

She nodded. That was exactly how she pictured the scene in her own mind, when she allowed herself to believe that he would come out of this alive.

"I'm taking you home."

"No." A protest rose automatically to her lips, and she shook her head with fierce determination.

"I'm going to have Manuela cook you something to eat and then I'm going to tuck you in bed and let you sleep. When you wake up, we'll talk. We have a good deal to discuss."

Something in the back of her head told Amy that she shouldn't be listening to Josh, that she shouldn't trust him. But she was so very tired, and much too exhausted to listen to the cool voice of reason.

She must have fallen asleep in the car on the way home from the hospital because the next thing she knew, they were parked outside her home and Josh was coming around to the passenger side to help her out.

He didn't allow her to walk, but gently lifted her into his arms as if she weighed less than a child and carried her in the front door.

"Manuela," he shouted.

The plump housekeeper came rushing into the entryway at the sound of Josh's voice. She took one look at him and mumbled something low and fervent in Spanish.

"Could you make something light for Amy and bring it to her room? She's on the verge of collapse."

"Right away," Manuela said, wiping her hands dry on her blue apron.

"I'm not hungry," Amy felt obliged to inform them. She would admit to feeling a little fragile and a whole lot sleepy, but she wasn't sick. The one they should be taking care of was her father. The thought of him lying so pale and so gravely ill in the hospital bed was enough to make her suck in her breath and start to sob softly.

"Mr. Josh," Manuela shouted, when Josh had carried Amy halfway up the stairs.

"What is it, Manuela?"

"I say many prayers you come back."

Amy wasn't sure she understood their conversation. The words floated around her like dense fog, few making sense. She lifted her head and turned to look at the housekeeper, but discovered that Manuela was already rushing toward the kitchen.

Josh entered her bedroom, set her on the edge of her bed and removed her shoes.

"I want a bath," she told him.

He left her sitting on the bed and started running the

bathwater, then returned and looked through her chest of drawers until he found a nightgown. He gently led her toward the tub, as if she needed his assistance. Perhaps she did, because the thought of protesting didn't so much as enter her mind.

To her consternation, Amy had to have his help unbuttoning her blouse. She stood lifeless and listless as Josh helped remove her outer clothing.

A few minutes later, Manuela scurried into the bedroom, carrying a tray with her. Frowning and muttering something in her mother tongue, she pushed Josh out of the room and helped Amy finish undressing.

Josh was pacing when Amy reappeared. She had washed and blow-dried her hair, brushed her teeth and changed into the soft flannel pajamas covered with red kisses.

Instantly Josh was at her side, his strong arms encircling her waist.

"Do you feel better?" he inquired gently.

She nodded and noted the way his eyes slid to her lips and lingered there. He wanted to kiss her, she knew from the way his gaze narrowed. Her heart began to hammer when she realized how badly she wanted him to do exactly that. Unhurried, his action filled with purpose, Josh lowered his head.

His mouth was opened over hers. Amy sighed at the pleasure and wrapped her arms around his neck, glorying in the feel of him until he broke off the kiss. "Manuela brought you a bowl of soup," Josh insisted, leading her to the bed.

Like a lost sheep, Amy obediently followed him to where the dinner tray awaited her. Josh sat her down on the edge of the mattress and then placed the table and tray in front of her.

After three bites she was full. Josh coaxed her into taking that many more, but then she protested by closing her eyes and shaking her head.

Josh removed the tray and then pulled back the covers, prepared to tuck her into bed.

"Sleep," he said, leaning over and kissing her once more.

"Are you going away again?"

"No," he whispered, and brushed the hair from her temple.

She caught his hand and brought it to her lips. "Promise me you'll be here when I wake up… I need that, Josh."

"I promise."

Her eyes drifted shut. She heard him move toward the door and she knew that already he was breaking his word. The knowledge was like an unexpected slap in the face and she started to whimper without realizing the sounds were coming from her own throat.

Josh seemed to understand her pain. "I'm taking the tray down to the kitchen. I'll be back in a few minutes, angel, I promise."

Amy didn't believe him, but when she stirred a little while later, she discovered Josh sitting in a chair, leaning forward and intently studying her. His forearms were resting on his knees.

He reached out and ran his finger down the side of her face. "Close your eyes, baby," he urged gently. "You've only been asleep a little while."

Amy scooted as far as she could to the other side of the mattress and patted the empty space at her side, inviting him to join her.

"Amy, no," he said, sucking in his breath. "I can't."

"I need you."

Josh sagged forward, indecision etched in bold lines across his tight features. "Oh, angel, the things you ask of me." He stood and sat next to her. "If I do sleep with you, I'll stay on top of the covers. Understand?"

She thought to protest, but hadn't the strength.

Slowly, Josh lowered his head to the pillow, his eyes gentle on her face, so filled with love and tenderness that her own filled with unexpected tears. One inglorious teardrop rolled from the corner of her eye and over the bridge of her nose, dropping onto the pillow.

Josh caught the second droplet with his index finger, his eyes holding hers.

"Oh, my sweet Amy," he whispered. "My life hasn't been the same from the moment I met you."

She tried to smile, but the result was little more than a pathetic movement of her lips. Closing her eyes, she raised her head just a little, anticipating his kiss.

"So this is how you're going to make me pay for my sins?" he whispered throatily.

Amy's eyes flickered open to discover him studying her with sobering intensity.

"Don't you realize how much I want to make love with you?" he breathed, and his tongue parted her lips for a deep, sensual kiss that left her shaken. She raised her hand and tucked it at the base of his neck, then kissed him back. Although she was starved for his touch, having him in bed with her didn't stir awake sexual sensations, only a deep sense of love and security.

He closed his hand possessively over her hip, dragging her as close as humanly possible against him on the mattress. He kissed her again.

Beneath the covers he slid his hand along her mid-riff. There was much she wanted to tell him, much she wanted to share. Questions she longed to ask but to her dismay, she was forced to stop in order to yawn.

He seemed to understand what she wanted. "We'll talk later," he promised. "But first close your eyes and rest."

She nodded, barely moving her head. Her lashes drifted downward, and before she knew what was happening, she was stumbling headlong on the path to slumber.

Sometime later Amy stirred. She blinked a couple of times, feeling disoriented and bemused, but when she realized that she was in her own bedroom, she sighed contentedly. The warm, cozy feeling lulled her, and her eyes drifted closed once more. It was then that she felt the large male hand slip wrapped around her middle.

With a small cry of dismay, her eyes flew open, and she lifted her head from the thick feather pillow. Josh was asleep at her side, and she pressed her hand over her mouth as the memories rolled into place, forming the missing parts of one gigantic puzzle.

"No," she cried, pushing at his shoulder in a flurry of anger and pain. "How dare you climb into my bed as though you have every right to be here."

Josh's dark eyes flashed open and he instantly frowned, obviously perplexed by her actions. He levered himself up on one elbow, studying her.

"Kindly leave," she muttered between clenched teeth, doing her best to control her anger.

"Angel Eyes, you invited me to join you, don't you remember?"

"No." She threw back the covers with enough force

to pull the sheets free from between the mattress and box springs. To add to her dismay, she discovered that her nightgown had worked its way up her body and was hugging at her waist, exposing a lengthy expanse of leg, thigh and hip. In her rush to escape, she nearly stumbled over her own two feet.

"Will you please get out of my bedroom...or I'll... I'll be forced to phone the police."

"Amy?" Josh sat up and rubbed the sleep from his eyes as though he expected this to be a part of a bad dream. "Be reasonable."

"Leave," she said tersely, throwing open the door to be certain there could be no misunderstanding her request.

"Don't you remember?" he coaxed. "We kissed and held each other and you asked me to—"

"That was obviously a mistake, now get out," she blared, unconsciously using his own phrase. She wasn't in the mood to argue or discuss this—or anything else—rationally. All she knew was that the man she'd been desperately trying to forget was in her bed and looking very much as though he intended to stay right where he was.

Chapter 12

"Amy," Josh said, his voice calm and low, as though he was trying to reason with a deranged woman.

"Out," she cried, squeezing her eyes shut as if that would make him go away.

"All right," he returned, eyeing her dubiously. "If that's what you really want."

The audacity of the man was phenomenal. "It's what I *really* want," she repeated, doing her level best to maintain her dignity.

Josh didn't seem to be in any big rush. He sat on the end of the bed and rubbed his hand down his face before he reached for his shoes. It demanded everything within Amy not to openly admire his brazen good looks. It astonished her that she could have forgotten how easy on the eyes Josh was. Even now, when his expression was impassive, she was struck by the angled lines of his features, as sharp as a blade, more so now as he struggled not to reveal his thoughts.

He stood, but the movement was marked with reluctance. "Can we talk about this first?"

"No," she said, thrusting out her chin defiantly.

"Amy—"

"There's nothing to discuss. I said everything the day you left."

"I was wrong," he admitted softly. "I'd give everything I own if I could turn back time and change what happened that morning. From the bottom of my heart, I'm sorry."

"Of course you were wrong," she cried, fighting the urge to forgive and forget. She couldn't trust Josh anymore. "I knew you'd figure it out sooner or later, but I told you then and I meant it—I don't want you back."

Manuela appeared, breathless from running up the stairs. "Miss Amy... Mr. Josh, the hospital is on phone."

In her eagerness to expel Josh from her room, Amy hadn't even heard it ring. "Oh no..." she murmured and raced across the room, nearly toppling the telephone from her nightstand in her eagerness.

"Yes?" she cried. "This is Amy Johnson." Nothing but silence greeted her. Frantically, she tried pushing on the phone lever, hoping to get a dial tone.

"I unplugged it," Josh explained and hurriedly replaced the jack in the wall. At her fierce look, he added, "I wanted you to rest undisturbed."

"This is Amy Johnson," she said thickly, her pulse doubling with anxiety and fear.

Immediately the crisp, clear voice of a hospital staff member came on the line. The instant Amy heard that her father was awake and resting comfortably, she slumped onto the mattress and covered her mouth with her hand as tears of relief swamped her eyes.

"Thank you, thank you," she repeated over and over before hanging up the phone.

"Dad's awake…he's apparently doing much better," she told Manuela, wiping the moisture from her face with the side of her hand. "He's asking for me."

"Thank the good Lord," Josh whispered.

Amy had forgotten he was there. "Please leave." She cast a pleading glance in Manuela's direction, hoping to gain the housekeeper's support in removing Josh from her bedroom.

"Mr. Chad come to see you," Manuela whispered, as though doing so would prevent Josh from hearing her. "I tell him you sleep."

"Thank you, I'll phone Mr. Morton when I get back from the hospital."

"I also tell him Mr. Josh is back to stay," Manuela said with a triumphant grin.

"If you'll both excuse me," Amy said pointedly, "I'd like to get dressed."

"Of course," Josh answered, as if there had never been a problem. He winked at her on his way out the door, and it was all Amy could do not to throw something after him.

She was trembling when she sat on the edge of her mattress. The emotions battling within her were so potent, she didn't know which one to respond to first. Relief mingled with unbridled joy that her father had taken a decided turn for the better.

The others weren't so easy to identify. Josh was here, making a dramatic entrance into her life when she was too wrapped up in grief and shock to react properly.

Instead, she'd fallen into his arms as though he was Captain America leaping to the rescue, and the memory infuriated her. He could just as easily turn and walk away from her again. She'd suffered through a good deal of heartrending pain to come to that conclusion. And once burned, she knew enough to stay away from the fire.

By the time she had dressed and walked down the stairs, Josh was nowhere to be seen. She searched the living room, then berated herself for looking for him. After all, she had been firm about wanting him to leave. His having left avoided an unpleasant confrontation.

No sooner had the thought passed through her mind when the front door opened and he walked into the house as brazen as could be.

Amy pretended not to see him and stepped into the dining room for a badly needed cup of coffee. She ignored the breakfast Manuela had brought in for her and casually sought her purse and car keys.

"You should eat something," Josh coaxed.

Amy turned and glared at him, but refused to become involved in a dispute over something as nonsensical as scrambled eggs and toast.

"I've got a rental car, if you're ready to go to the hospital now."

"I'll take my own," she informed him briskly.

Josh leaned across the table and reached for the toast on her plate. "Fine, but I assume it's still at the hospital."

Amy closed her eyes in frustration. "I'll take another vehicle then."

"Seems like a waste of gasoline since I'm going that way myself. Besides, how are you going to bring two cars home?"

"All right," she said from between clenched teeth. "Can we leave now?"

"Sure."

Any told Manuela where she could be reached and walked out to Josh's car, which was parked in front of the house. She climbed inside without waiting for him to open the door for her and stiffly snapped her seat belt into place.

They were in the heavy morning traffic before either spoke again. And it was Josh who ventured into conversation first. "I can help you, Amy, if you'll let me."

"Help me," she repeated with a short, humorless laugh. "How? By slipping into my bed and forcing unwanted attentions on me?" She couldn't believe she had said that. It was so unfair, but she would swallow her tongue before she apologized.

Josh stiffened, but said nothing in his own defense, which made Amy feel even worse. She refused to allow herself to be vulnerable to this man again, least of all now, when she was so terribly alone.

"I'd like to make it up to you for the cruel way I acted," he murmured after a moment.

Her anger stretched like a tightrope between them, and he seemed to be the only one brave enough to bridge the gap.

Amy certainly wasn't. It angered her that Josh thought he could come back as easily as if he'd never been away, apparently expecting to pick up where they'd left off.

"I'd like to talk to your father," he said next.

"No," she said forcefully.

"Amy, there's a good deal you don't know. I could help in ways you don't understand, if you'll let me."

"No, thank you," she returned, her voice hard and inflexible, discounting any appreciation for his offer.

"Oh, Amy, have I hurt you so badly?"

She turned her head and glared out the side window, refusing to answer him. The fifteen-minute ride to the hospital seemed to take an hour. Josh turned into the parking lot, and she hoped he would drop her off at the entrance and drive away. When he pulled into a parking space and turned off the engine, she realized she wasn't going to get her wish.

Biting back a caustic comment, she opened the door and climbed out. Whether he followed her inside or not was his own business, she decided.

She groaned inwardly when the sound of his footsteps echoed behind her on the polished hospital floor. The ride in the elevator was tolerable only because there were several other people with them. Once they arrived on the eighth floor, Amy stopped at the nurses' station and gave her name.

"Ms. Johnson, I was the one who called you this morning," a tall redheaded nurse with a freckled face said. "Your father is looking much better."

"Could I see him, please?"

"Yes, of course, but only for a few minutes."

Amy nodded, understanding all too well how short those moments would be, and followed the nurse into the intensive-care unit.

Harold Johnson smiled feebly when she approached his bedside. Her gaze filled with fresh tears that she struggled to hide behind a brilliant smile. His color was better, and although he remained gravely ill, he was awake and able to communicate with her.

"This is an expensive way to vacation," she said, smiling through the emotion.

"Hi, sweetheart. I'm sorry if I frightened you."

Her fingers gripped his and squeezed tightly. "I'm the one who's sorry...more than you'll ever know. Every time I think about what happened, I blame myself."

A weak shake of his head dismissed her apology. He moistened his mouth and briefly closed his eyes. "I need you to do something."

"Anything."

His fingers tightened around hers, and the pressure was incredibly slight. "It won't be easy, baby...your pride will make it difficult."

"Dad, there isn't anything in this world I wouldn't do for you. Don't waste your strength apologizing. What do you need?"

"Find Joshua Powell for me."

Amy felt as if the floor had started to buckle beneath her feet. She gripped the railing at the side of his bed and dragged in a deep breath. "Josh? Why?"

"He can help."

"Oh, Daddy, I'm sure you mean well, but we don't need Josh." She forced a lightness into her voice, hoping that would reassure him.

"We need him," her father repeated, his voice barely audible.

"Of course, I'm willing to do whatever you want, but we've gotten along fine without him this far," she countered, doing her best to maintain her cheerful facade. Then it dawned on her. "You think *I* need him, don't you? Oh, Dad, I'm stronger than I look. You should know by now that I'm completely over him. Chad and I have a good thing going, and I'd hate to throw a wrench into that relationship by dragging Josh back."

"Amy," Harold said, his strength depleting quickly. "I'm the one who has to talk to him. Please, do as I ask."

"All right," she agreed, her voice sagging with hesitation.

"Thank you." He closed his eyes then and was almost immediately asleep.

Reluctantly, Amy left his side, perplexed and worried. Josh was pacing the small area designated as a waiting room when she returned.

"How is he?"

"Better."

"Good," Josh said, looking encouraged. His gaze seemed to eat its way through her. "Did you tell him I was here?"

"No."

"You've got to, Amy. I can understand why you'd hesitate, but there are things you don't know or understand. I just might be able to do him some good."

She didn't know what to make of what was happening, but it was clear she was missing something important.

"We've got to talk. Let me buy you breakfast—we can sit down and have a rational discussion."

Amy accepted his invitation with ill grace. "All right, if you insist."

His mouth quirked up at the edges. "I do."

The hospital cafeteria was bustling with people. By the time they had ordered and carried their orange trays through the line, there was a vacant table by the window.

While Amy buttered her English muffin, Josh returned the trays. When he joined her, he seemed unusually quiet for someone who claimed he wanted to talk.

"Well?" she asked with marked impatience. "Say whatever it is that's so important, and be done with it."

"This isn't easy."

"What isn't, telling the truth?" she asked flippantly.

"I never lied to you, Amy. Never," he reinforced. "I'm afraid, however," he said sadly, "that what I'm going to tell you is probably going to hurt you even more."

"Oh? Do you have a wife and family securely tucked away somewhere?"

"You know that isn't true," he answered, his voice slightly elevated with anger. "I'm not a liar or a cheat."

"That's refreshing. What are you?"

"A former business executive. I was CEO for the largest conglomerate in the country for three years."

She raised her eyebrows, unimpressed. That he should mislead her about something like this didn't shock her. He had misrepresented himself before, and another violation of trust wasn't going to prejudice her one way or the other. "And I thought you were into oil. Fancy that."

"I was, or have been for the past several years. I left my former employer."

"Why?" She really didn't care, but if he was willing to tell her, then she would admit to being semi-curious as to the reason he found this admission to be such a traumatic one.

"That's not important," he said forcefully. "What is vital now is that I might be able to help your father save his company. These are dangerous times for him."

"He's not going to lose it," she returned confidently.

"Amy, I don't know how much you're aware of what's

going on, but Johnson Industries is a prime candidate for a hostile takeover by any number of corporate raiders."

"I know that. But we've got the best minds in the country dealing with his finances. We don't need you."

"I've been there, I know how best to handle this type of situation."

She sighed expressively, giving the impression that she was bored with this whole conversation, which wasn't entirely false. "Personally, I think it's supremely arrogant of you to think you could waltz your way into my father's business and claim to be the cure of all our ills."

"Amy, please," he said, clearly growing frustrated with her.

Actually she didn't blame him. She wasn't making this easy for a reason. There were too many negative emotions tied to Josh for her to blithely accept his offer of assistance.

"The next time you see Harold, ask him about me," he suggested.

The mention of her father tightened Amy's stomach. It was apparent that Harold already knew, otherwise he wouldn't have pleaded with her to find Josh. Nor would he have offered Josh a position with the firm. But they both had kept Josh's past a secret from her. The pain of their deception cut deep and sharp. Her father she could forgive. But Josh had already hurt her so intensely that another wound inflicted upon one still open and raw only increased her emotional anguish.

Valiantly, she struggled to disguise it. What little appetite she possessed vanished. She pushed her muffin aside and checked her watch, pretending to be surprised by the time. With a flippant air, she excused herself and hurried from the cafeteria.

Blindly, she stumbled into the ladies' room and braced her trembling hands against the sink as she sucked in deep breaths in an effort to control the pain. The last thing she wanted was for Josh to know he still had the power to hurt her. The sense of betrayal by the two men she'd loved the most in her life grew sharper with every breath.

Running the water, Amy splashed her face and dried it with the rough paper towel. When she'd composed herself, she squared her shoulders and walked out of the room, intent on returning to the intensive care unit.

She stopped abruptly in the hallway when she noticed that Josh was leaning against the wall waiting for her. Her facade was paper-thin, and he was the last person she was ready to deal with at the moment.

"I suppose I should mention that my father asked me to find you when I spoke to him this morning," she said when she could talk.

Josh's dark eyes flickered with surprise and then relief. "Good."

"You might as well go to him now."

"No," he said firmly, and shook his head. "We need to clear the air between us first."

"That's not necessary," she returned flatly. "There isn't anything I want to say to you. Or hear from you. Or have to do with you."

He nodded and tucked his hands in his pants pockets as if he had to do something in order not to reach out to her. "I can understand that, but I can't accept it." He paused as two orderlies walked past them on their way into the cafeteria. "Perhaps now isn't the best time, but at least believe me when I say I love you."

Amy pretended to yawn.

Josh's eyes narrowed and his mouth thinned. "You're not fooling me, Amy, I know you feel the same thing for me."

"It wouldn't matter if I did," she answered calmly. "What I feel—or don't feel for you—doesn't change a thing. If you and my father believe you can help the company, then more power to you. If you're looking for my blessing, then you've got it. I'd bargain with the devil himself if it would help my father. Do what you need to do, then kindly get out of my life."

Josh flinched as if she had struck him.

Amy didn't understand why he should be so shocked. "How many times do I have to tell you to leave me alone before you believe me?"

"Amy." He gripped her shoulders, the pressure hard and painful as he stared into her eyes. "Did I do this to you?"

"If anyone is at fault, I am. I fell in love with the wrong man, but I've learned my lesson," she told him bitterly. Boldly, she met his stare, but the hurt and doubt in his dark eyes were nearly her undoing. Without another word, she freed herself from his grasp and headed toward the elevator.

Josh followed her, and they rode up to the eighth floor in an uncomfortable silence. She approached the nurses' station and explained that her father had requested to talk to Josh.

She had turned away, prepared to leave the hospital, when the elevator doors opened and Chad Morton stepped out.

"Amy," he cried, as if he expected her to vanish into thin air before he reached her. "I've been trying to see you for two days."

"I'm sorry," she said, accepting his warm embrace.

"I stopped off at the hospital yesterday, but I was told you'd gone home. When I drove to the house, Manuela explained that you were asleep."

"Yes, I... I was exhausted. In fact, I wasn't myself," she said pointedly for Josh's benefit.

"With little wonder. You'd been here every minute since your father's heart attack. If you hadn't gone home, I would have taken you there myself."

Amy could feel Josh's stare penetrate her shoulder blades, but she ignored him. "I was just leaving," she explained. "I thought I'd check in at the office this morning."

Chad's frown darkened his face. "I... I don't think that would be a good idea."

"Why not?"

It was clear that Chad was uncomfortable. His gaze shifted to the floor, and he buried his hands in his pockets. "The office is a madhouse with the news and... and, well, frankly, there's a good deal of speculation going around—"

"Speculation?" she asked. "About what?"

"The takeover."

"What are you talking about?" She'd known that their situation was a prime one for a hostile takeover— in theory at least—but the reality of it caused her face to pale.

Chad looked as though he would give his right arm not be the one to tell her this. He hesitated and drew in a breath. "Johnson shares had gone up three dollars by the time Wall Street closed yesterday. Benson's moved in."

George Benson was a well-known corporate raider, the worst of the lot, from what little Amy knew. His reputation was that of a greedy, harsh man who bought out companies and then proceeded to bleed them dry with little or no compassion.

Amy closed her eyes for a moment, trying to maintain a modicum of control. "Whatever you do, you mustn't tell my father any of this."

"He already knows," Josh said starkly from behind her. "Otherwise, he wouldn't have asked for me."

Chad's troubled gaze narrowed as it swung to Josh. "Who is this?" he asked Amy.

Purposely, she turned and stared at Josh. "A friend of my father's." With that she turned and walked away.

Josh lost track of time. He and Lloyd Dickins had pored over the company's financial records until they were both seeing double. They needed a good deal of money, and they needed it fast. George Benson had seen to it that they were unable to borrow the necessary funds, and he had also managed to close off the means of selling some collateral, even if it meant at a loss. Every corner he turned, Josh was confronted by the financial giant who loomed over Johnson Industries like black death. Harold Johnson's company was a fat plum, and Benson wasn't about to let this one fall through his greedy little fingers.

"Are we going to be able to do it?" Lloyd Dickins asked, eyeing Josh speculatively.

Josh leaned back in his chair, pinched the bridge of his nose and sadly shook his head. "I don't see how."

"There's got to be some way."

"Everything we've tried hasn't done a bit of good."

"Who does George Benson think he is, anyway?" Lloyd flared. "God?"

"At the moment, he's got us down with our hands tied behind our backs," Josh admitted reluctantly. The pencil he was holding snapped in half. He hadn't realized his hold had been so tight.

"The meeting of the board of directors is Friday. We're going to have to come up with some answers by then."

"We will." But the confidence in Josh's voice sounded shaky at best. He had run out of suggestions. Years before, his ideas had been considered revolutionary. He never *had* been one to move with the crowd, nor did he base his decisions on what everyone else was doing around him. He had discovered early on that if he started looking to his colleagues before making a move he would surrender his leading edge to his business peers. That realization had carried him far. But he had been out of the scene for too many years. His instincts had been blunted, his mind baffled by the changes. Yet he had loved every minute of this. It was as if he was playing a good game of chess—only this time the stakes were higher than anything he had ever wagered. He couldn't lose.

"I think I'll go home and sleep on it," Lloyd murmured, yawning loudly. "I'm so rummy now I can't think straight."

"Go ahead. I'll look over these figures one more time and see what I can come up with."

Lloyd nodded. "I'll see you in the morning." He hesitated, then chuckled, the sound rusty and discordant.

"Looks like it *is* morning. Before much longer this place is going to be hopping, but as long as it isn't with Benson's people, I'll be content."

Josh grinned, but the ability to laugh had left him several hours ago. A feeling of impending doom was pounding at him like a prizefighter's fist, each blow driving him farther and farther until his back was pressed against the wall.

There had to be a way…for Amy's and her father's sakes, he needed to find one. With a determination born of desperation, he went over the numbers one last time.

"What are you doing here?"

Amy's voice cracked against his ears like a horsewhip. His eyes flew open, and he blinked several times against the bright light. He must have dozed off, he realized. With his elbows braced against the table, he rubbed the sleep from his face. "What time is it?"

"Almost seven."

"Isn't it a little early for you?" he asked, checking his watch, blinking until his eyes focused on the dial.

"I… I had something I needed to check on. You look absolutely terrible," she said, sounding very much like a prim schoolteacher taking a student to task. "You'd better go to your hotel and get some sleep before you pass out."

"I will in a minute," Josh answered, hiding a smile. Her concern was the first indication she still loved him that she'd shown since the morning she awoke with him in her bed. That had been…what? Two weeks ago? The days had merged in his mind, and he wasn't entirely certain of the date even now.

"Josh, you're going to make yourself sick."

"Would you care?"

"No...but it would make my father feel guilty when I tell him, and he's got enough to worry about."

"Speaking of Harold, how's he doing?"

"Much better."

"Good."

Amy remained on the other side of the room. Josh gestured toward the empty chair beside him. "Sit down and talk to me a minute while I gather my wits."

"Your wits are gathered enough."

"Come on, Amy, I'm not the enemy."

Her returning look said she disagreed.

"All right," he said, standing, "walk me to the elevator then."

"I'm not sure I should...you know the way. What do you need me for?" She held herself stiffly, as far on the other side of the office as she could get and still be in the same room with him.

"Moral support. I'm exhausted and hungry and too tired to argue. Besides, I have a meeting at nine. It's hardly worth going to the hotel."

"My dad has a sofa in his office...you could rest there for an hour or so," she said, watching him closely.

Josh hesitated, thinking he'd much rather spend the time holding and kissing her. "I could," he agreed. "But I wouldn't rest well alone." Boldly his eyes held hers. "The fact is, I need you."

"You can forget it, Joshua Powell," she said heatedly. She was blushing, very prettily, too, as she turned and walked out of Lloyd Dickins's office.

Josh followed her. When she stepped into her father's office, he dutifully closed the door.

"I...think there's a blanket around here somewhere."

She walked into a huge closet that contained supplies. Josh went in after her, resisting the temptation to slip his arms around her and drag her against him.

"Here's one," she said and when she turned around he was directly behind her, blocking any way of escape. Her startled eyes clashed with his. Josh loved her all the more as she drew herself up to her full height and set her chin at a proud, haughty angle. "Kindly let me go."

"I can't."

"Why not?" she demanded.

"Because there's something else I need far more than sleep."

She braced one hand against her hip, prepared to do battle. Only Josh didn't want to fight. Arguing was the last thing on his mind.

"What do you want, Joshua?" she asked.

"I already told you. We should start with a kiss, though, don't you think?"

Astonished, she glared at him. "You've got to be out of your mind if you think I'm going to let you treat me as though I was some brainless—"

Josh had no intention of listening to her tirade. Without waiting for her to pause to breathe, he clasped his hands around her waist and dragged her against his chest. She opened her mouth in outrage, and Josh took instant advantage.

Amy tried to resist him. Josh felt her fingernails curl into the material of his shirt as if she intended to push him away, but whatever her intent had been, she abruptly changed her mind. She may have objected to his touching her, but before she could stop herself, she was kissing him back and small moaning sounds were coming from her throat. Or was he the one making the noise?

"Oh...oh..."

At the startled gasp, Josh broke off the kiss and shielded Amy from probing eyes.

Ms. Wetherell, Harold Johnson's secretary, was standing in the office, looking so pale it was a wonder that she didn't keel over in a dead faint.

Chapter 13

Matters weren't looking good for Johnson Industries. Amy didn't need to attend the long series of meetings with Josh and the department executives to know that. The gloomy looks of those around her told her every-thing she needed to know. Lloyd Dickins, usually so pro-fessional, had been short-tempered all week, snapping at everyone close to him. His movements were sluggish, as if he dreaded each day, so unlike the vivacious man whose company she'd come to enjoy.

Twice in the past two weeks, Amy had found Ms. Wetherell dabbing at her eyes with a spotless lace han-kie. The grandmotherly woman who'd served her father for years seemed older and less like a dragon than ever.

Amy sincerely doubted that Josh had slept more than a handful of hours all week. For that matter, she hadn't either. In the evenings when she left the office, she headed directly for the hospital. Josh had made several visits there himself once her father was moved out of the intensive-care unit, but the older man always seemed cheered after Josh had stopped by. Amy knew Josh wasn't telling Harold the whole truth, but, despite their differences, she approved and didn't intervene.

For her part, Amy had avoided being alone with Josh since that one incident when Ms. Wetherell had discovered them. She had learned early on that she couldn't trust Josh, but he taught her a second more painful lesson—*she couldn't trust herself around him.* Two seconds in his arms and all her resolve disappeared. Even now, days later, her face heated at the memory of the way she had opened to his impudent kisses.

"How's he doing?"

Amy straightened in her chair beside her father's hospital bed. Josh, the very object of her musings, entered the darkened room. "Fine. I think."

"He's sleeping?"

"Yes."

Josh claimed the chair next to her and rubbed a hand down his face as if to disguise the lines of worry, but he wasn't fooling her. Just seeing him caused her heart to throb with concern. He looked terrible. Sighing inwardly, Amy guessed that she probably wasn't in much better shape herself.

"When was the last time you had a decent night's sleep?" she couldn't help asking.

He tried to reassure her with a smile, but failed. "About the same time you did. Amy, I'm sorry to tell you this but it doesn't look good. You know as well as I do how poorly that meeting went with the board of directors this afternoon. We're fighting even more of an uphill battle than we first realized. Half are in favor of selling out now, thinking we might get a better price, and no one's willing to speculate what Benson will be offering next week."

"We…we can't let my father know."

Josh shrugged. "I don't know how we can keep it from him. He's too smart not to have figured it out. We've done everything we can to hide it, but I'm sure he knows."

Amy nodded, accepting the truth of Josh's statement. She was all too aware of the consequences of the take-over. It would kill her father as surely if George Benson was to shoot him through the heart. Johnson Industries was the blood that flowed through her father's veins. Without the business, his life would lack purpose and direction.

Josh must have read her thoughts. His hand reached for hers, and he squeezed her fingers reassuringly. "It's going to work out," he told her. "Don't worry."

"It looks like you're doing enough of that for the both of us."

He tried smiling again, this time succeeding. "There's too much at stake to give up. If I lose this company," he said, his eyes holding hers, "I lose you."

Amy's gaze fell to her lap as his words circled her mind like a lariat around the head of a steer. "You lost me a long time ago."

The air between them seemed to crackle with electricity. Amy could almost taste his defeat. So much was already riding on Josh's shoulders without her adding her head as a prize. Whatever happened happened. What was between them had nothing to do with that.

"I can't accept that."

"Maybe you should."

"You can't fool me, Amy. You love me."

"I did once," she admitted reluctantly, "but, as you so often had told me in the past, that was a mistake. Chad and I—"

"Chad!" He spat out the name as if it were a piece of spoiled meat. "You can't honestly expect me to believe you're in love with that spineless pansy?"

A tense moment passed before she spoke again. "I think we'd best end this conversation before we both lose our tempers."

"No," he jeered. "We're going to have this out right now. I'm through playing games."

"Talk this out? Here and now?" she flared. "I refuse to discuss anything of importance with you in my father's hospital room."

"Fine. We'll leave."

"Fine," she countered, nearly leaping to her feet in her eagerness. She felt a little like a boxer jumping out from his corner at the beginning of a new round. Every minute she was with Joshua, he infuriated her more.

At a crisp pace, she followed him out of the hospital to the parking lot. "Where are we going?" she demanded, when he calmly unlocked the passenger side of his car door.

"Where do you suggest?" he asked, as casually as if he was seeking her preference for a restaurant.

"I couldn't care less." His collected manner only served to irritate her all the more. The least he could do was reveal a little emotion. For her part, she was brimming with it. It was all she could do not to throw her purse to the ground and go at him with both fists. The amount of emotion churning inside her was a shock.

"All right then, *I'll* decide." He motioned toward the open car door. "Get in."

"Not until I know where we're headed."

"I don't plan on kidnapping you."

"Where are we going?" she demanded a second time, certain her eyes must be sparking with outrage and fury.

"My hotel room."

Amy slapped her hands against her thighs. "Oh, brother," she cried. "Honestly, Josh, do I look that stupid? I simply can't believe you! There is no way in this green earth that I'd go to a hotel room with you."

He stood on the driver's side, the open door between them. "Why not?" he asked.

"You...you're planning to seduce me."

"Would I succeed?"

"Not likely."

Unconcerned, Josh shrugged. "Then what's the problem?"

"I..." She couldn't very well admit that he was too damn tempting for her own good.

"We're closer to my hotel than your house, and at least there we'll be afforded some privacy. I can't speak for you, but personally, I'd prefer to discuss this in a rational manner without half of Seattle listening in."

He had her there. Talk about taking the wind out of her sails! "All right, then, but I'd rather drive there in my own car."

"Fine." He climbed inside his vehicle, leaned across the plush interior and closed the passenger door, which he had opened seconds earlier for her.

The ride to the hotel took only a few minutes. There was a minor problem with parking, which was probably the reason Josh had suggested she ride with him.

Since there wasn't any space on the street, she found a lot, paid the attendant and then met Josh in the lobby.

"Are you hungry?"

She was, but unwilling to admit it. The hotel was the same one where he had been staying when she had first met him. The realization did little to settle her taut nerves. "No."

"If you don't object, I'll order something from room service."

"Fine."

The air between them during the elevator ride was still and ominous, like the quiet before a tornado touches down.

Josh had his key ready by the time they reached his room. He unlocked the door and opened it for her to precede him. She stopped abruptly when she realized that even the *room* was identical to the one he'd had months earlier. How differently she'd felt about him then. Even then she'd been in love with him.

And now…well, now, she'd learned so many things. But most of those lessons had been painful. She'd come a long way from the naive college graduate she'd been then. Most of her maturing had come as a result of her relationship with Josh.

"This is the same room you had before," she said, without realizing she'd verbalized her thought.

"It looks the same, but I'm on a different floor," Josh agreed absentmindedly. He reached for the room-service menu and scanned its listings before heading toward the phone. "Are you sure I can't change your mind?"

"I'm sure." Her stomach growled in angry protest to

the lie. Amy gave a brilliant performance of pretending the noise had come from someone other than herself.

Josh ordered what seemed like an exorbitant amount of food and then turned toward her. "All right, let's get this over with."

"Right," she said, squaring her shoulders for the coming confrontation.

"Sit down." He motioned toward a chair that was angled in front of the window.

"If you don't mind, I'd like to stand."

"Fine." He claimed the chair for himself.

Amy had thought standing would give her an advantage. Not so. She felt even more intimidated by Josh than at any time in recent memory. Garnering what she could of her emotional fortitude, she squared her shoulders and met his look head on, asking no quarter and giving none herself.

"You wanted to say something to me," she prompted, when he didn't immediately pick up the conversation.

"Yes," Josh reiterated, looking composed and not the least bit irritated. "I don't want you seeing that mamma's boy again."

Amy snickered at the colossal nerve of the man. "You and what army are going to stop me?"

"I won't need an army. You're making a fool of him and an even bigger one of yourself. I love you, and you love me, and frankly, I'm tired of having you use Chad as an excuse every time we meet."

"I was hoping you'd get the message," she said, crossing her arms over her waist. "As for this business of my still loving you," she said, forcing a soft laugh, "any feeling I have for you died months ago."

"Don't lie, Amy, you do a piss poor job of it. You always have."

"Not this time," she told him flatly. "In fact, I can remember the precise moment I stopped loving you, Joshua Powell. It happened when you stepped inside a taxi that was parked outside my home. I… I stood there and watched as you drove away, and I swore to myself that I'd never allow a man to hurt me like that again."

Josh briefly closed his eyes and lowered his head. "Leaving you that day was the most difficult thing I'd ever done in my life, Amy. I said before that I'd give anything for it never to have happened. Unfortunately, it did."

"Do you honestly believe that a little contrition is going to change everything?"

Josh leaned back in the chair, and his shoulders sagged with fatigue. "I was hoping it would be a start."

"A few regrets aren't enough," she cried, and to her horror, she felt the tears stinging in the back of her eyes. Before they brimmed and Josh had a chance to see them, she turned and walked away from him.

"What do you want?" he demanded. "Blood?"

"Yes," she cried. "Much more than that… I want you out of my life. You…you seem to think that…that if you're able to help my father, that's going to wipe out everything that's happened before and that… I'll be willing to let bygones be bygones and we can marry and have two point five children and live happily ever after."

"Amy…"

"No, Josh," she cried, and turned around, stretching her arm out in front of her in an effort to ward him off. "I refuse to be some prize you're going to collect once this craziness with George Benson passes and my father recovers."

"It's not that."

"Then what is it?"

"I love you."

"That's not enough," she cried. "And as for my not seeing Chad Morton again…there's something you should know. I…plan on marrying Chad. He hasn't asked me yet, but he will, and when he does, I'll gladly accept his proposal."

"You don't love Chad," Josh cried, leaping from his chair. "I can't believe you'd do anything so stupid!"

"I may not love Chad the way I love—used to love you, but at least if he ever walks out on me it won't hurt nearly as badly. But then, Chad never would leave me—not the way you did at any rate."

"Amy, don't do anything crazy. Please, Angel Eyes, you'd be ruining our lives."

"Chad's wonderful to me."

Momentarily, Josh closed his eyes. "Give me a chance to make everything up to you."

"No." She shook her head wildly, backing away from him, taking tiny steps as he advanced toward her. "Chad's kindhearted and good."

"He'd bore you out of your mind in two weeks."

"He's honorable and gentle," she continued, holding his gaze.

"But what kind of lover would he be?"

Amy's shoulders sagged with defeat. Chad's kisses left her cold. Josh must have known it. A spark of triumph flashed from his eyes when she didn't immediately respond to his taunt.

"Answer me," he demanded, his eyes brightening.

Amy had backed away from him as far as she could. Her back was pressed to the wall.

"When Chad touches you, what do you feel?"

The lie died on the end of her tongue. She could shout that she came alive in Chad Morton's arms, insist that he was an enviable lover, but it would do little good. Josh would recognize the lie and make her suffer for it.

Slowly, almost without her being aware of it, Josh lifted his hand and ran his fingertips down the side of her face. Her nerves sprang to life at his featherlight stroke, and she sharply inhaled her breath, unprepared for the onslaught of sensation his touch aroused.

"Does your Mr. BMW make you feel anything close to this?" he asked, his voice hushed and ultra-seductive.

It was a strain to keep from closing her eyes and giving in to the sensual awareness Josh brought to life within her. She raised her hands, prepared to push him away, but the instant they came into contact with the hard, muscular planes of his chest, they lost their purpose.

"I don't feel anything. Kindly take your hands off me."

Josh chuckled softly. "I'm not touching you, angel, you're the one with your hands on me. Oh, baby," he groaned, his amusement weaving its way through his words. "You put up such a fierce battle."

Mortified, Amy dropped her hands, but not before Josh flattened his against the wall and trapped her there, using his body to hold her in check.

Amy's immediate reaction was to struggle, pound his chest and demand that he release her. But the wild, almost primitive look in his eyes dragged all the denial out of her. His pulse throbbed at the base of his throat like a drum, hammering out her fate. He held himself almost completely rigid, but Amy could feel the entire length of him pulsating with tension.

It came to her then that if she didn't do something to stop him, he was going to make love with her. The taste of bitter defeat filled her throat. Once he became her lover, she would never be able to send him away.

Her breath clogged her throat and she bucked against him. Her eyes flew to his face, and he smiled.

"That's right, angel," he urged in a deep whisper. "You want me as much as I want you."

"No, I don't," she murmured, but her protest was feeble at best.

He kissed her then. Slow and deep, as if they had all the time in the world. Against every dictate of her will, blistering excitement rushed through her and she moaned. Her small cry seemed to please him, and he kissed her again, and she welcomed his touch, wanting to weep with abject frustration at the treachery of her body.

His hands were at the front of her blouse.

Knowing his intention, Amy made one final plea. "Josh…no…please."

His shoulders and chest lifted with a sharp intake of breath.

The polite knock against the door startled them both. Josh tensed and sweat beaded his fervent face.

"Josh," she moaned, "the door…someone's at the door."

"This time we finish," he growled.

The knock came a second time. "Room service," the male voice boomed from the other side. "I have your order."

"Please," she begged, tears filling her eyes. "Let me go."

Reluctantly, he released her, and needing to escape him, Amy fled into the bathroom. From inside she could hear Josh dealing with the man who delivered the meal. She ran her splayed fingers through her mussed hair, disgusted with herself that she'd allowed Josh to kiss and hold her. It shocked her how quickly she'd given in to him, how easily he could manipulate her.

"Amy. He's gone."

Leaning against the sink, she splashed cold water on her face and tried to interject sound reason into her badly shaken composure.

When she left the bathroom, it demanded every ounce of inner strength she possessed. As she knew he would be, Josh was waiting for her, prepared to continue as if nothing had happened.

She raised her shoulders and focused her gaze just past him, on the picture that hung over the king-size bed. "You proved your point," she said, shocked by how incredibly shaky her voice sounded.

"I hope to high heaven that's true. You're going to marry me, Amy."

"No," she said flatly. "Just because I respond to you physically…doesn't mean I love you, or that I'm willing to trust you with my heart. Not again, Josh, never again."

Before he could say or do anything that would change her mind, she grabbed her purse and left the room.

Amy spent the next four days with her father, purposefully avoiding Josh. In light of what had happened in his hotel room, she didn't know if she would ever be able to look him in the eye again. If the hotel staff hadn't decided to deliver his meal when they had, there was no telling how far their lovemaking would have progressed.

No, she reluctantly amended, she *did* know where it would have ended. With her in his bed, her eyes filled with adoration, her body sated with his lovemaking. Without question, she would have handed him her heart and her life and anything else he demanded.

"You haven't been yourself in days," Chad complained over lunch. "Is there anything I can do?"

No matter what Josh believed about the other man, Chad had been wonderful. He'd anticipated her every need. Amy didn't so much as have to ask. More often than not, he arrived at the hospital, insisting that he was taking her to lunch, or to dinner, or simply out for a breath of fresh air.

Rarely did he stay and talk to her father, and for his part, Harold Johnson didn't have much to say to the other man, either.

"How's everything at the office?" she asked, recognizing that she was really inquiring about Josh and angry with herself for needing to know.

"Not good," Chad admitted, dipping his fork into his avocado and alfalfa-sprout salad. "Several of the staff have turned in their resignations, wanting to find other positions while they can."

"Already?" Amy was alarmed, fearing her father's reaction to the news. She hoped Josh would shield him from most of the unpleasantness.

"When Powell left, most everyone realized it was a lost cause. I want you to know that I'll be here for however long you and your father need me."

"Josh left?" Amy cried, before she could school her reaction. A numb pain worked its way out from her heart, rippling over her abdomen. The paralyzing agony edged its way down her arms and legs until it was nearly impossible to breathe or move to function normally.

"He moved out yesterday," Chad added conversationally. "I'm surprised your father didn't say anything."

"Yes," she murmured, lowering her gaze. For several moments it was all she could do to keep from breaking down into bitter tears.

"Amy, are you all right?"

"No... I've got a terrible headache." She pressed her fingertips to her temple and offered him a smile.

"Let me take you home."

"No," she said, lightly shaking her head. "If you could just take me back to the hospital. I...my car is there."

"Of course."

An entire lifetime passed before Amy could leave the restaurant. On the ride to the hospital, she realized how subdued her father had been for the past twenty-four hours. Although his recovery was progressing at a fast pace, he seemed lethargic and listless that morning, but Amy had been too wrapped up in her own problems to probe. Now it all made sense.

When the going got tough, Josh packed his bags and walked out of their lives. He hadn't even bothered to say goodbye—at least not to her. Apparently, he hadn't been able to face her, and with little wonder. Harold had needed him, even if she didn't. But none of that had mattered to Josh. He had turned his back on them and their problems and simply walked away.

"Why didn't you tell me?" Amy demanded of her

father the moment they were alone. Tears threatened but she held them in check. "Josh left."

"I thought you knew."

"No." She wiped away the moisture that smeared her cheeks and took in a calming breath before forcing a brave front for her father's sake. "He didn't say a word to me."

"He'll be back," her father assured her, gently patting her hand. "Don't be angry with him, sweetheart, he did everything he could."

"I don't care if he ever comes back," she cried, unable to hold in the bitterness. "I never want to see him again. Ever."

"Amy…"

"I'll be married to Chad before Josh returns, I swear I will. I detest the man, I swear I hate him with everything that's in me." She had yet to recover from the first time he had deserted her, and then in their greatest hour of need, he had done it a second time. If her father lost Johnson Industries, and in all likelihood he would, then Amy would know exactly who to blame.

"There's nothing left that he could do," her father reasoned. "I don't blame him. He tried everything within his power to turn the tide, but it was too late. I should have realized it long before now—I was asking the impossible. Josh knew it, and still he tried to find a way out."

"But what about the company?"

"All is lost now, and there's nothing we can do but accept it."

Amy buried her face in her hands.

"We'll recover," her father said, and his voice cracked.

He struggled for a moment to compose himself before he spoke again. "I may be down, but I'm not out."

"Oh, Daddy." She hugged him close, offering what comfort she could, but it was little when her own heart was crippled with the pain of Josh's desertion.

Chapter 14

By the weekend, Amy came to believe in miracles. Knowing that her father was about to lose the conglomerate he had invested his entire life building, she had been prepared for the worst. What happened was something that only happened to those who believe in fairy tales and Santa Claus. At the eleventh hour, her father sold a small subsidiary company that he had purchased several years earlier. The company, specializing in plastics, had been an albatross and a money loser, but an unexpected bid had come in, offering an inflated price. Her father and the corporate attorneys leaped at the opportunity, signing quickly. Immediately afterward, Johnson Industries was able to pay off its bondholders, all within hours of its deadline. By the narrowest of margins, the company had been able to fend off George Benson and his takeover schemes.

The following week, her father was like a young man

again. His spirits were so high that his doctors decided he could be released from the hospital the coming Friday.

"Good morning, beautiful," Harold greeted his daughter when she stopped in to see him on her way to work Monday morning. "It's a beautiful day, isn't it, sweetheart?"

Not as far as Amy was concerned. Naturally, she was pleased with the way matters had turned out for her father, but everything else in her life had taken a sharp downward twist.

Carefully, she had placed a shield around her heart, thinking that would protect her from Josh and anything he might say or do. But she had been wrong. Having him desert her and her father when they needed him most hurt more the second time than it had the first.

Amy found it a constant struggle not to break down. She could weep at the most nonsensical matters. A romantic television commercial produced tears, as did a sad newspaper article or having to wait extra long in traffic. She could be standing in a grocery aisle and find a sudden, unexplainable urge to cry.

"It's rainy, cold and the weatherman said it might snow," she responded to her father's comment about it being a beautiful day, doing her best to maintain a cheerful facade and failing miserably.

"Amy?" Her father's soft blue eyes questioned her. "Do you want to talk about it?"

"No," she responded forcefully. It wouldn't do the least bit of good. Josh was out of their lives, and she couldn't be happier or more sad.

"Is it about Josh?"

Her jaw tightened so hard her back teeth ached. "What possible reason would I have to feel upset about

Joshua Powell?" she asked, making his question sound almost comical.

"You love him, sweetheart."

"I may have at one time, but it's over. Lately... I think I could hate him." Those nonsensical tears she had been experiencing during the past two weeks rushed to the corners of her eyes like water spilling over a top-full barrel. Once more, she struggled to disguise them.

Narrowing his gaze, Harold Johnson motioned toward the chair. "Sit down, sweetheart, there's a story I want to tell you."

Instead, Amy walked to the window, her arms cradling her waist. "I've got to get to work. Perhaps another time."

"Nothing is more important than this tale. Now, sit down and don't argue with me. Don't you realize, I've got a bad heart?"

"Oh, Dad." She found herself chuckling.

"Sit." Once more he pointed toward the chair.

Amy did as he asked, bemused by his attitude.

"This story starts out several years back..."

"Is this a once-upon-a-time tale?"

"Hush," her father reprimanded. "Just listen. You can ask all the questions you want later."

"All right, all right," she said with ill grace.

"Okay, now where was I?" he mumbled, and stroked his chin while he apparently gathered his thoughts. "Ah, yes, I'd only gotten started.

"This is the story of a young man who graduated with top honors at a major university. He revealed an extraordinary talent for business, and word of him spread even before he'd received his MBA. I suspect he came by this naturally, since his own father was a well-known stockbroker. At any rate, this young man's ideas were revolutionary, but by heaven, he had a golden touch. Several corporations wanted him for their CEO. Before long he could name his own terms, and he did."

"Dad?" Amy had no idea where this story was leading, but she really didn't want to sit and listen to him ramble on about someone she wasn't even sure she knew. And if this was about Josh, she would rather not hear it. It couldn't change anything.

"Hush and listen," her father admonished. "This young man and his father were apparently very close and had been for years. To be frank, the father had something of a reputation for doing things just a tad shady. Nothing illegal, don't misunderstand me, but he took unnecessary risks. I sincerely doubt that the son was fully aware of this, although he must have guessed some of it was true. The son, however, defended his father at every turn."

Amy glanced at her watch, hoping her father got her message. If he did, it apparently didn't faze him.

"It seems that the son often sought his father's advice. I suppose this was only natural, being that they were close. By this time, the son was head of a major conglomerate, and if I said the name you'd recognize it immediately."

Amy yawned, wanting her father to arrive at the point of this long, rambling fable.

"No one is exactly certain what happened, but the conglomerate decided to sell off several of its smaller companies. The father, who you remember was a stockbroker, apparently got wind of the sale from the son and with such valuable inside information, made a killing in the market."

"But that's—"

"Unethical and illegal. What happened between the father and son afterward is anyone's guess. I suspect they parted ways over this issue. Whatever happened isn't my business, but I'm willing to speculate that there was no love lost between the two men in the aftermath of this scandal. The son resigned his position and disappeared for years."

"Can you blame him?"

"No," her father replied, his look thoughtful. "Although it was a terrible waste of talent. Few people even knew what had happened, but apparently he felt his credibility had been weakened. His faith in his father had been destroyed, no doubt, and that blow was the most crushing. My feeling is that he'd lived with the negative effects of having money for so many years that all he wanted was to wash his hands of it and build a new life for himself. He succeeded, too."

"Was he happy?"

"I can't say for certain, but I imagine he found plenty of fulfillment. He served in the Peace Corps for a couple of years and did other volunteer work. It didn't matter where he went, he was liked by all. It's been said that he never met a man who didn't like him."

"Does this story have a punch line?" Amy asked, amused.

"Yes, I'm getting to that. Let me ask you a couple of questions first."

"All right." She'd come this far, and although she hadn't been a willing listener, her father had managed to whet her appetite.

"I want you to put yourself into this young man's place. Can you imagine how difficult it would be for him to approach his father eight years after this estrangement?"

"I'm confident he wouldn't unless there was a good reason."

"He had one. He'd fallen in love."

"Love?" Amy echoed.

"He did it for the woman, and for her father, too, I suspect. He knew a way to help them, and although it cost him everything, he went to his father and asked for help."

"I see," Amy said, and swallowed tightly.

"Amy." He paused and held his hand out to her. "The company that made the offer, the company that *saved* us, is owned by Chance Powell, Josh's father."

Amy felt as if she had received a blow to the head. A ringing sensation echoed in her ears, and the walls started to circle the room in a crazy merry-go-round effect. "Josh went to his father for us?"

"Yes, sweetheart. He sold his soul for you."

Although Amy had been to New York several times, she had never appreciated the Big Apple as much as she did on this trip. The city was alive with the sights and sounds of Christmas. Huge boughs of evergreens were strung across the entryways to several major stores. The city was ablaze with lights, had never shone brighter. A stroll through Central Park made Amy feel like a child again.

Gone was the ever-present need to cry, replaced instead with a giddy happiness that gifted her with a deep, abiding joy for the season she hadn't experienced since the time she was a child and the center of her parents' world.

With the address clenched tightly in her hand, Amy walked into the huge thirty-story building that housed Chance Powell's brokerage. After making a few pertinent inquiries, she rode the elevator to the floor where his office was situated.

Her gaze scanned the neat row of desks, but she didn't see Josh, which caused her spirits to sag just a little. She'd come to find him, and she wasn't about to leave until she'd done exactly that.

"I'm here to see Mr. Powell," Amy told the receptionist. "I don't have an appointment."

"Mr. Powell is a very busy man. If you want to talk to him, I'm afraid you'll have to schedule a time."

"Just tell him Amy Johnson is here...you might add that I'm Harold Johnson's daughter," she added for good measure, uncertain that Josh had even mentioned her name.

Reluctantly, the young woman did as Amy said. No sooner had she said Amy's name than the office door opened and Chance Powell himself appeared. The resemblance between father and son was striking. Naturally, Chance's looks were mature, his dark hair streaked with gray, but his eyes were so like Josh's that for a moment it felt as if she was staring at Josh himself.

"Hello, Amy," he said, clasping her hands in both of his. His gaze slid over her appreciatively. "Cancel my ten o'clock appointment," he said to the receptionist.

He led the way into his office and closed the door. "I wondered about you, you know."

"I suppose that's only natural." Amy sat in the chair across from his rich mahogany desk, prepared to say or do whatever she must to find Josh. "I don't know what Josh said to you, if he explained—"

"Oh, he said plenty," the older man murmured and chuckled, seemingly delighted about something.

"I need to find him," she said fervently, getting directly to the point.

"Need to?"

Any ignored the question. "Do you know where he is?"

"Not at the moment."

"I see." Her hands tightened into a fist around the strap of her purse. "Can you tell me where I might start looking for him?" Her greatest fear was that he'd headed back to Kadiri or someplace else in the Middle East. It didn't matter, she would follow him to the ends of the earth if need be.

Chance Powell didn't seem inclined to give her any direct answers, although he had appeared eager enough to meet her. He scrutinized her closely, and he wore a silly half grin when he spoke. "My son always did have excellent taste. Do you intend to marry him?"

"Yes." She met his gaze head-on. "If he'll have me."

He laughed at that, boisterously. "Josh may be a good many things, but he isn't a fool."

"But I can't marry him until I can find him."

"Are you pregnant?"

Chance Powell was a man who came directly to the point, as well.

The color screamed in Amy's cheeks, and for a moment she couldn't find her tongue. "That's none of your business."

He laughed again, looking pleased, then slapped his hand against the top of his desk, scattering papers in several directions. "Hot damn!"

"Mr. Powell, please, can you tell me where I can find

Josh? This is a matter of life and death." His death, if he didn't quit playing these games with her. Perhaps she'd been a fool to believe that all she had to do was fly to New York, find Josh and tell him how much she loved him so they could live happily ever after. It had never entered her mind that his father wouldn't know where he was. Then again, he may well be aware of precisely where Josh was at that very moment and not plan to tell her.

"Do you have any water?" she said, feigning being ill. "My…stomach's been so upset lately."

"Morning sickness?"

She blushed demurely and resisted the temptation to place the back of her hand to her brow and sigh with a good deal of drama.

"Please excuse me for a moment," Chance said, standing.

"Of course."

A moment turned out to be five long minutes, and when the office door opened, it slammed against the opposite wall and then was abruptly hurled closed. The sound was forceful enough to startle Amy out of her chair.

Josh loomed over her like a ten-foot giant, looking more furious than she could ever remember seeing him. His eyes were almost savage. "What did you say to my father?"

"Hello, Josh," she said, offering him a smile he didn't return. Bracing her hands against the leather back of the chair, she used it as a shield between the two of them. The little speech she had so carefully prepared was completely lost. "I… I changed my mind about your offer. The answer is yes."

"Don't try to avoid the question," he shouted, advancing two steps toward her. "You told my father you're pregnant. We both know that's impossible."

He looked so good in a three-piece suit. So unlike the man who had asked to share a picnic table with her along the Seattle waterfront all those months ago. He had been wearing a fringed leather jacket then, and his hair had been in great need of a trim. Now...now he resembled a Wall Street executive, which was exactly what he was.

"What do you mean, you changed your mind?"

"I'm sorry I misled your father. I never came out directly and told him I was pregnant. But he didn't seem to want me to know where you were, and I had to find you."

"Why?"

He certainly wasn't making this easy on her. "Well, because..." She paused, drew in her breath and straightened her back, prepared for whatever followed. "Because I love you, Joshua Powell. I've reconsidered your marriage proposal, and I think it's a wonderful idea."

"The last I heard you were going to marry Chad Morton."

"Are you kidding? Don't you know a bluff when you hear one?"

He frowned. "Apparently not."

"I want to marry *you*. I have from the day you first kissed me on the Seattle waterfront and then claimed it had been a mistake. We've both made several of those over the past months, but it's time to set everything straight between us. I'm crazy about you, Joshua Powell. Your father may be disappointed, but the way I figure it, we could make him and my father grandparents in about nine months. Ten at the tops."

"Are you doing this out of gratitude?"

"Of course not," she said, as though the idea didn't even merit a response. "Out of love. Now please, stop looking at me as if you'd like to tear me limb from limb and come and hold me. I've been so miserable without you."

He closed his eyes, and his shoulders and chest sagged. "Oh, Amy..."

Unable to wait a moment longer, she walked into his arms the way a bird returns to its nest, without needing directions, recognizing home. A sense of supreme rightness filled her as she looped her arms around his neck and stood on her tiptoes. "I love you too, Angel Eyes," she said for him.

"I do, you know," he whispered, and his rigid control melted as he buried his face in her hair, rubbing his jaw back and forth against her temple as if drinking in her softness.

"There're going to be several children."

Fire hardened his dark eyes as he directed his mouth to hers in a kiss that should have toppled the entire thirty-story structure in which they stood. "How soon can we arrange a wedding?"

"Soon," she mumbled, her lips teasing his in a lengthy series of delicate, nibbling kisses. She caught his lower lip between her teeth and sucked at it gently.

Josh fit his hand over the back of her head as he took control of the kiss, slanting his mouth over hers with a hungry demand that depleted her of all strength. "You're playing with fire, angel," he warned softly, his dark eyes bright with passion.

She smiled up at him, her heart bursting with all the love she was experiencing. "I love it when you make dire predictions."

"Amy, I'm not kidding. Any more of that and you'll march to the altar a fallen angel."

She laughed softly. "Promises, promises."

Epilogue

"Amy?" Josh strolled in the back door of their home, expecting to find his pregnant wife either taking a nap or working in the nursery.

"I'm in the baby's room," he heard her shout from the top of the stairs.

Josh deposited his briefcase in the den, wondering why he even bothered to bring his laptop home. He had more entertaining ways of filling his evenings. Smiling, he mounted the stairs two at a time, while working loose the constricting silk tie at his neck. Even after five years, he still wasn't accustomed to wearing a suit.

Just as he suspected, he discovered Amy with a tiny paintbrush in her hand, sketching a field of wildflowers around several large forest creatures on the nursery wall.

"What do you think?" she asked proudly.

Josh's gaze softened as it rested on her. "And to think I married you without ever knowing your many talents."

He stepped back and observed the scene she was so busy creating. "What makes you so certain this baby is a boy?"

Her smile was filled with unquestionable confidence. "A woman knows these things."

Josh chuckled. "As I recall, you were equally confident Cain would be a girl. It was darn embarrassing, bringing him home from the hospital dressed entirely in pink."

"He's since forgiven me."

"Perhaps so, but I haven't." He stepped behind her and flattened his hands over her nicely rounded abdomen. Her stomach was tight and hard, and his heart fluttered with excitement at the thought of his child growing within her. "I can think of a way for you to make it up to me, though," he whispered suggestively in her ear, then nibbled on her lobe. He felt her sag against him.

"Joshua Powell, it's broad daylight."

"So?"

"So…"

He could tell she was battling more with herself than arguing with him. Josh hadn't known what to expect once they were married. He had heard rumors about women who shied away from their husbands after they had spoken their vows. But in all the years he had been married to Amy, she had greeted his lovemaking with an eagerness that made him feel humble and truly loved.

"Where's Cain? Napping?"

"No…he went exploring with my father," she whispered.

"Then we're alone?" He stroked her breasts, and his loins tightened at how quickly her body reacted to his needs. No matter how many times they made love, it was never enough, and it never would be. When he was ninety, he would be looking for a few private moments to steal away with her.

"Yes, we're the only ones here," she told him, her voice trembling just a little.

"Good." He kissed the curve of her neck, and she relaxed against him.

"Josh," she pleaded, breathless. "Let me clean the brush first."

He continued to nibble at her neck all the while, working on the elastic of her jeans.

"Josh," she begged. "Please," she moaned.

"I want to please you, angel, but you need to take care of that brush, remember."

"Oh, no, you don't," she cried softly. "You've got to take care of *me* first. You're the one who started this." Already she was removing her top, her fingers trembling, her hurried movements awkward. "I can't believe you," she cried, "in the middle of the day with Cain and my father due back any moment. We're acting like a couple of teenagers."

"You make me feel seventeen again," Josh murmured. He released her and started undressing himself.

Amy locked the door, then turned and leaned against it, her hands behind her back. "I thought men were supposed to lose their sexual appetite when their wives were pregnant."

Josh kicked off his shoes and removed his slacks. "Not me."

"I noticed."

He pinned her against the door, his forearms holding her head prisoner. "Do you have any complaints?"

"None," she whispered, framing his face lovingly with her hands. She kissed him, giving him her mouth She looped her arms around his neck as she moved her body against him.

"I want you," he managed.

"Right here?" Her eyes widened as they met his. "Now?"

Amy closed her eyes, sagged against the door and sighed.

"You okay?"

"Oh, yes," she whispered.

By the time Josh had drifted back to earth, Amy was spreading kisses all over his face. He marveled at her, this woman who was his wife. She was more woman than any man deserved, an adventurous lover, a partner, a friend, the mother of his children, a keel that brought balance to his existence and filled his life with purpose.

Gently he helped her dress, taking time to kiss and caress her and tell her how much he loved her. Some things he had a difficult time saying, even now. Her love had taken all the bitterness from his life and replaced it with blessings too numerous to count.

As he bent over to retrieve his slacks, Josh placed a hand in the small of his back. "Remind me that I'm not seventeen the next time I suggest something like this."

"Not me," Amy murmured, tucking her arms around his neck and spreading kisses over his face. "That was too much fun. When can we do it again?"

"It may be sooner than you think."

Amy kissed him, and as he wrapped his arms around the slight thickening at her waist, he closed his eyes to the surge of love that engulfed him.

"Come on," she said with a sigh, reaching for her paintbrush. "All this horsing around has made me hungry. How about some cream cheese and jalapeños spread over a bagel?"

"No, thanks." His stomach quivered at the thought.

"It's good, Josh. Honest."

He continued to hold her to his side as they headed down the stairs. "By the way, my father phoned this afternoon," he mentioned casually. "He said he'd like to come out and visit before the baby's born."

Amy smiled at him. "You don't object?"

"No. It'll be good to see him. I think he'd like to be here for the baby's arrival."

"I think I'd like that, too," Amy said.

Josh nodded. He had settled his differences with his father shortly before he had married Amy. Loving her had taught him the necessity of bridging the gap. His father had made a mistake based on greed and pride, and that error had cost them both dearly. But Chance deeply regretted his actions, and had for years.

In his own way, Josh's father had tried reaching out to Josh through his sister-in-law, but he had never been able to openly confront Josh. However, when Josh had come to him, needing his help, Chance had been given the golden opportunity to make up to his son for the wrong he had done years earlier.

Amy set a roast in the oven and reached for an orange, choosing that over the weird food combination she'd mentioned earlier.

"Mommy, Mommy." Three-year-old Cain crashed through the back door and raced across the kitchen, his stubby legs pumping for all he was worth. "Grandpa and I saw a robin and a rabbit and a...a worm."

Josh waylaid his son, catching him under the arms and swinging him high above his head. "Where's Grandpa?"

"He said Mommy wouldn't want the worm inside the house so he put it back in the garden. Did you know worms live in the dirt and have babies and everything?"

"No kidding?" Amy asked, pretending to be surprised.

Harold Johnson came into the kitchen next, his face bright with a smile. "It looks like Cain gave you a run for your money, Dad," Amy said, kissing her father on the cheek. "I've got a roast in the oven, do you want to stay for dinner?"

"Can't," he said, dismissing the invitation. "I'm meeting the guys tonight for a game of pinochle." He stopped and looked at Josh. "Anything important happening at the office I should know about?"

"I can't think of anything offhand. Are you coming in on Tuesday for the board of directors' meeting?"

"Not if it conflicts with my golfing date."

"Honestly, Dad," Amy grumbled, washing her son's hands with a paper towel. "There was a time when nothing could keep you away from the business. Now you barely go into the office at all."

"Can't see any reason why I should. I've got the best CEO in the country. My business is thriving. Besides, I want to live long enough to enjoy my grandchildren. Isn't that right, Cain?"

"Right, Gramps." The toddler slapped his open palm against his grandfather's, then promptly yawned.

"Looks like you wore the boy out," Josh said, lifting Cain into his arms. The little boy laid his cheek on his father's shoulder.

"He'll go right down after dinner," Harold said, smiling broadly. "You two will have the evening alone." He winked at Josh and kissed Amy on the cheek. "You can thank me later," he whispered in her ear.

* * * * *

THE SOLDIER'S SECRET CHILD

Lee Tobin McClain

To my daughter, Grace, who shows me every day
that families aren't about bloodlines;
they're about heart.

Chapter 1

Lacey McPherson leaned back, propped her hands on the low white picket fence and surveyed the wedding reception before her with satisfaction. She'd pulled it off.

She'd given her beloved brother and his bride a wedding reception to remember, not letting her own anti-romance attitude show. But she had to admit she'd be glad when her half-remodeled guesthouse stopped being a nest for lovebirds.

"Nothing like a spring wedding, eh, Lacey?"

She jumped, startled at the sound of the gruff, familiar voice right behind her. She spun around. "Vito D'Angelo, you scared me!" And then her eyes widened and she gasped. "What happened?"

His warm brown eyes took her back to her teen years. She'd been such a dreamer then, not good at navigating high school drama, and her brother's friend had stepped in more than once to defend her from girls who wanted to gossip or boys who tried to take advantage. She and her brother had welcomed invitations to the D'Angelo family's big, loud Italian dinners.

But now the most noticeable thing about his face wasn't his eyes, but the double scar that ran from his forehead to his jawline. A smaller scar slashed from his lower lip to his chin.

Instinctively she reached out toward his face.

He caught her hand, held it. "I know. I look bad. But you should see the other guy."

His attempt at a joke made her hurt more than it made her laugh. "You don't look bad. It's just…wow, they barely missed your eye." Awkwardly, she tried to hug him with the fence in between.

He broke away and came inside through the open gate. "How're you doing, Lace? At least *you're* still gorgeous, huh? But you're too thin."

"You sound just like your grandma. And you're late for the wedding." Her heart was still racing from the surprise, both of seeing him and of how he looked.

She wanted to find out what had happened. But this wasn't the time or the place.

"Buck won't mind my being late. He looks busy." Vito looked past the wedding guests toward Lacey's brother, laughing and talking in the summer sun, his arm slung around his new bride. "Looks happy, too. Glad he found someone."

A slightly wistful quality in Vito's words made Lacey study her old friend. She hadn't seen him in almost ten years, not since he'd brought his army buddy home on a furlough and Lacey had fallen hard for the handsome stranger who'd quickly become her husband.

Back then, after one very stormy conversation, Vito had faded into the background. He'd been in the firestorm that had killed Gerry, had tried to save him and had written to Lacey after Gerry's death. But he'd continued on with another Iraq tour and then another. She'd heard he'd been injured, had undergone a lot of surgery and rehab.

Looking at him now, she saw that he'd filled out from slim to brawny, and his hair curled over his ears, odd for a career military man. "How long are you home?"

"For good. I'm out of the army."

"Out?" She stared. "Why? That was all you ever wanted to do!" She paused. "Just like Gerry."

"I felt awful I didn't make his funeral." He put an arm around her shoulders and tugged her to his side. "Aw, Lace, I'm sorry about all of it."

Her throat tightened and she nodded. Gerry had been dead for a year and a half, but the loss still ached.

A shout went up from the crowd and something came hurtling toward her. Instinctively she put her hands up, but Vito stepped in front of her, catching the missile.

Immediately, he turned and handed it to her.

A bouquet of flowers? Why would someone…

Oh. *The* bouquet. Gina's.

She looked across the crowd at her friend, glowing in her pearl-colored gown. Gina kept encouraging Lacey to date again. Happily in love, she wanted everyone to share in the same kind of joy.

The crowd's noise had quieted, and some of the guests frowned and murmured. Probably because Gina had obviously targeted Lacey, who'd been widowed less than two years ago. One of the older guests shook her head. "Completely inappropriate," she said, loud enough for most of those nearby to hear.

Well, that wouldn't do. Gina was a Californian, relatively new to Ohio and still finding her way through the unspoken rules and rituals of the Midwest. She hadn't meant to do anything wrong.

Lacey forced a laugh and shook the bouquet threateningly at Gina. "You're not going to get away with this, you know," she said, keeping her tone light. "I'm passing it on to…" She looked around. "To my friend Daisy."

"Too late." Daisy waved a finger in front of her face and backed away. "You caught it."

"Actually, Vito caught it," old Gramps Camden said. "Not sure what happens when a man catches the bouquet."

As the crowd went back to general talk, Lacey tried to hand off the bouquet to all the females near her, but they all laughingly refused.

Curious about Vito's reaction, she turned to joke with him, but he was gone.

Later, after Gina and Buck had run out to Buck's shaving-cream-decorated truck, heads down against a hail of birdseed, Lacey gave cleanup instructions to the two high school girls who were helping her with the reception. Then, after making sure that the remaining guests were well fed and happy, she went into the guesthouse. She needed to check on Nonna D'Angelo.

Having Nonna stay here was working out great. The light nursing care she needed was right up Lacey's alley, and she enjoyed the older woman's company. And the extra bit of income Nonna insisted on paying had enabled Lacey to quit her job at the regional hospital. Now that the wedding was over, she could dive into the final stages of readying the guesthouse for its fall opening.

Nonna D'Angelo had mingled during the early part of the reception, but she'd gone inside to rest more than an hour ago. Now Lacey heard the older woman crying and hastened her step, but then a reassuring male voice rumbled and the crying stopped.

Vito.

Of course, he'd come in to see his grandma first thing. He hadn't been home in over a year, and they'd always been close.

She'd just take a quick peek to make sure Nonna wasn't getting overexcited, and then leave them to their reunion.

Slowly, she strolled down the hall to the room she'd made up for Nonna D, keeping her ears open, giving them time. She surveyed the glossy wood floors with satisfaction. The place was coming along. She'd redo this wallpaper sometime, but the faded roses weren't half-bad for now. Gave the place its historical character.

She ran her hand along the long, thin table she'd just bought for the entryway, straightened her favorite, goofy ceramic rooster and a vase of flowers. Mr. Whiskers jumped up onto the table, and Lacey stopped to rub his face and ears, evoking a purr. "Where's the Missus, huh?" she cooed quietly. "Is she hiding?"

Hearing another weepy sniffle from Nonna D, Lacey quickened her step and stopped in the doorway of Nonna's room.

"My beautiful boy," Nonna was saying with a catch in her voice. "You were always the good-looking one."

Vito sat on the edge of the bed, looking distinctly

uncomfortable as Nonna sat up in bed to inspect his cheek and brush his hair back behind his ears.

She felt a quick defensiveness on Vito's behalf. Sure, the scars were noticeable. But to Lacey, they added to his rugged appeal.

Nonna saw her and her weathered face broke into a smile, her eyes sparkling behind large glasses. "There's my sweet girl. Come in and see my boy Vito."

"We talked already, Nonna." Vito was rubbing the back of his neck. "Lacey, I didn't realize you were taking care of my grandma to this extent. I'll take her home tomorrow."

"Oh, no!" Lacey said. "I'm so happy to do it!"

"I can't go home!" Nonna said at the same time.

"Why not?" Vito looked from Nonna to Lacey and back again.

"I need my nursing help," Nonna explained. "Lacey, here, is a wonderful nurse. She's practically saved my life!"

Lacey's cheeks burned. "I'm really a Certified Nursing Assistant, not a nurse," she explained. "And I haven't done anything special, just helped with medications and such." In truth, she knew she'd helped Nonna D'Angelo with the mental side as well as the physical, calming her anxiety and making sure she ate well, arranging some outings and visits so the woman didn't sink into the depression so common among people with her health issues.

"Medications? What's wrong?"

"It's my heart," Nonna started to explain.

Vito had the nerve to chuckle. "Oh, now, Nonna. You've been talking about your heart for twenty years, and you never needed a nurse before."

"Things are different now." The older woman's chin quivered.

He reached out and patted her arm. "You'll be fine."

Lacey drew in a breath. Should she intervene? Families were sometimes in denial about the seriousness of a beloved relative's health problems, and patients sometimes shielded their families from the truth.

"If you want to move your grandma, that's fine," she said, "but I'd recommend waiting a couple more weeks."

"That's right." Nonna looked relieved. "Lacey needs the money and I need the help."

Vito frowned. "Can we afford this?" He looked down at his grandma and seemed to realize that the woman was getting distressed. "Tell you what, Grandma, Lacey and I will talk about this and figure some things out. I won't leave without saying goodbye."

"All right, dear." She shot a concerned glance at Lacey.

She leaned down in the guise of straightening a pillow for Nonna. "I'll explain everything," she reassured her.

She led the way to the front room, out of earshot from Nonna D'Angelo. Then she turned to Vito, frowning. "You don't think I'm taking advantage of your grandma, do you?"

"No!" He reached for her, but when she took a step back, he crossed his arms instead. "I would never think that, Lacey. I know you. I just don't know if you've thought this through."

She restrained an eye roll. "You always did like to interfere when your help wasn't needed."

"Look, if this is about that talk we had years back..." He waved a dismissive hand. "Let's just forget that."

She knew exactly what he meant. As soon as Vito had found out Gerry had proposed, he'd come storming over to her house and pulled her out onto the front porch to try and talk her out of it. "You were wrong," she said now.

"I wasn't wrong." When she opened her mouth to protest, he held up a hand. "But I was wrong to interfere."

That wasn't exactly what she'd said, but whatever.

"But back to my grandma. I don't know what her insurance is like, but I know it hardly ever covers in-home nursing care. I'm living on limited means and until I get back on my feet—"

"It's handled. It's fine."

He ran a hand through his thick, dark hair. "She's always tended to be a hypochondriac—"

"A heart attack is nothing to take lightly."

"A *heart attack*?" Vito's jaw dropped. "Nonna had a heart attack?"

His surprise was so genuine that her annoyance about what she'd thought was neglect faded away. "About two weeks ago. She didn't tell you?"

"No, she didn't tell me. Do you think I'd have stayed away if I'd known?" His square jaw tightened. "Not a word. How bad was it?"

Lacey spread her hands. "Look, I'm just a CNA. You should definitely talk to her doctor."

"But from what you've seen, give me a guess."

Outside, she could hear people talking quietly. Dishes rattled in the kitchen, the girls cleaning up. She blew out a breath. "It was moderate severity. She had some damage, and there are some restrictions on what she can do. Changes she needs to make."

"What kind of changes?" He thrust his hands in his

pockets and paced. "I can't believe she had a heart attack and I didn't know. Why didn't you call me?"

"It's her business what she tells people."

His mouth twisted to one side. "C'mon, Lace."

"I'm serious. Patients have the right to confidentiality. I couldn't breach that. In fact," she said, stricken, "I probably shouldn't have told you even now."

"You're my friend. You can tell me as a friend. Now, what kind of changes? What does she need to do to get back on her feet?"

She perched on the arm of an overstuffed chair. "You can probably guess. It's a lot about diet. She needs to start a gentle exercise program. I have her walking around the block twice a day."

He stared. "Nonna's walking? Like, for exercise?"

"I know, right?" She smiled a little. "It wasn't easy to talk her into it. I make sure we have an interesting destination."

"How did you get so involved?"

She let her forehead sink down into her hand for just a second, then looked back up. Vito. He'd never take her seriously. He'd always been a big brother to her, and he always would be.

He held up a hand. "I'm not questioning it, Lacey. I'm grateful. And I feel awful having been out of the loop, not helping her. I've had lots of personal stuff going on, but that's no excuse."

His words flicked on a switch of interest in her, but she ignored it. "I worked her hall at the hospital, and since she knew me, we talked. She was worried about coming home alone, but she didn't want to bother you, and your brother's far away. I was looking to make a change, anyway, moving toward freelance home care so

I could have time to finish renovating this place." She waved an arm toward the unfinished breakfast area, currently walled off with sheets of plastic.

"So you made a deal with her." He still sounded a little skeptical.

"Yes, if that's what you want to call it." She stood, full of restless energy, and paced over to the fireplace, rearranging the collection of colored glass bottles on the mantel. "She's had a lot of anxiety, which is common in people recovering from a heart attack. She's on several new medications, and one of them causes fatigue and dizziness. The social worker was going to insist on having her go to a nursing home for proper care, which she couldn't afford, so this was a good arrangement." She looked over at him, mentally daring him to question her.

He rubbed a hand over the back of his neck. "A nursing home. Wow."

"It wouldn't have suited her."

"For how long? How long do you think she'll need the extra care?"

Lacey shrugged, moved an amber bottle to better catch the sun. "I don't know. Usually people take a couple of months to get back up to speed. And your brother's happy to pay for as long as we need."

Vito's dark eyebrows shot up. "She told him and not me?"

"She said you'd find out soon enough, when you came back home."

"And he's paying for everything?"

"He felt bad, being so far away, and apparently he begged her to let him help. Look, if you want to make a change in her care, I totally understand." It would mess up her own plans, of course; she'd given notice at the hospital only when she had this job to see her through, so if Nonna left, she'd have to apply for a part-time job right away. But Nonna was improving daily. If she had Vito with her, and he could focus on her needs, she'd probably be fine. A lot of her anxiety and depression stemmed from loneliness and fear.

Truth was, Lacey had found the older woman a hedge against her own loneliness, as her brother had gotten more and more involved in his wedding plans.

Now Buck and Gina and their dogs would be living in a little cottage on the other side of town. She'd see them a lot, but it wouldn't be the same as having Buck living here. "Whatever you decide," she said. "For now, we'd better go reassure your grandma, and then I need to attend to the rest of my guests."

Vito followed Lacey back into his grandmother's room, his mind reeling. Nonna had mostly raised him and his brother, Eugene, after their parents' accident, and she was one of the few family members he had left. More to the point, he was one of *her* only family members, and he should have been here for her.

Everyone treated him like he was made of glass, but the fact was, he was perfectly healthy on the inside. His surgeries had been a success, and his hearing loss was corrected with state-of-the-art hearing aids, courtesy of the VA.

He just *looked* bad.

And while the scars that slashed across his face, the worse ones on his chest, made it even more unlikely that he'd achieve his dream of marriage and a large family, he couldn't blame his bachelorhood entirely on the war.

Women had always liked him, yes—as a friend. And nothing but a friend. He lacked the cool charisma that most women seemed to want in a boyfriend or husband.

Entering his grandmother's room, he pulled up a chair for Lacey, and then sat down on the edge of Nonna's bed, carefully, trying not to jolt her out of her light doze. He was newly conscious that she was pale, and thinner than she'd been. A glance around the attractive bedroom revealed a stash of pill bottles he hadn't noticed before.

Nonna's eyes fluttered open and she reached out.

He caught her hand in his. "Hey, how're you feeling?"

She pursed her lips and glared at Lacey. "You told him about my heart."

"Yes, I told him! Of course I told him!" Lacey's voice had a fond but scolding tone. "You should have let him know yourself, Nonna. I thought you had."

He squeezed his grandmother's hand. "Don't you know I would've dropped everything and come?"

Nonna made a disgusted noise. "That's exactly why I didn't tell you. You and your brother have your own lives to lead. And I was able to find a very good arrangement on my own." She smiled at Lacey.

"It *is* a good arrangement, and I'm glad for it." Vito glanced over at Lacey, who had gotten up to pour water into a small vase of flowers.

With its blue-patterned wallpaper, lamp-lit bedside table and a handmade quilt on the bed, the room was cozy. Through the door of the small private bathroom, he glimpsed handicapped-accessible rails and a shower seat.

Yes, this was a good situation for her. "Look, I want

to take you back to the house, but we'll wait until you're a little better."

Nonna started to say something, and then broke off, picking restlessly at the blanket.

"I haven't even been over to see the place yet," he continued, making plans as he thought it through. "I just got into town. But I'll check it out, make sure you've got everything you need."

"About that, dear…" Nonna's voice sounded uncharacteristically subdued.

"I hope you don't mind, but I'm planning to live there with you for a while." He smiled. It was true comfort, knowing he could come back to Rescue River anytime and find a welcome, a place to stay and a home-cooked meal.

Lacey nodded approvingly, and for some reason it warmed Vito to see it.

"Neither one of us will be able to live there," Nonna said, her voice small.

Lacey's eyebrows rose in surprise, and he could feel the same expression on his own face. "What do you mean?"

"Now, don't be angry, either of you," she said, grasping his hand, "but I rented out the house."

"You *what?*"

"When did you do that?" Lacey sounded bewildered.

"We signed the papers yesterday when you were out grocery shopping," Nonna said, looking everywhere but at Vito and Lacey.

"Who'd you rent it to?" If it had just been finalized yesterday, surely everything could be revoked once the situation was explained. Lacey hadn't said anything about cognitive problems, but Nonna *was* in her early eighties. Maybe she wasn't thinking clearly.

Nonna smiled and clasped her hands together. "The most lovely migrant family," she said. "Three children and another on the way, and they're hoping to find a way to settle here. I gave them a good price, and they're going to keep the place up and do some repairs for me."

"Nonna…" Vito didn't know where to begin. He knew that this was the way things worked in his hometown—a lot of bartering, a lot of helping out those in need. "You aren't planning to stay here at the guesthouse indefinitely, right? How long of a lease did you sign?"

"Just a year." She folded her hands on top of her blanket and smiled.

"A year?" Not wanting to yell at his aged grandma, Vito stood and ran his hands through his hair. "Either you're going to have to revoke it, or I'm going to have to find another place for you and me to live." Never mind how he'd afford the rent. Or the fact that he'd named Nonna's house as his permanent residence in all the social services paperwork.

"No, dear. I have it all figured out." She took Lacey's hand in hers, and then reached toward him with her other hand. Once she had ahold of each of them, she smiled from one to the other. "Vito, if Lacey agrees, you can stay here."

No. She wasn't thinking clearly. "Nonna, that's not going to work. Lacey made this arrangement with you, not with me." And certainly not with the other guest he had in tow. No way could Lacey find out the truth about Charlie.

"But Lacey was thinking of getting another boarder for this period while she's remodeling. It's hard to find the right one, because of all the noise." Lacey started to speak, but Nonna held up a hand. "The noise doesn't bother me. I can just turn down my hearing aid."

Vito knew what was coming and he felt his face heat. "Nonna…"

"Vito's perfect," she said, looking at Lacey, "because he can do the same thing."

Lacey's eyebrows lifted as she looked at him.

No point in trying to hide his less visible disability now. "It's true," he said, brushing back his hair to show his behind-the-ear hearing aids. "But that doesn't mean you have to take us in." In fact, staying here was the last thing that would work for him.

He'd promised Gerry he'd take care of his son, conceived during the affair Gerry had while married to Lacey. And he'd promised to keep Charlie's parentage a secret from Lacey.

He was glad he could help his friend, sinner though Gerry had been. Charlie needed a reliable father figure, and Lacey needed to maintain her illusions about her husband. It would serve no purpose for her to find out the truth now; it would only hurt her.

Lacey frowned. "I *was* looking to take in another boarder. I was thinking of maybe somebody who worked the three-to-eleven shift at the pretzel factory. They could come home and sleep, and they wouldn't be bothered by my working on the house at all hours."

"That makes sense," he said, relieved. "That would be better."

"But the thing is," she said slowly, "I haven't found anyone, even though I've been advertising for a couple of weeks. If you wanted to…"

Anxiety clawed at him from inside. How was he

supposed to handle this? He could throttle Gerry for putting him into this situation. "I... There are some complications. I need to give this some thought." He knew he was being cryptic, but he needed time to figure it all out.

Unfortunately, Nonna wasn't one to accept anything cryptic from her grandchildren. "What complications? What's going on?"

Vito stood, then sat back down again. Nonna was going to have to know about Charlie soon enough. Lacey, too, along with everyone else in town. It would seem weirder if he tried to hide it now. "The thing is," he said, "I'm not alone. I have someone with me."

"Girlfriend? Wife?" Lacey sounded extremely curious.

Nonna, on the other hand, looked disappointed. "You would never get married without letting your *nonna* know," she said, reaching up to pinch his cheek, and then pulling her hand back, looking apologetic. It took him a minute to realize that she'd hesitated because of his scars.

"One of my finished rooms is a double," Lacey said thoughtfully. "But I don't know what your...friend... would think of the mess and the noise."

This was going off the rails. "It's not a girlfriend or wife," he said.

"Then who?" Nonna smacked his arm in a way that reminded him of when he'd been small and misbehaving. "If not a woman, then who?"

Vito drew in a breath. "Actually," he said, "I've recently become certified as a foster parent."

Both women stared at him with wide, surprised eyes.

"So I'd be bringing along my eight-year-old foster son."

He was saved from further explanation by a crash, followed by the sound of shattering glass and running feet.

Chapter 2

Lacey raced out of Nonna's bedroom, leaving Vito to reassure the older woman. A quick scan of the hall revealed the breakage: her ceramic rooster lay in pieces on the floor.

One of the kids, probably; they were all sugared up on wedding cake and running around. She hurried to get a broom and dustpan, not wanting any of the remaining wedding guests to injure themselves. As she dropped the colorful pieces into the trash, she felt a moment's regret.

More important than the untimely demise of her admittedly tacky rooster, she wondered about Vito fostering a child. That, she hadn't expected.

"Miss Lacey!" It was little Mindy, Sam Hinton's daughter. "I saw who did that!"

"Did you? Stay back," she warned as she checked the area for any remaining ceramic pieces.

"Yes," Mindy said, "and he's hiding under the front porch right now!"

Behind her, Lacey heard Vito coming out of Nonna's bedroom, then pausing to talk some more, and a suspicion of who the young criminal might be came over her. "I'll go talk to him," she said. "It wasn't Xavier, was it?"

"No. It was a kid I don't know. Is he going to get in trouble?"

"I don't think so, honey. Not too much trouble, anyway. Why don't you go tell your dad what happened?"

"Yeah! He's gotta know!" As Mindy rushed off to her important task, Lacey walked out of the house and stood on the porch, looking around. The remaining guests were in the side yard, talking and laughing, so no one seemed to notice her.

She went down the steps and around to the side of the house where there was an opening in the latticework; she knew because she'd had to crawl under there when she'd first found Mrs. Whiskers, hiding with a couple of kittens. When she squatted down, she heard a little sniffling sound that touched her heart. Moving aside the branches of a lilac bush, breathing in the sweet fragrance of the fading purple flowers, she spoke into the darkness. "It's okay. I didn't like that rooster much, anyway."

There was silence, and then a stirring, but no voice. From the other side of the yard, she could hear conversations and laughter. But this shaded spot felt private.

"I remember one time I broke my grandma's favorite lamp," she said conversationally, settling into a sitting position on the cool grass. "I ran and hid in an apple tree."

"Did they find you?" a boy's voice asked. Not a familiar voice. Since she knew every kid at the wedding, her suspicion that the culprit was Vito's new foster son increased. "Yes, they found me. My brother told them where I was."

"Did you get in trouble?"

"I sure did." She remembered her grandma's reprimand, her father chiming in, her own teary apology.

"Did they hit you?" the boy asked, his voice low.

The plaintive question squeezed Lacey's heart. "No, I just got scolded a lot. And I had to give my grandma my allowance to help pay for a new lamp."

"I don't get an allowance. Did you…" There was a pause, a sniffle. "Did you have to go live somewhere else after that?"

Lacey's eyes widened as she put it all together. Vito had said he'd *recently* become certified as a foster parent. So this must be a new arrangement. It would make all the sense in the world that a boy who'd just been placed with a new foster father would feel insecure about whether he'd be allowed to stay.

But why had Vito, a single man with issues of his own, taken on this new challenge? "No, I didn't have to go live somewhere else," she said firmly, "and what's more, no kind adult would send a kid away for breaking a silly old lamp. Or a silly old rooster, either."

Branches rustled behind her, and then Vito came around the edge of the bushes. "There you are! What happened? Is everything okay?"

She pointed toward the latticed area where the boy was hiding, giving Vito a meaningful look. "I think the person who *accidentally*—" she emphasized the word "—broke the rooster is worried he'll get sent away."

"What?" Vito's thick dark eyebrows came down as

understanding dawned in his eyes. He squatted beside her. "Charlie, is that you? Kids don't get sent away for stuff like that."

There was another shuffling under the porch, and then a head came into view. Messy, light brown hair, a sprinkling of freckles, worried-looking eyes. "But they might get sent away if they were keeping their dad from having a place to live."

Oh. The boy must have heard Vito say he couldn't live here because of having a foster son.

"We'll find a place to live," Vito said. "Come on out."

The boy looked at him steadily and didn't move.

"Charlie! I mean it!"

Lacey put a hand on Vito's arm. "Hey, Charlie," she said softly. "I grew up next door to this guy. I was three years younger and a lot smaller, and I did some annoying things. And he never, ever hit me." She felt Vito's arm tense beneath hers and squeezed. "And he wouldn't hurt you, either. Right, Vito?" She looked over at him.

His mouth twisted. "That's right." He went forward on one knee and held out a hand to the boy. "Come on out. We talked about this. Remember, I look meaner than I really am."

The boy hesitated, then crawled out without taking Vito's hand. Instead, he scuttled over to the other side of Lacey and crouched.

Vito drew in a breath and blew it out. His brow furrowed. "You're going to need to apologize to Miss Lacey, here, and then we'll find out how you can make up for what you did."

The boy wrapped his arms around upraised knees. A tear leaked out and he backhanded it away. "I can't make it up. Don't have any money."

"I might have some chores you could do," Lacey said, easing backward so she wasn't directly between Charlie and Vito. "Especially if you and your foster dad are going to be living here." As soon as she said it, she regretted the words. "Or living nearby," she amended hastily.

She liked Vito, always had. And she adored his grandmother, who clearly wanted her family gathered around her. But Lacey had been planning to have the next few months as a quiet, calm oasis before opening her guesthouse. She still had healing to do.

Having Vito and this boy here wasn't conducive to quiet serenity. On the other hand, young Charlie seemed to have thrown himself on her for protection, and that touched her.

"Can we live here? Really?" The boy jumped up and started hopping from one foot to the next. "'Cause this place is cool! You have a tire swing! And there's a basketball hoop right across the street!"

Vito stood, looking at her quizzically. "The grownups will be doing some talking," he said firmly. "For tonight, we're staying out at the motel like we planned. But before we go back there, I want you to apologize."

The boy looked at Lacey, then away, digging the toe of a well-worn sneaker into the dirt. "I'm real sorry I broke your rooster. It was an accident."

She nodded, getting to her feet. "That's all right. I think I can find another one kind of like it."

Her own soft feelings surprised her. Generally, she avoided little ones, especially babies; they were a reminder of all she couldn't have.

But this boy touched her heart. Maybe it was because his reaction to breaking the rooster was so similar to her own reaction when she'd broken the lamp. *Hide. Don't let the grown-ups know, because you never know what disaster will happen when grown-ups get upset.* She'd been fortunate, found by her grandma and father instead of her mom. Come to think of it, her brother had probably gone to them on purpose. He'd wanted her to get in trouble, but not from their volatile mother.

Lacey was beyond all that now, at least she thought so, but she still identified with the feeling of accidentally causing disasters and facing out-of-proportion consequences.

"And the other question you have to answer," Vito said, putting an arm around Charlie's shoulders lightly, ignoring the boy's automatic wince, "is how you got down here when you were supposed to be staying with Valencia."

Lacey moved to stand by Charlie, and her presence seemed to relax him.

"I asked her if we could take a walk," Charlie explained, a defensive tone coming into his voice. "When we came by here, she started talking to the people and I came inside. I just wanted to look around."

"You're not to do things like that without permission." Vito pinched the bridge of his nose. "You have another apology to make, to Valencia. And no dessert after dinner tonight."

The boy's lower lip came out, and Lacey felt the absurd impulse to slip him an extra piece of wedding cake.

An accented voice called from the other side of the yard. "Charlie! Charlie!"

"You run and tell Miss Valencia you're sorry you didn't stay close to her. And then wait for me on the porch."

As the boy ran toward the babysitter's anxious voice, Lacey looked up at Vito. "In over your head?"

"Totally." He blew out a breath. "What do I know about raising kids?"

"How'd you get into it, anyway?"

"It's complicated." He looked away, then back at her. "Listen, don't feel pressured into having us stay at your guesthouse. I don't expect that, no matter what Nonna says. And you can see that we'd be a handful."

She looked into his warm brown eyes. "I *can* see that. And I honestly don't know if it would work. But what are you going to do if you can't stay here?"

"That's the million-dollar question." He rubbed his chin. "We'll figure something out."

"Let me sleep on it. It's been a crazy day."

"Of course it has, and I'm sorry to add to that." They headed toward the rest of the guests, and he put an arm around her shoulders and squeezed. It was an innocent gesture, a friendly gesture, the same thing he'd done with Charlie.

But for some reason, it disconcerted her now, and she stepped away.

Something flashed in Vito's eyes and he cleared his throat. "Look, tomorrow Charlie has a visit with his birth mom up in Raystown. Let me take you to lunch. We can talk about Nonna and the possibility of Charlie and me staying here. Or more likely, how to break it to Nonna that we *won't* be staying here."

She'd planned to spend the next afternoon cleaning up and recovering from the wedding. "That'll work."

"The Chatterbox? Noon?" His voice was strictly businesslike.

"Where else?" She wondered why he'd gone chilly on her. "I'm looking forward to catching up."

And she was. Sort of.

The next morning, Vito pulled his truck into the parking lot at the Supervised Visitation Center and glanced into the backseat of the extended cab. Yes, a storm was brewing.

"Why do I have to do this?" Charlie mumbled. "Am I going back to live with her?"

"No." He twisted farther around to get more comfortable. "We talked about this. Your mom loves you, but she can't do a good job taking care of you, and you need to have a forever home." He'd practically memorized the words from the foster parenting handbook, and it was a good thing. Because apparently, Charlie needed to hear them a bunch of times.

"Then why do I have to visit? I wanted to play basketball with Xavier, that kid from the wedding yesterday. He said maybe I could come over."

Vito pulled up another memorized phrase and forced cheer into his voice. "It's important for you to have a relationship with your mom. Important for you and for her."

The whole situation was awful for a kid, and Krystal, Charlie's mother, wasn't easy to deal with. She'd neglected Charlie, and worse, exposed him to danger—mostly from her poorly chosen boyfriends—way too many times.

Someone who hurt a kid ought to be in prison, in Vito's mind, at the very least. But he had to keep reminding himself that Krystal was sick.

"You'll have fun with your mom," he said. "I think

you guys are going to go out for lunch in a little while and maybe over to the lake afterward."

"That doesn't sound fun." Charlie crossed his arms and looked out the window, making no move to get out of the car.

Vito looked that way, too, and saw Krystal getting out of the passenger side of a late-model SUV. Maybe things were looking up for her. He'd only met her a few times, but she'd been driving a car noticeably on its last legs.

The SUV roared off, passing them, with a balding, bearded, forty-something guy at the wheel. Vito looked back at Charlie in time to see the boy cringe. "What's wrong, buddy?" he asked. "Do you know that guy?"

Charlie nodded but didn't say anything.

Krystal strolled over to the back stoop of the Center, smoking a cigarette. Vito wished for a similarly easy way to calm his nerves.

He wished he knew how to be a father. He'd only had Charlie full-time for a month, most of which they'd spent in Cleveland, closing down Vito's previous life, getting ready to move home. Charlie had been well and truly welcomed by the Cleveland branch of Vito's family, though everyone had agreed on waiting to tell Nonna about Charlie until the foster care situation was definite. If everything went well, he'd be able to adopt Charlie after another six months and be the boy's permanent, real father.

Learning how to parent well would take a lifetime.

Vito got out of the car. The small, wire-supported trees around the brand-new building were trying their best, sporting a few green leaves. A robin hopped along the bare ground, poking for worms, and more birds chirped overhead. It was a nice summer day, and Vito was half tempted to get back in the truck and drive away, take Charlie to the lake himself.

But that wasn't the agreement he'd made. He opened the passenger door and Charlie got out. His glance in his mother's direction was urgent and hungry.

Of course. This visit was important. No matter what parents did, kids always wanted to love them.

Vito forced a spring into his step as they approached the building and Krystal. "Hey," he greeted her, and tried the door.

"It's locked, genius." Krystal drew harder on her cigarette. She hadn't glanced at or touched Charlie, who'd stopped a few steps short of the little porch.

Looking at the two of them, Vito's heart about broke. He considered his big, extended family up in Cleveland, the hugs, the cheek pinches, the loud greetings. He had it good, always had. He squatted beside Charlie and cast about for conversation. "Charlie's been doing great," he said to Krystal, not that she'd asked. "Going to sign him up for summer softball."

"Nice for you. I never could afford it." She looked at Charlie then, and her face softened. "Hey, kid. You got tall in the past couple months."

Vito was so close to Charlie that he could sense the boy's urge to run to his mom as well as the fear that pinned him to Vito's side.

The fear worried him.

But Charlie would be safe. This was a supervised visit, if the caseworker ever got here.

"You were Gerry's buddy," Krystal said suddenly. "Did you know about me, or did he just talk about *her*?"

What was Vito supposed to say to that, especially in front of Charlie? The boy needed to think highly of his father, to remember that he'd died a hero's death, not that he'd lived a terribly flawed life. "It's better we focus on now," he said to Krystal, nodding his head sideways, subtly, at Charlie.

She snorted, but dropped the subject, turning away to respond to her buzzing phone.

Focus on now. He needed to take his own advice. Except he had to think about the future and make plans, to consider the possibility of him and Charlie staying with the *her*—Lacey—that Krystal was mad about. Which would be a really rotten idea, now that the ramifications of it all came to him.

He wasn't sure how much Krystal knew about Lacey and Gerry, what kind of promises Gerry might have made to her. From what he'd been able to figure out, Krystal hadn't known that Gerry was married, at least not at first. No wonder she was angry. Problem was, she'd likely pass that anger on to Charlie. She didn't seem like a person who had a very good filter.

And if she talked to Charlie about Lacey, and Charlie was living at Lacey's boardinghouse, the boy could get all mixed up inside.

If Gerry were still alive, Vito would strangle him. The jerk hadn't been married to Lacey for a year before he'd started stepping out on her.

Krystal put her phone away, lit another cigarette and sat down on the edge of the stoop. She beckoned to Charlie. "Come on, sit by me. You scared?"

Charlie hesitated, then walked over and sat gingerly beside her. When she put her arm around him, though, he turned into her and hugged her suddenly and hard, and grief tightened her face.

Vito stepped back to give them some space and covertly studied Krystal. He didn't understand Gerry. The man had had Lacey as a wife—gorgeous, sweet Lacey—and he'd cheated on her with Krystal. Who, admittedly, had a stellar figure and long black hair. She'd probably been beautiful back then. But now the hair was disheveled. Her eyes were heavy-lidded, her skin pitted with some kind of scars. Vito wasn't sure what all she was addicted to, but the drugs had obviously taken their toll.

It looked like she'd stayed sober to visit with Charlie today, knowing she'd have to submit to a drug test. Maybe she'd had to stay clean a couple of days. That would put any addict into a bad mood.

Even before she'd been an addict, Krystal couldn't have compared to Lacey.

A battered subcompact pulled into the parking lot and jolted to a halt, its muffler obviously failing. The driver-side door flew open and the short, curly-haired caseworker got out. After pulling an overstuffed briefcase and a couple of bags from her car, she bustled over to them.

"Sorry I'm late! These Sunday visits are crazy. Maybe we can switch to Mondays or Tuesdays?" She was fumbling for the key as she spoke. "Come on in, guys! Thanks so much, Vito!"

"Charlie." Vito got the boy's attention, held his eyes. "I'll be back at three, okay?"

Relief shone on Charlie's face. He ran to Vito, gave him a short hug and whispered into his ear: "Come back for sure, okay?"

"You got it, buddy." Vito's voice choked up a little bit.

Charlie let go and looked at Vito. Then his eyes narrowed and he grinned purposefully. "And can we stay at that place instead of the motel?" he whispered. "With the cat and the nice lady?"

Vito knew manipulation when he saw it, but he also knew the boy needed both security and honesty.

"What's he begging for now?" Krystal grinned as she flicked her cigarette butt into the bare soil beside the building. "I recognize that look."

"I'm starting to recognize it, too," Vito said, meeting Krystal's eyes. Some kind of understanding arced between them, and he felt a moment of kinship and sorrow for the woman who'd given birth to Charlie but wouldn't get to raise him.

"Well, can we?" Charlie asked.

"We'll see. No promises." Vito squeezed the boy's shoulder. "You be good, and I'll see you right here at three o'clock."

In reality, he wished he could just sweep the boy up and take him home, and not just to protect him from an awkward day with his mom. Vito wasn't looking forward to the lunch date—no, *not* a date—he was facing in only a few hours. Whatever he and Lacey decided, it was going to make someone unhappy.

Chapter 3

"They left the two of us in charge of the nursery? Are they crazy?" Lacey's friend Susan put her purse up on a shelf and came over to where Lacey stood beside a crib, trying to coax a baby to sleep.

"I'm just glad it's you working with me." Lacey picked up the baby, who'd started to fuss, and swayed gently. "You won't freak out if I freak out."

Working in the church nursery was Lacey's counselor's idea, a way to help Lacey deal with her miscarriage and subsequent infertility. She needed to desensitize herself, find ways to be around babies without getting upset by them, especially if she was going to open a family-friendly guesthouse and make a success of it.

The desensitization had started accidentally, when Gina Patterson had showed up in town earlier this year with her son, Bobby, just ten months old at the time. With nowhere else to turn, she'd spent the early spring at the guesthouse, in the process falling in love with Lacey's brother, Buck. Being around little Bobby had made Lacey miserable at first, but she was learning. More than that, she was motivated; she wanted to serve others and get out of her own pain, build a well-rounded life for herself.

Which included being around babies. "I'm here to work through my issues," she told Susan, "but why are *you* here?"

Susan's tawny skin went pink. "Sam and I decided it would be a good idea for me to get comfortable with babies. I used to be terrified of even touching them, but… I guess I'd better learn."

Something in Susan's tone made Lacey take notice, and she mentally reviewed what Susan had just said. Then she stared at her friend. "Wait a minute. Are you expecting? Already?"

Susan looked down at the floor, and then met Lacey's eyes. "Yeah. We just found out."

Selfish tears sprang to Lacey's eyes as she looked down at the infant she held, feeling its weight in her arms. Something she'd never experience for herself, with her own child. A joy that Susan and many of Lacey's other friends would find effortlessly.

Susan would be a part of the circle of happy young mothers in town. Lacey wouldn't, not ever.

"I'm so sorry to cause you pain. News like this must be hard for you to hear."

Susan's kind words jolted Lacey out of her own self-centered heartache. Finding out you were having a baby was one of the most joyous times of a woman's life. She remembered when the two pink lines had shown up on her own pregnancy test. Remembered her video call to Gerry. She'd shown the test to him, and they'd both cried tears of joy.

Susan deserved to have that joy, too. She shouldn't have to focus on her friend's losses.

Lacey lifted the baby to her shoulder so she could reach out and put an arm around Susan. "It does hurt a little—I'm not going to lie. But what kind of friend would I be not to celebrate with you? I'm thrilled!"

"You're the best, Lace." Susan wrapped her arms around Lacey, the baby in between them, and Lacey let herself cry just a little more. Susan understood. She'd stayed a year at Lacey's guesthouse before the remodeling, the horrible year when Lacey had lost both Gerry and the baby. Susan had been an incredible comfort.

"Anyway," Susan added, "I'm going to need your help to fit in with the perfect mothers of Rescue River. You know I have a knack for saying the wrong thing."

"You'll be fine." And it was true. Susan was outspoken and blunt, but she gave everything she had to the kids she taught at the local elementary school, and people here loved her for it. "How's Sam handling the news?"

"Making a million plans and bossing me around, of course." But Susan smiled as she said it, and for just a moment, Lacey felt even more jealous of the happy-married-woman smile on Susan's face than of the tiny, growing baby in her belly.

"Hey, guys, can I leave Bobby here for a little while?" Lou Ann Miller, who was taking care of Gina's baby while she and Buck enjoyed a honeymoon at the shore, stood at the half door. "I want to go to adult Sunday school, but there's no way he'll sit through our book discussion."

"Sure." Lacey thrust the infant she'd been holding into Susan's arms. "Just hold her head steady. Yeah, like that." She walked over to the door and opened it. "Come on in, Bobby!"

"Laaasss," he said, walking right into her leg and hugging it. "Laaasss."

Lacey's heart warmed, and she reached down to pick Bobby up. "He'll be fine. Take your time," she said to Lou Ann. "Wave bye-bye to Miss Lou Ann, okay?"

Two more toddlers got dropped off, and then a diaper needed changing. Little Emmie Farmingham, who was almost three, twirled to show Lacey and Susan her new summer dress, patterned with garden vegetables and sporting a carrot for a pocket. Then she proceeded to pull the dress off.

Once they'd gotten Emmie dressed again, the infant sleeping and the other two toddlers playing side by side with plastic blocks, Susan and Lacey settled down into the tiny chairs around the low table. "Babies are great, I guess," Susan said doubtfully, "but I have to say, I like bigger kids better. I wish one could just land in my lap at age five, like Mindy did."

"Not me." Lacey looked over at the toddlers, another surge of regret piercing her heart. "I've always loved the little ones."

"I know you have." Susan's voice was gentle. "Hey, want to come over and have lunch with us after this? I think Sam's grilling. You could bring your swimsuit."

"You're sweet." The thought of lounging by Sam and Susan's pool was appealing. And Susan was a great friend; she'd stand by Lacey even as she was going through this huge transition of having a child. She wouldn't abandon Lacey, and that mattered.

Lacey shook her head with real disappointment. "Can't. I'm meeting Vito for lunch."

"Oh, *Vito*." Susan punched her arm, gently. "Is this a date?"

"It's not like that. We're old friends."

Susan ignored her words. "You should see where it leads. He seems like a great guy, from what I saw of him at the end of the reception. Good-looking, too. Even with the scars." Susan's hand flew to her mouth. "I shouldn't say things like that, should I?"

"Probably not." Lacey rolled her eyes at her friend, pretending exasperation. "But it's okay. You can't help but notice his scars. Anyway, we're just going to talk about this crazy idea his grandma dreamed up." She explained how Nonna had unexpectedly rented out her own house, and how Vito was newly a foster father. "Apparently, Vito had no idea that was her plan. He was counting on bringing his foster son, Charlie, to live in Nonna's big house out in the country. I actually got the feeling Nonna had kept it a secret on purpose, to make sure Vito ended up staying at the guesthouse."

"But that would be perfect!" Susan clapped her hands. "Vito could be with his *nonna*, and Charlie could get a sense of family, and they'd be right in town to get, like, reintegrated into the community."

"Yes, but—"

"And you wanted someone else to room in, right? He'd pay rent, which would help with your expenses. He and Charlie could have separate rooms, or those two connecting ones upstairs."

Lacey's response was cut off by the sound of crashing blocks and a wail, and they got busy playing with the babies. The subject of Vito moving into the guesthouse didn't come up again, but Lacey couldn't stop thinking about it.

Susan seemed to think it was a great idea, and Nonna had talked to Lacey over breakfast about how wonderful it would be to have Vito there and to get to know the newest member of the family. Her eyes had sparkled when she said that, and few enough things had brought a sparkle to Nonna's eyes since the heart attack.

There were all kinds of reasons to embrace the idea of Vito and Charlie moving in, but Lacey still felt uneasy about it.

She couldn't begin to articulate why, even to herself.

At lunchtime, Vito stood outside the Chatterbox Café, looking up at the town's outdoor clock, which clearly showed it was only eleven forty-five. He was early. Why had he come so early?

He loosened the itchy collar of his new button-down shirt. He shouldn't have worn a brand-new shirt today, should have at least washed it first, except that he was living out of a suitcase and he'd been rushing to get Charlie ready to go and there hadn't been the chance.

He could have just worn an old, comfortable shirt, but the fact was, he was trying to look good. Which was obviously a losing battle.

It wasn't about Lacey. It was about the fact that he'd probably see other people he knew here at the Chatterbox, and he needed to present a professional image. He had good benefits from the VA—they were paying for his online degree—but a man needed to work, and Vito would be looking for a part-time job just as soon as he'd found a place to live and gotten Charlie settled.

Maybe something with kids, since he was looking to become a teacher.

No, it wasn't about Lacey. He'd had some feelings for her once, but he'd turned those off when she'd married, of course. He'd been over her for years.

"Vito!" Lacey approached, a summery yellow dress swirling around her legs, the wind blowing her short hair into messiness.

She looked so beautiful that, for a moment, he couldn't breathe.

He crooked his arm for her to take it, an automatic gesture he'd learned at his *nonna*'s knee. The way a gentleman treated a lady. And then he remembered how she'd stepped away when he'd done the Italian thing and thrown an arm around her yesterday. He put his arm back at his side.

People are disgusted by your scars, he reminded himself. *And she hasn't seen the half of them.*

As they turned toward the café—Vito carefully *not* touching her—he caught a whiff of something lemony and wondered if it was her shampoo, or if she'd worn perfume.

Inside, everything was familiar: the smell of meat loaf and fries, the red vinyl booths and vintage tables trimmed with aluminum, the sight of people he'd known since childhood. Even the counter waitress, Nora Jean, had been here since he was a kid and called a greeting.

"Sit anywhere, you two. Lindy'll wait on you, but I'm coming over to say hello just as soon as these guys give me a break." She waved at her full counter.

Dion Coleman, the police chief, swiveled in his chair and stood to pound Vito on the back. "I'm glad to see your ugly mug," he joked. Which didn't feel awkward, because it was the exact same thing Dion had always said when Vito came home, even before his injuries. "Police business has been slow these past months, but with you home, it's sure to pick up."

Vito shook the man's hand with genuine pleasure. "I'll see what I can do about knocking down some mailboxes and shooting up signs, just to give you something to do. You're getting soft." He nodded down at Dion's flat belly and then at the grilled chicken salad on the counter in front of him. "Eating too much. Just like a cop."

"You never change." Dion was laughing as he sat back down. "Give me a call, you hear? We have some catching up to do."

Lacey had headed toward one of the few empty booths at the back of the café, and as he followed her it seemed to Vito that conversation stopped, then rose again when he'd passed. He rubbed a hand across his face, feeling the uneven ridges of his scars.

As soon as they sat down, they were mobbed. The young waitress could barely squeeze in to take their order. Everyone, friend or acquaintance, stopped by to say hello. They wanted to know where he was staying, how long he'd be in town, where he was stationed. Explaining that he wasn't in the army anymore felt embarrassing, since he'd always intended it to be his life's work. More embarrassing were the sympathetic nods and arm pats. People felt sorry for him.

But he kept it upbeat and answered questions patiently. Once people knew his story, they'd settle down some. And maybe someone would think of him when a job opening came up, so he made sure to let everyone know he was looking.

After people had drifted back to their tables and they'd managed to eat some of their lunch, Lacey wiped her mouth and smiled at him. "That got a little crazy. Are you wishing we'd gone somewhere else?"

He swallowed his massive bite of cheeseburger and shook his head. "Best to get it over fast. Let people get a good look."

She took a sip of soda. "You think they all came over to look at your scars?"

"That, and find out the latest news. But mostly to see how bad the damage is, up close and personal." His support group at the VA had warned him about people's reactions, how they might not be able to see anything but his scars at first.

"They're not looking at your scars in a bad way," Lacey said, frowning. "They're grateful for your service."

Of course, that was what most of the people who'd greeted them had said. And they weren't lying. It was just that initial cringe that got to him. He wasn't used to scaring people just by the way he looked.

His friend with severe facial burns had told Vito that you never really got used to it. "Older people do better, but young people like pretty," he'd said. "Makes it a challenge to get a date."

The waitress refilled his coffee cup and headed to a booth across the way. Vito gestured toward her. "You can't tell me someone like that, someone who doesn't know me, isn't disgusted when she first sees me."

Lacey looked at him for a long moment, her brown eyes steady. "Look over there," she said, pointing to a twenty-something man in an up-to-date wheelchair, sitting at a table with an older woman. "That's our waitress's brother," she said. "He served, too."

Vito blinked and looked more closely, seeing how the man's head lolled to one side, held up by a special support. He wore a hoodie and sweats, and as Vito watched, the older woman put a bite of something into his mouth.

"Wounded in service?"

Lacey nodded. "I think he was a Marine."

"Is a Marine," Vito corrected. "And I'm sorry. You're right. I need to get out of my own head. I'm more fortunate than a lot of guys." He met her eyes. "Gerry included, and I'm a jerk to focus on myself."

She shrugged. "We all do that sometimes."

Had Lacey always had this steady maturity? He couldn't help but remember her as a younger girl, pestering him and her brother when they'd wanted to go out and do something fun. And he remembered how flightily she'd fallen for Gerry, swept away by love and unable to listen to anyone's warnings.

Now though, there was real thoughtfulness to her. She was quieter than she'd been, and more assertive.

He liked that. Liked a woman who'd call him on his dumb mistakes.

And he didn't need to be thinking about how much he liked the new Lacey. Best to get to the real reason for their lunch. "So, I was looking into options for Charlie and me," he said. "I talked to the family Nonna rented her house to."

"And? Did you ask if they'd let her out of the contract?"

"I couldn't even bring it up." He lifted his hands, shrugging. "They're thrilled with the house and the price Nonna gave them, and they need the space. And she's pregnant out to here." He held a hand in front of his stomach.

"Well, look who's back in town!" Old Mr. Love from the hardware store, who had to be in his eighties, stopped by their table and patted his shoulder. "I'd recognize that voice anywhere!"

Vito stood and greeted the man, and then looked at the gray-haired woman with him. "Miss Minnie Falcon? Is that you?"

"That's right, young man. You'd better not forget your old Sunday school teacher."

"I couldn't ever forget." He took her hand, gently. Unlike some of the other kids in Sunday school, he'd actually appreciated Miss Minnie's knowledge of the Old and New Testament, and the way she brought the stories to life, infusing them with a sense of biblical history.

Mr. Love was leaning toward Lacey. "I was hoping you'd find romance." His voice, meant to be low, carried clearly to Vito and Miss Minnie. "Now that Buck's out of your hair, it's your turn, young lady." He nodded toward Vito, raising an eyebrow.

"Harold!" Miss Minnie scolded. "Don't make assumptions. Come on. Let's get that corner table before someone else takes it." She patted Vito's arm. "It was nice to see you. Don't be a stranger. We like visitors over at the Senior Towers." She turned and headed across the restaurant at a brisk pace, pushing her wheeled walker.

"When a lady talks, you listen." Mr. Love gave Vito an apologetic shrug as he turned and followed Miss Minnie, putting a hand on her shoulder.

After they were out of earshot, Vito lifted an eyebrow at Lacey. "They're a couple?"

"It's anybody's guess. They both say they're just friends, but tongues are wagging. It *is* Rescue River."

"Gossip central," he agreed, sipping coffee.

"And speaking of wagging tongues," she said, "imagine what people will assume about us if you come and live in the guesthouse. Just like Mr. Love assumed when he saw us together here. They'll think *we're* a couple. And I'm not comfortable with that."

"I understand." He looked down at his hands, traced a scar that peeked out from his shirt cuff. "I'm not exactly a blue-ribbon bronco."

"Vito!" She sounded exasperated. "You haven't changed a bit since you had to try on six different shirts for the homecoming dance."

The memory made him chuckle. He'd gotten her to sit on the porch and judge while he tried on shirt after shirt, running back to his room to change each time she'd nixed his selection.

Little did she know that Buck had begged him to keep her busy while he tried to steal a few kisses from cheerleader Tiffany Townsend, ostensibly at their house for help with homework.

"That was a long time ago," he said now. "And the truth is, I *have* changed."

She rolled her eyes. "You're still good-looking, okay? Women don't mind scars." Then she pressed her lips together as her cheeks grew pink.

His heart rate accelerated, just a little. Why was she blushing? Did *she* think he was good-looking?

But of course, she hadn't seen the worst of his scars. And even if there *was* a little spark between them, it couldn't go anywhere. Because he was living with a secret he couldn't let her discover.

"Look," she said, and then took a big gulp of soda. "Getting back to the idea of you and Charlie staying at the guesthouse. I'd be willing to consider it, for Nonna's sake, but... I'm trying to build a rich, full life as a single person, see, and I don't want everyone asking me questions or trying to match us up. I'm just getting over being Lacey, the pitiful widow. And now, if I have this good-looking man living in my guesthouse..." A flush crept up her cheeks again and she dropped her head, propping her forehead on her hand. "I'm just digging myself in deeper here, huh?"

She *did* think he was good-looking. All of a sudden, other people's curious stares didn't bother him half as much.

"Can I get you anything else?" The perky waitress was back, looking at Lacey with curiosity. "You okay, Lacey?"

"I need something chocolate," she said, looking up at the waitress but avoiding Vito's eyes.

"Right away! I totally understand!"

Vito didn't get women's obsession with chocolate, but he respected it. He waited until the server had brought Lacey a big slice of chocolate cream pie before blundering forward with their meeting's purpose. "I have an appointment tonight to talk to a woman who might want to rent me a couple of rooms in her farmhouse, out past the dog rescue. And there's the top floor of a house available over in Eastley."

"That's good, I guess." She toyed with the whipped cream on her pie. "But Nonna won't like having you so far away. And Charlie could make more friends in town, right?"

"He really took a shine to the place and to you, it's true."

"And Nonna wants you to live there. She pulled out all the stops at breakfast, trying to talk me into it again."

"She phoned me, too."

Lacey was absently fingering the chain around her neck, and when he looked more closely, he saw what hung on it.

A man's wedding ring. Undoubtedly Gerry's.

He wasn't worth it, Lace.

A shapely blonde in a tight-fitting dress approached their table. Tiffany Townsend. "Well, Vito D'Angelo. Aren't *you* a sight for sore eyes."

He snorted. "No." And then he thought about what Lacey had said: *Women don't mind scars.* And nobody, even a less-than-favorite classmate like Tiffany, deserved a rude response. He pasted on a smile. "Hey, Tiffany. It's been a long time."

"Where are you hiding yourself these days?" She bent over the table, and Vito leaned back in the booth, trying to look anywhere but down her low-cut dress. "We should get together sometime!" she gushed, putting a hand on his arm.

This was where a suave man would smile and flirt and make a date. But Vito had never been suave. He'd always been the one to console the girls whose boyfriends got caught on Tiffany's well-baited line. Always the friend, happy to take them out for coffee or a milk shake and to listen to them.

Unfortunately for his love life, it hadn't usually gone further than that.

Tiffany was looking at him expectantly. "Where did you say you're staying?"

"I'm not really…" He broke off. Did he really want to get into his personal business with Tiffany?

Lacey cleared her throat, grasped Vito's scarred hand and smiled up at Tiffany. "He's staying at my guest-house," she said sweetly. "With me."

"Oh." There was a world of meaning in that word, backed up by Tiffany's raised eyebrows. "Well, then. It was good to see you." She spun on her high heels and walked over to the counter, where she leaned toward Nora Jean and started talking fast and hard.

Vito turned his hand over, palm to palm with Lacey. "Thanks," he said, "but you didn't have to do that."

"Tiffany hasn't changed a bit since high school," Lacey said. "She'd break your heart."

"It's not in the market."

"Mine, either."

They looked at each other and some electrical-like current materialized between them, running from their locked eyes to their intertwined hands.

No, Vito's heart wasn't in the market. He had enough to do to rebuild a life and raise a boy and keep a secret.

But if it *had* been in the market, it would run more toward someone like Lacey than toward someone like Tiffany.

Lacey glanced toward the counter. "Don't look now," she said, "but Tiffany and Nora Jean are staring at us."

"This is how rumors get started." He squeezed her hand a little, then could have kicked himself. Was he flirting? With the one woman he could never, ever get involved with?

"That's true," Lacey said briskly, looking away. "And

we've obviously done a good job of starting a rumor today. So…"

"So what?" He squeezed her hand again, let go and thought of living at the guesthouse with Nonna and Charlie.

Charlie could walk to the park, or better yet, ride a bike. Vito was pretty sure there was one in Nonna's garage that he could fix up.

Vito could see Nonna every day. Do something good for the woman who'd done so much for him.

And he could get back on his feet, start his online classes. Maybe Nonna, as she got better, would watch Charlie for him some, giving him a chance to go out and find a decent job.

Soon enough, Nonna would be well and Charlie would be settled in school and Vito would have some money to spare. At which point he could find them another place to live.

He'd only have to keep his secret for the summer. After that, he and Charlie would live elsewhere and would drift naturally out of Lacey's circle of friends. At that point, it was doubtful that she'd learn about Charlie's parentage; there'd be no reason for it to come up.

How likely was it that Lacey would find out the truth over the summer?

"Maybe you could stay for a while," she said. "I'm opening the guesthouse this fall, officially, but until then, having a long-term guest who didn't mind noise would help out."

"How about a guest who makes noise? Charlie's not a quiet kid."

"I liked him."

"Well, then," Vito said, trying to ignore the feeling

that he was making a huge mistake, "if you're seriously making the offer, it looks like you've got yourself a couple of tenants for the summer."

Chapter 4

The next Wednesday afternoon, Lacey looked out the kitchen window as Charlie and Vito brought a last load of boxes in from Vito's pickup. Pop music played loudly—Charlie's choice. She'd heard their good-natured argument earlier. The bang of the front screen door sent Mr. Whiskers flying from his favorite sunning spot on the floor. He disappeared into the basement, where his companion, Mrs. Whiskers, had already retreated.

Some part of Lacey liked the noise and life, but part of her worried. There went her peaceful summer—and Nonna's, too. This might be a really bad idea.

She glanced over at the older woman, relaxing in the rocking chair Lacey had put in a warm, sunny corner beside the stove. Maybe she'd leave the chair there. It gave the room a cozy feel. And Nonna didn't look any too disturbed by the ruckus Vito and Charlie were creating. Her eyes sparkled with more interest than she'd shown in the previous couple of weeks.

"I'd better get busy with dinner." Lacey opened the refrigerator door and studied the contents.

"I used to be such a good cook," Nonna commented. "Nowadays, I just don't have the energy."

"You will again." Lacey pulled mushrooms, sweet peppers and broccoli from the fridge. "You'd better. I don't think I could face the future without your lasagna in it."

"I could teach you to make it."

Lacey chuckled. "I'm really not much of a cook. And besides, we need to work on healthy meals. Maybe we can figure out a way to make some heart-healthy lasagna one of these days."

As she measured out brown rice and started it cooking, she looked over to see Nonna's frown. "What's wrong?"

"What are you making?"

"Stir-fried veggies on brown rice. It'll be good." Truthfully, it was one of Lacey's few staples, a quick, healthy meal she often whipped up for herself after work.

"No meat?" Nonna sounded scandalized. "You can't serve a meal to men without meat. At least a little, for flavor."

Lacey stopped in the middle of chopping the broccoli into small florets. "I'm cooking for men?"

"Aren't you fixing dinner for Vito and Charlie, too?" Nonna's eyebrows lifted.

"We didn't talk about sharing meals." Out the window, she saw Vito close the truck cab and wipe his forehead with the back of his hand before picking up one of the street side boxes to carry in. "They *are* work-

ing up a sweat out there, but where would I put them?"
She nodded toward the small wooden table against the
wall, where she and Nonna had been taking their meals.
Once again, she sensed their quiet, relaxing summer
dissolving away.

At the same time, Nonna was an extrovert, so maybe
having more people around would suit her. As for Lacey,
she needed to get used to having people in the house, to
ease into hosting a bed-and-breakfast gradually, rather
than waiting until she had a houseful of paying guests
to feed in her big dining room. And who better than
good old Vito?

"There's always room for more around a happy home's
table," Nonna said, rocking.

"I guess we *could* move it out from the wall."

Vito walked by carrying a double stack of boxes,
and Lacey hurried to the kitchen door. "Are you okay
with that? Do you need help?" Though from the way
his biceps stretched the sleeves of his white T-shirt, he
was most definitely okay.

"There's nothing wrong with me below the neck."
He sounded uncharacteristically irritable. "I can carry
a couple of boxes."

Where had *that* come from? She lifted her hands and
took a step back. "Fine with me," she said sharply.

From above them on the stairs, Charlie crowed,
"Ooo-eee, a fight!"

Vito ignored him and stomped up the stairs, still carrying both boxes.

"You come in here, son." Nonna stood behind Lacey,
beckoning to Charlie.

Lacey bit her lip. She didn't want Nonna to overexert herself. And being from an earlier generation, she

might have unreasonable expectations of how a kid like Charlie would behave.

But Nonna was whispering to Charlie, and they both laughed, and then he helped her back to her rocking chair. That was good.

Lacey went back to her cutting board, looked at the stack of veggies and reluctantly acknowledged to herself that Nonna was probably right. If she could even get a red-blooded man and an eight-year-old boy to eat stir-fry, the least she could do was put some beef in it. She rummaged through her refrigerator and found a pack of round steak, already cut into strips. Lazy woman's meat. She drizzled oil into the wok, let it heat a minute, and then dumped in the beef strips.

"Hey, Lace." It was Vito's deep voice, coming from the kitchen doorway. "C'mere a minute."

She glanced around. The rice was cooking, Nonna and Charlie were still talking quietly and the beef was barely starting to brown. She wiped her hands on a kitchen towel. "What's up?" she asked as she crossed the kitchen toward him. "You're not going to bite my head off again, are you?"

"No." He beckoned her toward the front room, where they could talk without the others hearing. "Look, I'm sorry I snapped. Charlie's been a handful and…" He trailed off and rubbed the back of his neck.

"And what?"

"And… I hate being treated like there's something wrong with me. I'm still plenty strong."

"I noticed." But she remembered a similar feeling herself, after her miscarriage; people had tiptoed around her, offering to carry her groceries and help her to a seat in church. When really, she'd been just fine physically. "I'm sorry, too, then. I know how annoying it is to be treated like an invalid."

"So we're good?" He put an arm around her.

It was a gesture as natural as breathing to Vito as well as to the rest of his Italian family. She'd always liked that about them.

But now, something felt different about Vito's warm arm around her shoulders. Maybe it was that he was so much bigger and brawnier than he'd been as a younger man.

Disconcerted, she hunched her shoulders and stepped away.

Some emotion flickered in his eyes and was gone, so quickly she wasn't sure she'd seen it.

"Hi!" Charlie came out of the kitchen, smiling innocently. He sidestepped toward Nonna's room.

"Where you headed, buddy?" Vito asked.

"Lacey, dear," Nonna called from the kitchen. "I'd like to rest up a little before dinner."

"I'm glad she called me." Lacey heard herself talking a little faster than usual, heard a breathless sound in her own voice. "I try to walk with her, because I have so many area rugs and the house can be a bit of an obstacle course. But of course, she likes to be independent." Why was she blathering like she was nervous, around Vito?

"I'll help her." Vito went into the kitchen and Lacey trailed behind. "Come on, Nonna, I'll walk with you. Smells good," he added, glancing over to where the beef sizzled on the stove.

It *did* smell good, and the praise from Vito warmed her. She added in sliced mushrooms and onions.

For a moment, all she could hear was the slight sizzle of the food on the stove and the tick of the big kitchen clock on the wall. Peace and quiet. Maybe this was going to work out okay.

The quiet didn't last long. From Nonna's room, she could hear Charlie talking, telling some story. Vito's deeper voice chimed in. His comfortable, familiar laugh tickled her nerve endings in a most peculiar way. Then she heard his heavy step on the stairs. No doubt he was going up to do a little more unpacking while Charlie was occupied. Vito was a hard worker.

And just why was she so conscious of him? What was wrong with her?

She walked over to the sink and picked up the photo she kept on a built-in wooden shelf beside it. Gerry, in uniform, arriving home on one of his furloughs. Someone had snapped a photo of her hugging him, her hair, longer then, flying out behind her, joy in every muscle of her body.

She clasped the picture close to her chest. *That* was reality.

Reassured, she moved out the table and located some chairs for Charlie and Vito, almost wishing Buck hadn't taken her bigger kitchen table with him when he'd moved. She checked on the dinner. Just about done. She found grapes and peaches to put in a nice bowl, both a centerpiece and a healthy dessert.

"What's going on here?" She heard Vito's voice from Nonna's room a little later. He must have come back downstairs. She hadn't even noticed. Good.

Charlie's voice rose, then Nonna's. It sounded like an argument, and Lacey's patient shouldn't be arguing. She wiped her hands and hurried to check on Nonna.

When she looked into the room, both Nonna and Charlie had identical guilty expressions. And identical white smudges on their faces. Beside Nonna was a box from the bakery that someone had brought over yesterday. Cannoli.

"Dessert before dinner, Charlie?" Vito was shaking his head. "You know that's not allowed."

"Nonna!" Lacey scolded. "Rich, heavy pastries aren't on your diet. You know the doctor's worried about your blood sugar."

"She told me where they were and asked me to get them for her," Charlie protested. "And you told me I was supposed to treat older people with respect."

Vito blew out a sigh. "You just need to check with me first, buddy. And, Nonna, you've got to stick to your eating plan. It's for your health!"

"What's life without cannoli?" Nonna said plaintively. "Do I have to give up all my treats?"

Vito knelt beside his grandmother. "I think you can have a few planned treats. But sneaking cannoli before dinner means you won't have an appetite for the healthy stuff."

"I didn't anyway," Nonna muttered.

"Me, either." Charlie went to stand beside Nonna on the other side. Obviously, he'd made a new friend in Nonna, and that was all to the good for both of them—as long as it didn't lead to Nonna falling off the diet bandwagon.

It was up to Lacey to be firm, so she marched over and picked up the bakery box. "Whatever you men don't eat for dessert is getting donated tonight," she said firmly. "Obviously, it's too much of a temptation to have things like this in the house."

An acrid smell tickled her nose.

"What's that burning?" Vito asked at the same moment.

"Dinner!" Lacey wailed and rushed into the kitchen, where smoke poured from the rice pan. In the wok, the beef and vegetables had shrunk down and appeared to be permanently attached to the wok's surface.

All her work to make dinner nice and healthy, gone to waste.

She turned off the burners and stared at the ruined food, tears gathering in her eyes. In her head she could hear her mother's criticism of the cookies she'd baked: *you'll never be much of a chef, will you?*

She remembered Gerry shoving away his dinner plate the first night they'd come back from their honeymoon, saying he wasn't hungry.

Nonna was calling questions from her room and Charlie shouted back: "Lacey burned up dinner!"

The acrid smoke stung her eyes, and then the smoke detector went off with an earsplitting series of beeps.

This was not the serene life she had been looking for. She was a failure as a cook.

She burst into tears.

Vito coughed from the smoke and winced from the alarm's relentless beeping. He turned down the volume on his hearing aids and moved toward Lacey, his arms lifting automatically to comfort her with a hug.

She clung on to him for one precious second, then let go and looked around like she didn't know what to do next.

He needed to take charge. He shut off the smoke detectors, one after the other. Then he opened all the windows in the kitchen, gulping in big breaths of fresh air.

Lacey flopped down at the kitchen table, wiping tears. He beckoned to Charlie. "Run and tell Nonna everything's fine, but dinner will be a little late." As Charlie left the room, Vito scraped the ruined food into the garbage and filled the two pans halfway with soapy water. They'd need some serious scrubbing later.

Lacey was sniffling now, blowing her nose and wiping her eyes.

He leaned back against the counter and studied her. "How come this got you so upset? You're not a crier."

She laughed. "I am, these days. And I'm also a loser in the kitchen, in case you didn't notice. My mom always told me that, and Gerry concurred."

"Gerry?" That was a surprise. The man had eaten enough MREs in the military that he should have been grateful for any home cooking, however simple.

She pushed herself to her feet. "What'll we eat now? Nonna needs dinner. We all do. I guess, maybe, pizza? But that's not the healthiest choice for your grandma."

"Do you have canned tomatoes?" Vito asked her. "Onions? Garlic? Pasta?"

She nodded and blew her nose again. "I think so."

"Great. You sit down and I'll give you stuff to chop. I'm going to make a spaghetti sauce." He might not know what words to say to comfort her, but he could definitely cook her a meal.

"Spaghetti!" Charlie yelled, pumping his fist as he ran into the kitchen.

"That's right." Vito stepped in front of the racing boy. "And you, young man, are going to do some chores. Starting with taking out this garbage."

Charlie started to protest, but Vito just pointed at the

garbage can. Charlie yanked out the bag and stomped out of the house with it.

Lacey chopped and Vito opened cans of tomatoes and set the sauce to cooking. As the onions sizzled in olive oil, the day's tension rolled off him. When Charlie came back in, he had Gramps Camden, a weathered-looking, gray-haired man, with him.

Lacey gave the older man a hug, then turned to Vito. "You remember Gramps Camden, don't you?"

Vito stood and greeted the older man, who'd been a part of the community as long as he could remember.

"Wanted to pay a visit," he said in his trademark grouchy way. "See what you've got going on over here."

"You'll stay for dinner, won't you?" Lacey asked.

"Twist my arm," the old man said. "Cooking's good over at the Senior Towers, but nothing beats home-made."

Lacey asked Charlie to take a couple of bills out to the mailbox, and he went happily enough.

A knock came on the back screen door, and there was Gina, the woman Lacey's brother, Buck, had married, holding a toddler by the hand. "Hey, Lace, are you in there?"

"C'mon in." Lacey got up and opened the door for the woman, a rueful smile on her face. "Welcome to the zoo."

"Hey," Gina greeted Vito and Gramps Camden, and then turned to Lacey, holding the little boy by his shoulders as he attempted to toddle away. "Can you watch Bobby for ten or fifteen minutes? I have to run over to the Senior Towers to check out a few facts."

Vito's curiosity must have shown on his face, because she explained. "I'm doing some research on the town and the guesthouse. This place was a stop on the Underground Railroad and has a really amazing history."

"Laaaaas," the little boy said, walking into Lacey's outstretched arms.

"Hey, how's my sweet boy?" Lacey wrapped the child in a giant hug, and then stood, lifting him to perch on her hip. Her bad mood was apparently gone. "Look, Bobby, this is Vito. And this is Mr. Camden. Can you say hi?"

Bobby buried his face in Lacey's neck.

"Taking off," Gina said, and hurried out the back door.

Lacey cuddled the little boy close, nuzzling his neck, and then brought him to the window. "Look at the birdies," she said, pointing toward a feeder outside the window where a couple of goldfinches fluttered.

"Birdie," Bobby agreed.

"You're a natural," Vito said, meaning it. Lacey looked right at home with a child in her arms, and the picture made a longing rise in him. He wanted a baby. More than one.

And Lacey probably needed to have another baby. It would help her get over the pain of her devastating miscarriage.

Lacey set the table, having Bobby bring napkins along to help, letting him place them haphazardly on the table and chairs.

Vito tasted the sauce and frowned. "It needs something."

"I have basil growing outside. At least, I *think* it's still alive. Want some?"

"Fresh basil? For sure."

"Come on, Bobby." She helped the little boy maneuver across the kitchen and through the back door.

Could Vito be blamed for looking out the window to see where her herbs were planted? After all, he might do more cooking here. He was enjoying it.

And once he looked, and saw her kneeling in the golden late-afternoon sunlight, pointing and talking with Bobby, he found it hard to look away.

"Take a picture, it lasts longer," Gramps muttered. "Do I have to chaperone everyone around here?"

Vito blinked and went back to his cooking, but the image of Lacey, the curve of her neck, soft hair blowing in the breeze, stayed with him.

Who was he to think romantically about someone so beautiful, so perfect?

Half an hour later, they were about to sit down to a not-bad-looking dinner when Gina tapped on the back door.

"Mama!" Bobby cried and toddled toward the door.

She opened the door, scooped up her son and gave him a big loud kiss.

"You'll stay for dinner, won't you?" Lacey asked Gina.

"Oh...no. I would but... I need to get home." Her cheeks went pink and Vito put it together. She was a new bride, must have just gotten back from a brief honeymoon. She wanted to get home to her new husband.

Envy tugged at Vito's heart. Would he ever have a wife who was eager to return to him, or would he always remain just the best friend?

Dinner was fun. Nonna insisted they put on some Italian opera music—"the most romantic music on earth!"—and then got into a good-natured argument with Gramps Camden, who insisted that Frank Sinatra sang the best love songs. Her eyes sparkled with pleasure as everyone talked and joked and ate. Charlie enjoyed the company, too. Both of them would benefit from being part of a bigger family, Vito realized. He would, as well.

He just didn't know how to make it happen. But at least for the summer, it was something they could enjoy here at Lacey's. He would talk to her about having meals together as often as possible, splitting grocery bills and sharing cooking duties.

When he stood to clear the dishes, Lacey put a hand on his arm. "It's okay, Vito. You cooked, so I'll clean up."

"It's a lot," he protested, trying not to notice the delicate feel of her hand.

"I have an excellent helper," she said, letting go of Vito and patting Charlie's arm. "Right?"

"Sure," the boy said with surprising good cheer.

Of course. Lacey had that effect on every male of the species. Her charm wasn't meant specially for him.

"You can walk me back over to the Towers," Gramps said unexpectedly to Vito, so after a few minutes of parting conversation, the two of them headed down to the street. The Towers were almost next door to Lacey's guesthouse, and Gramps seemed plenty strong to get there on his own, but maybe he just wanted the company. Fine with Vito. He needed to get away from pretty Lacey, get some fresh air.

"How you handling those scars?" Gramps asked abruptly.

Vito felt the heat rise up his neck and was glad for

the darkness and the cool breeze. "Apart from terrifying women and children, no big deal."

Gramps chuckled. "It's what's on the inside that counts. Any woman worth her salt will know that. The kid over there seems like he gets it, too."

It was true; the few occasions Charlie still cringed away from Vito had more to do with leftover fears related to his mother's boyfriends than with Vito's looks.

They were almost to the front door of the Towers now, and Vito was ready to say goodbye when Gramps stopped and turned toward him. "Just what are your intentions toward Lacey?"

Vito pulled back to stare at the older man. "Intentions?"

"That's right. Some of us over at the Towers got to talking. Wondered whether you and she had more than a landlord-tenant friendship."

"Hey, hey now." Vito held up a hand. "Nobody needs to be gossiping about Lacey. She's had enough trouble in her life already."

Gramps propped a hand on the railing beside the door. "Don't you think we know that? For that matter, you have, too. The both of you have— What is it young folks call it?"

"Baggage," Vito said. "And we may be young compared to…some people, but we're not so young we need to be told what to do."

Gramps snorted. "Think you know everything, do you?"

"No. Not everything. Not much. But I do know my love life's my business, just as Lacey's love life is hers."

"Give it some thought before you mingle them together, that's all. I'd hate to see either Lacey or that boy hurt."

"I'd hate to see that, too." Vito lifted an eyebrow. "We done here?"

"We're done," Gramps said, "but have a care how you spend the rest of your evening over there."

And even though he found the warning annoying, Vito figured it was probably a wise one.

Chapter 5

When Vito walked back into the guesthouse, he heard dishes clattering in the kitchen. Lacey. Like a magnet, she drew him.

And maybe Gramps knew just what he was talking about. Being careful was the goal Vito needed to shoot for. A vulnerable woman and a vulnerable child were both somewhat under his protection, and Gramps didn't know the half of how any relationship between Lacey and Vito could cause damage to both of them.

He'd expected to see Charlie in the kitchen, but when he got there Lacey was alone, squatting to put away a pan.

"Hey," he said softly, not wanting to startle her. "Where's Charlie?"

She stood and turned toward him. "I told him he could watch TV. He was a good helper, but apparently, it's time for one of his favorite shows."

"Oh, right." Vito should go. He should go right upstairs, right now.

But in the soft lamplight, he couldn't look away from her.

She was looking at him, too, her eyes wide and confused.

He took a step toward her.

Leaning against the counter with one hip, she picked up a framed photo from the counter, studied it for a few seconds, and then placed it carefully on the shelf beside the sink.

"What's that?" He walked over but stopped a good three feet away from her. A safe distance.

She picked it back up and held it out for him to see. "It was Gerry's second time home on furlough. I'd missed him so much that when he came off the plane, I broke away from the other wives and ran screaming to hug him. Somebody caught it on film."

Vito studied the picture of Lacey and his friend, and his heart hurt. They *did* look happy, thrilled to see each other. "Could've been in the newspaper. Good picture."

"It was in the *Plain Dealer*," she said, smiling shyly. "That embarrassed Gerry. Me, too, a little. Everyone kept coming up to us to say they'd seen it."

"Gerry didn't like that, huh?" Vito felt sick inside, because he knew why.

Gerry had already been involved with Krystal at that point. Maybe she'd even been pregnant with Charlie. He thought about asking Lacey the year, and then didn't. He didn't even want to know.

How awkward for Gerry that his girlfriend might see his loving wife hugging on him.

Gerry had been such a jerk.

"He was everything I ever wanted," Lacey said dreamily, studying the picture. "Sometimes I don't think I'll ever get over him."

"Right. Look, I'd better go check on Charlie and catch some sleep myself." He turned and walked out of the room. An abrupt departure might be a little rude, but it was better than staying there, listening to her express her adoration of a man who'd not been worth one ounce of it. Better than blurting out something that would destroy that idealized image she had of Gerry.

Don't speak ill of the dead. It was a common maxim, and valid.

Was he making a huge mistake to stay here, even though that was what Nonna and Charlie both wanted?

He scrubbed a hand across his face and headed up the stairs. He needed to focus on his professional goals and forget about his personal desire to have a wife and a large family. He needed to make sure that personal desire didn't settle on Lacey, like Gramps seemed to worry it would.

He and Charlie were living in the home of the one woman he could never, ever be involved with. He'd promised Gerry at the moment of his death, and that meant something. It meant a lot. The sooner he got that straight in his head, the better.

On Friday, Lacey strolled along the sidewalk with Vito and Charlie and tried to shake the odd feeling that they were a family, doing errands together. It was a strange thought, especially given that her goal was to get her guesthouse up and running so that she could dive into her self-sufficient, single-woman life and make it good.

She just needed to keep in mind the purpose of this trip: to create a cozy room at the guesthouse for any child who came to stay for a night or a weekend.

It was only midafternoon, but with the arrival of summer, a lot of people seemed to be taking off work early on Fridays. A group of women clustered outside of the Chatterbox Café, talking. A young couple pushed their baby in a stroller. Several people she knew vaguely from the Senior Towers were taking their afternoon walk, and outside Chez la Ferme, Rescue River's only fancy restaurant, Sam Hinton stood with sleeves rolled up, talking to another man in a suit, smiling like he'd just tied up a deal.

"You're sure you don't mind focusing on Charlie's room right now?" Vito asked as Charlie ran ahead to examine a heavily chromed motorcycle in front of the Chatterbox. "It's not the project you were planning on, I'm sure."

"It's not, but it's a good change of plans. Having a room or two decorated for kids will only add to the guesthouse's appeal. And that little room off the big one is perfect for that."

"And you're being kind. Charlie's been in a mood, so maybe this will help." They reached Love's Hardware, and Vito held the door for her, then called for Charlie to come join them.

The front of the store was crowded with summer merchandise, garden tools and stacked bags of mulch and grass seed. A faint, pungent smell attested to the fertilizer and weed killer in stock. Farther back, bins of nails and screws and bolts occupied one wall while pipes and sinks and bathtubs dominated the other. Overhead, modern light fixtures, price tags hanging, intermixed with old-fashioned signs advertising long-gone brands of household appliances. The soft sound of R & B played in the background.

A string of small bells chimed on the door as it closed behind them, and the store's owner, Mr. Love, came forward immediately, one weathered brown hand extended, subtly guiding him through the store aisle. His vision wasn't the best, but he still managed his hardware store almost entirely on his own.

"Hey, Mr. Love, it's Lacey. And you remember Vito D'Angelo, right?"

"I sure do, sure do. Glad to see you folks on such a fine day." Mr. Love fumbled for their hands, and then clasped each in a friendly greeting.

"And this is his foster son, Charlie."

"Say hello," Vito prompted the boy, urging him forward.

Charlie scowled as if he might refuse. But as he looked up at Mr. Love, he seemed impressed by the man's age and courtly dignity. "Hi, it's nice to meet you," he said, holding out his hand to shake in a surprising display of good manners.

After Lacey had explained their mission, Mr. Love led them over to the paint section, where Charlie's momentary sweetness vanished. "I want this blue," he said, selecting a bold cobalt paint chip and holding it out as if the decision was made.

Lacey bit her lip. She'd told Charlie he could help pick out the color, but she and her future guests were the ones who'd have to live with it. "How about something a little lighter, Charlie? It's an old-fashioned house, and this is a pretty modern color." She offered up a sample card featuring various shades of blue. "I was thinking of something in this range."

"That's boring. I want this one."

"It's Lacey's decision, buddy," Vito said, putting a firm hand on Charlie's shoulder. "We're guests in her house, and she's nice to let you choose the color blue."

Charlie's lower lip stuck out a mile.

"Let's look at the cobalt in shades," Lacey suggested. "We could have that color, just a little lighter. Do you like this one?" She pointed at a shade halfway down the sample card.

"That one's okay." Charlie pointed at one toward the end, almost as bright as his original pick.

"Charlie. Lacey has the last word."

Lacey bent to see Charlie's downcast face. "I promise I'll take your ideas into consideration."

"Fine." Charlie gave Lacey a dirty look.

"Come on, let's go see the power tools," Vito suggested. "Guy stuff," he added, winking at Lacey.

Immediately, her distress about Charlie's attitude faded as her heart gave a funny little twist.

"I have to let my granddaughter mix the paint or she gets mad at me," Mr. Love said to Lacey. In a lower voice, he added, "I can't see the colors too well, but if you'd like, I can ask her to add in a little more white to whatever shade the boy picked."

"That would be fantastic," Lacey said gratefully. "Thank you."

"Don't you worry about young Charlie," Mr. Love said, patting her arm. "Kids usually come around."

That was true, and besides, Charlie wasn't her problem to worry about. But there was no point in explaining that to Mr. Love, so she let it go.

On the way home, they walked by a group of slightly older boys playing basketball in the park, and Charlie wanted to join in.

"No, buddy," Vito said. "We're painting today."

"I don't wanna paint! I wanna play outside!"

That made sense to Lacey, but Vito shook his head. "You can run ahead and play basketball outside the guesthouse for a while."

"That's no fun, playing by myself." But Charlie took off ahead of them, staying in sight, but kicking stones in an obvious display of bad temper.

Vito blew out a sigh. "Sure wish there was a manual on how to parent," he said.

"I think you're doing great," she said, reassuring him. "What's Charlie's background, anyway? Was it difficult?"

Vito looked away, then back at her. "Yeah. His mom's an addict. She loves him, but not as much as she loves to get high."

Poor Charlie. "What about his dad?"

Vito looked away again and didn't answer.

A sudden, surprising thought came into Lacey's head: was Charlie *Vito's* biological son?

But no. If Vito had fathered a child, he wouldn't deny it and pretend to just be the foster dad.

"His dad's passed," Vito said finally. "And Mom keeps getting involved with men who rough her up. It happened to Charlie a few times, too, which is why he originally went into foster care. His mom wasn't able to make a change, so Charlie's free for adoption. I hope we'll have that finalized within a few months."

"That's great, Vito." Even as she said it, she wondered how and why he'd gotten involved in foster care.

It was so good of him, but not something most single men in their early thirties would consider. "Why did—"

"Charlie learned a rough style of play in some of his old neighborhoods," Vito interrupted quickly, almost as if he wanted to avoid her questions. "And he doesn't have the best social skills. If he's going to play basketball in the park, I need to be there to supervise."

"You could stay with him now. You don't have to help me paint his room."

"Thanks, but no. It's only right that we help. And besides," he said, flashing her a smile, "it's what I want to do."

So they spent the afternoon painting as a team. Sun poured through the open windows, and birds sang outside. Stroking the brush, and then the roller, across the walls, soothed Lacey's heart. Again, more strongly this time, she got that weird feeling of being a family with Vito.

He was good around the house. He could fix things, he could paint, he could cook. And he liked to do those things with her.

Unlike Gerry, who'd always begged off family chores.

Charlie burst into the room, planted his feet wide and crossed his arms. He looked around the half-painted room, his lip curling. "That's not the color I wanted."

Something about his stance and his expression looked oddly familiar to Lacey, but she couldn't put her finger on what it was.

"The second coat'll make it brighter, buddy," Vito said. "Why don't you stay in here and I'll teach you to paint with the roller?"

"No way. That's boring." Charlie turned to stomp out and landed a foot directly in the tray of paint. When he saw what he'd done, he ran out of the room, tracking paint the whole way.

Vito leaped up and hurried after him, while Lacey raced to wipe up the paint before it dried on the hard- wood floors, chuckling a little to herself. With Vito and Charlie around, there would never be a dull moment.

"Oh, man, I'm sorry," Vito said as he returned to see her scrubbing at a last footprint. "Charlie's in time- out in the kitchen, since I can't exactly send him to his room, and he'll be back up in a few minutes to help. Neatly. To make up for this mess."

"It's okay. It's part of having a kid."

Vito sighed. "I guess it is, but I wasn't ready for it. I never know if I'm doing the right thing or not."

"You're doing a good job. Really good." She smiled up at him.

"Thanks. I don't feel so sure."

Just like the other night, their eyes caught and held for a beat too long.

Charlie burst into the room in sock feet and stood, hands on hips. "I'm here, but I ain't apologizing and I ain't helping." He lifted his chin and glared at Vito as if daring him to exert his authority as a father.

Vito opened his mouth to speak, but Lacey's heart went out to the hurting little boy, and she held up a hand. "Let me talk to him," she said, and walked over to Charlie. "It's been a rough day, hasn't it? But that paint came right off and it won't be a problem."

"So?"

In every stiff line of his body she read a need for a mother's comfort. "Hey," she said, putting an arm around him, "I'm glad you're here and I think this is going to be a great room for you. You can help decorate it."

For a second Charlie relaxed against her, but then he went stiff again and stepped away, his face red. "That's what you said about the paint, and then I got this baby color!" He waved a hand at the nearest wall.

"Oh, honey—"

"Don't call me that! Only my real mom can call me that!"

"Charlie…" Vito said in a warning voice, approaching the two of them.

"She doesn't have any kids! She's not a mom, so why is she acting like one?"

The words rang in Lacey's ears.

It was true. She wasn't a mom, and Charlie, with a child's insight, had seen right into the dream inside her head. On some barely conscious level she'd been pretending that Charlie was her child and Vito was her husband, and it had to stop.

Slowly, she backed away from Charlie just as Vito reached him.

"I want you to apologize to Miss Lacey," Vito said firmly.

"I'm not apologizing!" Tears ran down Charlie's reddened face, but he ignored them, frowning fiercely and thrusting his chest out.

"Charlie." Vito put a hand on the boy's shoulder.

"Don't you touch me! You're not my real dad. And you're ugly, too!" Charlie ran from the room.

Vito's hand went to his scarred face for just a moment, and then he followed Charlie.

Even in the middle of her own hurt feelings, Lacey wanted to comfort him, to tell him he *wasn't* ugly.

But that was exactly the problem. She wasn't the mom of the family. She wasn't the wife.

She never would play that role, and she needed to stop pretending and accept the truth.

Chapter 6

"Let's see if we can scare up a basketball game at the park," Vito said to Charlie the next day after lunch.

"Yeah!" Charlie dropped his handheld game and jumped up.

Vito laughed. He was still getting used to the time frame of an eight-year-old. "In ten minutes, okay? I have to clean up our dishes and make a phone call."

Vito had planned to spend Saturday setting up Charlie's room and looking for jobs online. But Charlie's behavior the previous day had changed his mind. Vito was no expert, but it seemed to him that Charlie needed structure, and chores, and attention. So they'd spent the morning weeding the gardens around the guesthouse, and with a little prodding Charlie had worked hard. He'd even taken a glass of lemonade to Lacey, who was sanding woodwork in the breakfast room, and Vito had heard her talk cheerfully to Charlie, which was a relief. Apparently, she wasn't holding a grudge against Charlie for yesterday's behavior.

So, amends made, Vito and Charlie half walked, half jogged to the park together, bouncing a basketball. Lawn mowers and weed eaters roared, filling the air with the pungent fragrance of vegetation, and several people called greetings from flower beds and front yards. Things weren't much different than when Vito himself had been eight, growing up here.

The call he'd made had been to Troy Hinton, an old acquaintance whose son, Xavier, was just Charlie's age. Troy and Xavier met them by the basketball courts at the park, and immediately, the boys ran out onto the blacktop to play. Vito and Troy sat down on a bench to watch.

Xavier played well for an eight-year-old, making a few baskets, dribbling without too much traveling. Charlie, though, was on fire, making well more than half of the shots he took. Paternal pride warmed Vito's chest. He'd make sure Charlie tried out for the school team as soon as he got to sixth grade.

"That's a good thing you're doing, fostering him," Troy said, nodding toward Charlie. "He seems like he's settling in fine."

That reminded Vito of yesterday, and he shook his head. "A few bumps in the road."

"Yeah?" Troy bent down to flick a piece of dirt off his leg.

"I think he misses his mom. He sees her once a week, but that's hard on a kid."

"Any chance of her getting him back?"

Vito shook his head. "No. Supervised visits is all."

"Gotcha." Troy was watching the two boys play.

Even at eight, Charlie used his elbows and threw a few too many shoves.

"Charlie!" Vito called.

When Charlie looked over, Vito just shook his head. Charlie's mouth twisted, and then he nodded.

"We talked about sportsmanship this morning. I don't know why he thinks he can play street ball here, in the park."

Troy chuckled. "It's a process. And Xavier's holding his own." Indeed, the boy did some fancy footwork and stole the ball from Charlie.

Which was impressive, considering Xavier's background. "How's his health?"

"Almost two years cancer-free."

"That's great." Although Vito had been overseas, he'd heard from Nonna about the careworn single mom who'd come to town to work at Troy's dog rescue, bringing her son, who was struggling with leukemia. Now Troy and Angelica were married, with another child, and it was great to know that Xavier was healthy and strong.

"He's doing so well that we can't keep up with him in the summer. So we've got him in a weekday program here at the park. Six hours a day, lots of activity. Charlie should join."

"Well…" Vito thought about it. "That's tempting, but Charlie has a few issues."

"People who run it are good with issues. And you should also bring him to the Kennel Kids." Troy explained the program for at-risk boys, helping once a week at the dog rescue farm Troy operated.

Vito had to thank God for how things were working

out here in Rescue River. It was a great place to raise kids. "Sounds perfect, if you've got a space for him."

"Might have one for you, too. I could use a little help."

"Oh, so that's how it is," Vito joked, but truthfully, he was glad to be asked. Vito liked dogs, and Troy. And most of all, he wanted to do positive things for Charlie, and with him. "Sure thing. I can help out."

The boys came running over, panting, and grabbed water bottles to chug.

"You guys should come play!" Charlie said, looking from Vito to Troy.

"Aw, Dad's too tired." Xavier bounced the basketball hard so it went back up higher than his head.

"Who says?" Troy got to his feet and grinned at Vito. "Hintons against D'Angelos, what do you say?"

"I'm not a D'Angelo," Charlie protested.

"But you're going to be, pretty soon." Vito stood, too, and ruffled Charlie's hair. "Meanwhile, let's show these Hintons how it's done."

After an hour of play that left them all breathless and sweating, Troy and Xavier invited Charlie to come out to the farm for a few hours, and Vito agreed. It was good for Charlie to make friends.

But that left Vito with a hole in his day. He'd finished the preliminary work for his online courses, and the term didn't start for another week. Nonna was spending the day visiting at the Senior Towers.

He thought of Troy Hinton, married, raising two kids, the town veterinarian and dog rescue owner, volunteering with the Kennel Kids. What was Vito contributing by comparison? And Troy had a big property to handle, a place for kids to run, while Vito was living in two rooms.

He walked through the park, feeling uncharacteristically blue. There was a soccer game going on, a coed team of kids a little younger than Charlie, and Vito stopped to watch. The game wasn't too serious. Parents chatted with each other in the bleachers while coaches hollered instructions, mostly encouraging rather than overly competitive. Nearby, a family with a new baby sat on a blanket, cheering on their kids who were playing while cuddling with toddlers who looked like twins.

Vito wanted that. Wanted a family, a large family. It was in his blood.

Suddenly, someone tapped his shoulder, and he turned to see Lacey and another woman, pretty, dark-haired, with Asian features.

"Hi!" the dark-haired woman said, holding out a hand. "I'm Susan Hinton. I've heard a lot about you."

What did that mean? He shook Susan's hand and shot a glance at Lacey. Her cheeks were pink. What had she been telling Susan?

"Vito D'Angelo," he supplied, since Lacey seemed to be tongue-tied. "It's a pleasure. Are you related to Troy?"

"Sure am. I'm married to his brother, Sam."

"I know Sam. Sorry to have missed the wedding." He'd been invited, but he'd been in the thick of his surgery at that point.

"Mindy could score," Lacey said, gesturing toward the soccer game. She looked like a teenager, dressed in cutoffs and a soft blue T-shirt. Her short blond hair lifted and tossed in the breeze, and Vito liked that she didn't glue it down with hair spray.

He felt an urge to brush back a strand that had fallen into her eyes, but that would be completely inappropriate. They weren't that kind of friends.

"C'mon, Mindy, go for it!" Susan yelled, and the little girl in question kicked the ball hard, making a goal. "Good job!"

"Susan's a teacher," Lacey said when the hubbub had died down. "She might have some good ideas about your career change."

"You're switching over to teaching?" Susan asked. "What age of kids?"

"I like the little ones," Vito admitted. "Seems like elementary teachers make a big difference."

"And we need more men in the profession," Susan said promptly. "Are you planning to stay local?"

"If I can find work."

Susan opened her mouth as if she were going to ask another question, but a shout interrupted her. Mindy, the child who'd scored a goal, ran over, accompanied by two little girls about the same age. "Did you see, Mama, did you see?"

"I saw." Susan hugged the little girl close. "You're getting better every day."

Vito was watching the pair, so it took a minute for him to become aware that the other two girls were staring up at him.

"What happened to the side of your face?" one of them asked.

"He looks *mean*," said the other little girl.

The remarks shouldn't have stung—he'd known that was how kids would feel, hadn't he?—but they did, anyway.

"Cheyenne! Shelby!" Susan spun and squatted right

in front of the other two girls. "You know it's not polite to make personal remarks about someone's appearance."

"I'm sorry, Miss Hayashi," one of them said right away.

"It's Mrs. Hinton, dummy," the other said. "Don't you know she got married?"

Susan put a hand on each girl's shoulder. "First of all, it's more important to be… Do you remember what?"

"More important to be polite than right," the two and little Mindy chorused.

"And furthermore, Shelby," Susan said sternly, "this gentleman got those injuries serving our country, and you *will* show him the respect he deserves."

Vito didn't know which felt worse: being told how bad he looked by a second-gradeish little girl, or being defended by a woman approximately half his size. "Hey, it's okay," he said, squatting down, too, making sure his better half was turned toward the girls. "It can be a surprise to see somebody who looks different."

Mindy shoved in front of him. "I'm *glad* he looks different. Different is cool." She reached up and unhooked something from her back and then started fumbling with her arm.

"Don't take it off! Don't take it off!" the other two girls screamed, sounding more excited than upset.

At which point Vito realized that Mindy had a prosthetic arm, which she seemed set on removing.

Other kids ran in their direction, no doubt attracted by the screams. Vito stood and glanced at Lacey, who gave him a palms up that clearly said she had no idea how to handle the situation.

"Mindy!" Susan's voice was stern, all teacher. "Don't you dare take off that arm. You know the rules."

Mindy's forehead wrinkled, and she and Susan glared at each other. Then, slowly, Mindy twisted something back into place and let go of her prosthetic. "I just wanted to show them that everybody's different, and that's okay," she said sulkily.

Susan knelt and hugged her. "That was a very kind impulse. Now, why don't you girls get back on the field? I think the second half is starting."

Vito took a step back. "Hey, it was nice meeting you," he said to Susan.

"Vito—" Lacey sounded worried.

"Got to go. See you later." What he really needed to do was to be alone. Today's little scene had hammered the truth home to him: he couldn't work with kids in person. His appearance would create a ruckus that would interfere with their learning.

The trouble was he liked kids. And interacting with them through a computer screen just didn't have the same appeal.

Lacey looked from where Susan was ushering the little girls back into the soccer game, toward the path where Vito was walking away, shoulders slumped.

"I'm headed home," she called to Susan, and then took off after Vito. She couldn't stand what she'd just seen.

He was walking fast enough that she was out of breath by the time she got within earshot. "Vito, wait!"

He turned around to wait for her.

"Where are you going? Are you okay?" she asked breathlessly.

"I'm going for a walk, and I'm fine." His words were uncharacteristically clipped.

"Mind if I come?" She started walking beside him, sure of her welcome. After all, this was Vito. He was always glad to see her.

"Actually…" He walked slowly, glanced over at her. "Look, I'm not fit company. Go on back and hang out with Susan."

She gave him a mock glare. "No way! You hung out with me plenty when I wasn't fit company. I'm just returning the favor to an old friend."

He started to say something, then closed his mouth, and mortification sent heat up Lacey's neck. She was being intrusive. It was one of her flaws, according to Gerry, and she half expected Vito to bite her head off.

But he didn't speak and his face wasn't angry. They walked quietly for a few minutes, past the high school. The fragrance of new-mown grass tickled Lacey's nose. From somewhere, she smelled meat grilling, a summer barbecue.

"Where are you headed?" she repeated, because he hadn't answered. "Can I tag along?" Then she worried she'd pushed too far.

"I'm going to the river. To think." He gave her shoulders a quick squeeze. "And sure, you can come. Sorry to be such a bear."

So she followed him down a little path between the grasses and trees and they emerged on the riverbank. As if by agreement, they both stopped, looking at the sunlight glinting off the water, hearing the wind rustle through the weeping willow trees overhead.

"I'm sorry that happened back there," she said. "That must be hard to deal with, especially…" She trailed off.

"Especially what?"

"Especially when you were always so handsome."

He laughed, shaking his head at the same time. "Oh, Lace. My biggest fan."

She had been, too. In fact, as a younger teen, she'd dreamed of a day when she'd be older, with clear skin and actual curves, and Vito would ask her out. A visceral memory flashed into her mind: lying on the floor of her bedroom, feet propped up on a footstool and CD player blasting out a sad love song, which in her fourteen-year-old brain she'd applied to herself and Vito's lost love.

"You were the best looking of all the guys in your class," she said. "Everyone said so."

He didn't deny it, exactly, but he waved a dismissive hand. "A lot of good it did me. I could barely get a date."

That had to be an exaggeration; she remembered plenty of girls noticing him. But it was true, he hadn't dated as much as you'd expect of a boy with his looks. "You were too nice. You weren't a player."

He laughed. "That's true, I never got that down." They turned and strolled along the river's grassy bank. "Now I look mean, like the little girl said. Maybe I should cultivate a mean persona to match. I'd get all the girls."

"As if that's going to happen." Lacey couldn't imagine Vito being mean. It just wasn't in his nature. "Is that what you want, Vito? All the girls?"

He gave her a look she couldn't read. "Not all. But I'd like to get married, start a family, and I'm not getting any younger."

"Is that why you're adopting Charlie?"

He lifted a shoulder and looked away. "That's part of it."

"As far as getting married," she said, "you could have any woman you wanted."

A muscle contracted in his scarred cheek. "Don't, Lace."

"Don't what?" She stumbled on a root and he automatically caught her arm, steadied her.

"Don't lie to me. If I couldn't get the girls before, I'm not going to get them now."

"I'm not lying. You have a…" She paused, considering how to say it. "You have a rugged appeal."

"Is that so?" He looked over at her, his expression skeptical.

For some reason, her face heated, and she lifted it to cool in the breeze from the river. She focused on the birdcalls and blue sky, visible through a network of green leaves, while she tried to get her bearings.

When she looked back at him, he was still watching her. "Think of Tiffany Townsend," she said, trying to sound offhand. "She was all over you."

He rolled his eyes, just a little, making her remember him as a teen. "Tiffany Townsend isn't what I want."

"What do you want?"

Instead of answering, he walked a few paces to the right and lifted a streamer of honeysuckle growing against a thick strand of trees. Beyond it was a cave-like depression in a natural rock wall. "Wonder if kids are still carving their names in here?"

She laughed. "Lover's Cave. I'd forgotten about it." She followed him inside, the temperature dropping a good few degrees, making a chill rise up on her arms.

Vito pinched off a vine of honeysuckle flowers, inhaled their scent, and then tucked them into Lacey's hair. "For a lovely lady."

Wow. Why wasn't Vito married by now? He was chivalrous, a natural romantic. Who *wouldn't* want to be with a man like that?

Inside the small enclosure, she turned to him, then stepped back, feeling overwhelmed by the closeness. *Make conversation; this is awkward.* "Did you ever kiss a girl in here?"

He laughed outright. "My *nonna* taught me better than to kiss and tell. Why? Were you kissed in here?"

"No." She remembered bringing Gerry down to the river, showing him the sights of her younger days. She'd hoped to finally get a kiss in Lover's Cave, but he hadn't wanted to follow her inside. Romantic gestures weren't his thing, but that was okay. He'd loved her; she was sure of that.

"What was wrong with the boys in your grade? Why didn't you get kissed here?"

"Guys didn't like my type." She turned away, catching a whiff of honeysuckle.

He touched her face, making her look at him. "What type is that?"

"Shy. Backward."

"Are you still?"

Lacey's heart was pounding. "I… I might be."

His fingers still rested on her cheek, featherlight. "Don't be nervous. It's just me."

A hysterical giggle bubbled up inside her, along with a warm, melty breathlessness. She couldn't look away from him.

He cupped her face with both hands. Oh, wow, was he really going to kiss her? Her heart was about to fly out of her chest and she blurted out the first nervous thought she had. "You never answered my question."

"What was it? I'm getting distracted." He smiled a little, but his eyes were intense, serious.

He was *incredibly* attractive, scars and all.

"I asked you," she said breathlessly, "what *do* you want, if you don't want someone like Tiffany?"

"I want…" He paused, looked out through the veil of honeysuckle vines and let his hands fall away from her face. Breathed in, breathed out, audibly, and then eased out of the cave, holding the honeysuckle curtain for her, but careful not to touch her. "I want what I can't have."

Suddenly chilled, Lacey rubbed her bare arms, looking away from him. Whatever Vito wanted, it was obviously not her.

Chapter 7

"Come on, Nonna, let's go sit on the porch." Vito was walking his grandmother out of the kitchen after dinner. Nonna hadn't eaten much of it despite his and Charlie's cajoling. Vito wished Lacey had stayed to eat with them, but she'd had something else urgent to do.

Most likely, urgently avoiding *him*. And rightly so. He was avoiding her, too, and kicking himself for that little romantic interlude in Lover's Cave.

"I'm a little tired for the porch, dear." Nonna held tightly on to his arm.

She sounded depressed, something Lacey had mentioned was common in patients recovering from a heart attack. Activity and socializing were part of the solution, so Vito pressed on. "But you've been in your room all day. A talk and a little air will do you good."

"Well…" She paused. "Will you sit with me?"

"Nothing I'd rather do." He kissed her soft cheek,

noticing the fragrance of lavender that always clung to her, and his heart tightened with love.

He and Nonna walked slowly down the guesthouse hall. She still clung to his arm, and when they got to the bench beside the door, she stopped. "I'll just…rest here a minute. Could you get me another glass of that iced tea? I'm so thirsty."

"Sure." He settled her on the bench and went back to the kitchen to pour iced tea, looking out into the driveway to see if, by chance, Lacey had come in without his noticing. He'd feel better if she were here. Only because Nonna wasn't feeling well.

When he reached the guesthouse door with the tea, he saw that Nonna was already out on the porch. "Charlie helped me out," she said, gesturing to where the boy was shooting hoops across the street. "He's a good boy."

He set their tea on the table between the rocking chairs and sat down. The evening air was warm, but the humidity was down and the light breeze made for comfortable porch-sitting. In fact, several people were outside down the block, in front of the Senior Towers. A young couple walked by pushing a stroller, talking rapidly in Spanish. Marilyn Smith strolled past the basketball hoop with her Saint Bernard, and Charlie and his friend stopped playing to pet it and ask her excited questions.

Evening in a small town. He loved it here.

"Tell me about your course work, dear," Nonna said. "Is it going well?"

"Just finished a couple of modules today. It's interesting material."

"And you like taking a class on the computer?"

He shrugged. "Honestly, I'd rather be in a classroom

where I could talk and listen, but we don't have a college here, and this is the easiest, cheapest option."

"That's just what Lou Ann Miller says. She's almost done with her degree. At her age!"

They chatted on about Vito's courses and Lou Ann and other people they knew in common, greeted a few neighbors walking by.

After a while, Vito noticed that Nonna had gotten quiet, and he looked over to see her eyes blinking closed. In the slanting evening sunlight, her skin looked wrinkled like thin cloth, and her coloring wasn't as robust as he'd have liked to see.

Lacey's little car drove into the driveway. She pulled behind the guesthouse, and moments later the back screen door slammed. Normally, she'd have come in by the front porch, stopping to pull a couple of weeds from the flower bed and say hello to Nonna. So she was still avoiding him, obviously, but at least she was home in case Nonna needed her.

Nonna started awake and looked around as if she was confused. "Tell me about your courses, dear," she said.

"We just talked about that." Vito studied her. "Are you feeling okay? Do you want to go inside?"

"I'm fine. I meant your job hunt. Tell me about your job hunt." She smiled reassuringly, looking like her old self.

"I keep seeing jobs that look interesting, but they're all in person." He paused, then added, "I want an online job."

As usual, Nonna read his mind. "You can't hide forever," she said, patting his hand.

"You're right, and I'm a coward for wanting to hide

behind the computer. Except…would you want your kids to have a scary teacher?"

"I'd want them to have a smart, caring teacher. And besides, once people get to know you, they forget about those little scars. I have."

It was what Lacey had said, too. It was what Troy had said. It was even what his friends in the VA support group said. He didn't know why he was having such a hard time getting over his scarred face.

And okay, he was bummed for a number of reasons. If things had been different, if Charlie hadn't needed a home and if he hadn't been so scarred, then maybe he and Lacey could have made a go of things. She'd seemed a little interested, for a minute there.

But things weren't different, and he needed to focus on the here and now, and on those who needed him. He glanced over at Nonna.

She was slumped over in her chair at an odd angle, her eyes closed.

"Nonna!" He leaped up and tried a gentle shake of her shoulders that failed to wake her. "Charlie, come here!" he called over his shoulder.

He lifted his grandmother from the chair and carried her to the door just as Charlie arrived and opened it for him. "Is she okay?" Charlie asked.

"Not yet. Get Lacey, now!" Vito carried Nonna into her bedroom and set her gently on the bed. He should never have encouraged her to go out on the porch. On the other hand, what if she'd fainted in her room, alone? What had brought this on? Up until tonight she'd seemed to be improving daily.

Lacey burst into the room, stethoscope in hand, and bent over the bed, studying Nonna. "What happened?"

"She wasn't feeling well, and then she passed out."

Lacey took her pulse and listened. "It's rapid but…" She stopped, listened again. "It's settling a bit." She opened Nonna's bedside drawer and pulled out a pen-like device, a test strip, and some kind of a meter. "I'm going to test her blood sugar."

Charlie hovered in the door of the room as Lacey pricked Nonna's finger, and Vito debated sending him away. But he and Nonna were developing a nice friendship, and Charlie deserved to be included in what was going on.

Nonna's eyes fluttered open. She was breathing fast, like she'd run a race.

Vito's throat constricted, looking at her. She was fragile. Why hadn't he realized how fragile she was?

Lacey frowned at the test strip, left the room and returned with a hypodermic needle. "Little pinch," she said to Nonna as she extracted clear liquid from a small bottle and injected her arm. "Your blood sugar is through the roof. What happened? It hasn't been this high in weeks!"

There was a snuffling sound from the doorway; Charlie was crying. Vito held out an arm, and Charlie ran and pressed beside him, looking at Nonna with open worry.

Lacey propped Nonna up and sat on the bed, holding her hand. "Are you feeling better? You passed out."

"Was it the cake?" Charlie blurted out.

Vito's head spun to look at the boy at the same time Lacey's did. "What cake?" they asked in unison.

Charlie pressed his lips together and looked at Nonna, whose expression was guilty.

"I… I gave him money…" Nonna broke off and leaned back against the pillow, her eyes closing.

"What happened?" Vito set Charlie in front of him, put his hands on the boy's shoulders and studied him sternly. "Tell the truth."

"She gave me money and asked me to get her cake from the bakery. I didn't know what to do! I wanted her to have a treat. She said it would be our secret. And she gave me the rest of the money so I could get something, too." Charlie was crying openly now. "I'm sorry! I didn't know it would hurt her.'"

Vito shook his head and patted the boy's shoulder, not sure whether to comfort or punish him. "Remember, you're supposed to come ask me, not just go do something another adult tells you to do. Even if it's Nonna."

"Is she going to be okay?"

"She'll be okay." Lacey gave Charlie's hand a quick squeeze. "But your dad's right. Don't ever bring her something to eat again without asking one of us."

Even in the midst of his worries, Vito noticed that Lacey had automatically called him Charlie's dad. He liked the sound of that.

But he was second-guessing himself for bringing Charlie to live here at all. The kid was eight. He didn't know how to properly assist in the care of a very sick elderly woman, and he didn't have an idea of consequences.

Nonna said something, her voice weak, and Lacey put a hand on Charlie's arm. "Let's listen to Nonna."

"I…told him…to do it. Not his fault." She offered up a guilty smile that was a shadow of her usual bright one.

"Nonna! This is serious. We're going to have to take you to the emergency room to get you checked out."

"Oh, no," Nonna said as Charlie broke into fresh tears. "I just want to rest."

Lacey bit her lip and looked at Vito. "I might be able to talk Dr. Griffin into coming over to take a look at her," she said. "It would be exhausting for her to go to the ER, and I *think* she's going to be okay once her sugar comes down, but I'm not qualified to judge."

"If you could do that, I'd be very grateful." He knew that old Dr. Griffin lived right down the street.

"Okay. Charlie, would you like to come help me get the doctor?"

Charlie nodded, sniffling.

"Could you run upstairs and get my purse out of my bedroom?"

"Sure!" Charlie ran.

Vito was grateful. Lacey had every reason to be angry at the boy, but she was instead helping him to feel better by giving him a job. But that was how she was: forgiving, mature, wise beyond her years.

"Doc owes me a favor," Lacey said quietly to Vito. "I'm sure he'll come, if he's home. Just sit with her until we get back. It'll only be five minutes."

He nodded, gently stroking Nonna's arm, and Lacey and Charlie went out the door.

Beside Nonna's bed was a photo of him and his brother as children. She'd taken them in and raised them after their parents' accident, putting aside her bridge games and bus trips to rejoin the world of PTA meetings and kids' sporting events. And she'd done it with such good cheer that he'd never, until recently, understood the burden it must have been to her.

Now it was time for him to return the favor. To make sure that she was getting the very best care she could.

Which meant that later tonight if, God willing, Nonna was okay, Vito needed to have a very serious talk with Lacey.

After ushering Doc Griffin out the door with profuse thanks, Lacey walked back into the guesthouse as Vito emerged from Nonna's room, gently closing her door behind him.

"She's already asleep," he said. "She's exhausted, but she said to tell you again that she's sorry."

Lacey shook her head and paced the hall. "I'm the one who should be sorry. I should have been keeping closer track of her food."

"She's an adult," Vito said. "She made a choice." But something in his voice told her he didn't completely believe what he was saying, and what he said next confirmed it. "If you have a minute, could we talk?"

"Of course." She gestured for him to come into the front sitting room as her heart sank.

She'd been avoiding him hard all week, since that crazy moment in Lover's Cave. She'd thought he was going to kiss her, and she was sure that expectation had shone on her face. But instead of doing it, he'd gently pushed her away from him.

He was too kind to give her a real rejection, but even his careful one had made her feel like a loser.

He stood in the middle of the room, looking more masculine than ever amidst the delicate Victorian furnishings, and she realized he was waiting for her to sit down first. Who had those kind of manners these days?

Vito, that was who. And she was starting to care for him more than she should. Even though he didn't return the feelings, and nothing would come of it, she felt guilty. What would Gerry think if he knew that she was looking at his best friend in a way she'd once reserved for him?

Or, if the truth be told, in a different way but with the same end game? Because there weren't two men in the world more different than Vito and Gerry. And while Gerry's confidence and swagger had swept her away when she was young, Vito's warm and caring style appealed to her now.

He was still standing, waiting, so she sank down onto the chesterfield and pulled her feet up under her, leaving Vito to take the matching chair. It was a little small for him. Good. Maybe this conversation would be brief.

He cleared his throat. "I was wondering if you've been avoiding me."

Lacey felt her eyebrows shoot up, and against her will, heat rose into her cheeks. "Avoiding you?"

He nodded patiently. "After what happened last weekend. You know, at Lover's Cave."

She blew out a breath. She'd hoped to avoid that topic, but here he was bringing it out into the open to deal with. "I, um…" She wanted to lie, but couldn't bring herself to do it. "Maybe a little," she admitted.

"I thought so." He leaned forward, elbows on knees, and held her gaze. "You don't have to worry about a repeat. And you don't have to stay away from your own house to keep me at bay."

Keep *him* at bay? But of course, chivalrous to the core, Vito would put it like that. Make it seem like she was the one rejecting him, when in point of fact, it had been the other way around.

She swallowed and tore her eyes away from his. And for the life of her, she couldn't think of what to say.

How could she respond when she didn't even know what she felt, herself? When these feelings about Vito tugged at her loyalty to Gerry, even making her question some of her husband's behaviors? When Vito didn't seem to share her attraction at all?

"The thing is," he said, "I'm worried about Nonna's care. If Charlie and I are keeping you from focusing on that, then we should move out."

"She wouldn't like that."

"But if you hadn't come home tonight, and known just what to do, and given her that injection, something much worse could have happened, right?"

Miserably, Lacey twisted her hands together, staring at the floor. "I'm really sorry. I can see why you think I've been neglectful."

"That's not it. I don't think you and she ever had an arrangement where you had to be here with her 24/7. Did you?"

"No." Honesty compelled her to add, "But part of the appeal of living here was that she'd have me around a lot while I remodeled. Which I usually am. It's just been a week of running errands instead of remodeling."

He nodded. "I've been too focused on my own stuff, too, and apparently, it's given Nonna and Charlie too much time to get into trouble together."

"Does Charlie understand that he's not to do that anymore?"

"Yes. He was pretty upset when he saw Nonna passed out. He's grown very fond of her." He looked into her eyes again. "And of you. You've been very kind to him."

"He's a good kid."

He nodded. "So, this arrangement is working out

well for Nonna, and well for Charlie. It's just you and me who need to manage our…interactions."

If he could be up front and honest, so could she. "I won't need to avoid you if you're serious about no re-peat of that. I… I'm not over Gerry, you see." She fin-gered the necklace where she wore his wedding ring. "I know it's been over a year, which some people say is enough time, but it's not. He was everything to me."

A shadow crossed Vito's face, and for the first time she realized that he didn't talk much about Gerry. She wondered why. They'd been close comrades, right? Close enough for Gerry to come home with Vito on leave from the army. "You know what he was like," she persisted. "What a great guy he was."

Vito nodded once. "I know what he was like."

"So you can see why…well, why it's hard to get over him. He'll always be my hero."

A muscle worked in Vito's scarred face. "I under-stand. And believe me, the last thing I want is to dis-place that feeling in you. So please, stay and care for Nonna and don't worry about Charlie and me."

He stood and walked quickly out of the room.

And Lacey stared after him, wondering why it seemed that he was leaving a lot unsaid.

Chapter 8

Vito was deep into finishing a research paper on the educator John Dewey when Charlie barged into his room. "Nonna's bored," he announced.

"Bored?" Vito came slowly back to twenty-first-century Ohio. "You're bored?"

"Well, yeah," Charlie said thoughtfully, "a little. But I came to tell you that *Nonna* is bored."

That brought Vito to full attention. "Did she ask you to get her sweets again?"

"No." Charlie shook his head vigorously. "She wouldn't. But she wants me to play a card game called Briscola, and it's too hard. And she wants me to watch TV with her, only I don't like her shows."

"I'll go spend some time with her." Vito ruffled Charlie's hair. "You probably want to go outside and ride that bike, don't you?" He'd fixed up an old one for Charlie over the weekend.

"Yeah," Charlie said, looking relieved that Vito understood. "Can I?"

"Let's see who's outside. If you stay on this block and be careful of cars, it's okay."

After he'd walked out with Charlie and made sure there were several parents in yards up and down the street, keeping an eye on the kids, Vito went back inside and headed toward Nonna's room. He'd stayed up late working on his research paper and spent most of the day on it, as well, and he felt like the letters on the computer monitor were still bouncing in front of his eyes. But it was all good. He was finding all the teaching theories extraordinarily interesting and it made him certain he'd done the right thing, enrolling in school.

Distracted, he tapped on the edge of Nonna's open door and walked in before realizing that Lacey was there, sitting beside Nonna, both of them engrossed in a television show.

A week had passed since Nonna's health scare and their talk, and they were settling into a routine in which Lacey spent more time at home. A routine that most emphatically did *not* include strolls to Lover's Cave. In fact, it barely included being in the same room together.

Lacey glanced up, saw him and looked away.

Nonna clicked off the television. "I can't believe he picked the blonde. I'm very disappointed in that young man."

"Well, she *was* the prettiest," Lacey said, laughing. "But you're right. I don't see the relationship lasting very long."

"Hey, Nonna." Vito bent over to kiss his grandmother's cheek, conscious that it was the first time he'd seen her that day. He'd been neglectful, working on this paper. He'd do better tomorrow.

The silver lining was that Lacey was spending more time with Nonna, staying home more. He'd heard her up at all hours, working on the renovations. Now, he realized guiltily that one reason she might be staying up late was that Nonna was needing her companionship during the day. Which was partly her job, but also partly his responsibility.

Lacey stood up. "I should go get some stuff done." It was clearly an excuse to get away from Vito.

Perversely, that made him want her to stay.

Apparently, Nonna felt the same. "Could you wait just a minute, dear? There's something I want to talk to you two about."

"O-kaaay." She sat down again with obvious reluctance.

Vito focused on his grandmother. "Charlie says you're bored, Nonna."

"Oh, my, bored doesn't begin to describe it." She patted Lacey's hand. "Although it's not for this one's lack of trying."

"I can't hang out as much as I'd like," Lacey said apologetically. "I've got to finish the renovations before the end of the summer, and there's so much to do. But I was thinking, maybe you're well enough to do more of the activities over at the Senior Towers."

"That's a great idea," Vito said, relieved. "Don't they have a bridge group?"

"Yes, and a drop-in lunch program, as well." Lacey smiled at Nonna. "You'd definitely get more exciting lunch choices over there than you get when I fix lunch.

And it would get you walking more, which would be great for your health."

"How does that sound, Nonna?"

She shrugged. "Good, I guess," she said. "But…" She trailed off, plucking at the edge of her blanket.

"But what?"

She looked up. "I need a project."

"Like what, a craft project?"

"No, I want to start something new. With people."

That made sense; Nonna wasn't a sit-home-and-knit type of person, or at least, she hadn't been. "Like when you started your baking club that burned everything? Or that barbershop quartet, back when we were kids?" Vito smiled, remembering the off-key singing that had emanated from the big old house's front room when the ladies came to practice. Both groups had been disasters, but entertaining for all involved. Everyone wanted to join in Nonna's projects because she was so much fun as a person.

It made all the sense in the world that she would want to do something like that again.

"Do you have any ideas of what you might want to do?" Lacey asked her.

"Well…" She smiled winningly.

Vito shook his head. "Nonna, when you get that look on your face, I get very afraid."

"What's the idea?" Lacey sounded amused.

Nonna pushed herself up, looking livelier than she'd been the past week. "All right, I'll tell you. You know the show we were just watching?"

"*Bachelor Matches*, sure," Lacey said. "But what's that got to do with you having a project?"

Nonna clasped her hands together and swung her

legs to the side of her bed. "I want to start a new match-maker service in Rescue River."

"What?" Vito's jaw about dropped. "Why?"

"I don't think—" Lacey began.

"You remember the stories from the old country," Nonna interrupted, gripping Vito's hand. "My Tia Bi-anca, she was a *paraninfo*. Known for matchmaking throughout our village and beyond. She continued until she died at ninety-seven, and the whole region came to her funeral."

Vito nodded, frowning. He did remember the stories, but he wondered what was behind this.

"I need to start with some test clients," she contin-ued, "and because of all you two have done for me, you can have the honor. For free!"

"Oh, Nonna, no," Lacey said. "I don't think this is a good idea. I don't want you to overexert yourself."

"She's right." Vito moved to sit beside his grand-mother. The last thing he needed was Nonna trying to match him up with some unsuspecting woman who would be horrified by his scars.

"If I don't do this, then what do I have to live for?" Nonna's chin trembled. "Why do I even get up in the morning? Of what use am I to the world?" She bur-ied her face in thin, blue-veined hands, her shoulders shaking.

Vito looked over at Lacey and saw his own concern mirrored on her face.

"Nonna, you have so much to live for!" she said.

"So many people who love you," Vito added, putting an arm around her shoulders.

"But none of it *means* anything!" she said, her face still buried in her hands.

Tears. Vito couldn't handle a woman's tears. "Oh, well, Nonna, if it's that important to you..."

"I could maybe see it if you get someone else involved to help you," Lacey said. "Someone sensible like Lou Ann Miller or Miss Minnie Falcon."

Nonna lifted her head, her teary face transformed by a huge smile. "Yes, they can help, both of them!"

"Good," Lacey said. "And not too much at once. Don't get carried away."

"It'll be just the two of you to start. Now, Vito. What do you want in a woman?"

Vito blinked. How had she recovered from her tears so quickly? Had he missed something?

Or had Nonna been hoodwinking them?

"Could you get me a tablet of paper, dear?" Nonna said to Lacey. "I don't want to miss a word."

"Here you go," Lacey said, handing Nonna a legal pad and a pencil. "And now I've got to get to sanding woodwork."

"Oh, stay, dear. I want to talk to you, too."

Lacey laughed. "Don't you think these interviews should be private?" She spun and walked toward the door.

Vito watched her go, thinking of Nonna's question. The truth was, he wanted someone like Lacey. But because of the secret he had promised to keep, he could never, ever have her.

The next Saturday, Lacey climbed out of her car at A Dog's Last Chance, Troy Hinton's animal rescue farm. As she stretched her arms high, she felt like a weight was gone from her shoulders.

Grasses blew in the soft breeze and looking off to the

fenced area by the barn, she could see one dog's shiny black fur, another's mottled brown and white coat. Beside her, the creek rushed, a soothing sound, and red-winged blackbirds perched on the fence.

It was good to get away from the guesthouse. Good to do something for others.

Good to get away from Vito and the constant tension of trying to avoid him.

He'd been in her thoughts so much lately, and in a confusing way. He was so hardworking—up late most nights at his computer, making steady progress toward finishing his degree. He spent time with Charlie every evening, getting involved in the life of the town, even lending a hand with the youth soccer team when one of the coaches had a family emergency.

And he was so patient with Nonna, whose matchmaking service was going full speed ahead, obviously giving the woman something fun to do, but in the process, making Lacey uncomfortable.

A shiny new SUV pulled up beside her car, and Lacey was surprised to see her friend Susan getting out. "Nice car!" she said, remembering the rusty subcompact that Susan had driven when she'd lived for a year at the unrenovated guesthouse.

Susan made a face. "Sam. Just because we're expecting, he thinks we need to have a huge vehicle. I had to talk him down from a full-size van."

"How are you feeling?" Lacey could now ask the question without even a twinge of pain, and that told her she was moving forward, getting over her miscarriage and ready to celebrate other people's happiness.

"I'm feeling great, but Sam treats me like I'm made of glass." Susan rolled her eyes. "He didn't want me to come today. He's afraid one of the big dogs will knock me down. Like I haven't done this eighty thousand times before. And like a stumble would hurt the baby!"

"He loves you."

"He does." Susan's eyes softened. "And he's a control freak. But speaking of men…how's Vito?"

Lacey shrugged. "He's fine. Seems busy."

"You don't see much of him?"

"Well, since he's staying at the guesthouse, of course I see him. But we keep to ourselves."

"By choice, or would you like to see more of him?"

Lacey met her friend's perceptive eyes and looked away. "It's by choice. He makes me nervous."

"Nervous? Why?"

Lacey shrugged. "I don't know. He's so…"

"Big? Manly?"

Lacey laughed and shook her head a little. "Something like that. Come on, you've got to show me the ropes before all the kids arrive."

Susan was a longtime volunteer at the Kennel Kids, and she'd talked Lacey into getting involved. Lacey's therapist thought it was a good idea, too—a way to be involved with others and kids, not necessarily babies but with people. Making a difference.

"Speaking of Vito…" Susan said as they approached the barn where the sound of dogs barking was more audible.

Or at least, that was what Lacey thought her friend had said. "What?" she called over a new wave of barking.

"He's here. Vito." Susan gestured toward the barn, where Vito and Charlie stood talking to Troy Hinton, who ran the place and the Kennel Kids.

Lacey swallowed. What was he doing here?

Just then, he turned around and saw her. "What are you doing here?" he asked, sounding surprised.

"My question, too." They both looked at each other, and Lacey saw in Vito's eyes the same ambivalence she felt herself.

Susan nudged her. "I'm gonna go get set up. Come over when you're ready. No rush."

"Charlie's doing Kennel Kids," Vito explained.

Relief washed over Lacey, along with something like disappointment. "Oh. So you're just dropping him off?"

"I'm…actually staying to help. Unless that's a problem?"

She lifted her hands, palms out. "No! No, it's fine."

Across the barn, Troy Hinton was hoisting a dog crate to his shoulder. "If anyone has a free hand, we could use your help here," he called.

Lacey moved forward at the same time Vito did, and they jostled each other. And then bounced apart like two rubber balls. "Sorry!" they both said simultaneously, and Vito stepped back to let her go ahead.

Lacey blushed as she hurried toward Troy. She started to lift a crate.

"Vito, could you help her with that?" Troy nodded her direction. "It's a heavy one."

So she and Vito took ends of the crate and followed Troy.

"Put it down there. We like to have a few crates out here for the dogs to get away from the kids. It's a tough gig for them. Could you two bring one more so I can get started with these kids?"

"Sure." Vito headed back, and then turned to see if she was coming.

She followed reluctantly. Why had she and Vito ended up together? Why wasn't it Susan over here with her?

"Hey, look, why don't you go ahead and help Susan?" Vito said, apparently reading her mind. "I can get that last crate."

"No, it's okay. I'll help you. It's too heavy."

Vito gave her a look. "I'm every bit as strong as I used to be, even if I do have a few injuries."

"I know that!" Then, ashamed of her exasperated tone, she followed him into the barn and took the bull by the horns. "I'm sorry if this is awkward, Vito. I wish it wasn't."

"You don't want to be around me?"

"It's not that. I just…" More seriously, she was worried he didn't want to be around her.

"Hey, D'Angelo, c'mon! We don't have all day here!" Troy sounded impatient.

Lacey flinched and stole a glance at Vito. That kind of thing had always made Gerry livid; he'd hated to be corrected. It was a guy thing.

Except, to her surprise, Vito laughed. "That's rich, coming from you, Hinton." And then he hustled over to the crate. "Guess we'd better get a move on."

She hurried to help him, wondering as she did what it meant that Vito hadn't gotten angry.

Had Gerry been unusually touchy?

She went to the crate and lifted the other side, breathing in the good smells—hay and animals. And maybe it was the thought of hay, but her necklace felt itchy on her neck.

"Dad!" Charlie ran over, his whole face lit up in a smile. "Can I get a dog? Mr. Hinton said they need homes." He jogged alongside them as they carried out the large crate.

Vito went still, looking at Charlie, then at Lacey. "It's the first time he called me 'Dad,'" he whispered.

Lacey wanted to hug both of them, but her hands were full, so she settled for a *"Wow"* mouthed across the crate as they continued carrying it out.

"Hey, Lacey," Charlie added, coming up beside her, obviously unaware of the emotions he'd evoked. "Want me to help with that? That's no job for a girl."

Lacey chuckled. "Girls can do a lot of jobs, including moving things. But yes, if you'd like to, you can take that corner." She winked meaningfully at Vito, warning him to slow down.

He gave a subtle nod, and something arced between them. It was nice to be able to communicate without words sometimes.

After they'd put the crate down, Charlie grinned at her. "*You* wouldn't mind having a dog around, would you, Miss Lacey?"

He was way too cute with that grin. She couldn't resist ruffling his hair. "I won't answer that on the grounds that it might incriminate me with your dad," she said, "but confidentially... I do like dogs."

"See, Dad?"

"Way to throw me under the bus," Vito complained, but there was a smile in his voice.

"Can we get one?"

Vito held up a hand. "That's not a decision we're going to make today."

Charlie looked like he wanted to whine, but shouts from a couple of newly arrived boys distracted him and he ran off. Vito watched him go, shaking his head. "It's hard for me to deny him anything."

A man Lacey knew vaguely emerged from the barn with two pit bulls on leads. As he approached the boys, Charlie took several steps back in obvious fear.

The man clearly noticed. "Hey, Troy," he called, "we have some new Kennel Kids here today. You want to give the bully breeds talk?"

She and Vito drifted over and listened while Troy explained that it was all in how the pit bull was raised, how some were taught to fight while others were raised in a gentle environment, how one always had to be careful in approaching a dog like this.

Troy's words triggered a thought. Charlie had apparently been raised in a rough environment, and he, too, acted out sometimes; he needed to be approached with care. But with love—the kind of love that Vito was so unselfishly offering him—he was starting, even now, to grow into his potential and to become the person God had made him to be.

She watched as one of the smaller pit bulls, a white female named Gracie, was brought out and went from boy to boy. The group started dissolving, some of the boys playing with puppies, others learning to clean kennels, others helping to leash and train dogs. Charlie knelt, and the white pit bull approached him slowly, cautiously.

"Hold out your hand so she can sniff it," Vito encouraged, and after a moment's hesitation, Charlie did.

Watching Vito, she saw someone so much more than the handsome older boy who'd protected her from school bullies when she was younger. He was fatherly now, a man, a hero. He accepted what had happened to him and ran with it, growing into a person of value.

But then again, the seed of the man he'd become had been present in the kind, handsome boy next door.

"Lacey!" Susan gave her a light punch on the shoulder, and she started and turned to her friend. "I've been trying to get your attention forever." She looked where Lacey was looking, and then a slow smile broke out across her face. "Are you *sure* you don't have feelings?"

"No! It's just Vito."

"Somehow, I'm not convinced."

"No way! The truth is, I keep thinking about Gerry."

One of the other volunteers turned. "Gerry McPherson? Boy, that guy was a piece of work."

Lacey cocked her head to one side, feeling her smile slip a little.

"What does *that* mean?" Susan asked, her voice protective.

Lacey looked at the other volunteer, and suddenly, she didn't want to hear what he was going to say.

And then Vito stepped up beside her. "Gerry McPherson was my friend and Lacey's husband." He put an arm around her, a tense arm. "And he died serving our country." His chin lifted a little and he gave the man a level stare.

The other guy raised his hands. "Hey, didn't mean anything." He turned and walked rapidly away.

Susan gave Lacey a curious look and went over to help one of the younger Kennel Kids, who was having trouble unhooking a black Lab's leash.

"Thanks." Lacey sidestepped away from Vito so she could see him better, and immediately he let his arm drop from her shoulders.

A chill ran over her where his arm had been.

What had the man meant, that Gerry was a piece of work?

She didn't want to face the tiny sliver of doubt that had pierced her.

A couple of hours later, Vito stood up from repairing a broken crate and was startled to find himself surrounded: Susan on one side and Troy's wife, Angelica, on the other.

"So, Vito," Angelica said, "what's going on between you and Lacey?"

"Not one thing. Why?"

"Oh, just wondering." The two women sat down beside him, each working on one of the broken crates.

He wasn't lying about nothing going on, at least not in a guy sense; there wasn't anything of the dating variety going on, that was for sure. On the other hand, there was a lot going on emotionally, every time he saw Lacey.

Man, that had been a close one with that stupid guy almost revealing something bad about Gerry. Lacey had looked so shocked and stricken that he hadn't been able to handle it.

She for sure still believed the best about Gerry. And that was good. He'd always remain a hero in her eyes.

And Gerry *had* definitely had a heroic side. In battle, there wasn't another man in the world Vito would've trusted more. They'd saved each other's skins more than once.

But the home front—specifically, women—had been Gerry's downfall. Something rotten in the way he was raised, or maybe the fact that he'd been so handsome and suave. Too many women had flocked to him, and Gerry hadn't ever been taught how to treat women with respect. To him, a woman who threw herself at him was fair game.

Any woman was fair game. Lacey definitely hadn't thrown herself at him; she wouldn't have known how. But she'd gotten swept away and before Vito could turn around and warn her, she'd gone and fallen for Gerry.

Vito had tried to talk her out of it, but that had been a miserable failure. Once someone was that far gone, you couldn't bring her back.

At that point, the only thing he could do was to insist that if Gerry wanted Lacey, he needed to marry her, not just use her and throw her away.

It had just about killed him to do it, because by that time, he'd thought Lacey was something pretty special himself. Talking his friend into marrying her was like cutting off his own arm. He'd had to admit, just to himself, that he'd been waiting for Lacey to get old enough that he could honorably ask her out.

Gerry had beaten him to it, had gotten in there and stolen her heart.

And he'd treated her despicably.

And now Vito was in a position of hiding Gerry's wrongdoing from the woman he still, if the truth be told, carried a torch for.

"Earth to Vito," Angelica teased, and he snapped back into the here and now. "You *sure* there's nothing going on?"

"I'm sure," he said heavily. "And there never will be anything going on."

Chapter 9

The next Friday, Vito heard a high-pitched shout from Nonna's room. "Vito! Lacey!"

He scrambled up from the computer and down the stairs on Lacey's heels. "What's wrong, Nonna?" she was asking as they both entered Nonna's room.

"Are you okay?" he asked his grandmother, who was sitting at the small writing desk looking perfectly fine. In fact, her color was better than he'd ever seen it.

Lacey put a hand on Nonna's shoulder. "You scared us. What's going on?"

"It's my first success," the older woman said. "I found you both dates for tonight!"

Vito had to restrain himself from rolling his eyes. Just what he needed, a blind date.

"Tonight?" Lacey sounded just as distressed as Vito felt. "I... I have plans."

Nonna's eyes sparkled behind her glasses. "The same

plans you've had for the past three Friday nights, young lady? A date with a paint can?"

Lacey smiled ruefully. "Actually...yes."

Nonna rubbed her hands together. "I hope you both have some dressy clothes. You'll need to be ready at six o'clock."

Vito groaned inwardly. The last thing he wanted was to put on a suit. "Why dressy? This is Rescue River."

"You both have reservations with your dates at Chez la Ferme."

"No way!" Vito said.

"That's not how you do a blind date, Nonna." Lacey's forehead creased. "For one thing, it's really expensive."

"You get coffee first," Vito added. And then he processed what Lacey had said and looked over at her. How would she know? Was she doing online dating?

He found her looking back at him with a similar question in her eyes, and he felt himself flushing. The truth was, he *had* put his profile up on a Christian dating site a couple of times. And he'd gotten no results worth pursuing, which he attributed to women being turned off by his ugly mug. Or his lack of wealth.

"What if we don't like them, Nonna? Then we're stuck spending hours together." Lacey sank down onto the edge of Nonna's bed, facing them both.

"Whereas with coffee," Vito added, "you can escape after half an hour."

"You're taking a negative attitude," Nonna said. "Why do you think you'll want to escape?"

Vito looked at Lacey, and she looked back at him, and they both laughed. And then he narrowed his eyes at her. So she *had* online dated. But when?

Nonna steepled her hands and stared down at the

floor. "I'm sorry," she said. "Do you want me to cancel the whole thing?" Her tone was desolate.

Vito looked at her bowed head and slumped shoulders and his heart melted. "No, Nonna, it's okay. I'm game. But just this once."

"Me, too," Lacey said with a sigh. "Who's my date?"

Nonna smiled gleefully up at them. "It's a surprise! You won't know until you get to the restaurant."

"Wait," Vito said. "We're *both* at Chez la Ferme tonight? Why there?"

"It's the only nice place in town. I'm so excited for you. You're going to have a wonderful time."

There was no trace of her former sadness, and Vito studied her narrowly. He had the feeling he'd just been manipulated.

"Be ready at six. You're meeting your dates at six thirty."

As they walked out, Vito couldn't help shaking his head. That Nonna. She really was a matchmaker, and she was also someone to whom he, at least, couldn't say no.

At five minutes before six, Vito came out of his room at the guesthouse. He'd driven Charlie over to a new friend's house, and as a result, he'd had to get ready quickly. Not that it mattered. Less time to spend in this necktie that felt like it was strangling him.

He needed to work on his attitude, he knew that. Maybe Nonna's matchmaking was God's way of finding him a partner, someone who'd help him fulfill his dream of building a loving family. Lacey wasn't the only woman in the world, despite what his heart said.

Halfway down the stairs, he caught his breath.

There was Lacey in a sleeveless blue dress that highlighted her figure and her coloring. She stood in front of an ornamental mirror, attempting to fasten a necklace.

Breathe. She's not for you.

He walked slowly the rest of the way down the stairs, watching her struggle with the small clasp. "Need some help?"

"Oh! Um, sure." She held out the ends of the necklace, her back to him, bowing her head.

Her neck looked slender and vulnerable. Her short hair brushed his fingers, soft and light as bird feathers.

He could smell her sweet, spicy perfume.

Breathe.

He fumbled a little with the tiny clasp, dropped one end, had to start over. "Sorry. Big fingers." But that wasn't really the problem. He knew how to fasten a necklace; he'd been doing it for his women friends forever.

Why did it feel so different with Lacey?

Why was he going slowly on purpose, trying to extend the moment, to stay close to her?

He finished and stepped back quickly, forbidding his hands to linger on her shoulders. "Whoever you're meeting tonight is going to be very happy."

She turned toward him, a smile curving her lips as she gave him an undisguised once-over. "Your date will be, too."

He laughed a little, shook his head. "My date is going to be in for a surprise, but not such a pleasant one."

"You look good, Vito." She reached up and, with one finger, touched his face. The bad side of it. "Except that there's a little shaving cream…right…here."

Their eyes met and her touch lingered on his face.

That soft, small finger, touching a place no one had ever touched, except in a medical capacity, made him suck in a breath. "It's hard to shave with...this." He gestured toward the ridged, scarred side of his face.

She let her hand open to cup his cheek. "I'm sure."

The moment lingered. He felt like he couldn't look away from Lacey's steady, light brown eyes.

Until Nonna opened her door and clapped her hands. From her room came strains of opera music. "Don't you both look gorgeous!"

Vito took a step backward and Lacey let her hand fall to her side.

"We clean up okay," he said, clearing his throat, trying to keep his cool. "How are we going to know our dates?"

"It's all set up at the restaurant."

Vito bit back a sigh and slid his hands into his pockets. "You're not going to tell us who, are you?"

"And spoil the anticipation? Of course not. That's just one of the things that will be unique about my matchmaking service. Now, you two had better get going."

That brought up another angle he hadn't considered. "Would it be awkward if we walked together to dates with other people?" he asked Lacey. "Or would you rather drive, with those heels?" *Which look spectacular*, he thought but didn't say.

"They're wedges—they're fine." Her cheeks were a little pinker than usual. "Um, sure, we can walk."

So they strolled together through the downtown of Rescue River, all dressed up. The evening air was warm, and shouts from the park indicated that families were enjoying the evening. Vito leaned just a little closer to Lacey to catch another whiff of her perfume, wishing with all his heart that he could spend this evening with her, as her date.

His thoughts toward his old friend Gerry, who'd

made him promise to keep Charlie's parentage a secret, were becoming more uncharitable by the minute. The man had been a hero and a friend, and Vito mourned the loss of him, but he couldn't deny resenting the promise that stood like a wall between him and the woman he was coming to care for more each day.

"Who do you think our dates are?" she asked, looking up at him with laughter in her eyes. "Will it be people we know or complete strangers?"

"Bound to be people we know. It's Rescue River. And Nonna knows the same people we do." He actually hoped it was someone who knew what he looked like, just to spare himself the awkward moment that often happened when people met him for the first time.

They approached Chez la Ferme to discover a small crowd of people waiting outside. "Looks like they're backed up. Hope Nonna really did make a reservation."

"Or not." Lacey made a wry face. "I do have that paint can waiting for me at home."

He chuckled. She wasn't any more into this whole game than he was. "Look, there's Daisy."

"And Dion." Vito lifted an eyebrow. Were the police chief and the social worker officially admitting they were a couple? Because being together at Chez la Ferme pretty much guaranteed that they'd be perceived that way.

"Hey!" Lacey hugged both of them, first Daisy, then Dion. "Long wait?"

"Not if you let them know you're here." Dion punched Vito's arm lightly. "Get with the program, my brother."

So Vito walked in to the hostess stand and gave his name.

"Oh, yes, Mr. D'Angelo. We've been expecting you."

The hostess gave him a broad smile. "Your table will be ready in just a few minutes."

Obviously, she was in on Nonna's secret.

Almost as soon as he'd exited the restaurant, while he was still walking toward his friends, the hostess came behind him. "Dion Coleman?" she called. "And Lacey McPherson?"

A slow smile crossed Dion's face. "Oh, your grandma," he said to Vito, shaking his head. And then he crooked his arm for Lacey. "Shall we?"

Lacey's eyebrows lifted as she looked up at the police chief. "Well, okay, then." She took his arm and the two of them turned toward the restaurant.

Vito's stomach seemed to drop to his toes as he watched the pair. He couldn't help noticing the details: the large squared-off college ring that glinted against Dion's dark skin, the expensive cut of his suit, the suave way he put a hand on the small of Lacey's back to guide her inside.

They were good-looking enough that several people in the crowd turned to watch. Or maybe the raised eyebrows were because Dion was linked with Daisy in the town's collective, gossipy mind.

Vito had known he couldn't be with Lacey himself, on account of Charlie. He'd almost—not quite, but almost—accepted that.

What he hadn't anticipated was how seeing Lacey with someone else would feel like a punch in the stomach.

And he should have known, because it had happened before, with Gerry. This exact same feeling: *You're not going to get her. She's going to choose someone else.*

*And you're going to have to stand there and be a man
about it. Do the right thing.*

Speaking of doing the right thing, he was being rude
to Daisy, standing there watching Lacey and Dion disappear inside the restaurant like a hungry dog, tongue
hanging out.

He schooled his expression before he turned to Daisy.
Was that a similar look on her face?

That brought him out of himself. He couldn't have
Lacey, and it was wrong to think she should save herself
for him, that she shouldn't find happiness with someone else. Dion was a good man, respected by everyone in town.

And now, he needed to go through with the evening's
plans as if he didn't feel gutshot. He didn't know Daisy
well, but he assumed that if Dion was set up with Lacey,
Daisy was probably set up with him. He turned to her.
"Any chance you're here for a blind date, too? Set up
by my grandma?"

"Yeah." She nodded. She didn't look enthusiastic.

He soldiered on, as he'd been trained to do. "Well,
you didn't get the prize," he said, "but you'll get a good
dinner. I think I'm your date."

"Oh. Okay." She didn't sound thrilled, but not horrified, either. "What do you mean, not the prize?"

He gestured vaguely toward the scarred side of his
face. "Only a doting grandma could love this mug."

She didn't deny the ugliness of his scars, but she
shrugged them away. "Most women care more about
what's inside. Whereas men…" She trailed off, and then
glanced down at her own curvy body. "I'm not the prize,
either, compared to her." She gestured toward the door
through which Dion and Lacey had disappeared.

It was true. Vito didn't find Daisy as attractive as he found Lacey. But then, he didn't find *any* woman that attractive. For better or worse, his heart had attached itself to Lacey, and he was realizing more every minute that his wasn't the kind of heart that could easily change directions. Still, Daisy—blonde, vivacious and with a killer smile—was something of a showstopper herself. And he wasn't going to be rude to her. "You *are* a prize. Anyone with any sense would wonder how someone like me got to go out with a knockout like you. I'm honored to be your date."

The crowd by the door was thinning out, and a bench opened up. "Want to sit down?"

So they sat, and talked about her work in social services, and his desire to become a teacher. She was a good conversationalist, easy to talk to. He found himself confessing his worries about scaring kids, his desire to work with them in person, and his pretty-sure decision to go with online teaching. When the hostess called them to go inside, she had to do it several times, apparently, from her expression when she came out to get them.

As they followed her into the restaurant, replete with stained glass and low lighting and good smells of bread and prime rib, they kept talking.

"Don't do online teaching if your heart is in the real classroom," she urged him as they crossed the restaurant behind the maître d'. "Kids respond to the whole person, not just how you look. I used to worry about them teasing me about my weight, but they're completely fine with it."

"As are most men," he assured her. "Women think we all like stick-skinny women, but that's not the case. You're beautiful."

"Your table, sir." The maître d' gestured, and Vito held Daisy's chair for her.

Only then did he realize that Dion and Lacey were just around a small corner from them, probably within earshot of most things they would say.

Not only that, but the two of them were leaning toward each other, sharing an appetizer and appearing to have a marvelous time.

Chapter 10

Lacey looked at the handsome man across the table from her and tried to ignore Vito and Daisy being seated practically right behind them.

Unfortunately, she couldn't ignore what she'd heard. "You're a beautiful woman," Vito had said to Daisy.

Which was true, and she didn't begrudge Daisy the praise, but the way it stung alerted her to something she hadn't quite realized before: she wanted Vito for herself.

"Hey," Dion said. "What's going on?"

She shrugged and toyed with her water glass.

"All of a sudden you're not comfortable," he said. "Is it something I said?"

"No! No, you're fine. What were we talking about?" She laughed nervously. "I'm sorry, I'm a little intimidated."

His forehead creased. "Intimidated? Why?"

"You're kind of known for your wisdom," she said, "not to mention that you're the police chief."

"Which is all a nice way of saying I'm an old man," he said, "who's fortunate to be out with a fine-looking young woman."

The words were gallant, but Lacey could tell Dion wasn't interested in her in *that* way. Rather than feeling insulted, she felt relieved and suddenly more comfortable. This was a little awkward, especially with Vito and Daisy so close, but at least she knew she wasn't misleading Dion.

"I'm the fortunate one," she said. "I might pick your brain about some Bible stuff. You're said to know everything there is to know."

"Who says that?"

"Angelica's husband, Troy. He thinks you're the font of all wisdom. And my brother's a fan, too."

"Don't you be thinking I'm perfect," he warned. "Nobody's perfect. Nobody's even close, right? That's what the good book says."

"See, you're making my point for me, quoting scripture at the drop of a hat." She frowned. "Anyway, of course, you're right. But I've spent my whole life trying to be good. Trying to be perfect."

"We all try," he said, "and that's not bad."

She did her best to ignore the rumble of Vito's voice behind her, but it played along her nerve endings like an instrument. She forced it away, forced herself to talk with Dion about her brother, with whom he'd had a good deal of official contact until Buck had dried out and they'd become friends. She forced herself to rave over the delicious, beautifully presented food: Dion's prime rib, her own organic grilled salmon.

"That was great," she said when they'd pushed away their plates.

"Yes, it was," he said, "but let me ask you something. Are you in this matchmaking thing for real?"

She looked at him and slowly shook her head. "Not really. I'm just doing it for Nonna. You?" She only asked the question to be polite, because she was pretty sure of the answer. "I always heard you were with Daisy."

"Everyone thinks that," he said, smoothly changing the subject. "You're a newish widow. It makes sense you're not ready to do a lot of dating."

"Yeah. I... I really loved my husband."

Dion didn't say, "He was a good guy." That would normally be the remark you made, wouldn't it? But instead, he said, "That's obvious. Gerry was blessed to have you. But—" he raised a finger and pinned her with a steady gaze "—at some point, you're going to have to move on. You're too young of a woman to give up on life."

She wasn't going to tell him about her infertility. Instead, she turned the tables. "Do you take your own advice?"

Dion cocked his head to one side, smiling at her. "Touché. I've been on my own a lot longer than you have, and I should probably be letting go of some baggage by now."

She wanted to ask him about his past, but the way his face closed when he mentioned it told her she shouldn't. "Moving on isn't as easy as it sounds, is it?"

"No," he said. "But let your feelings lead and you'll be fine. Your feelings and your heart. And most of all, the Lord."

Well, if she were to let her feelings lead... Involuntarily, she glanced over at Vito and then back at Dion. "I'm ashamed to say that I haven't spent much time consulting the Lord about this," she admitted.

The server took their plates away and promised to be right back with the dessert tray. "There's no time like the present," Dion said, "to take it to the Lord. Want to?"

So she let him take her hand in his, closed her eyes, listened to Dion's quiet words and said a few herself. Asked for forgiveness that she'd neglected to seek God's guidance in her feelings. Asked Him to lead her in the right direction.

When they were finished, she felt cleansed.

"And now," Dion said, "if we can get their attention, do you think we should move our table together with our friends for dessert?"

"I, um, I don't know if Nonna would approve."

"Nonna's not here, is she? Hey, Vito." Dion caught his attention and made the suggestion, and the servers rushed to help, assuring them it was no problem.

Once they were all sitting together, there was a slightly awkward silence, broken by the approach of the dessert tray. The waiter began to describe the offerings.

Lacey looked over at Daisy. "I need chocolate. Now. You?"

"I agree."

After a restless night, Vito woke Charlie up early, figuring they'd grab breakfast and go burn off some energy on the basketball court. But even before they reached the main floor of the guesthouse, delicious smells of cinnamon and bread wafted toward them.

Could Lacey be up baking cinnamon rolls?

But when they walked into the kitchen, there was

Nonna in her Kiss the Cook apron, bending over to check on something in the oven and looking like her old self.

At the table was Miss Minnie Falcon, matriarch of the Senior Towers and former Sunday school teacher to almost every child in Rescue River. Next to her was Lou Ann Miller, stirring sugar into a cup of coffee.

"You're looking good, Nonna," he said, walking over to the stove and giving his grandmother a kiss.

"And that smells good!" Charlie came over as Nonna removed the pan from the oven. "Can I have some?"

"Five minutes, *cùcciolo*." She patted Charlie's shoulder, smiling.

Vito felt a great weight lifting off him, a weight he hadn't known he was carrying. Nonna was going to be okay. Suddenly he could see it and feel it and believe it. Not only that, but she'd called Charlie by the same affectionate name she used to use on Vito and his brother. That, more than anything, meant Charlie was becoming part of their family. He swallowed against a sudden tightness in his throat and walked over to greet the ladies at the table.

As good as her word, Nonna brought a steaming loaf of cinnamon bread, along with small cups of butter and jam, and placed them in the middle of the table.

"Italian breakfast like the old days." Vito put an arm around Nonna, still feeling a little misty-eyed.

Charlie's hand froze in the act of grabbing a piece of the bread. "Why is it brown?" he asked.

"Because I used the healthy flour. It tastes just as good, so eat up."

Charlie grabbed a piece, slathered it with butter and jam and took a huge bite before anyone else had even secured a piece. "It's good, Nonna," he said, his mouth full of food.

Vito leaned close to Charlie's ear. "Good table manners will get you more food," he whispered.

Charlie raised his eyebrows. "What'd I do?"

"Don't talk with your mouth full." They'd cover the grabby behavior later. First things first.

Miss Minnie put a clawlike hand on Vito's arm. "I understand you were our first matchmaking client," she said.

"Yes, tell us all about it." Lou Ann Miller raised a slice of bread to her nose and inhaled, closing her eyes. "Fabulous, dear. You've outdone yourself."

As Nonna beamed, the door from the backyard opened and Lacey breezed in. She wore a red-and-white-checkered shirt and cutoff shorts and she looked as carefree as she had at twelve.

And he was a goner.

"That smells amazing, Nonna D'Angelo," she said, approaching the table. "And look, whole grains! I'm impressed."

"Hey, Miss Lacey, you're not wearing your necklace."

Lacey's hand flew to her throat. "Oh, wow, I'll run up and get it before I eat."

"Want me to get it for you?" The words were out of Vito's mouth before he realized that he didn't, in fact, want to get her the necklace. Didn't want her to wear Gerry's wedding ring around her neck anymore.

"Oh, it's okay. I'll get it." She half walked, half skipped out of the kitchen.

"My Vito." Nonna pinched his cheek—the second time someone had touched his scars in the past two days. "Always too nice for your own good."

"That's right," Miss Minnie said unexpectedly. "Being kind isn't all there is to life. Take a stand!"

"What are you ladies talking about?"

Lou Ann Miller glanced over at Charlie, who'd grabbed his handheld game and was immersed in it, still chewing on a huge mouthful of bread. She turned back to Vito. "Your love life is what we're talking about."

Vito looked from Lou Ann to his grandmother to Miss Minnie. "Seriously? Is that what I'm doing wrong? Being kind and nice?" But of course, they didn't know about his Charlie deception, which wasn't nice at all.

"Tell us about last night," Nonna said instead of answering his question. She removed her apron and sat down at the table and looked up at him expectantly.

"It was…fine. Daisy is great."

"And you don't want to date her."

"Well, of course he doesn't. For one thing, she's attached to Dion Coleman at the hip."

"And then there's the fact that Vito's affections are elsewhere."

"That's obvious. The question is what can we do about it?"

The three women's conversation was spinning out of control. "Nobody needs to do anything about it," he protested. "I can handle my own life."

The only good thing was that Charlie wasn't listening; he was just eating bread and playing with his game.

Lacey came back into the room and Vito didn't know whether to be glad or sorry. He got busy cleaning up the breakfast dishes and washing mixing bowls and bread pans.

"How was your date with Dion?" Lou Ann asked her.

Vito couldn't help tuning his ears to hear what she

would say. They'd all ended the evening together, on a friendly note and laughing about various people's efforts to play matchmaker over the years, but Vito still had a sinking feeling he couldn't compete with Dion, suave and good-looking and successful.

And he *couldn't* compete, he reminded himself. He couldn't have Lacey, because telling her the truth would destroy her world. Destroy her image of the husband whose ring she wore around her neck.

"It was great," she said easily. "He's a lot less intimidating on a date than when he's being the police chief. Mmmm, this bread is good."

Vito glanced over to see three gray heads turn toward Lacey. "So," Nonna said, "do you like Dion?"

"She means *like* like," Charlie supplied, his mouth full. "Like a boyfriend."

It seemed like everyone in the room—except Charlie—was holding their breath.

"No, I don't think so." Lacey seemed unconscious of how much interest her words were generating. "And I don't think he likes me that way, either, but I'm glad to get to know him better as a friend. He's a good guy and a wonderful Christian."

Vito let out a breath and his tight shoulders relaxed. He grabbed a dish towel and started drying cutlery with great energy.

"I'm not really ready to date," she continued, fingering her necklace. "I'm afraid you're going to have to find some other clients."

There was a little commotion outside the door, and then it opened, framing Buck, Gina and little Bobby, who toddled across the room toward Lacey. "Laasss," he crowed reverently, crashing into her leg and hanging on.

"Hi, honey!" She lifted him onto her lap and tickled his stomach, making him laugh.

She looked beautiful with a baby.

She would look beautiful with *his* baby.

Man, he had it bad and he had to stop.

"Mind if the dogs come in, Lace?" Buck asked.

She glanced down at Mr. Whiskers. "Run while you can, buddy," she said, and then beckoned for Gina to let the dogs in.

Immediately, Crater, a large black mutt with a deep scar on his back, galloped in. At his heels was a small white mop of a dog, barking joyously.

Charlie threw himself out of the chair and started rolling and roughhousing with them.

Vito looked at the ladies to see if they found the ruckus disturbing, but they were watching and laughing. Bobby struggled out of Lacey's lap and toddled fearlessly into the fray.

Buck and Gina came over to the table and talked above the kids and dogs, and all the noise created a dull roar Vito couldn't really follow, given his hearing loss. His aids worked well with individual conversations, but big noisy groups were still a challenge.

He was wiping down counters when Charlie came over and tugged at his arm. He bent down to hear what the boy had to say.

"Can we get a dog now, Dad?"

That had been predictable. "Of these two, which kind do you like?"

"Can we get two?"

"No!"

"Then, I like the big one. Can we get one like that? With cool scars?"

The phrasing made Vito lift an eyebrow. Cool scars, huh? That scars could be cool was a new concept to him. "We'll start thinking about it more seriously," he promised.

Given how strong his feelings for Lacey had become, he had some serious thinking of his own to do, as well.

When there was a knock on the front door, Lacey hurried to answer it, relieved to escape the busy kitchen and the probing questions of Nonna D'Angelo, Miss Minnie and Lou Ann. Not to mention Vito's thoughtful eyes.

It was Daisy. "Hey, I was walking by, and I thought I'd take the chance that you were here. Do you have a minute?"

"Um, sure." She and Daisy knew each other, but they weren't drop-in friends. She came out on the porch and gestured toward a rocking chair, tucking her feet under herself in the porch swing. "What's up?"

"I just wanted to make sure we're okay about last night."

Lacey forced a laugh. "We were clearly all victims of the grandma matchmaking brigade. What happened isn't your fault or mine, or any of ours."

"And it was fun in the end, right?"

"Sure." As she thought back, she realized that it *had* been fun, sitting and laughing with Vito and Daisy and Dion. Except for that nagging anxiety at the pit of her stomach.

Daisy was watching her, eyes narrowed. "But…" she prompted.

Lacey shrugged. "Nothing."

"It's not nothing. I *knew* something was bugging you last night. What's going on?"

"Nothing's going on." She paused. "If you're worried about whether I like Dion, I do, but not as a boyfriend."

Daisy waved a hand. "I know. I could tell. And it's not my business, anyway. I *wish* Dion would meet someone."

Lacey lifted an eyebrow, but didn't comment. She couldn't tell if Daisy meant it or not.

"And I'm not interested in Vito that way, either."

Lacey tried to school her facial expression, but she couldn't help feeling happy. "I...wasn't sure."

"I mean, he's great," Daisy said, "but I'm pretty sure he only has eyes for you."

Lacey had thought she couldn't get any more joyous, but an extra wave of it washed over her at Daisy's words. "You really think so?"

Daisy nodded. "I sat and had dinner with him, and he was great, he really was. So nice and flattering and kind. But he couldn't stop himself from looking over at you guys every time you and Dion laughed."

A breathless feeling took Lacey over then. Maybe this—her and Vito—could really happen. Maybe it would. "Do you think it's wrong for me to think about another man, so soon after losing Gerry? As a social worker, I mean?"

Daisy studied her thoughtfully. "It's been over a year, right?"

She nodded.

"And what have you done to get over the loss?"

"Well..." Lacey thought about it. "I've had counseling, with a psychologist and with Pastor Ricky. And with some of my friends, too, unofficially. I'm doing desensitizing things about kids, because...did you know I lost a baby, too?" She was amazed that she could say the words openly now, with only an ache instead of a sharp, horrific pain.

Daisy nodded. "I heard, and I'm sorry for your loss. That must have been terribly hard to deal with."

"Well…yeah. The worst. And I never thought I'd heal, but Buck, and little Bobby, and the church… Lots of people have helped me, and life goes on."

The door flew open and Charlie emerged. He threw his arms around Lacey and said into her ear: "I think Dad's getting me a dog!" Then he ran down the stairs and across the street to the basketball hoop where a couple of neighborhood kids were playing.

Lacey looked after him and blinked. "That came out of nowhere. I thought he didn't like me."

"If you seem to pose a threat to his relationship with Vito, he may act out. On the other hand, he might very well need a mother figure." Daisy leaned back in the chair, rocking gently.

"A mother figure?" Lacey laughed. "Why would he think of me that way? I'm not even dating his dad."

"Yet. Charlie may see something that the two of you won't yet acknowledge."

Heat suffused Lacey's cheeks and she didn't know how to respond. Because the truth was, she was interested in dating Vito. After last night, watching him with Daisy, she was sure of it.

There was a fumbling sound at the door and Miss Minnie Falcon made her way out, struggling a little with her rolling walker. Both Lacey and Daisy jumped up to help her.

"Would you like to sit a spell on your old porch?" Lacey asked. She'd bought the house from Miss Minnie two years ago when it had become too much for her to handle, and she tried to encourage the older woman to maintain her connection. It made Miss Minnie happy, and as her brother's wife, Gina, had discovered, Miss Minnie and the house itself were full of stories. Besides, Lacey enjoyed the sharp-tongued woman's company.

"Thank you, dear. I wouldn't mind."

Lacey made sure Miss Minnie was settled comfortably while Daisy folded her walker and put it against the porch railing.

"It got a little too noisy in that kitchen. I like children, but in controlled circumstances."

"I hear you," Daisy said. "It's probably just as well I don't have children." Then Daisy's eyes went round and she looked at Lacey apologetically. "I'm sorry. I guess this is a sensitive topic for you."

"Kind of," Lacey said. Then, to her own surprise, she added, "Especially since I can't have kids."

"Never?" Daisy's eyes widened, and she reached out to give Lacey's hand a quick squeeze.

"That's what they say." She lowered her head, and then looked from one woman to the other. "Please don't tell anyone, okay? I... I'm still getting used to it. And it's not common knowledge."

"It shouldn't be," Miss Minnie said, her voice a little sharp. "Young people share far too much about themselves these days. Some things are simply private."

Daisy laughed. "I take it you're not baring your soul on social media, Miss Minnie?"

"My, no." The older woman turned back toward Lacey. "There are other ways to nurture children, besides bearing them."

Lacey opened her mouth to disagree, and then realized she was wrong. Miss Minnie knew what she was talking about from personal experience. "You taught Sunday school for almost all the kids in Rescue River, so I guess you're right. That's one way."

"And you're sure getting close with Charlie, from the looks of things," Daisy said. "Kids need all kinds of people in their lives to grow up right. Not just their parents." She turned to Miss Minnie. "Did you ever regret not having kids?"

Lacey flinched a little. That was definitely a personal question. Daisy was the type to ask them, but Miss Minnie was the type to offer a sharp reply.

"Not that it's commonly known, but of course I did," the older woman said. "That's the reason I taught Sunday school all those years. If you don't have a family, you have to do a little more figuring to build a good life for yourself."

"You may not have much family, but I hear you do have a boyfriend," Daisy said slyly.

Lacey smiled, remembering what she'd seen at the Chatterbox. "Mr. Love, right?"

"You young people and your gossip tire me out. I need to get back home." But a faint blush colored Miss Minnie's cheeks.

"We're sorry." Lacey stood to help the woman to her feet. "We don't mean to tease. It's just nice to see..." She paused to clarify her own thoughts. "It's nice to see a single person having a fun, active social life."

"That's right," Daisy contributed, picking up Miss Minnie's walker. "We single ladies have to stick together. And what's more, it's crazy that any time you're friends with a man, people start linking you up romantically."

Lacey and Miss Minnie glanced at each other as

they made their way down the steps. Was Daisy talking about Dion? Was she or wasn't she involved with him?

After they'd walked Miss Minnie back to the Senior Towers, they stopped on the sidewalk to talk before parting ways.

"You going to the fireworks tonight?" Lacey asked.

"Yeah, I love the Fourth of July. You?"

Lacey shrugged. "I'll probably watch them from the front porch, with Nonna."

"And Vito?"

"Stop trying to match-make," Lacey scolded. "You heard what Miss Minnie said. We all share too much about our personal lives." But even saying that felt hypocritical, because the thought of Vito, of watching fireworks under the stars together, made a delicious excitement fill her chest. "I'm sure he and Charlie will watch the fireworks, one way or another."

"Then I'm sure you'll enjoy plenty of fireworks," Daisy teased.

"Hey, now!" She watched the woman—who was maybe going to become a closer friend—wave and stroll down the street.

A fluttery excitement filled her. Maybe it *would* be a night to remember.

Or maybe not. She herself was starting to feel like a relationship with Vito might be possible. But she wasn't sure how he felt. With Vito, it always seemed to be one step forward, one step back.

Chapter 11

On Monday afternoon, Vito was tempted to turn down his hearing aids as he drove home from the dog rescue with Charlie and his new dog going crazy in the back. Had he just made a big mistake? What was Lacey going to think of this new, and very loud, guest?

At a stop sign, he looked back to check on them. Wolfie, the new white husky mix, stood eager in the giant crate Troy had lent them, bungee-corded in place in the bed of the pickup. Charlie was turned around as far as his seat belt would allow, poking at the dog through the open back window, talking nonsense to it, turning back toward Vito to shout "look at him, *look* at him." The disbelieving thrill in his voice and his eyes melted Vito's heart.

Whatever the challenges, he thanked God that he could do this for Charlie.

When they pulled into the guesthouse driveway,

Lacey was outside on her knees, weeding the narrow flower garden that fronted the house. Dressed in old jeans and gardening gloves, she looked up and smiled, brushing blond bangs out of her eyes with the back of her hand.

Vito felt an unbelievable warmth just looking at her.

They'd finally relaxed around each other, watching the fireworks together, eating Nonna's new, healthy concoctions, hanging around the house. Homey, domestic stuff. It was dangerous territory, but he couldn't resist reveling in it for a little while, at least.

He stopped the truck, and Charlie jumped out. "Miss Lacey, Miss Lacey, come see my new dog!"

She stood easily and pressed her hands to the small of her back, smiling, then headed toward the vehicle where Vito was opening the back hatch. "I can't wait to meet him!"

Vito opened the hatch and the crate, and Wolfie bounded out. He leaped up on Lacey, his paws almost to her shoulders, nearly knocking her down. Then he ran through the yard in circles, barking, his big feet tearing at Lacey's flowers. Finally, he approached Charlie in a play bow, his blue eyes dancing, his mouth open in a laughing pant.

"Sorry, sorry!" Vito ran to hook the new leash on to Wolfie's collar, but the dog darted away.

Charlie tackled the dog, and the two of them rolled on the ground together like a couple of puppies, while Vito struggled to find the ring on the dog's collar to hook on the leash.

Finally, he attached the leash and put the looped end in Charlie's hand. "Hold on to him!" he told Charlie, and then stepped back beside Lacey to watch the pair. "I'm sorry about your garden. I'll fix it. He's a little excited."

"So what happened to the concept of a small dog?" she asked drily.

Vito inhaled the scent of wild roses that seemed to come from Lacey's hair. "I know. I'm sorry. I should have called to make sure a bigger dog was okay. It's just… We were playing with a bunch of the dogs, and it was as if they chose each other."

"He was the one, Lacey! Isn't he cool?" Charlie rose to his knees as the dog bounded around him in circles, barking.

A smile tugged at the corner of Lacey's mouth, and in that moment, Vito saw her tenderness for Charlie and fell a little bit more in love with her.

"Well…we did have Crater here, and he was as big as…what's this guy's name?"

"Wolfie!" Charlie shouted, pouncing on the dog again.

"Hold tight to that leash while I get his stuff out," Vito warned, and then turned back to the truck and started unloading dog food and dishes. Rather than an expensive dog bed, they'd stopped by the Goodwill store; a big blanket would do for the dog to sleep on.

He was carrying it all up to the porch when Nonna came out.

"What have we here?" she asked, smiling.

"It's Charlie's new dog." Vito looked over in time to see the dog pull out of Charlie's grip and head for the porch.

Before Vito could do anything, Lacey dived for the leash and held on. The dog actually pulled her for a couple of feet before she was able to stop it. "Sit, Wolfie!"

she commanded, but the dog just cocked his head at her, his mouth open in what looked like a laugh.

Lacey sat up cross-legged and held the leash firmly. "Nonna, this dog's a little crazy. Make sure you're sitting down when he's around, and wear long pants until he settles down." To Vito she added, "He's strong and he's got big claws. He could knock Nonna down in a second, and those claws could scratch her up pretty bad."

"He knocked me down," Charlie said, almost proudly. "And he scratched me, too." He held up an arm. Even from this distance, Vito could see the thin line of blood.

They'd definitely start training Wolfie today.

"Why was Wolfie at the shelter?" he heard Lacey ask Charlie. "He looks like a purebred, and he acts like a puppy."

"He's two years old, and the people who had him said he was un, un…" He looked up at Vito.

"Unmanageable?" Lacey asked drily.

"That's it!"

Lacey rolled her eyes at Vito, looking exactly like she had as a teenager.

He put down the supplies and spread his hands. "I know. I know, and I'm sorry. It was just something in his eyes."

"Wolfie's, or Charlie's?"

"Both. Charlie fell in love with Wolfie as soon as he saw him, for whatever reason." He noticed the "I found a home" placard they'd gotten at the shelter. "Supposedly, we have two weeks to test everything out. If he doesn't work for us, we can choose another dog."

"And two other families tried him and he didn't work out, so he was really sad," Charlie said. "I hope we can keep him. We can keep him, can't we, Dad?"

Vito blew out a breath. "We're going to do our best to give him a good home. With love and attention and discipline, he should settle down."

"Like me," Charlie said offhandedly, and went to hug Wolfie. "Don't worry, guy. Dad let *me* stay."

Lacey's hand flew to her mouth and Vito felt his throat tighten. They glanced at each other, and it was as if they agreed without words: this *had* to work.

His phone buzzed in his pocket, and seeing that the dog was safely under Lacey's control, he pulled it out for a quick look.

He didn't recognize the number, but it was local. "Hey, I'd better take this just in case it's about a job," he said to Lacey. "Can you…" He waved a hand at Charlie, the new dog and Nonna.

"Got it," she said instantly. "Come on, Charlie. Let's see if we can teach him how to walk nicely on a leash."

The fact that she had his back so readily and without complaint made Vito's heart swell with gratitude. He clicked on the call.

"Vito D'Angelo? This is Sandra Sutherland, head of the school district's summer programs. You interviewed with one of my people last week."

"That's right." He sank down onto the porch step to focus. "What's up?"

"I'd like to talk to you about a job opening for this summer, with a possibility of extending into fall. How are you with special needs boys? Older, say from eight to sixteen?"

Without even thinking about it, he laughed. "That's getting to be my specialty." He looked down the street at Charlie.

She went on to detail the job of Vito's dreams: part-time for now, sports centered, mentoring and counseling a small group four mornings per week. "We thought you'd be perfect for it."

"Can I ask why?"

She spoke slowly, thoughtfully. "Your background as a veteran, your leadership experience and the fact that you're familiar with the foster care system all play into it. And…" She hesitated.

Why would she sound so uncomfortable? Even as he thought of the question, Vito's hand went to his face and he knew the answer. "Do some of the kids have physical disabilities? Visible ones?"

"That's it," she said, sounding relieved. "We actually have two boys, siblings, who were in a terrible house fire. They lost their mother, and they have some disfiguring burns. They've been acting out, even within the small group, so when Marnie came to me and said she had a good interview with you, and she mentioned your scars…"

Vito blew out a breath and looked skyward. Was this what God was doing? He'd never thought his scarred face would be an asset.

"Look, if you're interested and available, we could set up a time to talk. Sooner rather than later, though. Their current group leader just quit."

He couldn't help chuckling again. Between Charlie, and Wolfie the dog, and these boys, it looked like he was headed toward a career in rehab. "I'm free later today," he said, and they set up a time.

He clicked his phone off and just sat a minute, thinking.

He wanted a career in education, with children. But with his looks, he'd figured he couldn't do anything but online teaching. Now, come to find out, there was a perfect job within reach—partly *because* of how he looked.

Special ed. Physical limitations. He hadn't thought about it before, but he was definitely strong enough to lift kids in and out of wheelchairs. At the VA, he'd gotten to know guys with all kinds of disabilities. And with his own very visible scars, the students would know instantly that he understood.

Father God, You work in mysterious ways.

His heart beating faster, he looked down the street and saw Lacey and Charlie coming back toward the house, laughing, trying to manage the unruly Wolfie. He stood up and headed toward them. He wanted nothing more than to tell Lacey the good news.

A job, Charlie, and maybe Lacey. Everything he wanted was within reach. Under one condition: he had to figure out a way to tell Lacey the truth about Charlie.

Lacey looked up from trying to contain Wolfie's enthusiasm and saw Vito walking toward them, face alight with some kind of excitement. The call he'd gotten must have been good news.

"Dad! Dad!" Charlie bounced toward Vito, leaving Lacey to try to hold Wolfie back with both hands as he lunged after the boy he seemed to know already was his.

Vito ruffled Charlie's hair. "How's it going? We better help Lacey, huh?"

They came toward her and Vito took hold of the out-of-control dog's leash. "We need to figure out how to work off some of his energy," he said.

"That's what me and Lacey were trying to do! Only, he's so crazy and he doesn't know how to walk on a leash and he ran after a squirrel and we almost couldn't hold on!"

"He's excited, buddy. We'd better let him run in the yard at the guesthouse, if that's okay with Lacey."

"Good idea," she said. "He was about to yank my arm off!"

Once they'd gotten him inside the fence, they all ran and played with him. It didn't take long to discover that the fence had a broken section; Charlie and Lacey ran after the dog and brought him back while Vito did a makeshift fix. After Wolfie's energy finally started to calm, Vito and Lacey sat down on a bench together while Charlie lay beside the dog, holding tightly to his leash.

"So, finally I can ask. What had you looking so excited after that phone call?"

Vito's face lit up. "I might have a job."

As he told her about the offer, Lacey nodded. It sounded perfect for someone as nurturing—and strong—as Vito.

"I'm going to have to set up some doggie day care for Wolfie, I think, and Charlie has his park program, so we'll be out of your hair a little more if this all works out."

She tilted her head to one side, studying him. "You're the least self-centered guy I know."

He looked blank. "What do you mean?"

"Most men would be crowing and bragging about getting a job, but you're all about how to take care of your responsibilities and how it'll affect other people. That's…refreshing."

His eyes narrowed. "You sound like you've had some experience with another type of guy."

She looked at the ground, nodding, feeling guilty.

Lately she'd been having some realizations that were altering her view of her marriage, and it wasn't at all comfortable.

"Gerry?"

She hesitated a moment. But she could tell Vito, couldn't she? "Yes. I hate to say it, but he tended to think of himself first. When the time came to reenlist, he didn't even ask me—he just did it and bragged about it. And I was pregnant!"

"You're kidding. That wasn't right. You deserved better." He touched her chin, forcing her to look at him. "You deserve the very best."

She met his warm brown eyes and her heart beat faster. She didn't know about deserving the very best, but she had the feeling that being with Vito would *be* the very best. Maybe even, in some ways, better than being with Gerry. It was a disloyal thought that made her look away from Vito, but that lingered in her mind long into the night.

Two days later, Vito set out lawn chairs at the lake and pulled a picnic lunch—courtesy of the Chatterbox Café—out of the back of the pickup.

It was his way of making it up to Lacey for all the hassles of having a giant new dog in her guesthouse. He'd talked her into taking the day off with them—his last day off for a while, as his new job started tomorrow.

"I wish we could've brought Wolfie," Charlie said, his face pouty as he reluctantly helped unload the picnic basket. Since Monday, he and the dog had been inseparable.

"This is a good way to test out the doggie day care

where he's going to spend mornings. And Lacey needs a break."

Charlie made a face, and Vito sighed. The boy and Lacey had been getting along great, but when he was in a bad mood, he tended to take it out on everyone. He hadn't wanted to come to the lake because it meant being separated from Wolfie. And probably because Vito's new job started tomorrow. Even though it wouldn't mean much of an adjustment for Charlie, even though he liked his summer parks program, anything new was tough on a kid who'd had too many changes and losses in his young life.

"I'll take over if you want to check out the water," Lacey said to Charlie, coming over to the table. "Man, it's hot! I'm coming in as soon as we get our stuff set up."

She was wearing a perfectly modest black one-piece and cutoff denim shorts. With her blond hair and sun-kissed, rosy face, the combination was striking.

Very striking.

"Hey, Charlie!" came a boy's shout from the beach area.

"Xavier's here!" Charlie's bad mood dissipated instantly. "Cool!" Without asking permission, he ran down toward the water.

"Stay in the shallow part," Vito called after him. He waved to Xavier's mom, Angelica, who was sitting with several other women right at the dividing line between grass and sand. He pointed at Charlie and she nodded, indicating she'd keep an eye on him.

"Can he swim?" Lacey asked.

"Not real well. His old life wasn't conducive to swimming lessons."

She spread a red-and-white plastic tablecloth on the splintery picnic table and anchored it with mustard, ketchup and pickle bottles. "Speaking of his other life, how are his visits with his mom going?"

"Okay, when she shows up sober." She and Charlie had had two supervised visits since the first Sunday one. One of the other planned visits she'd canceled, and once, she'd shown up high, causing the social worker to nix her seeing Charlie. "Whether the visit works out or not, he gets upset. Tuesdays are rough."

"Well, let's make his Wednesday better." She flashed a brilliant smile at him as she set out a big container of lemonade. "Man, I'm hot. I'm going to go say hi to Angelica and dip in the water."

"I'll probably be down." Vito wiped his forehead on his T-shirt sleeve.

Before Iraq, he'd have whipped off his shirt and jumped in the water in a heartbeat. Now, though, he hesitated.

For one thing, he'd have to take out his hearing aids. And while he could still hear some, especially if a person spoke clearly and was close by, he couldn't keep up with conversations, especially when there was a lot of background noise.

Add to that the dark, raised scars that slashed across his chest and back, ugly reminders of the plate glass window that had exploded beside him that last violent day in Kabul. He'd taken the brunt of the glass in his chest, with a few choice gashes in his face and back.

Outside of a hospital, the only person who'd ever seen the scars on his torso was Charlie, and he'd recoiled the first time Vito had taken off his shirt in his presence.

To have a whole beach full of people do the same might be more than Vito could handle.

It wasn't that he was vain, but he hadn't yet gotten used to turning people off, scaring kids. And mostly, he couldn't stand for perfect, gorgeous Lacey to see how he looked without his shirt.

Hearing young, angry voices shouting down at the water, Vito abandoned his load of beach towels and headed toward where Charlie and Xavier seemed to be in a standoff.

"It's not *fair*." Charlie clenched a fist and got into fighting position.

"Charlie!" Vito shouted, speeding up to a run.

"Take that!" Xavier let out a banshee scream and brought his foot up in an ineffectual martial arts kick, at the same moment that Charlie tried to punch him.

Somehow, both boys ended up on the ground, which seemed to end the disagreement.

Vito reached the boys. "Hey, Charlie, you know hitting doesn't solve any problems."

Angelica came over, not looking too concerned. "Xavier. You know you're not to practice karate on your friends. You need to apologize."

"You, too, Charlie."

Identical sulky lower lips came out.

Identical mumbles of "Sorry."

Then Xavier's face brightened. "C'mon, let's get in the lake!" he yelled, and both boys scrambled to their feet and ran to the water as if nothing had happened between them.

Getting in the lake sounded really refreshing. "Sorry about that," Vito said to Angelica. "I didn't see how it started, but I'll speak to Charlie."

"Don't worry about it. These things happen with boys, and they don't last but a minute." She smiled at him. "How's Wolfie working out?"

"He's a handful," Vito said, chuckling. "Bet Troy's glad to have him off his hands."

"There's a sucker born every minute," she teased. "Actually, he's a great dog. He just needed to find the right home." She nodded toward the other women. "Come on over and say hi."

The sight of Lacey, hair slicked back, perched on the end of someone's beach chair, was all the magnet he needed. He went over and greeted Gina and a woman named Sidney. They had their chairs circled around three babies, and as he watched, little Bobby held out his arms to Lacey and she lifted him up. "Such a big boy!" she said, nuzzling his bare stomach and blowing a raspberry on it, making the toddler laugh wildly.

Vito's heart seemed to pause, then pound. Lacey looked incredible with little Bobby, like she was born to be a mother. And suddenly, Vito wished with all his heart that she could be the mother of all the children he wanted to have.

If only he could tell her the truth about Charlie, cutting away the huge secret between them, he could let her know how he felt and see if there was any chance she'd be interested in him. But telling the truth would destroy her happy illusions about her husband and her marriage. Not to mention the impact the truth would have on Charlie, if he could even understand it.

And Vito didn't take promises lightly, especially deathbed promises.

The trouble was, he was having a hard time imagining a future without Lacey in it. Somehow, in these weeks of living at the guesthouse, she'd become integral to his life and his happiness.

"Dad! Come in the water!" Charlie and Xavier were throwing a beach ball back and forth.

"You should get in." Lacey smiled up at him. "The water feels great."

The sun beat down and he was sweating hard now, partly from the heat of the day and partly from the warmth he felt inside, being here with Lacey.

"Let's take the babies down to dip their feet in the water," Angelica suggested. The other women agreed, and soon they were all at the water's edge, wading.

"You're not worried about getting burned, are you?" Lacey asked him. "You're dark skinned. But I have some sunscreen back at the car if you need it."

"Why d'you have your shirt on, Dad?" Charlie asked, crashing into Vito as he leaped to catch the ball.

Vito's face heated, and to avoid answering, he splashed Charlie. That led to a huge splash fight and Vito was able to cool off some, even though he didn't dunk to get his shirt entirely wet. It was white, and his scars would show through.

When they got hungry, they headed back up to the picnic tables and Vito grilled hot dogs. The women and babies had declined to join them, but Xavier had come over to get a hot dog. It was fun and relaxing, just the kind of day he'd hoped they could have, a gift to Charlie and to Lacey, too.

"You nervous about starting your job tomorrow?" Lacey asked as they ate.

"A little," he admitted. "It's definitely going to be a challenge. I expect some testing."

"You'll handle it well," she reassured him. "You're great with kids."

Charlie grabbed the ketchup and squirted it on his hot dog. The bottle made a raspberry sound which Charlie immediately imitated, laughing.

"Let me do it!" Xavier cried, grabbing for the ketchup. As he tried to tug it from Charlie's hand, he accidentally squeezed the bottle. Ketchup sprayed around the table, painting a line across Charlie, Lacey and Vito's chests.

"That's enough!" Vito plucked the squirt bottle from Xavier's hand and set it at the other end of the table, away from the boys.

"I'm sorry," Xavier said, looking serious and a little frightened as he surveyed the damage.

"It looks like blood!" Charlie said. He and Xavier looked at each other. Charlie made another raspberry sound, and both boys burst out laughing.

Vito rolled his eyes. "Sorry," he said as he handed napkins to Lacey, and dabbed at the mess on his own shirt.

She shrugged and met his eyes, her own twinkling, and he was struck again with how great she was. She didn't get bent out of shape about boys and their antics. What a partner she'd be.

"This isn't coming off, and it stinks," she announced, gesturing to the ketchup on her shirt. "I'm getting in the water. And I bet I can beat you two boys." She jumped up from the picnic table and took off.

Immediately, the boys followed her, laughing and yelling.

Vito watched from the picnic table, alone and sweating in a now-even-smellier T-shirt. More than one male head turned to watch Lacey's progress. With her short hair and petite figure, laughing with the boys, she looked like a kid. But if you took a second look—as several guys were doing—she was all woman.

He dearly wanted to take his shirt off and follow her into the water. To be an easy, relaxed part of things. A partner she could be proud of.

He let his head drop into his hands, closed his eyes and prayed for insight and help. Insight to understand what to do, and help to do the right thing. Not just now, in regards to his ultimately silly shirt dilemma, but over-all, in regards to his promise.

The smell of warm ketchup got to him, though, and he lifted his head again without any answers.

Except a memory from his time rehabbing at the VA: had *he* ever lost esteem for someone because they had scars?

And the answer was glaringly obvious: of course not. He respected the way they'd gotten them, and he looked beyond.

Charlie and the other kids might not be mature enough to do that, but Lacey? Of all people, she was one of the least superficial he knew.

On the other hand, he wasn't just interested in gain-ing her respect. He wanted more. He wanted her to be drawn to him physically, as he was to her.

And why was he so obsessed with what Lacey thought of him, when their relationship couldn't go anywhere?

Like a slap in the face, it hit him: he was in love with her.

Not just a crush, a remnant of high school attraction.

Full-fledged, grown-up *love*.

Wow.

He just sat and tried to wrap his mind around that

concept for a while, until the boys got out of the water and started throwing a football and Lacey came back toward the table.

"Hey, lazy," she said, grabbing his hand and tugging it. "The water feels great. Come get in!"

He let her pull him up and she laughed and let go of his hand, walking toward the water with a flirtatious smile over her shoulder.

All of a sudden, he didn't want to be the good friend anymore. For once, he wanted to follow his instincts and desires, to be the main man. To try and see whether his scars were really the turnoff he feared they'd be.

He pulled off his T-shirt, removed his hearing aids and located their case, all the while psyching himself up for an encounter in some ways more terrifying than heading into battle.

Chapter 12

Lacey's cheeks heated as she headed down toward the lake. Had she been too forward? What was she thinking, insisting that Vito come swimming?

She glanced over her shoulder to see if he was following her. When she saw him fiddling with his ear, her hand flew to her mouth.

She usually didn't even remember that he wore hearing aids. But of course, he couldn't wear them into the water.

Was that why he'd been reluctant to come in?

She glanced again. Or was it the scar that slashed across his back, dark and very visible?

Pushing him had been a mistake. He was such a good sport he'd come if begged, but she hoped she hadn't caused him to do something he didn't want to do.

Kids shouted as they ran and splashed in the shallow part of the lake. As she walked by a group of teen girls, she inhaled the fragrance of coconut oil, something every dermatologist in the world would blanch at. Some things never changed.

She just hoped the kids and teens would be tactful about Vito's scars.

She waded into the lake, waist deep, then looked back to see whether he was following. And sucked in her breath.

The front of his chest, which she hadn't seen before, was crisscrossed with scars. Long ones and short ones, visible even with his dark Italian skin.

Their eyes met, and Vito's steps faltered a little.

Should she say something? Walk back toward him? Tell him his battle scars didn't affect her feelings toward him, except maybe to warm her heart that he'd sacrificed for his country?

But instinct told her to treat him just as she always had. Meaning, how they'd all acted at the lake as kids, since they hadn't been here together since.

He'd reached the water's edge now, and she grinned in invitation and flicked water at him with her hand. "Scared?" she taunted.

"A little." There seemed to be a double meaning in his words. "But I can play scared." He took a few steps toward her. Suddenly, he dived underwater. A few seconds later, she felt a hand wrap around her ankle, and then she was under, giggling into the green water.

She surfaced, shaking her wet hair out of her eyes. Hooked a toe around Vito's ankle and pushed hard.

He toppled backward and came up, grinning and holding up his hands. "Truce! Peace!"

Their playfulness attracted Xavier and Charlie, who came splashing toward them. "Dad, gross—put a shirt on!" Charlie yelled loud enough for the whole beach to hear.

And apparently, despite his hearing impairment, Vito could make out the words, too.

Around them, a few kids and teens stared openly at Vito. One boy, a little older than Charlie and Xavier, said something that made the nearby kids laugh.

A flush crawled up Vito's face. "I never claimed to be a beauty queen," he said to Charlie with a half smile.

He was handling it well, but she ached for him. He'd earned those scars defending his country, and she honored him for it.

Xavier studied him thoughtfully. "Kids used to tease me for being bald, when I had cancer. Mom said to ignore them."

Vito didn't respond.

Charlie went up and tugged his arm. "Hey! Are your hearing aids out?"

Vito looked down at Charlie. "What?"

"Can't he hear?" Xavier asked.

This was getting to be a little much, and Lacey decided to intervene. "Have you boys ever heard of chicken fights?"

Neither had, so she knelt in the water and told Xavier to climb up on her shoulders. "Get on your dad's shoulders, Charlie," she said, deliberately speaking loudly. "The game is, try to knock each other off."

"Get down, Dad!" Charlie yelled into Vito's ear.

Vito grinned at her, kneeled and took Charlie onto his powerful shoulders. When he stood, he and Charlie towered over Xavier and Lacey.

"Come on, Xavier. We may be short, but we're fast," she said, and went in low.

They splashed and played for a while, with both boys getting thoroughly and repeatedly dunked. Lacey's shoulders ached from carrying a heavy, wiggling boy, but she didn't mind. The water was cool and she hadn't laughed so hard in a long time.

Most of the rest of the swimmers drifted away, except for a few kids who talked their parents into participating.

Best of all, nobody was talking about hearing problems or scars.

Finally, Angelica called the boys to come and rest, and when she offered up watermelon as an enticement, they splashed their way to shore.

"Do you want to go get some?" Vito asked.

She shook her head. "I'm not hungry."

"Swim out to the dock?"

"Sure, and I'll beat you!" Lacey plunged her face into the water and started swimming fast.

It felt good. She seemed to have some extra energy saved up, a shaky excitement that made her want to move.

She was starting to feel such a mix of things for Vito. Admiration. Desire to protect. Caring.

Maybe even love.

She shoved that thought away and swam faster. She couldn't be falling in love with Vito, could she? Vito, her old friend and high school crush. Vito, the guy who'd always been around, always ready to lend an ear or a smile or a hand with whatever you were working on, be it figuring out algebra problems or speaking up against bullies or healing a broken heart.

Was he spending time with her now just to help her

get over Gerry? It seemed like, in his eyes, she'd been seeing something more.

She reached the dock at the same moment he did, but touched it first. "I won!" she crowed into his ear.

"You did." He grinned at her as he hoisted himself out onto the wooden platform.

She found the ladder and climbed up, narrowing her eyes at him. "Wait a minute. Did you try your hardest?"

"Let's just say the D'Angelos are swimmers. And gentlemen."

"You *did* let me win!"

He didn't admit to it, but he flashed a grin that took her breath away. Standing above her dripping wet, his teeth flashing against dark skin, his eyes laughing, he looked like a hero from some ancient, epic tale.

She couldn't seem to move. She just knelt there transfixed, halfway up the ladder, staring up at him.

He extended his hand toward her. "Come aboard, milady," he said, and helped her to the dock.

She needed the help. She couldn't seem to catch her breath.

They lay side by side, faces toward the blue sky, the sun warming their wet bodies. Beside them, a little railing shielded them from those on the beach, though their shouts were still audible. Lacey was exquisitely conscious of Vito, the warmth of his arm close to hers, the even sound of his breathing.

She couldn't understand what was going on inside her. This was Vito, her old neighbor, comfortable and safe. Vito, who'd always seemed out of reach because he was older.

Yet he was someone else, too, someone new. The things he'd been through had forged him into a man of strength and valor, a man she couldn't help but admire. It was starting to seem like she both wanted and needed him in her life.

"Do you remember coming out here as kids?" he asked unexpectedly.

"Sure." She watched a cloud laze across the sky, and then turned so she could speak into his ear. "Buck and I came with Dad pretty often when we were little."

"How come your mom never came? Was she…sick, even back then?"

"I don't know. She never wanted to do family things. Always busy with her dreams and plans, I guess."

Vito didn't answer, but he reached over and patted her hand, warm on the dock beside her.

"I don't know when she started with the pills." Lacey followed the swooping path of a dark bird, thinking about it. "I think she was okay when I was real small, but then she just started going in her bedroom and shutting the door." As she said it, she got a visceral memory of standing outside the closed door, hand raised to knock. She'd tried not to do it, knowing that Mom didn't like to be disturbed, but she hadn't been able to stop herself from knocking, then pounding on the door.

Where had Buck and her father been? Why had she been there alone for so long, with just her mother?

"If I had a kid," she said, still speaking into his ear to help him hear her, "I just hope I'd have more sense than to leave her to fend for herself like Mom did to me."

"You would. You're great with Charlie."

His automatic, assured response touched her. "Thanks, Vito."

"It's not about having the sense, it's about heart," he said with a shrug. "And heart, you've got."

His words surprised tears into her eyes. "I appreciate that."

He propped himself on one elbow to look at her, shading the sun. He was all she could see. "I can't say enough about you, Lacey. You were always sweet, and likable, and cute…"

She snorted. "Cute like a little brat, you mean."

He cocked his head to one side. "No, not exactly. I found you…appealing, as you grew up."

"You *did*?"

"Uh-huh." He reached out and brushed back a strand of her hair.

"Why didn't you ever, you know, ask me out?"

His eyebrows drew together. "You were three years younger! That wouldn't have been right."

She laughed up at him. "You're such a Boy Scout."

His eyes narrowed. "If you could read my mind, you'd know that's far from true."

"Then, or now?"

"What do you mean?"

"Are you talking about what was in your mind then, or now?" Something, some magnetic force field, drew her to reach toward his chest, the thick, luxuriant mat of hair sliced through by scars.

He caught her hand, held it still. "Don't."

"Why not?"

Shaking his head, he continued to hold her gaze.

"Because of this?" She tugged her hand away from him and traced the air above one of the multiple fault lines on his chest. Almost, but not quite, touching it.

He sucked in a breath, his eyes still pinning her. "Do you have any idea of what you're doing?"

"What am I doing?"

He caught her chin in his hand and let his thumb
brush across her lower lip.

She drew in a sharp breath, staring at him. Every
nerve felt alive, every sense awake.

"You have no idea how long I've wanted to do this."
He leaned closer, studying her face as if trying to read
her thoughts, her mood, her feelings.

"Do what?" she asked, hearing the breathy sound
of her voice.

"This." He slid his hand to the back of her head and
pressed his lips to hers.

The next Saturday, Vito's head was still spinning.

Kissing Lacey had been the sweetest and most promising moment of his life. Now he just had to figure out
what was next.

He'd been busy with his new job for the past couple
of days, and Lacey had been taking up the slack, spending extra time with Nonna and Charlie. She hadn't said
anything about their kiss, but she'd given him some secret smiles that burned right into his soul.

He had to talk to her, and soon. But this morning, to
give her privacy and time to get some detailed renova-
tion work done, he'd taken Nonna and Charlie out for
breakfast at the Chatterbox.

Now, seeing Charlie wave to a friend, hearing Nonna's
happy conversation with a woman at a neighboring table,
he felt full to the brim. His new life in Rescue River was
working out, and he had a lot to be thankful for.

"Hey, Dad," Charlie said. "Am I still seeing Mom on
Tuesday, now that you're working?"

"Yes. I'll drive you, and then we're going to see if
the social worker can bring you home. If she can't, I

can take off early." He'd explained his commitment to Charlie's schedule during his job interview, and his new employer was willing to be flexible.

"Mom said maybe she could drive me, only there's a lady she doesn't like in Rescue River."

"That's nice of her to offer, but your mom isn't allowed to transport…" All of a sudden Vito processed what Charlie had said and his heart skipped a beat. "Did she say anything about the lady?" he asked, carefully keeping his voice even.

"I think it was because of my dad. My other dad," Charlie clarified around a mouthful of pancakes. "Hey, Rafael asked if I could go to the park and play basketball, and they're leaving now. Can I?"

"Um, let me talk to his mom." His thoughts spinning, Vito slid out of the booth and made arrangements with Rafael's mother, forcing himself to focus. Charlie's social skills were improving rapidly enough that he felt okay about letting the boy go play some ball without him—after a stern warning about sportsmanship and manners.

Once that was settled, he paid the check and escorted Nonna out of the restaurant.

As they walked slowly toward the guesthouse, Vito wondered what Krystal had said to Charlie. If she was talking that openly about the past—what did it mean?

He took Nonna's arm when the sidewalk got bumpy. Quite possibly, it meant the whole truth could come out soon.

The woman in Rescue River whom Krystal had told Charlie she didn't like—and who was connected to Charlie's other dad—could be no one else but Lacey.

But Krystal didn't know Lacey, did she? Was there

a chance she'd say enough that Charlie would put it all together?

He looked over at Nonna. "What if there were something you needed to tell the truth about, only you'd made a promise not to?"

"Ah, difficult," she said, looking at him with sharp, curious brown eyes.

Clearly she was waiting for him to say more, but he didn't. If he was going to tell the truth, it had to start with Lacey. So he focused on watching a couple strapping twin babies into a double stroller.

A pang of envy swept through him. He wanted what they seemed to have. A happy, uncomplicated relationship of raising children together.

"Have you prayed about this problem?" Nonna asked.

Had he prayed? He nodded slowly. He'd sent up some urgent, brief pleas to God, for sure.

"And listened to the response?"

He blew out a breath. "Not really. I guess I need to."

They reached the guesthouse in time to see Lacey hauling a big load of trash to the curb, struggling a little. Vito jogged over and took the boxes out of her hands, earning a smile.

Lacey went to Nonna. "Are you going around the block another time? I can walk with you if Vito's got things to do." Lacey didn't look at him, but her cheeks were pink and he didn't think it was just the exertion. There had been a tentative, sweet promise in their interactions since their kiss earlier this week.

Nonna put a hand on Lacey's arm and another on Vito's. "I've had enough for now. Why don't you two walk?" She gave Vito a meaningful look, and when Lacey turned away, she mouthed, *"Tell her!"*

How had Nonna guessed that his secret had to do with Lacey?

Was he supposed to tell her *now*?

As soon as they'd gotten Nonna settled on the porch with her latest large-print library book, Vito and Lacey headed out, strolling toward the park. Behind them, Wolfie barked a request to go along.

"Should we go back and get him?" Lacey asked, clearly unaware of Vito's inner turmoil. "He's about to break through the fence again."

"Not this time. I put another nail in it yesterday."

"Thanks. I'll have to get somebody to do a real repair soon." Lacey lifted her face to the sun. "I've been inside all morning, painting woodwork. The fresh air smells good."

"I'm glad you could come." He wanted to put his arm around her. He wanted to build a family with her! But the wretched secret stood between them.

Should loyalty outweigh love? He pondered the question, watching a jogger and his golden Lab loping across the park.

"We haven't had a chance to talk since you started your new job," Lacey said. "How'd it go, really? Did the kids give you a hard time?"

The cowardly side of him was grateful for the distraction. This was territory he could handle. "It went well. The kids are a challenge, for sure, but I liked working with them."

"And your scars didn't make one bit of difference, did they?" She was smiling smugly, obviously sure she was right.

And she *was* right. "The kids made a couple of comments, but it was no big deal. I didn't overreact and the whole discussion just went away." He hesitated, then added, "You've helped me feel okay with how I look, especially because of...of how you responded to me the other day, at the lake."

She stared down at the sidewalk, but the corner of her mouth curved up in a smile.

He needed to tell her the truth about Charlie. He was going to tell her.

"I admire your being able to handle a big group of kids like that," she murmured, so quietly he had to lean down to hear her.

Thinking about how he could break the truth gently, he gave a distracted answer to her comment. "I like big groups of kids. In fact, that's my dream—to have enough kids of my own to form a baseball team."

He was about to add "with you" when she stopped still. The smile was gone from her face.

"You know what," she said, "I just realized I left something cooking on the stove. I need to run back and get it. You keep walking, okay? I don't want to interrupt your morning exercise."

She turned and hurried back toward the guesthouse.

Vito looked after her, puzzled by her abrupt departure. His *morning exercise*? And he was surprised to learn she had something cooking when she'd been painting woodwork.

He'd been about to tell her the truth. Was that God, letting him know it wasn't the right time yet?

And if so, why had Lacey suddenly started acting so weird?

Chapter 13

Numb from Vito's comment about wanting a large family, Lacey stirred canned soup on the stove and tried not to think.

If she didn't think, maybe it wouldn't hurt so much that she could never, ever give Vito what he wanted.

"Miss Lacey! Miss Lacey!" Charlie barged through the screen door, letting it bang behind him. He threw his arms around her. "Guess how many baskets I made today in one-on-one?"

She clung to him for a minute, relishing the feel of sweaty boy, and then resolutely untangled herself from his arms and stepped back. Charlie was getting way too close to her, given that she'd just learned she and Vito should never, *could* never, be a couple.

"Maybe you and Dad can come watch me play," he continued, unaware of her turmoil. "And Dad said sometime we could go see a real live Cavaliers game, all three of us!"

There is no "us."

She needed to be truthful. That was kinder in the long run.

Wolfie whined at the back door and Lacey let him in, figuring the dog could comfort Charlie in the face of what she was about to say. "I don't think that's going to happen," she said, crossing her arms, deliberately keeping her distance. "You and your dad are going to move out soon, and then we won't all see so much of each other."

Charlie visibly deflated, sinking down to put his arms around Wolfie's neck. "But I don't want to move."

How quickly he accepted the truth of what she said, and her heart broke for this child, who'd seen too much change and loss. She didn't know much about Charlie's background, but she knew his mom wasn't reliable enough to raise him. That had to hurt him right at the core.

And it meant he shouldn't get overly close to Lacey, because she was just going to be another loss. "You and your dad are going to be a forever family," she said, resisting the urge to hug him. "But that's not going to happen here." She forced herself to add, "It's not going to happen with me."

He looked at her with wide, sad eyes and she felt like she'd kicked a puppy. And even if her words had been for Charlie's own good, she hated that she was hurting him.

"Later," he said, then turned and straightened his shoulders. "Come on, Wolfie." And then both dog and boy ran up the stairs.

Tears rose in Lacey's eyes, and one spilled over and ran down her cheek. She wanted to call him back, to hug him and tell him that yes, they'd still be close, and yes, they could do things together in the future.

But that would just prolong the pain. Vito needed someone who could give him and Charlie a family, and he *would* find someone.

And that someone wouldn't be her.

Automatically, for comfort, she felt for her necklace. But she wasn't wearing it. After kissing Vito, she'd decided that it was time to remove it. Time to stop focusing on Gerry, and start focusing on life ahead.

She'd been wrong.

She turned off the soup, for which she had no appetite, and trudged up the stairs. Went into her room, opened her old jewelry box and pulled the chain back out.

She'd thought she was going to make new memories with Vito and Charlie, but she was going to have to stick with the old memories. Of Gerry and the child she'd lost. Memories that didn't seem like nearly enough to build a life on now that she'd tasted what love and family could mean at Vito's side.

But Vito wanted a big family. He'd be wonderful with a big family, and she wasn't going to deny him that.

The chain and ring settling around her neck felt heavy in a way they never had before.

Suddenly bereft of energy, she closed her bedroom door, pulled the shades and lay down in the semidarkness, too tired and miserable even to pray.

Saturday afternoon, Vito arrived at the church food distribution late and out of sorts.

Lacey had been scheduled to volunteer, too, he was sure of it; she'd come out onto the porch, car keys in hand.

But when she'd realized that he and Charlie were planning to go, she'd turned abruptly and gone back inside, shutting her door with a decisive click.

Not only that, but Charlie was on his worst behavior. After Lacey's defection he'd refused to go and, when Vito had insisted, he'd let loose with a tantrum that had surely roused the neighborhood. Now he wore a sneer better befitting a teenage delinquent than an eight-year-old boy.

"Hey, Charlie's here!" Angelica waved from where she and Troy were sorting out boxes of doughnuts and pastries. "C'mon, the Kennel Kids scored the best place on the line. We get to give out the desserts, and eat whatever's left over!"

Charlie scowled, but he walked down to the end of the line where several other boys from the group stood joking and roughhousing. Troy and Angelica seemed to have them under control, though, and Xavier greeted Charlie enthusiastically.

Relieved, Vito scouted around for a role that didn't involve a lot of chitchat. He wasn't in the mood today. As the line of food bank patrons entered the church's fellowship hall and picked up boxes to fill, Vito started carrying crates of produce from the loading dock at the back of the building to resupply those on the front lines.

He tried to distract himself from his gloomy thoughts by focusing on the scent of sun-ripened tomatoes and bundles of green onions, but it didn't work. He kept going back to Lacey's pale, strained face, to the definitive click of her door closing.

Had their new connectedness been an illusion? Had she had second thoughts about pursuing a relationship with someone who had disabilities and a challenging child to raise?

Was there some way she could have found out the truth about Charlie?

But they'd walked together this morning, and she'd been perfectly fine, seeming interested in him, his job, their conversation.

"Hey, Vito!" The father of the migrant family who was renting Nonna's house—was his name Vasquez?—took the empty crate Vito handed him and started filling it with bundles of kale. "Thanks for working today."

"Thank *you*." Vito tried for a good humor he didn't feel. "I'm impressed that you're helping, as busy as you must be with the new baby."

"The bambino has not arrived yet, and my wife, she is very uncomfortable." The man worked deftly as he spoke, lining up the bundles for maximum space in the box. "She cannot work now, so I will have to join the food line this month. But at least I can help others, too."

"Good plan." Vito took the crate from Mr. Vasquez and reminded himself that his weren't the worst problems in the world. Some families struggled to scrape together enough food to eat.

He walked back toward the line, focusing on the friendly chatter between helpers and recipients. Interesting that the line between the two sometimes blurred, as with Mr. Vasquez.

He'd just put the crate down when a highly irate voice sounded behind him. "Vito! I need to talk to you!"

It was Susan Hinton, and she tugged him over toward a quiet corner of the fellowship hall. "What did you say to Lacey?"

"What do you mean?"

Susan's hands were on her hips. "She's been doing so well, but when I stopped by the guesthouse to pick her up for volunteering, she looked awful. Said she couldn't come, and when I asked her if she was sick, if she needed anything, she said no and went back in her room. She *never* misses."

Vito lifted his hands, palms up. "I could ask you the same question. She's backed off from me, just today, and I don't know why."

Susan's eyes narrowed. "Since when? What went on?"

"I have no idea."

She actually smacked him on the arm. "Come on. Don't be a typical guy. What did you say to her?"

"I don't know." He leaned against a stack of boxes, trying to recreate the scene of their walk this morning in his mind. "I was talking about my new job. And not just because I was going on and on about myself. She wanted to know. She was fine one minute, and then boom, she lit out of there like I'd insulted her best friend."

"What, exactly, did you say?" Susan leaned back, crossing her arms over her chest. "And I'm not just being nosy. Lacey's had a lot happen to her, and she went through a pretty bad depression. I'd hate to see her sink back into that."

"Me, too." He frowned, thinking. "I was talking about working with the kids, and she said she didn't know how I could handle working with that many. I told her I love kids, want to have a passel of them myself someday, and it was about then that she seemed to back off. Was that…do you think I somehow offended her?"

Susan threw her hands up and snorted with disgust. "Vito!" Several people turned to look at them, and she tugged him closer and lowered her voice. "Look, I don't know that it's my place to tell you this, but Lacey *can't* have kids."

That hit him like a blow to deflect, news that had to be wrong. "But...she got pregnant with Gerry, right?"

She looked from one side to the other, making sure they weren't overheard. "When she miscarried, there was some damage. She's infertile now, and that's been really, really hard for her to deal with."

Pain sliced through him just as if it were he, himself, who couldn't have kids. Lacey would be such a great mom. Sometimes, life just wasn't fair.

"And so when you said..." Susan trailed off.

Understanding broke through. "Did she back off because I said I wanted a lot of kids?"

"I don't know. She's the type who'd sacrifice her own desires so other people would get what they wanted."

"Wait a minute, I'm confused. What *are* her own desires?"

"She really likes you, Vito, if you haven't wrecked it. Talk to her. That is, unless her infertility means you aren't interested in her, like some ancient king who only likes women so he can get a son."

Vito lifted his hands, palms up. "Whoa. That's not me. Not at all." His mind was reeling, but this was something he could maybe fix. "Look, I have to go. Can you tell them... Do you think they can handle the rest without..."

"Go." Susan actually shoved him toward the door. "The line's short today and it's almost done."

"Thanks. Thanks, Susan. Let me get Charlie, and I'm outta here."

Despite the sad news he'd learned about Lacey, hope was rising in him. If she cared for him so much that she'd sacrifice her own desires so he could have kids… But didn't she see that what he wanted was her? Kids came into families in all kinds of ways. Just look at Charlie.

The boy wasn't with the rest of the Kennel Kids. "He said he needed to talk to you," Angelica said. "Didn't he come over?"

"No…" Vito turned and scanned the room. "I'll find him. Thanks."

Alongside his excitement about possibly working things out with Lacey, self-blame pushed at him. He'd been paying so much attention to Susan's story that he'd forgotten to keep an eye on Charlie.

Finally, he thought to talk to the other Kennel Kids. "He said he was outta here, going home," one of the younger ones finally volunteered.

"Thanks." Vito blew out a breath, quickly left the church and walked the three blocks to the guesthouse at record speed. He'd told Charlie he had to stay and help the whole time. What did this new wave of defiance mean?

Nonna was at the front gate, headed out for lunch with Lou Ann Miller. "Did you see Charlie come in?" Vito asked.

"No, but I've been getting ready. I wouldn't have heard him if he went right upstairs. Is anything wrong?"

"Everything's fine. He's just in trouble."

"Don't be too hard on him, dear." Nonna patted Vito's arm, and then the two women headed down the sidewalk.

He trotted up the stairs. Noticed the door to Lacey's room was still closed. Was she in there?

He *really* wanted to talk to her, but he had to deal with Charlie's disobedience first. He pounded on the door to Charlie's room, and when there was no answer, flung it open.

The lecture he'd been about to give died on his lips.

The room was empty. Not just empty of people, but empty of stuff. Charlie's stuff.

He opened the closet door. There was a hamper of dirty clothes, but the clean ones were gone. As was Charlie's suitcase.

His heart pounding, he ran out onto the landing. "Charlie! Charlie!"

No answer, but Lacey's door opened. "What's wrong?"

He looked from window to window, searching the yard on both sides of the guesthouse, but they were quiet, empty.

"Vito? What's going on?"

"Have you seen Charlie?"

"Not since you guys left for the church. Where is he?"

"That," Vito said grimly, "is the million-dollar question. I think he's run away."

Chapter 14

Vito continued searching even as he explained the situation to Lacey, trying to stay calm.

"I just can't believe he'd run away. He's so happy here, and with you." Lacey walked into Charlie's room. She opened the closet door, and then squatted to look under the bed—all places Vito had already checked.

Vito strode into his adjoining room. He flung open the closet door and checked it top to bottom. "I never thought of him running, either, but he's not here. And his suitcase is gone." Quickly and methodically, he searched the rest of his room. News stories of all the bad things that could happen to kids played through his head, one after another.

A thought struck him and he went back to the window, lifted the screen and leaned out. He gave a whistle, and Wolfie trotted over to that side of the yard, panting, looking up expectantly.

"It's okay, boy," he said, and shut the window. Surely Charlie wouldn't have left without his beloved dog.

When he looked back into the room, Lacey was at Charlie's little desk, rifling through papers and magazines and empty potato chip bags.

"I'd better call Dion." He had his phone out to punch in the police chief's number when Lacey cried out softly.

"Look at this. Is this his handwriting?"

Vito took the torn piece of notebook paper from her and scanned it quickly, his heart sinking with every word he read.

I thot I cud have a mom and dad. I need a mom.
Take care of Wofie.

And he'd signed it, "Love, Charlie."

Vito's heart seemed to stop in his chest.

"What does it mean?" Lacey clutched her arms around herself. "'I need a mom.' And who did he think would be his mom? Was it…was it me?"

"Maybe." He caught Lacey's eye, held it. "Believe me when I say I didn't try to plant that idea. But right now I'm more worried about where he's headed."

"Could he have gone to his mom?"

"That's what I'm afraid of." He turned toward the door. "I can't even imagine how upset he was, to leave without Wolfie."

"But you said she's an addict…"

"She is, and she isn't very selective about her boyfriends. I've got to find him." He headed down the stairs.

She followed behind. "Where does she live? Where has he been meeting her?"

"He's been meeting her at a center in Raystown. But

432   *The Soldier's Secret Child*

she actually lives in Barnsdale. Way too far to walk, and he knows that."

Lacey grabbed his arm, stopping him. "There's a bus that goes to Barnsdale. We were talking one day, Charlie and Nonna and me, and we looked over the bus route together. He was sounding out the words, and when he came to Barnsdale, he said that's where he used to live."

Vito groaned. "I have a feeling that's exactly what he did. Is the bus stop still at the front of Cramer's Drugstore?"

She nodded. "Let's go. Maybe we can catch him before he gets the bus. I don't even know the schedule anymore, but the bus can't run very often."

They each grabbed phones, wallets and keys and rushed out to Vito's car. As they climbed in, Wolfie howled his distress at being left behind.

"Let's drive slow and watch. He could be headed back home. I doubt a bus driver would even take a kid as young as Charlie."

"I don't know. He can be pretty smart about figuring out ways to do things and making up stories."

They were at the drugstore in minutes, and Lacey got out of the car and rushed in before Vito even had a chance to park. By the time he got inside, seconds later, she was in heated conversation with a teenage clerk.

"Why didn't anyone stop him?" she was lamenting. "A little boy, alone?"

"Kids eight and over can ride unaccompanied." The young woman shrugged. "He had the right paperwork, looked like. The driver always checks."

Vito's heart sank. Charlie was perfectly capable of talking an adult into filling out a form for him. "How long ago did the bus leave?"

The teenager looked at the wall behind her, taking what seemed like an extremely long time to skim over a schedule. "Must've been about…an hour ago?"

He and Lacey looked at each other. "Let's go," she said.

As they reached the truck, the ramifications of what might be in front of them rushed into Vito's mind. Krystal, Lacey, Charlie. All together. "Lace…you might not want to go along. Someone should stay back at the guesthouse, in case he comes back."

"I'll call Lou Ann on the way and ask her and Nonna to go back."

"It's not safe—"

"*Charlie's* not safe. And you need backup."

He pulled out of the parking lot and headed toward Barnsdale. "I need backup I don't have to worry about. You can only come if you stay in the truck and be ready to call the police if needed. That's it, Lacey. I don't want you tangling with Krystal and her boyfriends, or whoever else is crashing at her place."

"Fine."

As they drove in silence, Vito's mind hopscotched from topic to topic. How would Charlie get from the bus stop to his house on the poorer side of town? Should he explain the whole situation about Charlie and Krystal and Gerry so that Lacey could be prepared? Why had Charlie run away, really?

He heard a small sound from the seat beside him. When he glanced over, he saw Lacey brushing her forefinger under her eye. "What's wrong?"

"I think I know why Charlie ran away," she said with a hitch in her voice. "I think it's my fault."

"How could it be your fault?" He kept his eyes on the rural road before him, pushing the speed limit.

"Because I told him we couldn't keep doing things together." She fumbled in her purse, found a tissue and blew her nose. "I told him we couldn't be a family."

Whoa. "How did you get into that conversation? When?"

"Just this morning." She paused, took a breath. "He came in from basketball, talking about all the things we three were going to do together, and I thought... I thought he'd better not expect that. So I just...told him it wasn't happening."

"Why?"

"Because it can't." He could barely hear her voice, low and hoarse.

He risked taking a hand off the steering wheel and gave her arm a quick squeeze. "We have to talk. Susan told me some stuff."

"What stuff?" She shifted to face him, sounding uneasy.

A passing road sign told Vito they were halfway to Barnsdale. "Look, I'm sorry if this is none of my business, but apparently Susan thought I should know about your infertility."

She drew in a little gasp, her hand rising to her mouth.

There was probably a tactful way to have this conversation, but he didn't know it, not now. "I'm sorry, hon. That's got to be tough, maybe the toughest thing for a woman."

She didn't say anything, and when he glanced over, her lips were pressed tightly together and her body rigid.

"But there are all kinds of ways to be a parent. It's not just biological. I mean, look at me and Charlie."

She didn't answer, and they rode without talking into Barnsdale, passing the automobile factory on one side of the road and a couple of small machine shops on the other.

He tried again. "When all this is over, when we find Charlie and get him home safe, I want to have more of a conversation about this. Okay?"

She nodded, reached over and squeezed his arm. "We'll find him."

Vito pulled onto the street where Krystal had been renting a place, the last address he had for her. Dingy cottages and overgrown yards lined both sides of the street. "This isn't going to be pleasant. Remember, I want you to stay in the car."

"I know. I'm ready to call the cops." She looked around uneasily.

He stopped the truck in front of Krystal's place. "And, Lace..."

"What?"

He hooked an arm around her neck, pulled her to him and gave her a fast, hard kiss. Then he pulled back to look into her eyes. "Remember, whatever happens, I want this with you." He got out of the truck before he could say too much.

There was a bang as the screen door flew open and back on broken hinges, slamming into the front of the house.

"Hey, what's going on, my man Vito!" Krystal came out on the front stoop, started down the concrete steps, and then grabbed the railing and sat down abruptly.

A man appeared in the doorway behind her, the same one Vito had seen driving the SUV. The balding, bearded one who'd made Charlie cringe.

Vito strode up the narrow walkway. "Is Charlie here?"

"Yeah, he's here." Krystal held up a can of beer like she was making a toast. "Decided he'd rather live with his good old mom after all."

Relief that he'd found Charlie warred with worry about the situation the boy had gotten himself into. "I'd like to talk to him."

The bearded man came out onto the stoop, his face unfriendly. "What's your business here?"

"Just looking for my son." Vito visually searched the place, glancing around the weedy yard, up at the little house's windows.

A curtain moved in one. Was it Charlie?

"You been stepping out on me?" The man nudged Krystal with his knee, none too gently.

"Aw, cut it out, Manny."

"You've got it wrong." Vito kept his voice calm, because he could tell that the man was volatile. "I'm just an acquaintance of Krystal's. Taking care of her son."

"You the daddy?" Manny asked.

Behind him, Vito heard the window of his truck being lowered. Lacey.

"I'm not his dad yet, but I'm going to adopt him. Let's just get him down here and I'll be on my way."

"Maybe I don't like the way you look." Manny shoved past Krystal and came down the steps. "Maybe I want you to leave right now."

Vito automatically straightened up, his fists clenching. He wanted to punch the jerk, but for Charlie's sake he couldn't. He needed to stay calm and keep things peaceful. "I'd be glad to leave you people to your own business as soon as I have Charlie."

Then everything happened at once.

Manny drew back a fist, but Krystal rushed up and grabbed it. Manny shook her off and shoved her back, roughly, causing her to fall back onto the steps. At the same moment Charlie came running out of the house. He crashed into his mother, who reached out reflexively to grab him.

Manny, unaware what was going on behind him, threw a punch that Vito dodged, but landed a second one on Vito's shoulder, knocking him back.

Behind him, the truck door opened. "Charlie!" Lacey cried. "Over here!"

Manny advanced on Vito, and with no time to regret the violence, Vito threw a one-two punch, connecting with Manny's ribs and then the side of his throat. Manny fell to the ground, gasping for air.

Vito spun to help Charlie just in time to see the boy extract himself from his mother's grip and run to Lacey. She was turning to usher him into the truck when Krystal spoke up.

"Hey!" she called, her voice slurred but plenty loud. "Wait a minute. I know who you are!"

Vito's heart skipped a beat and he ran toward Lacey and Charlie, intent on getting them into the truck so they didn't find out the truth this way.

Her heart pumping, her adrenaline high, Lacey ushered Charlie into the backseat. Then she turned to see where Vito was. She'd drive Charlie away herself if she needed to, even if it meant temporarily leaving Vito behind. He could fend for himself better than Charlie could.

Vito was approaching the truck at a run, so Lacey went around to get in the passenger's seat.

The dark-haired woman, Charlie's mother, reached the truck just as Lacey opened the passenger door. "I know who you are," she said, her tone angry.

Vito came back around from the driver's side. "Come on, Krystal, we'll talk another time. When you're sober."

"I'm sober enough to recognize *her*."

Lacey studied the woman. "How do you know me? I don't think I've met you."

"Krystal—" Vito started.

She held up a hand and interrupted him, still glaring at Lacey. "*You're* the woman who stole my man away."

That was so far from anything Lacey expected that she could only stare at Krystal.

"Hey, now," Vito said, "this can wait. Charlie doesn't need to hear this."

Lacey stepped away from the truck door. Before she could close it in an effort to block Charlie's hearing them, Krystal slammed it shut.

Someone clicked the locks. Vito.

She looked past Vito to Krystal, filled with a sinking feeling she didn't understand. "How do you know me?"

"Guy named Gerry McPherson sound familiar?"

"Ye-e-e-s," Lacey said slowly. "He was my husband."

"Well, he was *my* fiancé. And the father of my child."

"The father of your…"

"Him." Krystal pointed toward the backseat. "Charlie."

Lacey looked at Vito, who should be denying what this madwoman said, but Vito's face was a stone.

The edges of her world started to crumble. "Gerry was Charlie's father?"

"That's right. I gave him more than you ever did."

The words stabbed her, but she ignored the pain. She

had to explain to the woman how wrong she was. "But Charlie's eight. I was married to Gerry when…" She stared at Krystal.

Krystal threw up her hands. "You didn't even know, did you?"

Slowly Lacey shook her head. What she was hearing couldn't possibly be right.

"Yeah, he was seeing me on the side. At first, I didn't know about you, either." The anger was draining out of the woman's voice. "When I figured out that he was married, I tried to break it off, but he said your marriage was on the rocks and he was leaving. It was only when I saw that photo in the paper that I realized he'd been lying. You two were hugging each other like lovebirds, all happy." She shook her head, her expression bitter. "He wasn't worth the time I put into him."

"At least you got… Charlie." She heard the choked sound of her own voice as if from a distance.

Gerry had been cheating on her?

Could it be true?

She cleared her throat. "How long were you seeing him?"

"Couple of years. He didn't come around as much after Charlie was born. To be fair, he was overseas a lot after that."

"Don't be fair to him!" Lacey snapped. "Did he see you when he came home, too?"

"Yeah. Some. Not much." Something like compassion had crept into Krystal's voice. "Charlie doesn't remember him."

Lacey sagged back against the truck, unable to process what she was hearing.

Gerry had been unfaithful during the whole course of their marriage.

He'd conceived a son with this woman in front of her.

He'd met the son and seen the woman when he came home on leave.

And she'd known none of it.

She put her hands over her face, trying to block it out, trying to preserve the memory of the husband she'd adored, of the happy marriage she'd thought she had.

Vito cleared his throat.

The sound brought a whole new betrayal into focus, and she dropped her hands away from her eyes and turned to stare at him. "You knew."

Slowly, he nodded.

"You knew, and you stayed in my house, brought Gerry's son into my house, and you didn't tell me."

"Cold, Vito," Krystal said.

"Lacey, I wanted to tell you. Started to, so many times. But I promised Gerry I wouldn't."

Krystal snorted. "Yeah, well, we all made promises, didn't we? And look how much good that did."

Lacey stared from Krystal to Vito, trying to process it all.

Vito was still talking. "I promised that I'd take care of Charlie and look out for you, too. He knew how much it would hurt you…"

"Oh, that's rich," Krystal said.

Lacey just stared and shook her head. He'd kept the truth from her so as not to *hurt* her? At Gerry's behest?

There was a sound from inside the truck, and she turned to see Charlie knocking on the window and mouthing words, his face anxious.

Lacey just stared at him, the boy she'd come to care

for so much. The boy whose eyebrows arched high and dark, just like Gerry's had.

He was Gerry's son.

Gerry *had* a son. She herself had had so much trouble conceiving, and when she'd finally gotten pregnant, it had been too late: Gerry had been killed, and she had lost the baby.

Charlie was rattling the truck door now, and Vito and Krystal were arguing about something, but the words blurred into a mishmash she couldn't understand.

It was all too much. She had to get out of here.

She spun away and started walking down the road, faster and faster until she was nearly at a run.

Chapter 15

For a few seconds, Vito was paralyzed, watching Lacey disappear down the street.

Charlie's rattling of the door and the sounds of Krystal's voice speaking to Manny, who was waking up, snapped him out of it.

He needed to go after Lacey. He needed to reassure and help Charlie. And he probably needed to make sure Krystal was okay, too.

The confusion of prioritizing made his military training kick in. *Secure those closest and most vulnerable.*

He opened the truck door and leaned in toward Charlie. "Listen, we're going to talk this through and figure it all out."

Charlie slumped. "Am I in trouble?"

"Yes, you're in trouble, but everyone gets in trouble. It's okay." He knew what Charlie would ask next, and he held up a hand to forestall it. "You're not getting sent

away. You're still going to be my son and you can still
see your mom every week."

"What about Miss Lacey?"

Vito blew out a breath. No dishonesty. That was what
had gotten him in trouble in the first place. "I just don't
know, Charlie. She's pretty mad at me right now."

"How come?"

"Grown-up business. We'll talk about it later." He
stood, patted Charlie's shoulder, and then reached in
and gave the boy a hug. "Sit tight. I've got to check on
your mom and then we'll go make sure Lacey is safe."

He shut Charlie's door gently, and then walked a few
steps toward Krystal. "You going to be okay?" he asked,
nodding toward Manny. "I can call the cops for you."

"I got this," she said. "Go after her."

He took her word for it and drove out in the direction Lacey had gone, scanning the road. It was late afternoon and clouds were rolling in, thick and ominous.
He had to get her before this storm started—or, given
the neighborhood, something worse happened. "Help
me watch for Lacey," he told Charlie.

A moment later, Charlie leaned forward in the seat
and pointed. "Is that her?"

He could see her yellow shirt. She was desperately
waving down a truck. No. She wouldn't get in a stranger's
vehicle. Would she?

Did she want to avoid him that badly?

The truck stopped. The passenger door opened, and
Lacey climbed in.

Vito hit the gas. "Do you know anyone who drives
a blue pickup?" It seemed to have writing on the side,
but Vito couldn't read it.

His stomach was lurching. If something happened to Lacey...

He got behind the truck, which was traveling at a normal rate of speed, and was relieved to see it was headed toward Rescue River, rather than away. Maybe she'd known the person and was getting a safe ride. But he still followed, just to be sure.

His head was still spinning from the way it had all gone down. Lacey had found out the truth about Gerry in the worst possible way.

Why hadn't he told her before? The betrayal in her eyes had just about killed him.

How awful for her to find out about her adored, war hero husband from his lover, screaming jealously at her.

And normally, she'd have turned to him for comfort. But instead, she'd looked at him as the betrayer, and rightly so.

Except he'd promised Gerry he wouldn't tell.

He tried to think of how it could've worked out differently. What all he'd done wrong. He shouldn't have made the promise. He shouldn't have moved in with Lacey. But that had been for Nonna...

There was a sniffle from the seat behind him, and Vito pulled his attention away from his thoughts and to Charlie. "Hey, buddy. What's the matter?"

"I thought Mom would want me," Charlie said in a subdued voice. "But when I got to her house, she told me to go away because Manny would get mad. And then Manny saw me."

"Did he hurt you?" Vito would kill the man if he had.

"No, but he made Mom shut me in the bedroom. And they said I couldn't come out. And they were gonna call you, but then they started fighting and kind of forgot about me."

"You can't do that, buddy. You can't run away. And you can't live with your mom." As he spoke, he was watching the truck in front of him, relieved to see it taking the exit that led to the guesthouse.

"I know." Charlie's voice was subdued.

"We're gonna figure this out, talk about it." Vito reached over and ruffled Charlie's hair. "Right now, though, we've got to check on Lacey."

He followed the truck, and when it pulled up in front of Lacey's place, he pulled up behind it.

"Do I have to stay in the truck again?" Charlie's voice was quiet.

"No, buddy, but you have to let me talk a little bit to Lacey. Grown-up business. Go see Wolfie. Okay? Take him out and walk him down the street, but stay where you can see me. We'll go inside in just a minute."

"Good, because I'm hungry."

They both got out of the truck, and Vito watched to make sure Charlie was safely out of earshot. He turned in time to see a dark-haired man walking beside Lacey toward the front door.

Jealousy burned inside him. He didn't want anyone else walking with Lacey. Especially not some tall, buff, thirty-ish guy with no scars and, probably, no baggage.

He followed them up the steps. "Lacey, I need to talk to you."

She ignored him and turned to the dark-haired man. "Thank you for the ride."

"Would you like me to stay?" the man asked in a courteous voice with just a trace of a Spanish accent.

She glanced toward Vito without meeting his eyes.

"Maybe for a few minutes, if you don't mind. I just need to talk to…my other boarder, without him bothering me, and make a couple of arrangements."

"It's no problem." He sat down in the porch chair Vito had begun to consider his own.

Lacey turned to go inside.

Vito started to follow. "Lacey—"

"The lady prefers that you don't come in," the other man said, standing up to block Vito as Lacey continued on inside.

Vito stopped, lifted an eyebrow, wondered if he was going to have to fight again that day.

"She's an old friend, and she told me on the way home that she doesn't want you around. Not my business why." The man shrugged. "Sorry, man."

Vito sat down heavily on the front steps. He could smell someone barbecuing for Saturday dinner. He and Lacey had done the same just last week.

Before everything had fallen apart.

Charlie came back into the yard, tugging Wolfie. He started up the steps. "Let's go in. I'm starving."

"Can't. Not yet."

"Why not?"

"Lacey is… She doesn't want us to come in just yet, but we can in a little while."

Charlie's lower lip began to stick out. "I want to go to my own room."

Except it wasn't his own room. "Just a little while, buddy."

The dark-haired man stood and went down to his truck. He came back with a sandwich encased in plastic wrap and an apple. "Here," he said to Charlie. "It's good. Turkey and cheese."

"Thanks!" Charlie grabbed the sandwich and started unwrapping it.

"That's your lunch, man," Vito protested.

"I have kids. I understand." He sat back down in the same porch chair.

"Hey, you don't have to wait around. I won't bother her."

"I said I'd wait," the man said quietly. "No offense."

So they sat in silence while Charlie scarfed down the sandwich, and then played in the yard with Wolfie. It was another forty-five minutes before Lacey came out the door.

"Thanks, Eduardo," she said, still not looking at Vito. "I'm sorry to keep you from your work. I'm fine now."

"You're sure?"

"I'm sure."

They both watched as Eduardo trotted down the steps and swung into his truck. Charlie came over, holding Wolfie tight on his leash, in control for once. "Hi, Miss Lacey," he said uncertainly.

She knelt in front of him, giving Wolfie a quick head rub, and then turning her full attention to Charlie. "I need to talk to you about something serious," she said. "Can you listen?"

He nodded, eyes wide.

"I like you a lot," she said. "I'm really sorry it didn't work out for me and your dad, but that's not your fault."

Charlie swallowed hard, and Vito did the same.

"You always have a safe home with your dad. That isn't changing. You don't run away from him anymore, okay?"

"Okay." Charlie's voice was low.

"And because I really like you, this is hard, but...you and your dad are going to need to move out."

Charlie looked down at the floor, nodded and turned away, nuzzling his face in Wolfie's fur. Wolfie, seeming to understand the boy's sadness, whined a little and licked Charlie's face.

Vito felt like he'd been punched in the stomach, hard.

Lacey stood and faced him. "Vito, I've made arrangements for Nonna to stay at the Senior Towers. They have a room open for her for however long she needs, and they can help her move in tomorrow. I have a call in to a friend of mine, a nurse, who'll check on her every day."

"You didn't have to—"

"Let me finish." She held up a hand. "You're going to have to find another place for you and Charlie to stay. I'm going away for a few days, and I want you out when I get back." Her voice was cold and distant.

She didn't wait for an answer, but turned and walked into the house, letting the door bang behind her.

Vito's shoulders slumped and he felt like collapsing down onto the porch and burying his head in his hands.

She was really, truly rejecting him. He loved her, and he'd lost her. Despair clutched his stomach with strong, cold fingers.

But he had a son to care for.

He swallowed the lump in his throat and straightened his shoulders. Looked out across the lawn.

There was Charlie's basketball. They couldn't forget that.

He walked down the steps, heavily, to pick it up.

"We gonna play, Dad?" Charlie asked eagerly.

"No, son." Vito carried the basketball up the stairs,

not even bouncing it. "We're going to have to start packing, and I have to start looking for a new place for us to live."

He went to the front door, held it open for Charlie, and then followed the boy inside.

He felt utterly broken. And the only reason he was standing upright, trying to be strong, was because Nonna and Charlie depended on him.

It was Lacey's fifth day at the Ohio Rural Retreat Center, and she was finding some small measure of peace.

She'd cried so much that her eyes felt permanently swollen. She'd prayed almost continually. She'd sought counsel with the center's spiritual advisors.

She knew now that she needed to put her faith in God, not men.

She knew she wasn't healed yet, not even close.

The thought of Fiona Farmingham coming to visit with her today was terrifying. It wasn't that she didn't like Fiona; she barely knew her. And she had Fiona to thank for the idea of coming here. When she'd blurted out a piece of an explanation to Eduardo in that horrible truck ride home—"my husband wasn't who I thought he was"—Eduardo had urged her to get in touch with Fiona, who'd had something similar happen to her. And then he'd gone further and called Fiona, who'd texted her the address of the retreat center where she'd stayed when her world had fallen apart.

There was a knock on the door of her small, monk-like cell. "Your visitor is here," came the quiet, soothing voice of the retreat receptionist.

Trying not to show her reluctance, Lacey went out to

the reception area and greeted Fiona with a handshake, then an awkward hug.

"Would you like to walk?" Fiona asked. "When I was here, I always liked the trail around the pond."

"Um, sure." She hoped Fiona didn't plan to stay long, that she wouldn't say anything to burst the fragile, peaceful bubble Lacey had built around herself.

But it couldn't last forever, of course. She was going to have to get back to renovating the guesthouse. To rebuilding her life in Rescue River as a strong single woman.

That had been her goal all along. When and why had she let that fade? But she knew the answer: it was when Vito and Charlie had come. Ever so gradually, they'd slipped into her heart so that now, having lost them, she didn't feel strong. She felt weak and vulnerable and raw.

"Thanks for agreeing to a visit," Fiona said as they walked toward the center's small pond, separated from the main building by a stand of trees. "I just felt really led to talk to you. And if your nights have been anything like mine were, you're not sleeping well, so I figured an early morning visit would be okay."

"I appreciate it," Lacey lied politely. "Where are your kids?"

"With the nanny," Fiona said, sounding apologetic. It was no secret that she was quite wealthy after her scandalous divorce settlement, but she didn't flaunt her money; in fact, people said she didn't like mentioning it.

A red-winged blackbird, perched on a cattail at the pond's edge, let out its trademark "okalee, okalee" before taking flight, bright red and yellow wing patches flashing in the early morning sun. "This is an amazing place," Lacey said, meaning it. "Thank you for telling me about it."

"Of course. How are you doing?" The question wasn't a surface platitude, but a real inquiry.

"I'm…managing, but barely," Lacey admitted.

"That's normal," Fiona said matter-of-factly. "When I found out my husband had a whole other family, it took a year to even start to feel normal again."

Her blunt words reached Lacey in a way the retreat counselors' soothing tones hadn't. Fiona had been there, had experienced the loss and humiliation Lacey was going through. "Did you ever feel like it might have been a dream, like you were going to wake up any minute and none of it would be true?"

Fiona nodded. "All the time. And then you keep on realizing, no, it's true, my life wasn't at all like what it seemed to be."

"Exactly. It's like my memories were stolen. The happiness I had with Gerry was all a huge lie."

"Well." Fiona reached out to run her fingers alongside the reeds that rimmed the pond. "I don't know if it was all a lie. My therapist said that men who lead double lives can really believe they love both women. Or in my case, both families."

Lacey inhaled the rich, damp-earth fragrance of the wetlands. "I don't know how you stood it, with four kids to watch out for. I'm barely managing with just myself."

"You do what you have to do. For me, the betrayal was the worst part. It messed with my whole image of myself as a woman, like I wasn't enough."

Lacey looked over at Fiona, tall, with long, wavy

red hair and an hourglass figure. *She* had felt like she wasn't enough? "Did you get over that?"

Fiona shook her head. "You will, I'm sure, but I didn't. I've got my hands full with my kids and starting a business. Even if I felt like I could trust a man again—which I don't—I wouldn't have time for it."

"I hear you. My guesthouse is yelling for me to get back to renovations."

They walked in companionable silence for a few minutes. Green-headed mallards flew down and landed on the pond, skidding along. Overhead, the sky turned a brighter blue.

"I just wonder if everyone in town knew but me," Lacey burst out finally.

"I wondered the same thing, and I found out as soon as the truth started getting publicized. People *did* know, and they rushed to tell me how they'd suspected, or what they'd heard." She sighed. "That was bad enough, but when my kids started getting teased and bullied, I'd had it. I had to leave. It's why I moved to Rescue River."

"Oh, how awful for you *and* your kids!" Lacey felt almost ashamed for being upset about her own situation. Fiona, with her four kids suffering, had it so much worse.

"It was awful, but things are better now. Much better. What happened with your husband? How did you find out?"

So Lacey explained the whole situation. "And then Vito, he brought Gerry's child into my home! He was living there all along, knowing that secret."

"Ouch."

The sun was rising higher, and Lacey slipped off her

sweatshirt and tied it around her waist. "He was an old friend, but he lied to me."

"Did he actively lie? He seems like a really nice guy, but you never know."

Lacey thought back. "No, he never actively lied. I think the subject of Charlie's dad might have come up once, but he told me Charlie's father had died. And that he was Vito's war buddy. All of which was technically true. But—" she lifted her hands, palms up "—why did he come to live in the guesthouse—with my husband's son—when he had to know how much the truth would hurt me? And then we…" Tears rose to her eyes and she blinked them back. "We started getting close. I thought he cared for me." She almost choked on her words.

Fiona put an arm around her, giving her a quick shoulder-hug. "That sounds so hurtful. But do you think he did it on purpose, to be mean?"

Unbidden, an image of Vito's kind face swam before Lacey's teary eyes. She thought back over the time when he'd decided to stay at the guesthouse. "Nooooo," she said slowly. "He was actually reluctant to stay, and only agreed because his grandma was so keen on it."

"So he didn't exactly come knocking on your door, looking for a place to live."

"No. But he should have told me the truth!"

"He should have." Fiona hesitated. "That's a pretty hard thing to tell."

"I guess." Lacey didn't want to look at Vito's side, not yet. She was still too angry at him.

"And the thing is, were you perfect? That's what my counselor made me look at, in my situation. Were there any mistakes you made, in your marriage?"

"I was stupid," Lacey said bitterly.

"Well…yeah. You kind of were."

Lacey blinked, surprised. Not many people would speak that bluntly to someone who wasn't an old friend.

"We weren't wise as serpents, were we?" Fiona stared off into the distance. "Neither of us. And people suffered because of it."

Lacey had never thought of it that way. She'd focused on how she was an innocent victim, not on how she'd had a responsibility to be wise as well as gentle and kind.

And yes, people had suffered. She thought of Charlie's hurt face when she'd told him she wouldn't be doing things with Vito anymore. It was a big part of why he'd run away.

Kicking him and Vito out on the street… Making Nonna move to the Towers… Yeah. "I've made a lot of people miserable, dragged them down with me."

They were coming to the end of the loop around the pond. "Don't beat yourself up. That's not what I mean at all. I'm really sorry for what happened to you. It's just…we're all a mix, right? Nobody's perfect. Not your husband, not you. And not Vito, either."

"True."

They walked quietly for a few more minutes, and when they reached the parking lot, Fiona stopped. "I've got to get back to the kids. But I just want you to know, there's life after this. You can come back, live well. Keep on praying, and I'll pray for you, too."

They hugged, for real this time. "Thanks for coming to see me," Lacey said. "It helped. A lot."

And as she waved, and then headed back inside, she

felt better. Not healed, but better. And it was a good thing, because tomorrow she had to go back to town, hold her head high and probably encounter Vito and Charlie.

Chapter 16

A week later, Vito parked in front of the Senior Towers and headed inside. He'd been so busy with Charlie and his job that he hadn't visited his grandmother for the past couple of days, and he felt guilty.

That wasn't the reason for the heaviness in his soul, though. *That* came from his unresolved issues with Lacey. Even now, if he looked down the street, he could see her on the porch of her guesthouse, talking and laughing with a couple of visitors.

He hoped to catch her eye, but she didn't even glance his way.

He trudged inside the Senior Towers, trying to look at the bright side. Charlie was doing well; Vito had explained the whole situation to his social worker, and a couple of sessions with her, Vito, and Charlie had helped the boy to understand as much of the truth as an eight-year-old needed to know. They'd talked over running away, and Charlie had promised to make a phone call to his social worker if he ever felt like doing it again.

They'd found half of a double to rent on the edge of town, with a huge fenced yard and a dog-friendly neighbor in the other half of the house. So that was another good thing.

His course work was going well, and his new job even better. He loved working with the at-risk boys, and already his supervisor had talked with him about a possible full-time opening once he had his degree.

The scars weren't really an issue, in the job or otherwise. In fact, he felt almost foolish about how much he'd let them get in his way when he'd first returned to Rescue River. Now if a newcomer stared or a kid made a comment, he could let it roll off him, knowing that to most people, it was what was inside that mattered.

Lacey had helped him see that first. He owed her a debt of gratitude, but it was one he couldn't pay. To approach her again, after what he'd done, would be an insult to her.

He straightened his shoulders and ordered himself to focus on what he could do, not on what he couldn't. He'd go spend time with Nonna, help her feel better and recover from the move.

He walked into the Senior Towers and crossed the lobby. He was about to push the button on the elevator when he distinguished Nonna's voice, and he turned to see her emerging from the exercise room in the midst of a crowd of women. She wore hot pink sweats and a T-shirt that said… He squinted and read the words, Vintage Workout Queen.

She walked to him and gave him a strong hug. "My

Vito! Come on. Sit down here in the lobby. I can spare a few minutes before I meet with my business partners."

Vito blinked. "Business partners?"

"Yes, Lou Ann and Minnie. The matchmaking business is taking off. Now, tell me what's new with you, and you know what I mean."

He tried to deflect the conversation to his work, and to Charlie, but Nonna saw right through it.

"I'm glad those things are going well, but what about Lacey? Have you mended that fence yet?"

He shook his head. "No, and I don't think it's going to get mended. Some things just can't be fixed." Nonna didn't know the details of what had happened between them, didn't know about Charlie's parentage, but she knew something serious had split them apart.

"Bella? Are you ready?" It was Lou Ann Miller, and it took Vito a minute to realize she was talking to Nonna. He'd almost forgotten his grandmother had a first name. "Oh, hello, Vito."

"Go rouse Minnie," Nonna instructed the other woman. "We have to do a quick consultation with our first client, Vito, here, before we start working on our business plan."

That was the *last* thing he needed. "Nonna... I was really just coming to check on you, not to talk about my own troubles. How are you feeling?"

She waved a hand. "I'm fine. Better every day, and these ladies—" she waved toward Lou Ann and Minnie, now both coming down the hall, talking busily "—they keep me in the loop. Lou Ann knows about all the news outside the Towers, and Minnie knows what's going on inside. I love it here!"

Vito felt a pang. He wasn't really needed by his

grandma, not anymore. Nonna was making a new life
for herself.

The other two women reached the cozy corner where
Nonna and Vito sat, and Lou Ann pulled up chairs for
both of them, leaving Vito surrounded and without an
escape route.

Immediately, Nonna launched an explanation. "Vito,
here, is estranged from the woman he most loves, because of some kind of fight. He thinks the relationship
is doomed."

"Do you still have feelings for her?" Lou Ann demanded.

He was torn between telling the three interfering
woman to go jump in the lake and embracing them for
taking his troubles seriously. He chose the latter. "I still
have feelings. But I did something that hurt her terribly."

"Did you apologize?" Miss Minnie asked.

"Yes, of course. But she kicked me out of the guesthouse, and she isn't speaking to me."

"Why did you do it?" Lou Ann asked.

He shrugged helplessly. "Loyalty, I guess. Loyalty to
an old friend."

"Loyalty is an important value," Miss Minnie said.
"But love…remember your Bible, Vito. The greatest
of these is Love."

It was true. He saw that now, too late.

"So he's just backing away. Out of politeness!"
Nonna leaned forward and pinched his cheek. "My Vito.
Always the best friend. Always so nice."

"Too nice," Miss Minnie declared.

Lou Ann Miller looked thoughtful. "If you give up
on her, maybe you just don't care enough. Why, I know
a couple right here in Rescue River who had to keep

huge secrets from each other. But they pushed through their problems. Now they're happily married."

Happily married. If there was any possibility at all of that for him and Lacey...

"The choice is yours," Nonna said. *"Coraggio, ragazzo mio."*

Lacey was what he wanted most in the world. Could he risk another try, a heartfelt apology, a grand gesture that might sway her back in his direction?

What did he have to lose?

Nonna seemed to see the decision on his face. "If you need any help," she said, "we're here for you."

He stood and kissed her cheek. "I will most definitely take you up on that."

From a high-backed chair that faced away from their corner, Gramps Camden stood and pointed a finger at Vito. "For once, the ladies are right. Being polite doesn't get a man much of anything."

As the ladies scolded Gramps for eavesdropping, Vito waved and headed for the door, feeling more energy with each step he took.

He had some serious planning to do.

A week later, Lacey hugged Nonna at the door to the Senior Towers, glad to feel that the older woman was gaining weight and strength. "Don't worry," she said. "I'll take you to the party next week. Are you sure you don't want me to walk you upstairs?"

"I'm fine. And I'm sorry I got the date wrong. Maybe I'm losing my marbles." Nonna shrugged.

"It's all right. I enjoyed spending some time with you." Truthfully, the excursion had filled a gap in Lacey's week. Even though she'd tried to rebuild her life, to spend time with girlfriends and focus on her work, she still found herself lonely.

Still found herself missing Vito and Charlie.

Nonna reached up and straightened Lacey's collar, plucked a stray hair off her shoulders. "Do you know what we always said in Italy? *Si apra all'amore.* Be open to love."

"Um, sure." Maybe Nonna *was* getting a little confused, because that remark had been apropos of nothing.

She drove the half block to the guesthouse and parked in the driveway, taking her time. She didn't want to go inside an empty house. Without Charlie roughhousing and Wolfie barking, without Vito's deep voice, the place felt empty.

But delaying wouldn't solve her problem. She clasped the cross she'd hung around her neck, in place of the wedding ring she'd worn before. It was a reminder: she could do all things through Christ.

Including survive loneliness.

She climbed out of the car and walked slowly toward the front entrance, checking her flower beds, which were doing great. Looked reflexively at the broken fence. She really needed to...

She stopped. Looked again.

The makeshift fix they'd done weeks ago, when Wolfie had escaped, wasn't there. Instead, the fence was repaired.

She knelt down, awkward in her dress and heels, and examined it. The two broken pickets had been replaced with new ones, painted white. Only when you were very close could you see that the paint was a little brighter on the new pickets.

She frowned. Who would have repaired her fence?

Wondering, she walked toward the front of the house. As she rounded the corner, she heard music.

Opera music. *Italian* opera music.

What had Nonna called it? *The most romantic music on earth.*

What in the world?

The wonderful smell of Italian food—lasagna?—wafted through the air.

As she climbed the front steps, she saw something pink.

Her heart pounding, she reached the top of the steps. A trail of rose petals led her across the porch to a table set for two, topped with a white tablecloth.

She stared at the centerpiece, and tears rose to her eyes.

A ceramic rooster, exactly like the one Charlie had broken the day she'd met him.

No longer could she doubt who was responsible for what she was seeing.

She turned toward the front door. At the same moment, Vito emerged through it, a bowl of salad in one hand and a tray of pasta in the other. He wore dress trousers, a white dress shirt and an apron. Focused on balancing both dishes, he didn't notice her at first, but when he did, a strange expression crossed his face.

"Lacey," he said his voice intent. "Wait." He turned and carefully put down the two items on a side table.

Then he undid his apron and took it off, his eyes never leaving hers.

"How did you…" She broke off.

Walking slowly across the porch, he stood before her, not touching her. "I trespassed. Nonna gave me her key."

"Nonna…" She cocked her head to one side and reviewed the afternoon. Nonna's sudden invitation to a party, her insisting that Lacey dress up, the realization that it was the wrong date… "She was in on this. And you fixed my fence."

"For a good cause."

"What do you mean?"

He walked around her and pulled out a chair. "Explaining will take a minute. Would you like to sit down?"

She hesitated, feeling a little railroaded, but curious, too. "Oka-a-a-ay."

He poured iced tea, the raspberry flavor she always ordered at the Chatterbox, looking for all the world like a handsome Italian waiter. But then he pulled a chair to face her and sat down, close enough that their knees almost touched. Almost, but not quite. "The good cause is…an apology. Lacey, I am so sorry for what I did to you. There's no excuse for dishonesty."

She wanted to forgive him instantly. The music, the tea, the rose petals, the mended fence, the ceramic rooster—all of it created a romantic little world. But she couldn't just succumb to it. She needed to be as wise as a serpent, not just gentle as a dove. Not just go with her heart. "I would like to hear why you did what you did. I wasn't in a condition to listen before."

He drew in a breath and nodded. "Of course. You deserve that." Still, he seemed reluctant to speak.

"I can take it, Vito! Whatever happened, it's probably better than what I've been imagining."

"Right." He reached for her, then pulled his hand back. "It was only in the last couple of months of Gerry's life that I found out he'd been unfaithful to you."

The word stung, even though she knew it was true. "How did you find out?"

"He was burning letters," he explained. "Building a fire was dangerous over there, so I went to stop him. He said he had just a few more to burn, and he was turning over a new leaf. I still had to stop him—I was his commanding officer by then—and I happened to see a...suggestive card. It didn't look like something you'd send, so I asked him about it."

The thought of another woman sending racy cards to her husband made Lacey's face hot with anger and humiliation. Was that what Gerry had wanted in a woman? Hadn't her tame, loving letters been enough?

Vito was watching her face, and he reached out and wrapped his hand around her clenched fist. "He was *burning* it, Lace. He'd had a couple of risky encounters that had made him think about his life, and he wanted to get a fresh start."

"Either that, or he was afraid of getting caught."

"No, I think he was sincere. He really did love you. He just wasn't used to..." Vito seemed to cast about for the right word. "To monogamy, I guess. That's why I regret introducing you two."

"That's why you tried to warn me about him. You knew what he was like."

Vito nodded. "But you were in love, and I hoped marriage would change him. And it did. It just took a while. When you let him know you were expecting a baby, it made him want to change his ways, be a better husband and father."

"He already had a child!"

"Yeah." Vito sighed. "I found out about that at the very end. You sure you want to hear?"

"Tell me."

"Okay." He looked out toward the street, his shoulders unconsciously straightening into military posture. "Three of us were cut off from the others, and both Gerry and Luiz were hit and bleeding pretty bad. When Luiz died and Gerry realized the medics might not get there in time for him, either, he told me about Charlie. He asked me to take care of Charlie if Krystal couldn't. And he asked me to look out for you, and to keep you in the dark about who Charlie was, because he thought it would kill you to know. Before I could make him see it wasn't possible to do all those things together, he was gone."

Lacey just sat, trying to process what Vito was saying.

"I tried to save him, Lace. And I tried to do what he asked, though I didn't succeed very well." He sighed. "I thought things were okay for Charlie and Krystal. I thought it might be best for you if I stayed away. But then I got injured, and there was the rehab, and then everything hit the fan with Krystal and I found out Charlie was about to be put into the system... Well, first things first, I thought. Charlie is a kid."

"Of course." Lacey stared down at the porch floor. "It was my own fault I was so foolish, marrying Gerry. I was vulnerable to anyone."

"I was foolish, too, but I've learned. I've learned that honesty and...and *love*...trump loyalty to a bad cause."

She froze, not daring to look at him. "Love?"

He squeezed her hand, then reached up to brush a finger across her cheek. When he spoke, his voice was serious. "I love you, Lacey. I... Maybe I always have, kind of, but now it's grown-up and serious and forever."

Cautiously she looked at him through her eyelashes, not wanting to let her joy and terror show. She drew in a breath. "I have an apology to make, too. I was wrong to kick you and Charlie out. I was angry at Gerry, really, and at myself, and I took it out on you."

"Understandable."

"Is Charlie okay?"

He nodded. "We've had a few sessions with his social worker to talk it all through. She helped me understand how much to tell Charlie. Right now, he knows that his dad was a hero, but made some mistakes. That he felt ashamed he wasn't married to Charlie's mom. And that none of it is Charlie's fault. That seems like about as much as he can take in, right now."

"That's good." She bit her lip. "I shouldn't have taken out my hurt on you, and especially on an innocent child."

"For whatever you did wrong, I forgive you."

"And I forgive you."

They looked at each other. "Are we good?" he asked.

"We're good." She felt a strange breathlessness as he stood and pulled her gently to her feet.

And into his arms.

Being held by him, seeing and believing how much he cared, soothed some deep place inside her that wanted to be cared for and loved.

His hand rubbed slow circles on her back. "I hated being at odds," he said, and she felt the rumble of his voice against her cheek. "I want to be your friend. At *least* your friend. I want to be more."

She pulled away enough that she could look up at his face. "What kind of more?" she murmured in a husky tone that didn't even sound like her.

"This kind." He leaned down and pressed his lips to hers.

After a long while he lifted his head, sniffing the air, and then pulled away.

Lacey smelled it at the same time he did. "Something's burning!"

They ran inside and Vito pulled a scorched cake from the oven. "Oh, man, it was chocolate, too!"

She burst out laughing.

And then they were both laughing, and crying, and hugging each other, and kissing a little more. "It was so awful being apart from you. I never want that to happen again," he said.

"I don't, either." She pulled back. "But Vito. That nice meal is getting cold."

He laughed. "It'll warm up just fine. Come here."

He was right, of course. She stepped forward into his arms. "I love you," she said.

Epilogue

One Year Later

"I predicted this as soon as I saw you catch that bouquet," Susan Hinton said, looking around the guesthouse lawn with satisfaction.

"You couldn't have!" Lacey laughed. "Vito wasn't even back yet."

"I saw him come up behind you and I knew."

Gina, Lacey's sister-in-law, came over to where Lacey and Susan sat, under the party tent they'd put up against a summer shower. "Vito and Buck are exchanging fatherhood tips with Sam."

Lacey craned her neck and saw Sam Hinton, holding three-month-old Sam Jr. as if he were made of glass. Buck squatted to wipe the cake from little Bobby's face. And Vito was bending down to speak to Charlie, who looked adorably grown-up in his junior tux.

Lacey felt fully recovered from the devastating news about Gerry being Charlie's father. There even seemed to be a strange rightness in her helping Vito to raise Gerry's child.

Nonna approached Vito and took his arm, pulling him toward Lacey. She seemed years younger than she had after her heart attack; indeed, she was helping to teach heart attack recovery classes at the Senior Towers and was so happily enmeshed in the social circles there that she'd decided to live at the towers full-time.

"I need to talk to the bride and groom," Nonna said as she reached Lacey and her friends. "Alone."

Vito lifted an eyebrow and reached to pull Lacey from her reclining position. The very touch of his hand gave her goose bumps. They'd spent glorious time together during the past year, getting to know each other as the adults they were now. Vito had finished his online studies and student teaching, and had the offer of a job for the fall. Meanwhile, he'd been working with Lacey at the guesthouse, which had become so successful that she'd had to hire help—help that would now manage the place while she and Vito honeymooned.

The thought of their honeymoon on a South Carolina beach made Lacey's skin warm. She couldn't even regret that they could only manage a long weekend, with the guesthouse to run and Charlie to parent. She was so, so ready to begin married life with Vito.

"I'm afraid I've been interfering again," Nonna said, a twinkle in her eye.

"Nonna! What now?" Vito's tone was indulgent.

"You have that look on your face," Lacey added. "What have you been up to?"

Nonna looked from Vito to Lacey and bit her lip.

"First, I have a confession to make." She hesitated, then added, "My interfering has been going on for a while."

"What do you mean? The matchmaking date?" Lacey had suspected for some time that Nonna had arranged for her and Vito to go out with Daisy and Dion, knowing it would push them into acknowledging their feelings for each other.

Nonna patted Lacey's arm as if she were a bright student. "Yes, the whole matchmaking service was a scheme to get the two of you together. Of course, it's grown beyond that." Lou Ann and Miss Minnie had become Nonna's first lieutenants, matching up the singles of Rescue River.

"I'm just wondering when you three ladies will do some matchmaking on each other," Vito said. He didn't sound particularly surprised about Nonna's interference, either.

"Oh, no!" Nonna looked shocked. "We're having far too much fun to weigh ourselves down with cranky old men."

That made Lacey burst out laughing. "You're incorrigible."

"Well, and it didn't begin with the matchmaking service, either."

"What else?" Vito put on a mock-serious tone. "Tell us everything."

"I...well, I may have arranged for Lacey to take care of me, and my home to be unavailable, when I found out you were coming home, dear." She looked up through her glasses at Vito, her face tender. "You're going to be a wonderful husband, but I was afraid you'd be my age before you figured it out. When I ended up on Lacey's floor at the hospital, and heard about her history, and saw how lovely she'd grown up to be…well, I may have done a little scheming."

"Nonna D'Angelo!" Indignation warred with laughter in Lacey's heart. Laughter won on this glorious day.

"I have a way to make it up to you," Nonna said hastily. "You both know I came into a small inheritance when my cousin Paolo died last year."

Vito nodded, and Lacey just looked at Nonna, wondering where this was going. What would Nonna think of next?

"I've been trying to decide what use to make of it. What can I do, at my age? I have a few plans, but the first one is I want to give you this." She reached into her handbag and pulled out a small, gift wrapped box. She handed it to Lacey. "Open it."

The box was featherlight, and inside, there was nothing but paper. "I think you forgot to put the gift in—"

"Nonna!" Vito had pulled out the papers and was scanning them. "You can't do this!"

"I can, and I've already done it. You're booked for a week at a villa in Tuscany, and then a week in Rome and Venice. You leave tomorrow." She crossed her arms and smiled with satisfaction.

"But…our reservations in South Carolina…"

"Canceled. That was the interfering part." Nonna looked only slightly abashed. "You'll still get a wonderful honeymoon. It's just the destination that'll be different."

Lacey stared at Nonna and then at Vito. "Italy?" she asked faintly. "I've never been out of the country."

"And that's why your brother had to check into whether you had a passport. You do. Some trip to Can-

472   The Soldier's Secret Child

ada that didn't materialize?" Nonna waved her hand as if the details didn't matter.

Lacey looked at Vito. "Italy."

"Together." A smile spread across his face. "I've never been, either."

"And that's why you need two weeks," Nonna said firmly. "Everything's all arranged. The guesthouse, Charlie, reservations in *Italia*."

Lacey looked up to see Buck, Charlie, Susan and Sam all crowded together, looking at them, coming over to congratulate them on their changed honeymoon schedule and destination. It looked like everyone had been in on the surprise. Even Charlie knew that he and Wolfie would get to spend a little longer at the dog rescue farm with Xavier.

A regular clinking and ringing sound came, the traditional instruction to kiss. Vito pulled Lacey into his arms and kissed her tenderly, then held her against his chest.

"Is this what it's going to be like to be married to you?" he rumbled into her ear. "Surprises and adventures?"

"Enough to keep you on your toes." She laughed up at him as he pulled her closer, and then looked beyond, to the clear blue sky. Vito was amazing, and life with him and Charlie was going to be an adventure.

But she knew deep inside that none of this was a surprise to her heavenly father, who'd orchestrated all of it and would guide them through the rest of their days.

* * * * *

Get 3 FREE REWARDS!

We'll send you 2 FREE Books plus a FREE Mystery Gift.

FREE Value Over $20

Both the **Love Inspired**® and **Love Inspired**® Suspense series feature compelling novels filled with inspirational romance, faith, forgiveness and hope.

YES! Please send me 2 FREE novels from the Love Inspired or Love Inspired Suspense series and my FREE gift (gift is worth about $10 retail). After receiving them, if I don't wish to receive any more books, I can return the shipping statement marked "cancel." If I don't cancel, I will receive 6 brand-new Love Inspired Larger-Print books or Love Inspired Suspense Larger-Print books every month and be billed just $6.49 each in the U.S. or $6.74 each in Canada. That is a savings of at least 16% off the cover price. It's quite a bargain! Shipping and handling is just 50¢ per book in the U.S. and $1.25 per book in Canada.* I understand that accepting the 2 free books and gift places me under no obligation to buy anything. I can always return a shipment and cancel at any time by calling the number below. The free books and gift are mine to keep no matter what I decide.

Choose one:
- ☐ **Love Inspired Larger-Print** (122/322 BPA GRPA)
- ☐ **Love Inspired Suspense Larger-Print** (107/307 BPA GRPA)
- ☐ **Or Try Both!** (122/322 & 107/307 BPA GRRP)

Name (please print)

Address   Apt. #

City   State/Province   Zip/Postal Code

Email: Please check this box ☐ if you would like to receive newsletters and promotional emails from Harlequin Enterprises ULC and its affiliates. You can unsubscribe anytime.

Mail to the Harlequin Reader Service:
IN U.S.A.: P.O. Box 1341, Buffalo, NY 14240-8531
IN CANADA: P.O. Box 603, Fort Erie, Ontario L2A 5X3

Want to try 2 free books from another series! Call 1-800-873-8635 or visit www.ReaderService.com.

---

*Terms and prices subject to change without notice. Prices do not include sales taxes, which will be charged (if applicable) based on your state or country of residence. Canadian residents will be charged applicable taxes. Offer not valid in Quebec. This offer is limited to one order per household. Books received may not be as shown. Not valid for current subscribers to the Love Inspired or Love Inspired Suspense series. All orders subject to approval. Credit or debit balances in a customer's account(s) may be offset by any other outstanding balance owed by or to the customer. Please allow 4 to 6 weeks for delivery. Offer available while quantities last.

Your Privacy—Your information is being collected by Harlequin Enterprises ULC, operating as Harlequin Reader Service. For a complete summary of the information we collect, how we use this information and to whom it is disclosed, please visit our privacy notice located at corporate.harlequin.com/privacy-notice. From time to time we may also exchange your personal information with reputable third parties. If you wish to opt out of this sharing of your personal information, please visit readerservice.com/consumerschoice or call 1-800-873-8635. **Notice to California Residents**—Under California law, you have specific rights to control and access your data. For more information on these rights and how to exercise them, visit corporate.harlequin.com/california-privacy.

LIRLIS23

HARLEQUIN
PLUS

Try the best multimedia subscription service for romance readers like you!

Read, Watch and Play.

Experience the easiest way to get the romance content you crave.

Start your **FREE TRIAL** at
<u>www.harlequinplus.com/freetrial</u>.